I COULD FEEL
THE ELECTRIC TENSION OF HIS BODY
IN THE AIR ALL AROUND ME—

"I haven't wanted anything in this world but to take you in my arms and spend a solid week trying to tell you and show you how very much I love you, Grania Kirk. Do you know why I haven't?"

"You've had too much to cope with, and you knew I'd keep."

"My God, was I that sure of myself?"

"You knew—when you'd kissed me—that I was in love with you. If you'd thought I wouldn't wait, you'd have been insulting me."

"Why?"

"Thinking I kissed just any man with that much fervor," I said frankly.

"I forget precisely how much fervor that was," he said, and took me with both hands on my waist and kissed me on the mouth long and gently, then long and heartily. Finally, with my head on his shoulder as I caught my breath, he murmured, "I have had all I could handle, Grania, in the way of emotions and plans and hopes and fears but now I intend to annoy you with my attentions at all odd hours. . . ."

THE CLIFFS OF NIGHT

"SPELLBINDING DRAMATIC SUSPENSE!"
—*South Bend Tribune*

"EXCEPTIONALLY GOOD . . . HAS EVERYTHING!"
—*Jackson Daily News*

Big Bestsellers from SIGNET

- [ ] **ECSTASY'S EMPIRE by Gimone Hall.** (#E9292—$2.75)
- [ ] **FURY'S SUN, PASSION'S MOON by Gimone Hall.**
  (#E8748—$2.50)*
- [ ] **RAPTURE'S MISTRESS by Gimone Hall.** (#E8422—$2.25)*
- [ ] **GLYNDA by Susannah Leigh.** (#E8548—$2.50)*
- [ ] **WINTER FIRE by Susannah Leigh.** (#E8680—$2.50)
- [ ] **LORD SIN by Constance Gluyas.** (#E9521—$2.75)*
- [ ] **THE PASSIONATE SAVAGE by Constance Gluyas.**
  (#E9195—$2.50)*
- [ ] **MOMENTS OF MEANING by Charlotte Vale Allen.**
  (#J8817—$1.95)*
- [ ] **GIFTS OF LOVE by Charlotte Vale Allen.** (#J8388—$1.95)
- [ ] **THE RAGING WINDS OF HEAVEN by June Lund Shiplett.**
  (#E9439—$2.50)
- [ ] **REAP THE BITTER WINDS by June Lund Shiplett.**
  (#E9517—$2.50)
- [ ] **THE WILD STORMS OF HEAVEN by June Lund Shiplett.**
  (#E9063—$2.50)*
- [ ] **DEFY THE SAVAGE WINDS by June Lund Shiplett.**
  (#E9337—$2.50)*
- [ ] **CLAUDINE'S DAUGHTER by Rosalind Laker.**
  (#E9159—$2.25)*
- [ ] **WARWYCK'S WOMAN by Rosalind Laker.** (#E8813—$2.25)*

* Price slightly higher in Canada

Buy them at your local bookstore or use this convenient coupon for ordering.

THE NEW AMERICAN LIBRARY, INC.
P.O. Box 999, Bergenfield, New Jersey 07621

Please send me the SIGNET BOOKS I have checked above. I am enclosing
$_____(please add 50¢ to this order to cover postage and
handling). Send check or money order—no cash or C.O.D.'s. Prices and numbers
are subject to change without notice.

Name _____

Address _____

City_____ State_____ Zip Code_____
Allow 4-6 weeks for delivery.
This offer is subject to withdrawal without notice.

THE
CLIFFS
OF
NIGHT

by
Beatrice Brandon

A SIGNET BOOK
NEW AMERICAN LIBRARY
TIMES MIRROR

Of course this book is for my Be

All of the characters in this book are fictitious, and any resemblance to actual persons, living or dead, is purely coincidental.

1

Bring no ill will to hinder us,
My hapless heart and me,
Dread spirits of the blackened water,
Cold hag and wild banshee . . .
 —The Castle of Dromore

I REMEMBER AS THOUGH IT WERE YESTERDAY my first hour on that cruel crag, the wall that lifts from a sea whose water is cold and hostile as the rock itself.

The winter was closing for that year. Slowly, reluctantly, and with frequent outbursts of tired old anger, it was loosing its hold on the western edge of Ireland. But there seemed no promise of spring anywhere you looked; there was only the lingering death of a season, not the approaching birth of another. It was a time straight out of the gray and gloomy middle of the nineteenth century. You'd never have guessed that we were into the 1970's, with a brutal war agonizing Belfast only a hundred and eighty miles to the northeast.

I sat on my heels at the brink of the Cliffs of Moher as the dark afternoon waned into evening. Far below me the ocean smashed itself viciously against the walls of stone, time after time after endless time. The swooping gulls cried out harshly, and somewhere at my back a cold lonesome crow let a single plaintive squawk out of himself and then was silent. I might have been crouching on a planet that had never known another human soul.

My soul was mired just then in a melancholy that suited the climate and the desolation. I had brought it all the way from New York: a bleak, nearly hopeless state of mind which I recognized as the result of overwork and disappointment, yet which I could not shake off. Perhaps I didn't honestly want to be rid of it. Why else would I avoid the green and cheerful places of this lovely island, to drive like a monomaniac from one raw seascape to the next?

And now this winter of my spirit had brought me at last to the terrible Moher cliffs, which had been calling to me all my life; and here I believed, or half believed, that I was going to find either a new beginning or the salvation of a finale.

The Cliffs of Moher are the bastions of County Clare against the Atlantic. They begin down where the strand curves smoothly around from the Inagh River till it's stopped by the black rock rising abruptly four hundred feet to make the promontory called Hag's Head. From here the great cliffs run north and east for five full miles: a vast ragged wall of dark sandstone crowned with forty feet of jet shale, the two wedded rocks forming what is called a mural precipice, so nearly vertical that no climber could ever manage to scale it, supposing he were able to get himself out of the sea that rages at its base. It is not the height that is terrifying, but the incredible sheerness.

The image that occurs to me in trying to describe the cliffs, probably because of my theatrical background, is that of a gargantuan black velvet curtain. It is half drawn, so that its folds go in and out, in and out all along the miles. Here and there the vast drapery is too long and pushes against the stage—in this case the ocean floor—so that it bulges out somewhat and you cannot see the lower edge from the top; and the material is very old and has faded in spots and become a moldy green in others. I have never seen this vast curtain from the ocean, but I think that it would be a formidable sight. You would always be expecting the curtain to open all the way and disclose some revolting vision, like the entrance to a medieval hell ... at least you would if your nerves were in as rotten shape as mine were.

The long headland ends, as I've said, some five miles north of Hag's Head; it has been lifting gradually all the way, and the old view tower on the far crest is nearly seven hundred feet above the water. Beyond this the cliffs drop a little, the land retreats inward, and slowly the coastline achieves a more normal, less spectacular cast.

To get to this end of the place, if you're coming from Shannon Airport, say, you take the easy drive through Ennis and Ennistymon and then follow the signs on route L54. They say "Cliffs of Moher," and I may as well admit now that I have no idea who or what Moher was. Near the northern boundary you turn off and up, seaward, through the rippling green of the hills that are the land side of the cliffs, until you come to a tiny car park, called a lay-by. There is a row of enormous olive-tinted flagstones edge-up around this, and I understand that some visitors stop there, look at the view, and go away. How disappointed they must be! That's like staring at the Grand Canyon from your automobile. The thing to do—and I discovered this by accident—is to clamber past the protecting flags and down a few yards of grass onto the huge platform that a sensible Providence has laid there for you. Here the stone is perfectly flat, light brown, and without a vestige of a safeguard. You must march out and sit down at the threshold of the air. Then you may inhale the contemptuous majesty of the cliffs and truly appreciate it.

The platform's longest side faces roughly to the southwest. At the edge, toward the center of this side, is a cluster of reddish-black spikes, whose purpose I did not then know. Below, down the sheer and overwhelmingly frightful face, the noisy ocean waits impatiently for you to fall into its clutch. The sea, though, is less terrifying than the cliffs, which are silent and aware.

Now the wind was rising; I felt it rocking me on my heels, and impulsively I stretched at full length on the cold shelf with my head sticking out over the gulf. The spindrift was reaching up toward me, but it had a long way to mount before I'd begin to feel it on my face. I wondered if a real gale were brewing. I could not yet read the Irish weather well enough to know. But it felt like the dying old winter making a comeback.

I was dressed as warmly as I could be. Over my Limerick-bought Aran sweater I wore a brown fleece-lined leather jacket belted tight with thongs; under my old maxiskirt of sea-green wool I had on the long johns I used to wear for skiing before I broke my clavicle and gave up *that* idiocy; and the heavy walking brogues I'd acquired in Cork covered thick socks that would have kept a family of newborn mice snug in a hailstorm. In fact, I was actually sweating as I lay there, for I remember stripping off my driving gloves and tucking them into a pocket. I never wear hats, and my hair, which is brown and straight and two feet long, give or take an inch, flew and whipped in the wind.

A vast broken rack of purple-brown cloud swept inland and the sun shone for a few moments, down near the misty line of western ocean. Then it was hidden again. I told myself that it was time to leave. I had no reservation for that night, but it was the off season and I would find a bed in Lisdoonvarna, which was only seven miles away on L54. I'd slept there last night and the hotel was anything but crowded.

Perhaps I gave a thought to my handsome Quinn Griffin then. I think I did. Recalled the high tea and the kisses we'd shared in Lisdoonvarna. Wondered whether—hoped that?—he'd still be there. After all, for a few hours he'd dissipated my gloom and fidgets for me.

But the cliffs were too strong in their grip on my heart. I'd waited a lifetime to see them. I didn't move, watching the sea rise and fall and rise and the gulls dip aimlessly above it, hundreds of feet below me. If you look down at birds flying you can little by little breed the idea that you yourself are a bird, hanging suspended at the top of the world. I like that. . . .

My name is Grania Kirk. I was christened Grania at the urging of my maternal grandmother, an O'Doherty from Donegal who'd emigrated at nineteen to marry a Pennsylvania Dutchman. The other children in Freeport, when they wanted to tease me, would chant ferociously, "Grania, Grania, we'll jump *on* ya!"—which I recollect and put here because it explains how to pronounce my name, rare in the States though common enough in Ireland. I was not named for the fair, fickle Grania of the ancient legend (who would have spelled her name Gráinne, supposing she had been real, and able to spell), but for the grand pirate queen Gráinne Ni Mháille, who was very real indeed, and once upstaged Elizabeth I, a hard lady to snoot with impunity. I've always been pleased about that, though I do not remotely resemble a pirate queen.

What I do resemble, although I'm twenty-three, is a teen-ager. I stand five feet nine in sandals, and my best weight is a hundred twenty-eight. My face, all bones and green eyes and long full lips, is as photogenic as a thoroughbred horse's. I do not think I am beautiful by any stretch of anyone's imagination: at my best, I consider that I look interesting.

I am a television actress. I usually pass for very young

in my roles (and inadvertently in real life) because I inherited those fine-drawn looks that stay the same till the deep wrinkles come. That is the reason for my popularity with casting directors, because I'm not all that marvelous an actress. I am to them, depending on the current fad in young people, the Rebellious Girl, the Flower Child, the Freaked-Out Genius, the Pitiful Addict, and so forth. Which is, of course, a lot of moonshine, because I'm just an ordinary woman who is sometimes scared in Greenwich Village at night; who wouldn't recognize pot if she smelled it; and who has remained, despite the hoked-up glamour and promiscuity of my profession, incurably Middle American and vaguely proud of it.

The source of the depression that sent me to Ireland is quickly told. I was suffering from the effects of what most people might consider a delightful malady: continuous employment in show business. For three solid years I hadn't been out of work for more than a couple of days at a time. With all the up-front periods necessary for memorizing lines and studying characters, plus the frequent eighteen-hour stretches in front of Cameras One, Two, and Three in Studio D saying the same thing over again and again, my nerves had been stretched until suddenly there were far too many people in my world, and all of them nagging at me. I was ready, as we say, to wrap up everything and never go back.

This ramshackle state of my health (mental, not physical, for I'm tough as commissary beef) was aggravated by a passion for a fellow actor that lasted all of a month and was just going to turn into mutual love and/or marriage when for no imaginable reason he dropped me as if I'd burst into flames in his hand. Like a fool, I went around asking friends what was wrong, and eventually learned that someone had spitefully told him I was eighteen. By then it was no use assuring him that I was actually an old hag of twenty-three; he'd been whisked off by a lady, nameless here forevermore, who was forty-seven if she was a day.

My mother, who shared my apartment, told me a day or so later that I was coming down with nerves and should take a vacation. "Why not Ireland?" she said. "Go look up your cousins. There must be plenty there."

"I will," I said on impulse. A quick trip to Freeport to see my grandparents, and then it was only days until the

Aer Lingus jet dropped through the rain to Dublin's airport. In the capital, most of whose historical sites I skipped as not my cup of tea, I found a rental agency that could let me have a tiny Ford with an automatic shift (the clutch is life's ultimate mystery so far as I'm concerned), and headed south for my first Irish ruin, the eight-hundred-year-old Norman castle on the River Slaney.

I had a clear idea of what I would be, as inaccurate as such premature plans usually are. I'd be the opposite of an ordinary tourist. I'd go and mingle with the people, the simple yet subtle folk of the roads and farms. I'd get back to nature with the landscapes, and back to humanity with the kindly Irish. But fear does not vanish so simply, when all you've done to escape it is to cross an ocean. And I *was* afraid of people. It was an aspect of my nervous exhaustion that they made me cringe if they came within arm's length.

Well, I'd found the right place. Ireland is the land for few people if you want her that way. I drove and stared at the country, specifically the seaside cliffs and the uncountable ruins of the olden time. Day after day I spent shut fast in my little car, night after night I locked myself in hotel rooms and read myself to sleep. Timidly I made my way through Counties Wexford and Waterford, down through Cork and over to Kerry, following the coast and getting out of the car to enjoy the views only when there were none of my fellow creatures nearby. Slowly I ceased to hear my nerves snapping one by one, and was enveloped by the melancholy aspect of my illness, which was more bearable. By the time I came to the wonderful Ring of Kerry with its titanic sea panoramas, I was taking a gloomy but genuine pleasure in my ruins and cliffs, like any gentlemaiden out of an eighteenth-century story. But I never really talked to anyone until I came to Limerick Town on the Shannon, where I met Quinn Griffin.

I'd checked into a rosy pink brick hotel near the city's heart. It had turned cold that day—indeed, I had run through a flutter of snow this side of Croom, such an ineffectual handful of it sifting down from a bruise-colored cloud that it gave me a sweetly homesick shiver, for snow is rare in Ireland. That evening I put on my favorite and most wintry outfit, which was a long high-waisted soft-pleated skirt of velvet with a fitted bodice in metallic knit jersey, deeply V-necked and with full-length sleeves and a velvet belt tied in a large bow, the whole affair being one luscious shade of light powder blue; and I went down to the pseudo-Georgian splendor of the hotel's dining room.

The entrance to this was around a sharp corner from the lift (a conscious "word of the country" that came easily to me because of its basic sense), where I nearly bumped into a tall broad man coming from the other direction. We both stopped short and smirked with surprise, and I said "Chilly!" as though I'd been passing an old friend on Madison Avenue. Then I said, "It snowed today," for it seemed churlish not to pass on this earth-shaking news.

No, that's a feeble joke, because I'm sick of writing about the state of my nerves. The plain fact is that almost ramming into a stranger had startled me, and I was babbling. But that's what started it, started everything.

"Snowed?" he repeated, lifting one of his eyebrows, which were very long and thick and black. *"Où sont les neiges?"*

That was an odd enough question to hear in a Limerick hotel, and even odder when delivered by an obvious Irishman. Automatically I answered the old chestnut. "Downtown," I said.

"Come and have dinner," he said, taking me by the arm.

"What?" I said.

"Dinner," he said. "You know. Food and drink."

"But wait," I said, and was ushered to a seat.

"Are there Dublin Bay prawns?" he asked the waiter. "Good. We'll have a cocktail first. You *are* an American?" he asked me. "Yes, two martinis, fantastically dry." Then he smiled at me, a smile that involved everything from the wide, mobile lips past the broad cheekbones to the vivid blue eyes and even the bulky forehead, which creased straight across in a dozen lines. It was an altogether charming smile. "Matter a damn, of course," he said lightly, "but you're the finest-looking girl, darlin', in Limerick this night, and that's the sober truth of it."

"I really think I'd better find another table," I said faintly.

"Why would you do a thing like that?" he asked, looking bewildered.

I was already aware that I was not going to walk away from this engaging, handsome, take-charge guy. It would have been too embarrassing. And disappointing, yes. "I've never experienced an Irish pickup before," I muttered, for want of anything better.

"Didn't I say the right thing?"

"Is there a formula that has to be followed?"

He looked at me as though he were thinking quickly and hard, and blinked rapidly. His eyes with their thick fringe of sooty lashes would have been too beautiful for a man with a less rugged face. "I shouldn't think so, not to excess. My name is Quinn Griffin."

"I'm Grania Kirk."

"Grania is a grand name to bear, and you're the girl to bear it. I never expected anyone like you."

"Well, you're quite a shock to me, too."

"Shock? Who were you expecting?"

"Why, nobody!" I said.

Again there was the strange little pause and blink, which evidently indicated rapid thought. "I wonder," he said slowly.

"Wonder what?"

"How these drinks will be," he said, as the martinis were set reverently before us, "and why a woman with your face and figure, gowned in that glorious fashion, should not foresee that any man would ask you to dine with him." It was the only thing he'd said that did not sound wholly impulsive.

"You're flattering me outrageously."

"I never flatter," he said, after the *slainté* toasts and the first icy, delicious sips. "I merely speak the absolute truth as I see it." He gave me a slow wink that would have melted a brick at thirty paces. "Grania. You're of Irish descent."

"A quarter of me."

"Been here before?"

"No. I'm on my way to Moher."

He nodded as if he'd expected it. "Intriguing place, the Cliffs of Moher. But you'll not see much snow there."

I said lightly and rudely, "I didn't come looking for snow, you dope, but for cliffs."

If I had thought he'd ask why cliffs, I'd been wrong. "Dope. That's what you Americans call drugs, isn't it?"

"I guess so. That wasn't my meaning, though. It was a vulgarity, and I'm sorry. But an American coming here for *snow*—"

"Yes. Snow. That's another." He paused, and said, rather irrelevantly, "Lots of foxes up there at Moher," eyeing me over the rim of his glass, "especially dog foxes."

"What's a dog fox? A what's-it, a hybrid? Like ligers and tiglons?"

"No, just a male fox." Without explaining why there should be more males than females among the vulpine population of my fabulous cliffs, he went on. "Do you know anyone in Limerick?"

"I don't know anyone in Ireland."

"Is that the way of it?" murmured Quinn Griffin. This is what the Irish say where a New Yorker would say "Oh?"

"I'm quite old enough to be on my own," I said defensively.

"A man who'd doubt that would not have eyes in his head, Grania Kirk," he said. "What do you do by way of making a living in this harsh world?" His eyes slid over my expensive clothing. "Have you means?"

So of course that brought out that I was an actress, and for some reason I began, though I'm ordinarily as close-mouthed with strangers as an oyster, to babble of my inadvertent masquerade as an eighteen-year-old; and it was such a release and relief to talk about it that I might have gone on to describe my infancy and adolescence if the marvelous prawns had not appeared.

"And so you came over to see Ireland and forget," he said. "And you headed straight for Moher, of all places."

"No, I've been shilly-shallying around the Republic for nearly three weeks, staring at—"

"Let's see whether you can explain your burning desire to visit Moher, without laughing," he said.

I reminded myself that a mutual language between aliens can sometimes be a barrier to communication. What he meant to imply by his last two words I could not guess. Doubtless it was some piece of Irish jargon. I said slowly and carefully, "I'm a lover of precipices. A connoisseur of cliffs. They're my equivalent of a child's terror movies, my living ghost stories—a source of healthy dread. A reminder of my size and unimportance in the universe, maybe. I know that I always feel refreshed and bouncy when I come away from an hour or two on some deliriously awful verge. Everybody is a nut about something, after all." I paused. "I've heard"—and I thought how silly it was for a grown woman to come thousands of miles because of ghost stories—"I've heard that the Cliffs of Moher are very rewarding."

"Yes. Some would say rewarding indeed. But why not Slieve League instead of Moher? It's the highest cliff in the whole world, as you must know," said Quinn Griffin seriously.

"I will see it, afterwards. It's in Donegal, isn't it?"

"It is. Are you going into the North, then?"

"Only Donegal. That's where Grandmother came from." I was watching his face and suddenly I believed that I saw enough intelligence and sympathy there to risk the chance that I'd convince him I was a raving loony. "It was Grandmother who sold me on Moher, too."

"How was that?"

"Well, she used to tell me stories at night. First they were about Irish fairies, the Shee—"

"The *Sidh*, yes," he said, nodding quite soberly.

"But when I'd started to school she decided that I could stand tougher meat, so we left the silly little fairies behind and progressed to the Cliffs of Moher."

"Do not speak ill of the Good People," he said, lifting one finger. Then he gave me his smile again. "How do we know what's true and false? Go on, Grania Kirk."

I swallowed a bite of delectable prawn. There was champagne now, too. "First she told me about the Dread Women. I adored them. I'm not sure why."

"Because you have the true folk-feeling. There must be awe for such things. We know that, here in the island, and you inherited the knowledge."

"Are you kidding me?"

"I am not. Who are we to claim that the world isn't full of ghouls and demons? Must man have a monopoly on evil? Have the beings that haunted the night for ten thousand years really been explained into oblivion by a few decades of 'science'? I think not. And if they're out there, as our ancestors believed, then imagine how lonely they must be! Why wouldn't you feel sorrow for them, or even kinship?"

I was sure that he was merely playing with ideas; I went along. "Exactly. And there's always the fascination of the utterly grotesque. You know about the Dread Women, then? I used to believe, after I was grown, that Grandmother O'Doherty made them up."

"She didn't. They go back into the dank fogs of Celtic

myth—or Celtic fact—and probably beyond, perhaps into the Stone Age of Ireland. Time out of mind they're said to have laired in the cliffs up there. They are the Harpies of this land."

"Oh, yes, but worse than the Greek Harpies, far worse," I said. "Part human, part ogress, part formless evil, right?"

He nodded. "They are the true powers of darkness, Grania. It's heaven's mercy that they only emerge from sleep rarely. My father used to frighten me with them, too. Deathless, feasting on death, winged and savage, as full of malevolence as the sea is full of water! They are indeed like the Harpies, but there's cold earth under their nails, and warm blood in their veins." He sat back and laughed, so that people turned to look. "I must tell you that my mother's family, having an O to their name and therefore of royal descent, own a banshee; and so I half believe in *everything*."

"That's marvelous," I said. "I wish I could."

"Oh, but I think you do, and are afraid to admit it. Tell me more about Grandmother O'Doherty and her tales of hellish enormities."

"Well, when she ran out of stories about the Dread Women, which must have been soon, because I pestered her for them every evening, she told me about the pooka who patrols the cliffs, a huge black dog—"

"With eyes of flame," Quinn nodded.

"And the ghostly regiment of gallowglasses, mercenary soldiers, that tramps eternally along the brink—"

"I don't know that one," he said, sipping champagne.

"And a lot of other horrors that made me lie awake, enthralling me so much that I'd be back for more the next night."

"Your granny was wrong. There are only the Women and the pooka. But I take it that you know that now?"

"Yes. Not long ago, at the height of my overwork and overworry, when I'd half forgotten the Cliffs of Moher, I found a blurry photo of them in a travel brochure. I was astonished. When I was small I believed in two places, the Land of Oz and the Cliffs of Moher, and naturally you could not photograph either one. But it seemed that the cliffs were real. I went home just before I came to Ireland, and asked her about them. 'They're real right enough,' " I said in my grandmother's voice, " 'and as bad as Cromwell.' "

"How on earth do you do that?" asked Quinn.

"What?"

"Make your voice that of a seventy-year-old woman."

"I told you I'm an actress."

"You should be doing mimicry in the clubs. Go on."

"I said, 'Did Finn Mac Coul really—' and she said, 'Ah, he never saw the Cliffs of Moher.' I said, 'But when the Dread Women attacked Queen Macha—' and she said, 'What would the ruler of Ulster be doing *there?*' I said, 'And when Cuchulainn himself came down the coast to fight them?' and she said, 'Why, the Hound never even heard of 'em! Grania, you had those cliffs so solid in your imagination that nothing would ever do you but a Moher story. I invented forty thousand for you, it was the only way to keep you quiet.' "

Quinn Griffin clapped his hands. *'Óbh óbh! Gráinne abu!'*

"What?"

"Splendid, hooray for Grania! said I. You haven't the Gaelic?"

"No. Thanks," I said after an awkward pause, being unused to such extravagant praise for what I consider a very minor gift.

"And so you traveled here to meet the Dread Women."

"Hardly. I'm on my way to look up family in Donegal. But wouldn't it be a shame to come all this way and not stop at Moher?"

Now I'd been very frank and quick to tell this stranger all about my broken affair, and although that was as unlike myself as possible, it was explicable enough: I'd carried around the misery of it so long that I neded a confessional. Besides, he hadn't been a stranger for more than ten breaths. But no amount of reliance on his discretion and understanding was going to make me admit to my complete emotions about Moher.

By virtually depopulating the cliffs, Grandmother had made them an even more haunting spot than before. The tales that had been spun of them in the Celtic Dawning were the best of the lot. They had created a kind of gray, half-hysterical, half-hypnotized desire in me, a sickly sort of longing to go and stand on that incredible brink and ... and what? Glimpse an airborne hag? Or become airborne myself, if only for five or six seconds? I wasn't sure. I'm not sure now. I only know that I was ill, more so than I realized, and groping for an answer to a question that I didn't dare ask myself straight out. I was retreating, it may be, into a childhood world of safe fear and grisly untruths; longing to run away to the only fairyland I knew that had a location you could reach by a plane and a hired car.

How could I explain to Quinn Griffin that the child is mother to the woman, and that fancies can persist into sensible afterlife, even when you're a fairly tough-minded actress with a high threshold of credulity?

I might have said, "Look, I'm having a nervous breakdown all to myself inside this placid crust, so don't laugh if I assure you that I'm going up to meet a monstrosity that only a four-year-old would credit." But I didn't know I was that badly off. And he hadn't laughed at me even slightly.

He was nodding. "It would be a great pity not to see the Cliffs of Moher. Ah, the *tournedos*. They do it well here." He waited till the plates were put down. Then he bent forward and said quietly, "If you're playing with me, it will be the worse for you," and for a fingersnap of time something looked out from behind his eyes that I could have sworn, had it not been so impossible, was naked rage.

"I beg your pardon?" I said faintly.

He laughed, wholeheartedly and openly and so loud that heads turned again. "Nothing, Grania. An obscure quotation that fits, if you know the context. I've a weakness for obscurity. Now let me tell you of the day when I saw the ghost!"

And from there the conversation grew so light and so packed with Gaelic charm that I was sorry, more than an hour later after the sherry trifle, when he took me to the lift and said, "Good night, Grania Kirk, sleep sound," with a single flash of that enchanting smile as he turned on his heel.

I thought about him as I got ready for bed. Particularly I ran through the early part of our conversation, which seemed to have followed a curious course, as though we'd been talking for a few minutes at cross-purposes. As though, I said to myself as I crept gingerly into the cold bed, almost as though he'd mistaken me for someone else.

I decided that I was happy that he had, if he had, because I'd thoroughly enjoyed the dinner. Only his abrupt departure had been a disappointment.

"I'm coming alive again," I said to myself with sleepy surprise, and fell straight into a dream of dancing with Quinn Griffin on the rim of a ten-thousand-foot precipice made of blue and sparkling rock that matched his intense eyes. There were foxes playing all about our feet.

The next day was full of rain, and after dawdling around Limerick till midafternoon I drove northwest to Ennis and Ennistymon and then north to Lisdoonvarna, which is a tiny town on the edge of the fantastic limestone desert called the Burren. I found a delightful little hotel that was open (but rather startled, I think, to receive an American guest at that time of year) and I moved in. Tomorrow, unless the weather was really horrible, I would see my cliffs at last.

As I was signing the register, noting that ballpoints had not yet penetrated to Lisdoonvarna, someone murmured, "Now what I was saying about your vast towering height is that I feel if a girl is shorter than a man's chin she won't suit him——" and I jerked the pen and made a blot.

"Mr. Griffin!"

"Only last night it was Quinn this and Quinn that," he said, picking up my bags. "How quickly women forget." He strode off with my luggage so that I had to trot to keep up. "I came along to finish whatever it may have been that we were speaking of."

"You followed me here? Fifty miles?"

"Forty-eight. I preceded you. You said you were coming to Lisdoonvarna, and as there's only the one place open, I felt certain of meeting you. I saw a dog fox on the way," he said idly, looking down at me as we stopped beside a door. "Did you?"

"In this rain?" I said. "Why always *dog* foxes? Does one hunt them? Are they awfully clever?"

"Yes and yes, and oh yes." He leaned his shoulder against the door and swung it open, ducking to enter. He was about six feet three, and the doorway was less; his big frame filled it as he went in. "You have an hour till high tea." He set down the bags and tipped up my face and kissed me on the nose. "You're to look desperately ravishing," he said, and departed, leaving me as round-eyed as an owl.

He was waiting, sixty minutes later, with an Irish coffee in front of him and another at his left. "Sit down if you have a thirst on you," he said, "and drink that. I *like* that gown. They serve a superb high tea here. The sausages are so fine that you'd name your first-born after them. Mr. O'Carmody, this is Miss Kirk. O'Carmody is the grandest barman between Kilshanny and Ballynalacken."

"Mr. Griffin will have his joke," said the barman, shaking my hand. He was a small round man, obviously straight out of Dickens and designed by George Cruikshank. He was, I discovered, also the owner of the hotel. "Them places are three miles from here, Miss Kirk."

Quinn now turned his attention full on me, where it remained through the coffee and an inexhaustible supply of lamb chops, eggs, liver, bacon, the celebrated sausages (oh marvelous!), chips galore, and a flan of fruit, washed down with strong black tea. At last I leaned back and gasped that I couldn't handle another bite.

"You want a walk," said Quinn, solicitous. "How about Moher?"

"It's night," I objected.

"Many prefer them at night, when the dog foxes come out."

"But it's raining gallons," I said.

"Oh well, if you shrink or melt," he said carelessly. "What about Saturday?"

"I haven't any notion whether I'll be here then. I may not even be here *tomorrow* night."

"Yes, you did say you'd been stopping rather briefly everywhere. But I assumed that Moher . . ."

"One look may be enough. I may be frightened out of my obsession."

"Not you. You'll hang about till you've sighted a Dread Woman. Or at least a dog fox, I should think," he added, grinning. He led me into the lounge to a huge sofa. There was a television set blasting away in one corner, which he thoughtfully clicked off despite the people who were watching it. "You've had enough telly for a lifetime, I daresay," he told me, sitting down.

"Quinn," I said, "we've talked up a storm, and I still don't know the first thing about you, do you realize that?"

"Nonsense. You know that I have a banshee, that I once saw a ghost, that I find you immensely alluring—"

"But I know nothing about *you,* and I'm practically dating you!"

"I'm not married nor ever was, if that's what you mean," he said. He put a long arm over my shoulders. "Nor do I habitually roam the countryside in search of American actresses with banks full of money, on whom I can prey, however lovely they look."

I was suddenly, happily conscious of looking my best: the new rose brocade gown with its floor-length A-line skirt, jewel neck, and angel sleeves was an unqualified success, and let me appear to be almost my real age. "I've told you my life story. What about yours? What do you do for a living?"

"There's some would say one thing and some another."

"Don't make mysteries. You're glamorous enough."

He widened his elegant eyes at me. "That's a thing I've not been called before! Handsome, often and often, naturally. But glamorous!"

"You're laying on the brogue and blarney with a trowel again, and you *know* you look just like Peter O'Toole, only wider. What's your profession?"

"I'll tell you one day." He stared at me from quite close, and my head reeled slightly. "I honestly can't at present."

"A few years ago, then, I'd have guessed you were James Bond."

"I won't tell you yet, Grania, but only to keep from lying to you, which is a thing I'd hate to do. My business is not reprehensible."

"You make me shiver," I said, which was true, and delicious. "I can't help wondering now, can I? You traveled here from Limerick just to see me . . . or did you?"

He continued to study my face as though memorizing it. That's always flattering. "Partly," he said at last.

"You're impossible." I discovered that we were holding hands. "Do you have a cigarette?"

"I don't smoke. If I did, I'd never have caught that violet scent you're wearing."

"But I'm not. I forgot it."

"Then you wore it yesterday. I whiffed it last night, too."

"I've had a bath since then," I said indignantly.

"But the scent clings. I think perhaps in this," he said, lifting a strand of my hair. "Strange, I'd have thought

you'd be the spice type, not the floral. Yet it suits you."
Disregarding some passing people and a few disgruntled
ex-TV-viewers who were glaring at us, he bent forward
and kissed me ever so softly on the lips. "You are a most
fantastically attractive woman, Grania, and it's time you
forgot your obtuse and blind actor love and came into the
world again, isn't it?"

"Yes," I said, holding fast to his hand, "yes it is."

"And so you shall." He turned himself round on the big
brown sofa and lay with his head in my lap.

I chuckled. "You're the least inhibited Irishman in public that I've ever seen. Can't we be arrested for such behavior?"

"Oh, the folk here are used to me. Tell me what you
think of things, Grania. All things in the universe, all
things both great and small. We've the night before us."

"Yerra, the night is it," said I.

"You got that one from your grandmother."

"I did so."

"And that one, perhaps, from me?"

"Why not?"

"You talk back like a bloody Irishman. Repeat after
me: 'Oi'll give yez a puck in the wind if yez doubt for an
instant that Oi'm heels over head in love wid that grand
Misther Griffin.' "

"You're distracting me on purpose. Tell me, *are* you a
spy?"

He closed his eyes leisurely, smiling. "I ferret out state
secrets in Lisdoonvarna and sell them for untold amounts
to the governments of Morocco and Tunisia. Do you like
children, Grania Kirk?"

"Very much. Children and dogs—"

"We shall have seven," he murmured, his eyes shut and
his voice dreaming, "for there's luck in odd numbers. Children, I meant, not dogs."

"Well, then," I persisted, teasing, "are you a smuggler?"

His eyes clicked open and he looked up. Had I actually
struck a nerve? "What would a man smuggle out of this
country?" he laughed.

"Leprechauns. Wetback leprechauns."

"Or into it?"

" 'Brandy for the parson—' "

" 'Baccy for the clerk.' Yes. A vast fortune there'd be in
that. You were warmer on the spy tack, darlin'."

"I don't think so. You jumped. Do you smuggle in refugees from the North?"

He snorted. "All they need do is walk across the border. You Americans have weird notions of what's happening up there."

"Not drugs?" I ventured. And as he sat erect and glared at me, I knew that I had been, without recognizing it, half serious; for in him I could sense the strange wild currents moving all the time, as though behind the conventionally cut silk jacket beat a rakish, renegade heart, pumping blood that flowed in different rhythms from that of ordinary men's.

"What is it that you know about drugs?" he asked harshly.

"Why, nothing more than everyone does these days. They're the curse of the times, aren't they? I understand," I said, faltering now that his eyes had been on me so long, "there's a great deal of money in them, and . . ."

"Yes. There is that. Lashins of money, as we say."

"Quinn, you don't really, you aren't—"

He burst into a quick laugh. "Once a year I have the mother and father of all hangovers. You may guess after which night. And I'm prone then to take aspirin. Nothing more." His face had cleared. "I'm sorry, love," he said, watching me closely, "but no, I don't bring in curraghloads of marijuana on stormy nights to peddle round the streets of Dublin." Our stares were locked for another moment. Then he glanced down at his watch. "Grania, I hate to end this evening. But there will be others."

"You told me that we had the night before us," I said lamely, like a child being packed off early to bed. It was an abrupt and almost insulting exit line for him. "Don't tell me you've recollected an engagement."

"I have not. I didn't want the emotion of a sadly premature ending to invade our time till the last possible minute. Come along, I'll see you home," he said, and lifted me gently and firmly by an elbow and walked me to the hallway and down to my room. "I'm not being mysterious, not viciously so, any road; but I have an appointment."

Then he kissed me again, in front of my door, as if I were anything in the world but a casual friend. Afterward I was standing inside with my lips feeling bruised and my mind the same.

I got out of the rose brocade gown and into the bed. I

was disappointed, peevish, intrigued, and bewildered. Why had he suggested a walk at Moher if he'd had no more than those few minutes before whatever tryst he was now keeping? I suppose I went to sleep more mad than anything else. In spite of the kiss.

The next day I paid my small bill and drove into the Burren. This is as much of a desert as Ireland runs to, and in the spring it blooms with gorgeous flowers, as our own deserts do; but today, which was cloudy but not rainy, it showed little color beyond the browns and grays of its rock. It is full of caves, though I did not explore them because you're not supposed to do that alone, and because I am terrified of being underground; and there are plenty of stone forts and dolmens, many of which I did inspect. I was putting off the cliffs, now that I was in their neighborhood: working up to them via the Burren in the same spirit of self-tantalizing as that in which one slowly eats a hot fudge sundae and leaves the enormous maraschino cherry till last.

I had an idea that my maraschino cherry might be poisonous.

At a general store in the middle of nowhere I drank a bottle of milk and bought some ginger nuts (we call them snaps) and candy bars. Then I drove downcountry to the cliffs, whose stunning presence sent Quinn Griffin out of my thoughts entirely, and when I did recall him it was only in relation to high tea and Lisdoonvarna.

2

*And sure, my heart was throbbin'
for the blessed morning's light ...*
—Rising of the Moon

THE SWELLS CAME IN FROM MEASURELESS DISTANCES beyond my sight to destroy themselves at the foot of my great curtain-wall, and slowly, slowly I began to notice something.

Nobody can explain that feeling, of course. But anyone who's experienced it knows that there is no mistaking it. Raw nerves or not, when it happens, you *know* it.

I turned my head quickly and scanned from east to north, rolled onto my back and sat up to glare at O'Brien's Tower high on the crest, then past the lay-by where my small Ford sat alone, and over the land to the distant lavender-dusted hills. Nothing moved anywhere.

The feeling drained away.

But someone, or something, had been eyeing me. I would have bet ten Irish pounds on that.

I stood up. I did want to inspect the tower before I drove away, and the sun had only half an hour of life in it. I'd be back here tomorrow, but I wanted to see all that I could today. Indeed, if I'd arrived earlier, I would have tried the long walk down the brow of the cliffs all the way to Hag's Head to visit its old abandoned signal tower, which from here resembled one of the numberless castle ruins that pervade Ireland. But O'Brien's Tower was hardly five minutes to the north, and I set off for it, across the broad platform and up the short scramble; between the upended flagstones that keep timid folk well back from the drop; then onto the soggy ground and all the puddles that must be leaped in the ascent, until I'd topped the rise and walked a few hundred feet on the level to arrive at the tower.

24

What if there *had* been someone watching me? The Republic of Ireland is one of the safest countries in the world, despite what horrors occur in Ulster. Muggers do not lurk in its parks and lonely places, nor rapists lie in wait for unwary girls traveling alone. I had met precisely one unfriendly soul in three weeks, a waitress in County Wexford. If someone were curious about me, lying like a lunatic on the icy shelf above Moher's vast wall, they had a perfect right to stare. The platform is out of sight of the road, but maybe it had been a farmer, so far off that I hadn't spied him. Or a fox? Quinn had said that the place was full of them.

O'Brien's Tower looks as though it had been built by the Norman invaders; actually it is less than a century and a half old. But it is only a stone hull of a tower now, and as I walked around it and then stepped inside, I was disappointed to see that there was no way to climb to the viewing place on top, and that by no effort of imagination could it even be considered a haunted site. It is picturesque only from a distance. And cattle had been browsing about it, and I had to be careful where I stepped.

I went out into the freshening wind again, and looked north. There was time to walk a short distance farther. So I set off over the boggy humps of green—imagine a country that shows bright green all through a cold winter!—and crested the low rise and caught my breath. For here, on the last jut of the cliffs of Moher, was a *real* ruin, as romantically spectral a sight as the Rock of Cashel is in the twilight.

It had been a castle. In places it rose to what may have been half its original height, in others it lay like stone bones scattered over the barren rock from which it had once risen proud and whole and free. This great, jagged, broken, powerful creation of arrogant dead hands stood before me, and I caught my breath and leaned against the rushing gust from the sea while my hair streamed out in a plume over my right ear and my eyes watered with wind and emotion. The thing was as elemental and menacing as the cliffs themselves. I laughed aloud and ran toward it, hoping to surprise a ghost.

It was I who was surprised. So much so, I admit, that I gave a yip of fear as I caught sight of her.

She was perched on a merlon of the battlement, twenty yards ahead of me and perhaps twenty-five feet above my head. I slowed to a walk, feeling like a fool of a tourist, and approached her, while she stared at me without any amazement.

She was a girl of somewhere near my age, dressed in blue jeans and a red Connemara coat belted with a green criosanna, and she sat cross-legged on that towering chunk of stone as placidly as if she'd been on a pub stool. Her shining blond hair, as long as mine, was a bright banner in the wind. She never took her eyes off me, and her expression did not change as I halted just below.

"Hi!" I said brightly. I wondered how she had climbed up so far; there was nothing on my side of the shattered wall to make for an easy scaling.

She looked down for a minute and then said, so clearly and coolly that I could hear the capital letters, "Casual Visitors Are Not Encouraged."

I was taken aback, and felt my cheeks flush with embarrassment, even under their Irish windburn. "I just wanted to—why not?" Surely this wasn't private property.

"In the first place, the ruins are extremely dangerous," she said. Her voice was soft, but carried well, and I speculated that she might be an actress, to project that easily into the teeth of a gathering gale. "You'd likely break your neck. In the second place, they're haunted. How do you know that I'm not a ghost?"

"Too twentieth-century," I said. If it hadn't been for her calm hostility, this would have been friendly banter. But it wasn't. "I only want to poke around. Say, were you watching me a little while ago?"

"No. Go back to your car," she said. She rose lazily to her feet, which were cased in a pair of the most magnificent fur-topped black boots I'd ever seen. Standing there in the rays of the drowning sun, a very pretty girl indeed, she watched me for five or six seconds longer, and repeated her curious warning, her gentle voice gone all flat and menacing. "Casual visitors are *not* encouraged." Then she turned her back, with the radiant wind-lashed hair a perfect glory around her small head, and stepped away from me and vanished.

I stood thinking, and I was angry. Ruins in Ireland are there to be seen, to be inspected and marveled at and fingered and dreamed over. No one warns you away from them unless they lie in a private estate, where you can nearly always beg viewing permission anyway. And the

Cliffs of Moher belong, so far as I know, only to the Republic and to God—or, perhaps, to the Devil. So I went tramping along the southern edge of the ruin, looking for the marker that you find on many such places that tells you this is the protected property of the Irish government, and not to commit atrocities therein, et cetera. I could not find one. I glanced toward what remained of the sun and realized that dusk was practically here.

Well, I'd be back tomorrow, and after paying my respects to the cliffs again, I'd come up here and stroll all over the frayed old wreck of a castle, being as casual an unencouraged visitor as I liked. My Scotch-German-Irish dander was up, not to mention the faint dash of Iroquois I can boast of.

I trudged back across the marshy ground, splashing irritably right through the wettest places, slopping up my long skirt with muck and not giving a damn.

To compose myself after that preposterous rebuff, I descended past the big flagstones and went out right onto the western brink of the platform once more. I sat tailor-fashion—unconsciously, I imagine, to show *her* that *I* had the nerve to perch on high places, too—and tried to light a cigarette, but the wind was far too strong. I fished out my gloves and put them on, for my fingers were numbing by this time. I listened to the gulls mewing far down the steep, and let the black cliffs soothe me with their prodigious disdain as the daylight faded.

Finally I went back to the car. I'd left a window partially rolled down, and it was colder inside than out, it seemed to me; and the wind had got into my box of facial tissues and scattered them prodigally throughout the car. I bundled them roughly up and stuffed them into their box, blew my nose on two of them, rolled the window shut, stepped on the gas pedal, and turned the key.

And nothing happened.

The engine did not emit that throaty protracted clunking that it makes when a run-down battery is trying its best to obey you. It uttered no sound at all. There was just the click in the ignition and the faint squeak of the foot lever. I turned it off and pumped gently twice, and tried again.

My car did not start.

I felt no panic at first. I did not instantly connect this mysterious obstinacy of my faithful rented machine with the belligerent girl in the ruins, or with my sense of being watched, or with the legendary Harpies of Moher, or even with the mischievous leprechaun, whom you never hear of in that country anyway. I simply said several words that I had picked up around the television studios, and got out to lift the hood, which I'd learned rather self-consciously to call the bonnet. I peered in at the engine, which lay there quietly, an intricate, unfathomable, lifeless mess. I went back to find my flashlight—no, I corrected myself: my torch. When in Erin, speak as the sons of Patrick speak; besides being protective coloration, it gets things done quicker.

With the torch and a screwdriver, I poked and nudged everything that looked movable. All the time I realized that I was just showing off, in front of whom I wasn't sure—probably myself. Because I know nothing about engines. I can handle a steering wheel, even when it's on the wrong side of the car, and I can stand on the brake at a stop sign with the best of them, but the workings of the brute are a closed book. I could as easily repair a watch as start a balky motor.

"Wires," I said aloud. I was fairly sure that wires connected all sorts of vital parts, nameless parts to me, perhaps, but vital. I could make out a tangle of them back near the panel that separates the jumble of fans, coils, magnets, boxes, and paraphernalia from the car's interior. I zipped up my jacket to protect my clean sweater, being mortally certain that everything under the bonnet was coated with oil; and leaning as far over as I could, pulled at each wire in turn with the tip of the screwdriver. It had a plastic handle and I did not think I was in much danger of being electrocuted.

Everything was attached. I looked up forward. There was a square thing that must be the battery. Two thickish wires lay on it. Their tips were shielded in erratically shaped pieces of dull gray metal, and they were just lying there on the battery. I sighed. Obviously they were meant to be attached to each other, and they had been jarred loose. Feeling proud and brave, and hoping that my gloves would not conduct electricity, I fitted them together as well as I could. It was an odd fit, and very loose. A metal rod nearby was probably intended to hold them together. I worked one bit of metal under this rod and shoved in the second one next to it. It looked right. That must have been the cause of the trouble. I took a last squint at the tortuous enigma that is an internal-combustion engine, shut the bonnet, and hustled myself into the car away from the tearing wind.

By this time it was quite overcast and dark. I pulled a comb through my hair to free my eyes and then with an air of confidence started the engine, which didn't start.

Well, there was no use in the world in going out and scowling at the hodgepodge. I had made my effort in that direction.

I thought; and felt for my cigarettes and couldn't find them; and tried to turn on the ceiling light, which wasn't working either. I was sitting in a cold steel box which would keep the wind off, but would do nothing further than that to help me.

I looked out the windows to see if there might be a tiny twinkling light in some cottage within walking distance. There was none. I couldn't remember seeing any houses out yonder when I'd driven up. Even if there were some, they might be empty. People walk away and leave their homes in Ireland and the houses stand there, undisturbed, silent, looking the same, for years, decades, even centuries, until the roofs fall in or the venerable walls collapse at last.

Could I be out of gas? I had never run out of gas before in my life, but I might not have noticed. . . . I could not recollect when I had checked it last. Wait, though— I'd filled the tank just outside Limerick. The gauge in the light of my torch showed more than half full, but I couldn't be sure that *it* was working either. Maybe I'd had a leak in the fuel line, if English-made Fords had fuel lines. I emerged once more and knelt to inspect the roadway under the machine. Two or three tiny spots showed damp, which must be oil. Remembering the garage floor at home, I assumed that this was normal. I got back into the car.

It was growing colder. I tightened all the windows and, on a hunch, locked both doors. This was safe old Ireland, yes, but who could be sure how far across its borders the I.R.A. and the U.V.F. might carry their insanities?

Oh, the "wee folk, good folk, trooping all together," they had hexed me good and proper!

I might walk to Lisdoonvarna. Seven miles isn't far to walk . . . except on a night that's working up to a storm, when you can't see two paces ahead. My torch was manifesting symptoms of failure, too; its beam had been distinctly yellow during those minutes under the bonnet. I ought to have laid in fresh batteries days ago.

Aimlessly, to be doing something, I tried to start the motor again. After that time I stopped trying. The uselessness of it was too frightening.

What was the worst of the matter? I'd have to spend the night here. I shouldn't freeze, for it wouldn't go below forty; I had a pound of ginger nuts, so I wouldn't be too hungry; and in the morning I'd walk, or hitch a ride, to the garage in town. Hitchhikers are always picked up in Ireland—there is no danger whatever, to them or from them.

I struggled into the back seat and folded up my traveling rug for a pillow. I disposed myself as comfortably as possible (I'm too tall to lie straight in one of those miniature automobiles) and then my brain began to work. Wickedly.

I thought of the strange girl on the ruins, and she became in a surmise the moll of a gang of I.R.A. men who were ... what did I.R.A. men *do*, besides throwing nail bombs and Molotov cocktails at the British or the Protestants in Ulster? And what would they, or anyone, be doing on the Cliffs of Moher, out here at the back of beyond? Yet the girl had been here.

Was she getting ready to sack out somewhere over north in those eerie ruins? A preposterous idea. She must be on her way home now, wherever that was. But where had her car been parked? She certainly didn't live on a nearby farm. She was as different as I was from the countrywomen of County Clare, who still run to red flannel petticoats and gray shawls; especially the boots and the American-influenced blue jeans, they'd stamped her as—well, at least Limerick, and more likely Dublin. Her accent was soft and cultivated.

She was growing into an obsession. Why had she been so coldly forbidding? I was only an innocent stranger.

"Go away, witch," I mumbled. There was absolutely nothing to be frightened about. With my constitution, I wouldn't even catch a cold. And Fords are indubitably witchproof.

Witch. Cliffs of Moher. Right out *there*. I could hear the surf at their base—no, that was only the wind.

Why had I even thought the word "witch"? It was witches that had brought me here, really—a peculiar breed of witches, that I hadn't believed in since I was a child, but that frightened me silly as I lay here a few yards from their home base.

"Don't be a dad-blamed fool," I said loudly in the voice of a wonderful old character actor I'd worked with in a Western last year. "There ain't nothin' in the dark except the dark, and you consarned well know it!"

I ate a dozen ginger nuts, slightly stale but delicious. I breathed regularly, deeply, and reviewed all the improvements that this vacation had wrought with my nerves, imaginary or not; and by and by I did feel better, and knew that it had been only the perfectly reasonable shock of finding myself immobilized that had agitated me. After a while I fell into an uncomfortable doze, to waken with a start from some half-recalled dream and find my body stiff and cramped. The luminous hands of my watch said it was nearly half past midnight. Some doze! I'd slept for hours.

I searched for my cigarettes again, the torch now shining more brightly than before. They were nowhere in my clothes or on the floor. I must have dropped them on the rock shelf. The light showed the windows thick with condensation, and the air was choking and stale from my breath; that little car was as tight as a corked bottle. I rolled down both windows and got out to stretch my legs. There was moisture outside too, but it was much fresher and not too cold. There had been no storm. The wind had dropped to a gentle breeze, and the moon was out, nearly full. It would have been clear enough to walk to Lisdoonvarna, but coming up in the west I could see more heavy clouds. I was getting along quite well in my steel box, at any rate. I no longer minded waiting for morning. It was almost an adventure.

I ordinarily smoked about three cigarettes a day, but just now I wanted one badly. Taking the torch, I flicked it on again and started toward the big platform. The night was almost wholly silent, save for a muted surf. Every good Irishman was long abed. There were no such things as witches.

"Doggoned right they ain't," I said in my old friend's voice, to keep myself company as I scrambled down among the huge slabs of flagstone and onto the platform.

And abruptly, without even a warning dim and flicker, the light went out.

My eyes adjusted promptly to the moon, and I realized that I hadn't needed the torch. I set it on the stone and walked toward the edge where I'd been sitting at sundown. I remembered that I'd taken out the pack there, and stuffed it carelessly into a pocket when I'd found that my matches couldn't buck the wind. I must have missed the pocket.

Then it occurred to me that my half-empty pack would have been blown a mile inland by the wind. Unless I was lucky, and it had gotten itself stuck in some crevice or against the wall of grass that rose to the east. I turned left, searching the wet dark stone as far as I could see.

The moon was abruptly covered by a cloud like a mile-thick blanket, and the world disappeared around me.

I wailed with frustration, and turned to glare up at the sky where my only light had been shining. I saw the edges of the vast cloud lit for a moment, and then it swept on and even the silver lining vanished. I was standing alone in the middle of the blackest night I had ever experienced. It was so thick and palpable a darkness that if I had rubbed two fingers together, they might have been smudged as if with soot.

I pivoted and walked toward the path to the car park. The platform was quite flat, and if I tripped over anything it would be my feet. When I had walked about as far a distance as I thought I'd come from the incline and the rampart of flagstones, I slowed my pace. It was an unearthly sensation, and certainly a little frightening, to be walking along through that damnable ink, seven hundred feet above the ocean. I recalled the sheer drop, and shuddered. It was colder than I'd noticed. And maybe even blacker. And—

And I had surely come far enough to be at the path?

Then I stopped moving, because I realized that in turning to look at the moon that was no longer there, I'd changed the position of my feet. Then I had veered partially round again, toward where I believed the way back lay. But I hadn't taken the first turn into consideration when I started off. And now I did not truly know in which direction I had been walking so boldly and idiotically.

I was lost. How could I be lost, only a hundred yards from my car, I demanded indignantly, and an echo answered from the back of my dumfounded brain: Very easily.

Good Lord, I might have walked straight off into eternity!

All my outlandish, extravagant emotions about these cliffs came back to me with a rush, but this time they were laced with a deep and practical fear. I did not dare move a foot, an inch, a centimeter from my position. I stood there, feeling my body sway with the shivering dread. What should I do? How soon till that cloud passed beyond the moon? Would I grow giddy and fall down before I could see again? And *where* would I fall, onto the rock or into the ocean?

I remember feeling grateful for the fact that I had never fainted in my life, and was unlikely to do so now.

Wait a minute: I could step backward a short distance, and get down to all fours and—no, I really was so rattled that I couldn't be sure I hadn't shuffled around nervously after halting the last time.

As slowly as I could manage, I squatted until I was sitting on my heels. Just as timidly I put one hand out and lowered it, and my fingertips touched the wet stone of the platform. I swept them around, as far as I could reach, and my hand felt only rock.

I tried to get my bearings, but when you can see nothing—and oh, but that night was tropical in its lack of visibility, if not in its temperature—then you cannot aim yourself with any assurance. I listened to the noise of the sea. At last I thought I had located it, behind and off to my left. On hands and knees I began to crawl, about as briskly as a wounded earthworm, straight forward.

How far I crept along in this fashion I cannot guess.

Strangely enough, my fear had now retreated, leaving me rather wobbly but much eased in mind. I wouldn't fall off the cliffs now, and if I couldn't find the path, I would at least arrive eventually at some nice, soppy grass, where I could sit down and shiver until the moonlight returned.

I stopped moving. For a breath of time, I did not know why. Then it came to me that the air on my sweating, clammy face was different. The breeze had all but died, yet there was a curious touch on my cheeks and lips that had not been there a few seconds before. I could not analyze the change; perhaps it was mere imagination. I was about to go on, and then I realized that I could see something on the platform before me.

Gradually I extended my legs behind until I was in the posture that one assumes when doing push-ups. Then I shoved with my toes, leaned forward without moving my hands, and lowered my face to squint at whatever it was.

A curious dim milky-silver radiance, in spots and streaks and smears, moved and melted away and came in sight again. What was it? I thought of glowworms, which I had never seen. Had I come on a nest of them, here in a hollow of the stone? Would they bite?

Glowworms. *Glow.*

Oh my God, it was the phosphorescence of the breaking sea! My hands were at the lip of the fall, and my head was thrust out over the edge!

No wonder the air on my face had felt different. It was the freshness of the ocean, coming straight up those terrible walls.

I backed off like a spooked crab, and after a couple of yards, simply fell on my chest and gasped for sanity and breath.

I would not have started off on my stupid journey again, I told myself, even if I'd had my flashlight full of fresh batteries in my sweaty hand.

I was going to lie there, catching pneumonia or not, until the moon came out. No, the sun.

Of course I had been in no danger. One cautiously placed hand encountering no solid stone would have shot me backwards just as fast as the sight of that dully burning sea had done. But somehow, I thought, it would not have been half so horrifying.

It was then that I heard the noise. Small, perhaps innocent, but plain and clear above the surf. It came from somewhere behind me. It was the sound of pebbles rattling down over rock.

At once I thought of the blond girl. Was she wandering around, had she inspected my car and found me missing and—

That was nonsense. How could she see any better than I could in this murk? And why would she come searching for me at one o'clock in the morning? She'd only been mean about the ruins. . . .

It might be a fox—Quinn *had* made such a point of it

that the place was overrun with foxes—or a badger. Did badgers attack people? I didn't know.

I lifted myself a little and peered over my right shoulder in time to see, or to think that I saw, a pale yellow-white light shine briefly and go out. It happened so quickly that I could not even judge how far away it was.

But now I had my bearings. I knew where the platform ended. Shaky as a pillar of custard, I stood up and walked toward the lay-by. I covered two yards, six, ten. I must be near the rising ground. Somehow I was sure that this time I wasn't heading off the cliff. It was the irrational positiveness of desperation.

The rattling pebbles and the small flash of light had proclaimed something, but not until my foot touched earth beyond the rock did I dare to admit it to myself in words. I was not alone on the Cliffs of Moher. Something, human or demoniac, was there with me. And I felt mortally confident that whatever it was, it knew that I was there, too.

I heard someone whimpering. It was me. I bit my lip, a last bubble of panic slipped out, and then I was still. I began to move up the slope, my brogues sliding on the muck. I had never been so afraid in my life. The appearance of a luminous Irish ghost with his head on backward would have been a relief, because I would not have believed in him for a moment. What I had often read was true: the unseen, the unknown is more terrifying than anything visible can possibly be.

I heard another sound, and this time it was not my own sniveling. Out there in the dark, not far, not far at all, whatever had kicked the pebbles was making a noise at me. With my mouth wide open and my blind eyes bulging—yes, I was conscious in that awful instant of my face, for I was trying my best to scream and to see, and I could do neither—I faced the thing.

It was uttering a low, broken sound, a threatening noise without words. I realized with hideous clarity that it must be an idiot, a poor maimed soul that could only voice its hatred in a kind of blubbery snarling. Horrified beyond my power to tell, I whirled round to run. My foot slid sideways in the muddy grass and I fell to one knee. Then my vocal cords unfroze and I let out the scream of a lifetime.

The maniac slavered and snarled again. I was flailing my arms and trying to get to my feet. There was the steely chinking noise of hobnailed brogans on rock. Then a deep soft voice said, "Shut up, Balor," and at the same time my arms were gripped above the elbows. I yelled again, this time in a half-throttled whine, for my throat had clogged with fear.

I was lifted and set on my feet. A head came so close to my own that even in this tar barrel of a night I could see it, though I could not distinguish the features. And the man said, in the same quiet, level tone, "Well, now we have you, don't we?"

3

What are you doing here, miss,
Here, miss, here, miss?
What are you doing here, miss,
Where foxes bark and the hounds bow-wow!
— Child's Song

THE WORDS AND THE CRUEL GRIP were calculated to pet-
rify anybody who was standing on witch-haunted cliffs in
the middle of a rayless night in a foreign land. As a matter of fact, I believe they cheered me up considerably. I
was not thinking with any logic, admittedly; but I know
that I pressed myself forward into that man's arms and
gave a sigh, or a grunt, of relief. Then I said, "Oh, help,"
in a faint voice. For I was more afraid of the slavering
maniac than of any sane soul, threatening or not.

It must have baffled him. His clutch on my arms
relaxed and he cleared his throat loudly and said, "What
the devil?" uncertainly.

"There's some kind of *thing* out there," I said, my face
pushed into his chest, which smelled of damp wool and tobacco smoke.

"There's only us," he said. "Look here, this girl is shaking with ague."

"It's Balor that's frightened her," said another man
behind him.

"What, the hound?" said the one holding me.

And it all came together in my muddled head. "Is that
what it is?" I said, drawing back a little. "I thought it was
an idiot."

"Can't you see he's only a dog?"

"I can't see *anything*." I squinted hard at the Rorschach
blot that was his head. "You mean you can?"

"There's plenty of starlight," he told me with rough patience. "I suppose you're not used to it yet."

"Come here, Balor," said a woman's voice. The dog

whined happily and I heard its claws click on the rock as it moved.

"You're still shaking," said the man. "Are you ill?"

"No, you fool, I'm scared," I snapped. "I've been scared for an hour. I almost pitched off the damn cliffs, and crawled around for a mile on my stomach, and then your light flashed and your dog blustered at me and you came leaping out of nowhere, and I'm scared!"

"The dog would not harm you even if I told him to do so," said the man, "and we flashed no light. Why are you out here if you can't see at night?"

"I came to look for my cigarettes."

"Is that the way of it?" said the second man dubiously. "Did you find them, then?"

"No."

"That's your car back there, isn't it?" the first man said.

"Yes. It won't start. I don't know what's wrong with it."

"Where are your friends?"

"What friends?" I asked, wriggling in his grasp. "Do you have to stop my circulation like that? It must be obvious that I'm not going anywhere unless you guide me."

"When are they coming?" he demanded.

"Who?"

"You know perfectly well who!"

"I don't have any idea what you're talking about, and I'm not sure that you do, either."

"This conversation is heading nowhere by hops and bounds," said the other man. "Why don't we inspect the car? There's just a chance she's speaking the truth."

"I wish you'd tell me what's going on," I said, and felt ashamed of the distinct whine in my voice.

"Come along, we'll look at the car."

"You'll have to lead me."

"Don't worry," he said, "I wouldn't let loose of you for a hundred pounds."

We moved up the wet slope. "I left my torch someplace," I said. "It needs batteries. It went out on me."

"I have it," said the woman. There was a click. "It's dead, that much is true."

"Were you to signal with it?" asked the man sharply. I didn't even answer him, I was so mad. After a few stumbles over rocks that I couldn't see, we were on the smoothness of the car lay-by. The man still held me firmly.

"Give us our torch then, love," said the other. And there was a huge beam of light, blessed white light, and I felt my whole frame relax as the three figures sprang into view, as well as my poor little inert Ford.

"Where's the dog?" I said.

"Behind you."

"Will he bite when he sees me?" I am not afraid of animals, but there still clung to this invisible beast the aura of the menacing idiot.

"Certainly not. Balor is a gentleman." The man who was not holding me unlatched the bonnet and shone his torch inside. "Well, of course the bloody thing won't start," he said. "Look here, Dog."

I was so far from any sane reality by that time that I fully expected the hound to come paddling past me and peer into the workings of the car; but the first man shoved me forward ungently, and bent over it himself. I must have misunderstood the name he'd been called. "Didn't you even look at it?" he asked me, turning his face toward me. It was a square red-brown face, one of the most weather-beaten I'd ever met, and brown eyes scowled out of it upon me. "Didn't you look at the battery?"

"Yes. The wires were loose, so I joined them. You can see that."

"She joined them," said the second fellow. "Look at that, will you. She speaks the solemn truth. Bones of great Brian!"

"Do you expect us to believe that you found both these wires loose, and stuck 'em together like that, and thought the motorcar would then move?" said the leathery man angrily.

"Yes, I do. No, I don't! I don't expect anything from the three of you but sheer howling insanity." I was frightened and confused, but I was angry, too, as much at the sneer as at his tight grip on my arm. "But it's what I did, anyway. Is it wrong?"

The second man took a pair of pliers and a screwdriver from his hip pocket, freed the wires, and attached them to what I was informed were the battery terminals.

"How was I to know?" I said. "Do I look like a mechanic?"

"You look like a liar," said the first man coldly.

What I said then I will not repeat. I had never said it to another human being, and don't expect to do so again, but

I was driven far beyond the point of sweet forbearance. I was in an appalling situation and I am not the bravest woman in the world, but sometimes I seem to exude belligerence when I'm alarmed. It isn't pluck. It's some kind of terror reaction that I can hardly control. And I do think that most of us tend to get mad after being scared for a long time, as I had certainly been. At any rate, I said it.

"My, she has a vile tongue on her," said the second man calmly, shutting the bonnet. "Where would the keys be?"

"Why should I tell you? For all I know, you're a gang of car thieves. I hoped I'd left you all behind when I came to Ireland, too."

"She keeps it up well, you must give her that," he said to the man holding me. "You'd swear she was innocent as a bedtime story. But the wires contradict her, I think." He turned to the girl. "What do you say, love?"

I looked at her for the first time and saw that she was the blonde from the ruins. She said in her dove's voice, "The American girls *I* know are better acquainted with engines than their boy friends are. She could have had this car in motion in thirty seconds."

"It's the first thing anyone would look for," said the weathered man, nodding.

"My arm is getting numb," I told him. "But I suppose that'll only make you pinch it."

He took his hand away and said to the dog behind me, "Guard, Balor." The brute growled. I had not looked at him yet, and if I had my way, I never would. He would likely be the pooka, with eyes all yellow flame. "Don't try to run," said the man to me.

"Have some sense. Where would I go?"

"To your friends. If they're out there yet."

"My friends are about thirty-five hundred miles out there," I said sulkily, waving an arm in the general direction of the west. "I wish you'd tell me what this is all about, and who you think I am. I have a passport, after all."

"What do you think?" asked my captor.

"I think the wires clinch it," said the girl. "She disconnected them so she'd have an excuse to be here at night, if we came by. She's been waiting for Griffin."

I was glad that the dark brown man wasn't holding me then, for I started with surprise. But I had learned some caution. I said, "I was waiting for the moon to come back so I could see. There isn't anybody else around, I'm sure of it. I heard nothing at all until you kicked those pebbles, and then I saw your light."

They stared at one another, and the second man, a lean young six-footer with gigantic Dundreary whiskers separated by a firm chin, said to me, "When exactly was that?"

"You know perfectly well. A minute before your hound growled at me."

"That wasn't us," said the girl soberly. "We didn't kick any pebbles, did we? Nor show a light."

"We'd best get away out of this," said the brown one. "Where are the keys?"

"I won't tell you. I don't know who you are, or why—"

"All right," he said impatiently. "I am Roddy McCorley, and this chap is Kevin Barry, and the lady is Nell F. Drake. Will that do you?"

I said, "And I'm Kelly, the girl from Killann."

Whiskers chuckled, the nicest sound I'd had out of any of them yet. "She knows our songs, or our history."

"I get the invasions and the rebellions all mixed up," I said. I was thinking of Quinn Griffin, and what these people might be to him; enemies, that was plain. So I said the first thing that came onto my tongue.

"Who doesn't?" said the girl. She opened the door of the Ford and got in. "The keys are in the ignition."

"Bring them. Bring her gear, too," said the brown man, who seemed to be their leader. He moved to the car and looked in; the light had gone on when the door was opened, so I knew that they'd been right about those wires. "Is this tartan rug yours? Good. Hand it out," he said to the girl. "And the purse."

"Of all the highhanded thieves I have ever met," I said, shifting my feet but afraid to move because of the animal behind me, "you three take the prize. Will you tell me—"

"All in good time, madam," said Whiskers. "Give me the keys, love, and I'll look into the boot."

"There's some ginger nuts," said the girl. "Will I bring them?"

"Lord, yes, I'm famished to the point of oblivion and beyond," said Whiskers.

"There's a candy bar in the glove box, too." They were really cleaning me out. "Is the screwdriver yours?" she asked me.

"No," I said, and felt mildly surprised when she put it

back. They were differentiating between what belonged to me and what had come with the hired car. A unique set of thieves indeed. Who were they? Who did they think *I* was?

But assuredly they were not thieves at all in the ordinary sense; whatever they wanted, it was not to rob me.

They set down my two bags and the rest of my paraphernalia at the front of the car. "Anything else?" said the brown man to me. "Speak up, because you may not be seeing this car again."

"Nothing else," I said, after noting that the girl had my purse, my food, and even the box of tissues.

Their torch went off and the blackness descended.

"She didn't have a pistol, then, unless it's in her luggage."

"It's tucked into my belt," I said with as much sarcasm as I could put into my tone, and was abruptly grabbed and slapped all round my waist before I could bleat indignantly, "I was joking!"

"Ho ho ho," said the leader heavily. "Can we all see now?"

"I can't," I said.

"You're not expected to. Put your hand under Balor's collar. He'll guide you."

"Eat my arm off, more like," I said. My hand was grasped and moved upward; I felt damp shag and leather under my fingers, and gripped the collar. The dog moved restlessly. His head must have reached nearly to my breast. He was a monster; probably a wolfhound, I thought. The homey touch of him, a real dog, began to drive off some of my fear. I smoothed a great skull with my free hand. "Hello, Balor," I said softly, and was answered by a bang on the abdomen as he threw his head sideways in the same motion my old cat used to make when she was pleased with me. At least the dog and I would get along, it seemed. Yes, he actually did perk me up.

We set off through the charcoal-colored night, the dog going carefully at my side. Soon my ankles were soaked, as we tramped upward along the path to O'Brien's Tower. After the others had been silent for a few moments and the presence of the great hound had encouraged me further, I remarked quietly to him, "We waded through red blood to the knee."

"For all the blood that's shed on earth runs through the streams of this countree," said a voice behind me, where Whiskers labored with my pair of suitcases.

"What's someone who can misquote Thomas the Rhymer doing in a gang of kidnapers?" I asked him.

"I've come down a long way," he said cheerfully. "It's wicked companions that does it."

"Shut it up," said the brown man.

"I was just going to tell her how I was stolen by the gypsies," said Whiskers. I began to feel some reluctant affection for him. He had a beautiful voice, with that Dublin pattern of speech that is almost a universal English like Olivier's, sharp and clear and with few of the Irish vowels in it. If I had not once known an actor from the Abbey Theatre who spoke the same way, I would have guessed that Whiskers was a wellborn Englishman. And he had more gentleness about him than the other two.

We were on near-level ground. We must be passing the tower. We were making for the ruins, then.

"Dog," said Whiskers distinctly. Balor and I took two more paces and bumped into the brown man, who was standing still.

"What is it?"

"Don't know. Off to the right."

We all stood silent, me as blind as a mole and the others undoubtedly peering across the countryside. Balor put his huge head against my ribs and rubbed me affectionately.

"Nothing now," said Whiskers. "Thought I heard a noise, as of someone tripping over a stone."

We continued our eerie progression through the "murk, murk night" of the poem I'd remembered, although to my city-dulled senses there was "nae starlight" whatever.

That was twice that Whiskers had called the other man "Dog," and this time I could not have mistaken it. It was a queer sort of nickname, perhaps a shortening of Patrick O'Doggins or the like. More probably, I thought crossly, short for Dirty Dog.

"I'll take you from here," he said, beside me. My grip was loosened, not without some instinctive resistance on my part, from the old leather collar. "It's tricky over the stones."

"Are you going to tell me—"

"Oh, *do* be quiet," he said wearily.

We were within the shattered walls of the castle. I could not tell how I knew that; I don't suppose there is any aura of the ancient times that can be felt in a ruin if you can't see anything, but still, I knew we were there. The smell was the same as it had been all night: the salt of the sea. Perhaps the surf thunder was more muted, that was all.

"Stand here." He left me, and I stood obediently, afraid of falling if I should step out alone. Balor, the hound, nuzzled my palm. Evidently he had taken a fancy to me. I patted his rough, curly, wet shoulders. "All right, come along. Put your hands on my back and follow me closely."

I did so. We walked across flat tilted stone and then I could sense that we were within a much smaller enclosure. There was the heavy scraping of rock behind me, and a grunt of effort. Then a creak and a noise like the closing of a door. Snick of a lock . . .

"Who has the bloody torch? Lord, it's pitch," said Whiskers. How could he distinguish between this blackness and that which we'd just left? These people were part bat.

A light made me tighten my eyes. We were standing, the five of us, in a square room made of rocks sealed with old, old mortar. Whiskers was just inside an oaken door, holding my cases. The blond girl went to a table made of stacked pieces of broken flagstone and started to pump a big green Coleman lantern. While Dog held the torch aimed upward, she struck a match and pumped a little more, and the chill white fierce blaze of the Coleman spread out over us. Dog went over to a fireplace and bent to blow at some ashes on its hearth, where turf had been smoldering. The whole place—which was about eighteen feet to a side, with such a low roof that Whiskers, the tallest, had to stoop to avoid thumping his head—smelled richly of the sweet-and-bitter smoke of turf. Dog built up the fire, vermilion flames licking the fresh dark sods. The girl said coolly, "Welcome to the enemy camp."

"Why 'enemy'?" I asked. "Why on earth 'enemy'?" What did they imagine that I'd done to them? And, for the zillionth time, I asked myself, what were they to Quinn Griffin, and how had they linked me up with him?

Whiskers came gently to my defense. "Yes, we don't know that yet, love. She may be simply what she pretends to be."

"What *do* you pretend to be?" asked Dog, his back to me.

"I pretend to be a tourist," I said furiously, for there was something about the man's ennuied tone that drove me wild. They'd called me a liar and an enemy, and they didn't even know my name. It was such a maddening experience that I was quivering with shock. "I pretend to be an American," I said, "but actually I'm a double agent for several alien governments." I remembered telling Quinn that he must be James Bond; I rattled on. "The Cliffs of Moher is where the invading armies are going to attack, and I'm to give the signal, after I knock you all to pieces with my cigarette lighter. Twenty thousand dacoits and thugs are waiting out there in their sampans. We're going to take over the Republic. My God!" I exploded. "What kind of lunatics are you all, anyway?"

He turned around. "What's your name?"

"Grania Kirk."

"What do you do? Is it Mrs. Kirk?"

"Miss. I work in New York."

"How long have you been in Ireland?"

"About three weeks, and I loved it until tonight."

"Look through her purse," said the oaf. "See if there's a passport."

The girl opened my bag. I loathe someone doing that. I started toward her and the man said, "Guard, Balor," and the wolfhound stepped into my path and looked up at me. I saw that he had the sight of only one eye; the other was a discolored, milky ball in the big gray head. "Ah, you poor fellow," I said impulsively, putting both hands out to him. He licked them.

"Grania Kirk." She was reading my passport. "That's true."

"How do you come to be called Grania?" asked Whiskers.

"I have an Irish grandmother."

"Everyone in the blessed world has an Irish grandmother," said the man called Dog. "Have you ever met anyone who didn't?"

"Once," said Whiskers; "chap in Mesopotamia."

"He was lying," said Dog tiredly. "He didn't want to seem boastful. What else is in that purse?"

"Three pounds of gelignite," I snapped. I started toward them again and the hound moved across my path, polite but firm.

"Stand quiet and don't worry the poor beast," said

Whiskers. "He has to carry out his orders, you see, but he likes you, and it embarrasses him if you keep trying to walk."

I stood. Balor was very sweet and I had no wish to embarrass him; plainly, Whiskers was telling the truth. "I hate people digging in my private belongings," I said, "but if you must, go ahead. You're four to one against me."

"New York driver's license, Grania Kirk too, born—"

"Is it vital for everyone to know when I was born?"

"You're older than you look," she said.

"And I'm sick to death of hearing about it."

"Touchy, touchy," said Whiskers, grinning. "Must be over thirty."

"Twenty-three," said the girl, which was rather nice of her.

"I've seen you before," said Dog, scowling. "I can't think where." He came over to me. I realized why he spoke so wearily. The man was bone-tired. His eyes were reddened and sunken, and he slumped as he sat down on the edge of the rock table, although something in his carriage suggested that he did not ordinarily slouch. He must not have slept in days. "How long did you say you'd been in this country, Miss Church?"

"Three weeks," said the girl, checking my passport.

"Kirk," I said.

"Same thing," he said heavily. "I like 'Church,' it's so ironical if—Alanna, what about it?"

The blond girl came closer and inspected my face. She was half a foot shorter than I, and beautiful in a rounded, cuddly fashion. She wasn't wearing the marvelous boots of the previous afternoon, but a pair of brogans like my own. "Yes," she said, "definitely this is the one."

"The one what?" I demanded, as my skin crawled with apprehension; there'd always been the hope that seeing me in a good light would show them their mistake.

"The one who's friendly with Quinn Griffin," she said in that soft, cold voice. "The one who was prying around the keep this afternoon."

"Who is Quinn Griffin?" I asked. They were not going to get any more out of me than I could help, not till I discovered what was happening.

"You're a poor actress," said Dog. "Actress," he repeated. The bloodshot brown eyes riveted me. "That's it,

the telly. I've seen you—in black and white, I think—
when was it?"

"I was carrying a sign in a picket line," I said at random. I'd done that often enough, of course, as the Rebellious Girl or the Protester for Peace. He nodded, satisfied;
he hadn't actually believed the actress bit, and must have
assumed that he'd glimpsed me in a news shot. I saw no
point in enlightening him. I would go on the theory that
the less they knew about me, the better; that would hardly
hurt matters at this point. To distract him, I said, "You
look awfully beat. Don't you ever sleep? Are you on the
run?"

.The three stared at one another and then at me. "How
quaint and curious of you to suggest that," said Whiskers.
"Yet you are an American tourist, know nothing whatever
about motorcars, and never heard of Quinn Griffin. The
fact that Alanna saw you last night in the middle of
O'Carmody's place, shamelessly necking with Griffin, is
not important." He paused and then said lightly, "Surely,
though, 'Nothing that actually occurs is of the smallest importance.'"

"Oscar Wilde," I footnoted for him, while my mind
raced. That's why they'd linked me with Quinn; we'd been
seen. If I hadn't been so shaken up I'd have realized that
this would have been the only possible reason for the girl
Alanna to have suggested that I was waiting down on the
platform for Quinn. So much for the policy of keeping
secrets; anyway, for heaven's sake, I had nothing to hide!
If I could have gone back in the conversation I would instantly have told them that I was a television actress, and
had met Quinn, yes; and anything else at all. *Whatever*
they suspected me of, despite all my nervous decisions to
the contrary, the truth couldn't hurt me, could it? Though
it might hurt Quinn. I didn't know. I simply didn't know a
thing about anything.

Meanwhile, Whiskers' face had brightened out of all
proportion to what I'd said. "Brilliant!" he exclaimed.
"Dog, I don't care if she's the wickedest woman on earth,
if she can spot Wilde himself like that, she has *some* good
in her."

"I have a lot of good in me, if I do say so, and I wish
that you'd all stop playing silly games and tell me what's
happening. I feel like Alice down the rabbit hole."

"Some Alice," said the leader. "Look here, Miss Kirk,

suppose you tell us the facts. For a start, Alanna identifies you as the woman who was kissing Quinn Griffin in O'Carmody's lounge in Lisdoonvarna with half the scandalized town looking on. That doesn't speak to me of innocence."

"Innocence of what?" I shouted. "All right, he was lying with his head on my lap. I couldn't help that. And he kissed me, not vice versa."

"Yet you don't know him. Bit promiscuous with strangers, aren't you?"

What were they, moral vigilantes? Was I to be tarred and feathered, or have my head shaved? I'd seen the pictures of those poor girls in Ulster . . . but that was for political and religious reasons. "He was *not* a stranger! I met him in Limerick the night before last. I've had two meals with him, and being a wild Irishman, he did kiss me in public, but like a brother. We weren't necking, as your friend puts it."

"I like the term 'wild Irishman,'" murmured Whiskers. "Everyone knows what *they* are."

"It wasn't said in a sneering way," I apologized, though why I bothered I could not have told; after all, it was I who'd been kidnaped by these madmen, I who surely had reason for complaint.

"So you were lying before," said Dog, his words slower than ever. I thought the man was going to come apart. "Go on."

"Go on with what? I don't know who you think I am, or what Quinn is to you, or anything! I don't know what you want of me," I said, and suddenly, without meaning to, I sat down on the floor and put my arms around the wolfhound's neck. "I believe Balor is the only sane one of the whole mess of you," I said, leaning my face against his damp coat and crying in spite of myself.

"Dog," said Whiskers uncertainly, after a short silence, "do you think we may have made a hideous mistake?"

"It was always possible. We couldn't take the chance. Miss Kirk, do stop snuffling. Here." A handkerchief, fairly clean, was pushed under my fingers.

"He did kiss *her*," Alanna said. "They weren't really making love. It could have been just a, well, a brotherly gesture. Or he might have been making a pass that she didn't pick up. I never meant to exaggerate."

"Will you tell us exactly what there is between you and

Griffin?" the brown man asked me, less world-weary hardness in his tone than before.

I sat back and blew my nose. Then I recited the facts of how Quinn and I had met, accidentally, in the Limerick hotel, and become friends, and how he'd appeared in Lisdoonvarna the next night, evidently to attend to some business of his own as well as to see me again. When I'd finished, I asked them, "Won't you please tell me what this all means?"

"In a moment." Dog was leaning forward on the rock table, watching me. His expression was so much more pleasant that I began to cheer up. It had all been an error. They'd mistaken me for someone else. Lord knows who. But not me. "Miss Kirk, did Griffin mention us?"

"He talked about half the people and things in Ireland. I don't know whether you were among them. How could I? I don't know who you are!"

He glanced at his companions, and seemed to make up his mind. "This is Alanna Blake. This is her husband, Terence Blake."

I shook my head. "He never said either of those names."

"Sure?"

"Positive. I'd have remembered. In school I always thought that Blake, the poet I mean, was a certified nut. I'd have retained the name."

Whiskers—Terence, that is—drew himself to his full height, bumping his head on the ceiling. "*He* was English. No relation of mine. *We* have been in Ireland since the year 1230."

I giggled, because he had not meant his arrogance to be taken seriously. "Who are you?" I asked the tired brown man.

"My name is Thomas O'Flaherty."

"Oh," I said.

My voice had lent some meaning to the word that I hadn't intended, for he said sharply, "Griffin mentioned me, then."

"No. Really, he didn't. I was thinking—I'm sorry, I keep insulting all of you, and I don't mean to—of the thing on the gate."

"What?" said Alanna, perplexed.

The leader, still eyeing me, said, "A prayer that's supposed to have been carved over one of the gates of Gal-

way when it was a walled city. 'From the fury of the ferocious O'Flahertys, good Lord deliver us.' "

"You'll admit that it's an appropriate sentiment," I said
in a humble voice.

He looked into my eyes for what seemed like five minutes. Then, for the first time, his weather-beaten face
managed to smile. The motion did not extend to his eyes,
it was far from being the splendid all-encompassing expression of Quinn, but it was a smile. "I admit it. Miss
Kirk. My ancestors earned that reprimand ... richly, yes,
and I've done the same with you. If you had only told us
the truth at first—"

"Would you, in her place?" That was Terence Blake. "I
think not, Dog. We did rather burst on the girl with vague
accusations and implied menaces."

"You certainly did. You came out of the night and
called me a liar and an enemy and a wicked woman. And I
hadn't any idea of who you were or ... of course I still
don't."

"Let's say that we're not exactly boon comrades of
Quinn Griffin."

"I gathered that." I got off the floor, which was of earth
pounded to the hardness of metal. "Is that a reason to kidnap a person?"

"Let us say further," went on O'Flaherty, "that it
seemed to us a sufficient excuse."

"Well, will you tell me what's going on, then? So I can
find out what I should have confessed to you before you
ever bothered to ask me anything?"

Terence walked across the room and unlocked the oak
door with an enormous iron key. He pulled it open. I expected blackness on the other side, but there was nothing
but more rock. It was as though they had enchanted me
and led me straight through the side of a mountain into
this old chamber. "You aren't kidnaped any longer, I
think," Terence said. O'Flaherty nodded.

"But I haven't proved anything," I said. It sounds stupid
now, but my mood had lightened to such a degree that I
felt safe, and I wanted to discover what lay behind the
charade.

"We think you're telling the truth," said Alanna, "that's
all." The chill was off her voice, and I realized that it was
one of the most pleasant voices I had ever heard. I

wanted to ask her if she had ever acted, but that should come later. I would not babble with relief.

"Your story's reasonable," said O'Flaherty. He stood up, too, motioning the hound away from my side. He was just about my own height, and not a menacing man at all. As a matter of fact, he would have been rather attractive if he hadn't been half-covered with dried mud and on the verge of falling down with fatigue. "If you promise not to tell your friend Griffin about this, you may leave now. We'll take your word."

"But you can't simply kick me out in the middle of all this mystery!" I said indignantly. "You owe me something for scaring me, don't you?"

"Really, the less you know, the better," said Terence. "Only don't go and lodge a complaint with the gardai or anything like that. We are sorry, and we'll carry all your gear to the motorcar and see you safe on the way to where you're going. It was an honest mistake we made."

"If it hadn't been for us, you'd still be stranded on the cliffs," said Alanna reasonably.

O'Flaherty snapped his fingers. "Wait a tick," he said, "we're all so groggy that we're not thinking. If she didn't tamper with those wires, *who did?*"

"By the kneecaps of Finn himself," said Terence slowly into the silence.

"I did not—" I began.

"I wasn't accusing you, Miss Kirk. I'm saying, if you are as innocent as we've decided you are, then there's someone who wanted you to stay the night on the Cliffs of Moher. And why? And where is he, or she, or they, now? That's all I'm saying."

"Oh, come on," I said.

"What do you mean?"

"You know that you unscrewed those wires to keep me there."

"No, we did not."

"But then who did?"

"You know no one in Ireland, you said? Even after three weeks in the country?"

"Except Quinn."

They all stared back and forth. "No sense in it, is there?" Terence asked of nobody in particular. "Why should it have been him?"

"There's no knowing," said Thomas O'Flaherty. He sat

down again. "I have to think," he said sadly, "and I am too bloody tired to do it properly."

As much as I held against this man, my heart went out to him then. I had been in the same fix often enough lately, with the lights blazing savagely on me for the eighth or tenth consecutive hour, and the director shouting, "Damn it, Grania, you're not thinking! What's wrong with you?"

I could hardly put my arms around him and give him a soothing "There, there." I compromised by patting Balor and saying, "Once I'm in the car I'll be all right. If you can just walk me that far?"

"No, we must think this through. Alanna, what do you say? You've the clearest head of the three, you slept yesterday." There was a world of pathos in the sentence, though he didn't mean it that way.

Alanna said, "I can't imagine what's going on."

"Then you know how I feel," I said. She grinned in sympathy.

"Look here, Dog," Terence began. And I yelped, for something clicked in memory and I began to make a little sense out of two words that had haunted me.

If I hadn't spoken then, I think everything would have turned out quite differently. But I did blurt out, "Dog!"

They all gazed inquiringly at me.

"Dog *fox!*" I exclaimed. For Quinn Griffin's odd and frequent remarks about male foxes on the Cliffs of Moher suddenly snapped into focus. He must have been talking about this O'Flaherty person. Nothing else explained it. "Do they call you Dog Fox?" I demanded.

His face hardened into a mask like dark old clay, and I knew that I was right. And I also knew, with sickening clarity, that I should have bitten my tongue bloody before I'd asked him that.

"Terence," said Thomas O'Flaherty slowly, "I think you had best lock the door again." He stood up, weary and hostile and dangerous. "That's one too many loose ends that I cannot tie up tonight. My brain is decayed and rotten with the exhaustion. Miss Kirk, it seems, will be staying the night." He sighed. His dull sunken eyes held me as helpless and mute as though he *had* been a dog fox, and I a stupid newborn lamb. "The night, or longer," he said. "Or much longer."

And then I began to be truly afraid.

4

But yet they dare not slay me
For fear of the country round.
— Bold McDermott Roe

THE COLEMAN LANTERN HISSED AWAY; there was no other sound to break the hush.

We were all standing except Balor, who had lain down at my feet and put his huge gray head on his paws. The three of them did not speak for a long while, and I could not. But there was communion that could be sensed by an outsider; I began to comprehend that they had known one another for a long time. At last O'Flaherty said, "It's this way: we're all too stupid with the working to think. Or we'd never have allowed a few counterfeit tears to befuddle us. Let's get some sleep."

"I can explain—" I began.

"What about her nicky-noos?" Terence asked him, pointing to my bags. "If she has a weapon in there . . ."

"Oh, yes." He looked at me. "Understand this, Miss Kirk. We are of two minds about you, but now tend toward the distrustful. You will spend the night here. When we're fresher, we'll go into the matter of what's to be done with you. I hope it needn't be violent. This odd knowledge of yours may be totally explicable. I'm not able to make such judgments any longer. Is there anything you'll be wanting in those cases for now?"

"Of all the swaggering, contemptible, domineering gangsters I ever met," I said, and stopped, because my tone was such a terrified squeak that the effect of bravery was negligible. "No," I mumbled.

"Are the keys in your purse?"

"Yes."

He reached me my bag. "Give them to me, please." I

dug them out and handed them over. "Terence, lad," he said, throwing them across the room, "Just see that the cases are locked, and hang on to these, eh?" Yawning, he walked to one of the three sleeping bags that were strewn carelessly against the wall. "What time would it be?"

Alanna said, "Half one," which is Irish for one-thirty.

"Somebody wake me at half nine, then. I'm truly destroyed with the drowsiness." He maneuvered his body into the padded depths as though every movement hurt him, and I believe was asleep before Terence had finished locking my bags.

I opened my mouth and Alanna said softly but sharply, *"Please* don't make any more noise than you can help. He hasn't rested since—I've forgotten when. Are you hungry?"

"I'm too scared to be hungry," I told her frankly.

"I'll make you a sandwich anyway," she said, and did, while Terence, humming to himself, shed his gray jacket and high laced boots. As you often do when you know you're too frightened or tired or worried to be hungry, I discovered that food tasted ambrosial. It was buttery-soft Irish beef between thick chunks of soda bread, washed down with water from a keg. Terence ate three sandwiches and Alanna and I two apiece. We sat on the floor, passing things around like so many friendly campers. My fluttering died away.

"It's easy to account for my knowing the name," I said quietly, when Terence was helping himself lavishly to my ginger nuts for dessert.

"Tomorrow," said Alanna. She looked at me. "Please accept the fact that we can't take chances. There's too much at stake. So you're a hostage."

"Hostage for whom?"

"Tomorrow," said Terence. "Good night, darling." He kissed his wife, a long unashamed lover's kiss, and crawled into a sleeping bag.

"You can have mine," said Alanna. "I'll do fine with that rug of yours."

"That's all right, I'll take the rug." Pride, I suppose: if I'm to be a prisoner in your dungeon, then hang me in chains on the wall; that sort of asinine swank.

She unzipped the third sleeping bag and opened it with the flannel lining upward and flattened it before the hearth, on which the turf was burning gaily. She spread my tartan rug over it. "We'll share. These things are as good as a mattress if you're tired enough. Come on, I'll show you the loo." She took me into the far corner, behind a long heap of turf, and pointed out the primitive sanitary arrangements, which were mainly an apparently bottomless hole in the hard floor. "Be careful and don't fall in. We don't know where it goes, but we think into the sea." She grinned at me. "Nobody looks," she said, reading my mind, "they're both gentlemen."

"Not the word *I'd* have used for Mr. O'Flaherty," I said tartly. "Why is the air so fresh in here? Surely not simply the fireplace?"

"There's a flue sort of thing over there," she said, gesturing toward the ceiling. "We don't get much of a draft, but evidently the opening fronts on the ocean, because we can smell the salt air strongly if there's no fire going. It's a pretty clever piece of medieval engineering, this room."

"Do shut it off, love," said Terence from his bag. "I'm so used up that I'm flaking away in great chunks."

They may have been gangsters and kidnapers, but that was no excuse for me to be needlessly churlish. Shucking some of my clothes, I crept under my half of the rug and stretched out with a sigh. Alanna extinguished the Coleman and joined me. Reflecting that I had never shared a bed with a desperado before, I watched the darkness brighten as my eyes grew used to the flames of the turf fire. Dismally, I wondered if I would sleep at all. I began to go over the incredible events in order, to try and make some sense of them. Then I was asleep.

Sometime during the night Balor came and lay down beside me. I woke slowly with a tingling, half-numb arm; his head was pillowed cozily on the muscle. I wriggled the arm free and massaged it. The place was cold, and dead dark. I looked at my watch. It showed eight o'clock.

Balor licked my face moistly. I groped for his head and, sitting up, began to wool at his ears. I had been reared with red setters, and as Balor was Irish, too, I hoped he would appreciate their favorite caress. He did.

I was glad that I'd left my Aran sweater on; I could not reach my leather jacket or brogues. Shivering a little, I lay back, clutching Balor for his doggy-smelling warmth.

If I could get the key to the oak door—it would do me no good whatever. Beyond that door I had clearly seen rock. I supposed, thinking more sensibly at this hour than

I had in the frightened and angry bewilderment of last night, that the rock was actually a kind of second door beyond the wooden one. I had heard the scraping of heavy stone against stone, which must have been Terence closing it up. How the thing was managed I couldn't guess. In any case, I would have had to locate Terence, abstract the key from him, find the doorway, and open both doors before I had a chance at freedom; and any one of those steps was perfectly impossible.

I would have attempted to get the fire blazing if I could have seen anything, and was actually going through the process in my head, when I realized that I would run slap into the rock table on my way to the fuel stack. And then fall down the bottomless "loo." Besides, I had never dealt with a turf fire. It was probably beyond my amateurish capabilities. I'd read that it took practice, I recalled this now; and also that there was always a glowing heart beneath the ashes in the morning, so that the fire could be brought up again without matches. I had read, too, that in some Irish homes the turf fires have not gone out for literally centuries. Now that I was lying about two feet from one of them, I found this a fascinating fact, and thought about it for some minutes. A lifeline of fire to match the human line that tended it. Incredible. . . .

I was trying not to dwell on the sticky and inscrutable maze into which I had somehow blundered. I *must* think about it. Roughing Balor's ears gently, while his breath came heavy on my neck, I tried to recall exactly what Quinn had said about dog foxes each time he'd brought them up. It was all too cryptic to yield a glimmer of sense. All I knew was that he had sounded me out on whether I knew O'Flaherty. No hint of what O'Flaherty was to him, none at all.

Damn.

I tussled with the problem and finally came to the conclusion that O'Flaherty, and perhaps Terence, too, believed that I was in with Quinn on something whose nature I could not surmise, and that my use of the nickname had clinched the belief. Surely, when they'd given my story some thought, they'd understand how innocent of anything I must be?

Who under the misty Irish sun *were* they?

One thing sure, they weren't officials of any sort. They were hiding in these ruins like hunted jailbreakers.

The idea of Alanna in jail in those expensive boots made me smile in the dark.

Yet they were hiding. They had asked me not to go to the gardai, who are the police of Ireland. They had actually searched me for weapons. No, O'Flaherty had. The Blakes had treated me, at least physically, with respect.

O'Flaherty, I thought with a shudder, looked capable of killing me out of hand and chucking my body off the precipice. Even his acts of courtesy, loaning me his handkerchief and letting me find my keys in my own purse, had been done with a weary contempt. I had never seen such hostility in a man's eyes.

I had, come to think of it, never in my adult life actually encountered real, personal hostility before last night. Anger, dislike, yes, but positive enmity never. It was a sensation that I could have lived without.

The stresses and pressures of a busy life that had nearly resulted in a breakdown seemed now rather petty. Like mosquito bites that I'd been complaining about, just before I was trodden on by the passing hippopotamus.

I hope we needn't be violent, he'd said.

They wouldn't dare, would they?

The Republic of Ireland can boast of having fewer murders than any other country.

Terence was plainly a gentle soul, however suspicious of me.

It takes a terribly hard woman to connive at killing, and Alanna was not of that breed. Anyone could see that.

But O'Flaherty . . .

Oh, the police would be on them in a minute if—

At whose suggestion? Quinn's? He didn't even know that I'd meant to be in Lisdoonvarna on Saturday—tomorrow night—come typhoon or high water. If I vanished, he'd shrug it off as a woman's whim; I'd said I was heading for Donegal.

But when my corpse washed up on the strand there'd be investigations, and Thomas, the hereditarily ferocious O'Flaherty, would be dug out of this burrow like the red beast he called himself, and he must know that. He wouldn't dare use violence. Would he?

I was giving myself goose bumps to no purpose. I tried to switch my mind to something else. How to escape? I got absolutely nowhere.

There is a certain feeling that comes on you in a

strange place (in this case a positively outlandish place), and especially in a foreign country. I had felt it only slightly on the Cliffs of Moher, but now it overcame me to such a degree that I buried my face in Balor's shag and cried once more in the dark and the cold. It is the clear realization that you are *alone*. Just how alone, I cannot put into adequate words. I had never been truly alone in all my life before. There can be few emotions more poignant. Crusoe must have experienced it fully the first time he saw the cannibals; he wasn't really *alone* until then.

If this had happened in Arizona or Pennsylvania, I doubt that I'd have been nearly as panic-shaken as I was for a few minutes in that black cell, a couple of inches from a pretty blond girl, with my arms around a friendly dog that weighed as much as I did. But this place was far from home, I was isolated by a whole ocean from every thing I knew, and oh Lord but I was scared!

I wept it out, and gradually felt better.

And then I must have fallen asleep, for the next thing I remember is Terence uttering one of his old-fashioned curses, something about the thighbones of Oonagh, because the blessed turf would not stack properly. I opened my eyes to the light of the lamp, and they all were moving about except Balor and me.

"Good morning, Miss Church," said O'Flaherty. "If you'll unhand the hound, I'll give him his breakfast."

I unhanded the hound, sat up, and discovered my jacket and brogues beside my feet where I'd dropped them. "Hello," I said in a whisper.

"I hope you've decided to make a clean breast of things."

"If you'd given me the chance I would have last night. I'm sorry I lied to you at first; I was frightened and confused."

"That's understandable," said Terence, blowing on the ashes fiercely. "My very sideburns have terrified strong men before this day."

"Terry, this is bloody serious," said O'Flaherty.

"I know that. We'll end in Mountjoy Jail now for certain, instead of the fifty percent chance we had before." He looked at the other man over his shoulder. "So don't complain if I whistle softly in the gloom now and then," he said, "to cheer myself a little."

I looked at him more particularly than I had last night.

He was, as I've said, a good six feet, solid but slim, weighing no more than a hundred fifty-five or sixty; his luxuriant hair, and the huge Dundreary whiskers, were auburn with tiny black curls in them, and his eyes were a candid blue-gray. He had the very light and clear coloring of the real Irishman, buffed up to deep rose on the cheeks where the wind had apparently been at him all winter. His nose and lips were large and handsomely made, and he wore a habitual expression of slight and pleasurable surprise. In any other circumstances I would have adored him on sight.

O'Flaherty was as different as—well, as a glass of porter is from a goblet of champagne. (I thought of the simile at that moment: then I thought, you'd believe they wouldn't mix, but pour them together and they make a strong drink called Black Velvet. The Black Velvet Gang.) The Dog Fox was three inches shorter and six wider. His brown eyes, no longer red or dulled or sunken into his square face, were as alert as those of a wild animal. His nose could only be called snub, and he held his lips so firmly together that they seemed thinner than they were. His hair and brows were just a shade more brown than his skin. Where Terence Blake had an elegance, a kind of natural flamboyance, this man was all compact power. He might have been a dock worker. I think he was the only man I ever met of whom it could be said in strict truth that he did seem all bone and muscle. His carriage this morning was that of a career sergeant who had purposely swallowed his bayonet.

With reluctance I admitted to myself that I'd been right; now that he'd slept, he *was* immensely attractive in a hard, very masculine fashion, though quite without the flair of Quinn Griffin or Terence Blake.

"Miss Church," he said, staring at me across a couple of yards of bare earth floor.

"Mr. O'Fogarty," I said.

He had the grace to grin. "All right, Kirk. Will you tell us, then, who you are?"

"I have. Grania Kirk of New York City, a tourist."

"And what is your connection with Quinn Griffin?"

"Just what I told you. Acquaintances. No, I think friends, but only of two days' standing."

"What about the name Dog Fox?"

I told him how Quinn had dragged that phrase into our

conversations time after time, and how it had made no sense to me until I'd connected it with "Dog."

He grunted.

"Am I allowed to ask questions now?" I said.

"I think not."

"Come on, Tommy," said the blond girl, who was making tea, "that isn't fair."

"Wilde says that women have wonderfully primitive instincts," added Terence, "and so I imagine that Miss Kirk's intuitively decided that we aren't the larky young innocents we seem. I can't find any harm in a few questions. What do you want to know, Miss Kirk?"

"Only what's going on. Why I'm a prisoner."

"Because we made a mistake," said Alanna.

"Jump, jump," said the Dog Fox, "but beware of conclusions just yet. I'm not convinced."

"Oh, why don't you throw me into the sea and be done with it?" I snapped at him. Whenever the others began to make sense, there was this lout with his skepticism.

"Because there would be awkward inquiries by the gardai. And you may not accept this, Miss Kirk, but I have rarely thrown a woman into the sea, no matter how much I yearned to do it." He bit into the slice of bread and jam he was carrying, and went on with his mouth full. "If you are in league with Griffin, I would expect you to be an intelligent and crafty young baggage."

"You sound like a boys' adventure story," I said scornfully.

"I sound like a man who's had a lot of trouble in the past with Quinn Griffin," he said, swallowing and then cramming in the rest of the bread. "Has anyone seen my pipe?"

"It's over among the crowbars and spades," Alanna told him. He went to a big clutter of miscellaneous tools in the far corner and picked up a briar pipe and a black tobacco pouch. I had not noticed the tools before, but was given no time to wonder about them now. He came back and sat down on the table.

"Let's assume that you're telling the truth. Tell it all. Leave out no word, not a facial twitch or a start of surprise or anything you can remember," he said.

"Now you sound like Sherlock Holmes," I said.

"If you're determined to pick a fight with me, you bloody American brat," he said in that deep, rich voice that went so oddly with his rough looks, "I warn you I'm of the old school, and I'll spank a saucy child as quick as kiss her."

"Try either one with me and lose yourself an ear," I said. I was not full of fear as I had been in the cold darkness. There was no longer an atmosphere of menace, what with Alanna domestically brewing her tea and Terence meditatively brushing his whiskers in front of a piece of mirror by the Coleman's clean bright glare.

"I think you'd try. Fair enough," he said, which is a kind of Irish equivalent of "okay," "will you then tell me, like a sweet lady, the story of your life from the time you met Griffin?"

I asked for a bite of something, and Alanna gave me a slice of the soda bread thick with butter and strawberry jam. "Tea in a few minutes," she said.

I thought. "I came out of the lift," I said, "and bumped into him around the corner. We passed a few pleasantries—"

"Can you remember what they were, at all?"

"Yes." I didn't mention that being an actress, I have a memory that automatically registers conversation and keeps it intact for several days as though it were printed dialogue; which is in its way a curse. "I said, 'Chilly! It snowed today,' and he said, *'Où sont les neiges?'* and I said, 'Downtown.' "

"You mean *d'antan*," said Terence.

"No, I mean 'downtown.' It's an old gag."

"I never heard it."

"I have," said Alanna. "It's American."

"Why would Griffin know that? What did he say to it?"

" 'Let's eat.' "

"You haven't touched your bread and jam yet."

"Oh, I mean he said that, or 'Come have dinner,' or something of the sort."

"Just like that?"

"Just like that. And I went along, being overpowered by the Irish charm of it all."

"Not precisely *Irish* charm, I'd say." He frowned. "Go on."

I went through the business of Quinn flattering me and then trying the dog-fox thing, and said, "After that it was all blarney and have-you-been-where-the-Mountains-of-

Mourne-sweep-down-to-the-sea and my life story and a lot of Celtic ghosts and whatnot."

"Go back to that French. What does it mean?"

"It's from Villon," said Terence. "Where are the snows of yesteryear?"

"But the way they said it, it comes out 'Where are the snows?'—'Downtown.'" That was Alanna, hovering over her tea water.

"I didn't know Griffin spoke French," said O'Flaherty.

"He doesn't," I said. "His accent was terrible. As if—"

"Yes? As if what?"

I said reluctantly, feeling that I was perhaps acting as a traitor to my friend, who after all just *might* be James Bond, "As if he'd memorized the line without knowing the language, that's all."

O'Flaherty looked at his companion. "Terry?"

"Yes. A password."

"That's it. It must have been so. And when you answered it with your nonsense, he must not have realized it wasn't the word he'd expected. I admit it sounds much the same to me."

"How on earth do you figure that? A password," I said dubiously.

"Griffin may be stuffed to the eyebrows with fraudulent Irish whimsy when he wants to be, Miss Kirk, but he's not the sort of adolescent who goes about picking up girls at the flick of a false eyelash. He has other fish to fry."

"They are not false!"

"Then you are exceedingly lucky," he said, which I suppose was some kind of compliment. "I meant to suggest that Griffin has other things on his mind than women these days, and he mistook you for someone else he'd been waiting for, someone he didn't know by sight. He's too old to go chatting up a bird when there's—well, more important game in view."

"Too old? He's younger than you are," I said scornfully.

He smiled, very wryly. "He's half a dozen years older than I."

"He's thirty-two!"

"Precisely."

"Oh," I said, disconcerted. "Well, you don't look your age, as people keep saying to *me*." I'd have sworn he was pushing forty.

"I've been out in the gales a bit lately." He chuckled. "I think we're quits in the insult department, Miss Kirk."

"I'm sorry."

"How many people could finish that quotation of yours—properly, that is?"

"I should think a few million. Besides all the French people."

"But how many of them would do so at once, as you did?"

"About the same number." I thought. "If I said to you, 'I met with Napper Tandy'—"

" 'And he took me by the hand,' yes. I see. It was a bad choice for a password. And your bad luck that you mentioned snow at the instant of meeting him. Why did you?"

"I was rattled, and it *had* snowed, the first time I'd seen it here; that's all."

"Logical," said Terence.

"I didn't argue." said O'Flaherty. "It is." He lit his pipe. "Exactly when did he bring up dog foxes?"

"When I'd said I was on my way to Moher."

"I'm damned. There's something looking us in the face, and it won't show itself distinctly. Terry?"

"Was it yesterday you were born?" asked Terence in a thick stage-Irish accent. "Griffin leaped to the notion, probably from something she said besides the Moher thing, that *she* was one of *us*. Coming from America to join us. He must have realized early on that she wasn't the person he'd meant to meet." He laughed. "How he must have writhed over that password!"

O'Flaherty sent out a long plume of gray-blue smoke that smelled delightful and made me long for a cigarette. "Ye-es. Just possible. Well. What about the second night, in Lisdoonvarna?"

I told him about that, too.

"So he left you very suddenly, after exhibiting shock or amazement at some remark you made."

"Yes, something about smuggling drugs."

"That's odd. There used to be smuggling on this coast—you can see the spikes where they hung their ladders, down there on the platform, even yet—but drugs! Maybe it was another subject you mentioned, and he was covering himself. Or if he saw Alanna."

"He didn't," she said positively. "I went out by the rear door."

"Think now, Miss Kirk: what else had you mentioned?"

"Children, brandy, tobacco, dogs . . ."

"More Dog Fox?" asked Alanna, handing me a mug of hot, strong tea, but looking at O'Flaherty.

"No, that might be Balor. He knows him of old." This man could use the most antiquated expressions at times, and his native accent, which was thicker than Terence's by far (I learned later that he was from County Galway), made them seem right. "Hardly enough there, though. What else?"

"Leprechauns. Dancing. That's all I recollect."

He stared at his pipe, which had gone out. "Think again: did either of you mention castles?"

"I had, a couple of times, but not then."

"Relics?"

"Relics? I don't think so."

"Treasure?"

"No, definitely not. What—"

"Forget about it. Had you the occasion to refer to Northern Ireland, Trinity College Library, Marsh's Library in Dublin, or the Irish Antiquities Division of the National Museum?"

I could not help laughing. It was a bizarre list. "No. I'm sure we never spoke of them."

"Not even Belfast?"

"No. I did say something about refugees coming over the border."

"Terry?" he said again.

"Don't appeal to me! You've always told me that Griffin is quite mad."

"He's not!" I said.

O'Flaherty lit his pipe with that judicious, all-important concentration that drives mere cigarette-smokers wild. Then he said, "Miss Kirk, I do begin to believe that you've fallen into this farrago, and added another tangle to it, through no fault of your own. But you are no longer harmless to us. I can't let you loose, not for a while. In your situation, almost anyone would go screeching to Griffin or the gardai, and we'd be in the stew."

"If you told me what you're afraid of Quinn for, perhaps I'd understand."

"Not afraid, cautious. I could tell you, but you'd have no reason to think I was speaking the truth. You admit to being fond of the swine."

"He isn't a swine!"

"See what I mean?" he asked, smiling.

"Yes. But—"

"Be fair. All we know of you is that you're an irritable, quarrelsome, belligerent young freak-in with no reason to do us any favors."

"Freak-out," said Alanna. "She isn't, you know. She's quite normal and nice."

"In, out, I cannot comprehend the American jargon."

"I thought I'd been pretty cooperative, considering that your gang is an absolute puzzle to me."

"I always go by first impressions. It saves time."

He was deliberately baiting me. I wasn't being caught in that web. "I won't go to the gardai," I said in my demurest voice, "and if you are really in danger from Quinn, I promise I won't say a word to him. Because it was all a mistake, and I like your friends and your wolfhound, if not yourself, Mr. Dog Fox."

"There is, too, the second possibility," he said. "Which is that Griffin had sent for an ally, or been told that he was to look out for her—we can't guess what manner of organization is behind him, if there is one—complete with password and innocuous appearance and all. And that this ally is yourself, Miss Kirk. And that you're being as clever as clever can be, after a long night of thinking it out. Why would Griffin need a confederate, unless it was to worm her way into the center of things? Of course," he exclaimed, snapping his fingers, "that would account for the battery wires. No, I'm afraid you'll have to stay with us for a time."

"How long?" I demanded.

"Perhaps a day or two. We can't prophesy. Perhaps a few weeks. The tourist season will—"

"Weeks!" I said at the top of my voice, which is no small noise when I project.

"Mountjoy, we are coming," said Terence lugubriously. "Keep the gruel warm for us. Twenty years' worth of it."

"Well, what else can I do?" said O'Flaherty.

"Let her go," said Alanna. "Griffin's known about us for a month. She can't tell him much more than he's aware of already."

"If I were positive she was in with him, I would, I suppose," said O'Flaherty after a long pause. "But if she's innocent, whacko! she's off to the friendly policeman in Limerick."

"No, honestly, I won't."

"I cannot chance it. I'm sorry. You will be a pain in the ear to me, Miss Kirk, and I choose that phrase deliberately; you'll be an expense and a bother and a constant worry, but it can't be helped."

"Let's vote," said Alanna.

"No." He shook his head. "This is my department, the safety of the band, and my decision is that we keep her."

"As if I were a fish," I said bitterly. "As if you'd found me under a damp rock."

"I wouldn't keep a fish I'd found under a rock, believe me."

Terence chuckled. "'A simile committing suicide is always a depressing spectacle,' as Wilde says."

O'Flaherty stood. "We're behind by the width of an hour. Let's get at it."

"What are you going to do with Miss Kirk? Put a chain on her leg and drag her around after us?" asked Alanna. I flashed a dim smile at her.

"Leave her in here for today." He faced me. "Can you feed a turf fire properly? No? Terence will show you how to put sods on it when it goes low. You can have anything to eat you like. There are some books over there."

"I have books with me, thank you," I said coldly. There was no use pleading with the wretch, and at least I could take heart, for there was dissension in his own ranks; neither of the Blakes wanted to hold me prisoner, and maybe they would bring him around during the day. "Please show me about the fire," I said to Terence.

He chose two lumps of turf and demonstrated the knack to me. "See where there's a hole in the center, where the highest glow is? Take the tongs, so, and lay in your sod, so. That's all." He told me not to scatter the fine white powdery ash, which would be used at night for damping the fire; and also not take the bricks of fuel from the left end of the great stack, where they were darker and oilier than the rest. "Those haven't dried yet; they'd burn badly. What books have you?" he asked eagerly. "I've not read a new book in so many weeks that I'm killed and speechless with the lack of wisdom."

"If I can have the keys to my bags, I'll show you."

He went at once and unlocked both my cases, handing

me the keys thereafter. O'Flaherty watched rather sourly—he must have felt the allegiance of his friends slipping—as I fished out my old *House at Pooh Corner,* Yeats's *Fairy Tales,* a ghost book of O'Donnell's, and *Stephen Hero.* Terence fell on them with a growl of pleasure.

"Check for weapons," O'Flaherty said to Alanna. She shrugged and we turned over my clothing and sundries together.

"Not so much as a Sten gun," she told him.

"For the love of God, a little less heavy sarcasm," he said, picking up some of the tools. "Come along, there's work out there."

They left with Balor at their heels, both the Blakes smiling sadly at me. I had been right about the outer gate, which was a tall flagstone that slid sideways under the pressure of both of O'Flaherty's hands; it must run in a groove, I thought, hearing its muffled groaning as they shoved it back in place to hide the relocked oaken door. I was alone.

I'd listened very particularly to the noise of the rock slab closing. I knew that I would have a moment's warning when they came back. That meant a lot, because if there was one thing I didn't intend to do, it was to sit in this stone box all day reading fairy stories and twisting my hankie. I meant to get out.

I finished my mug of tea, which was strong enough, as they say in Ireland, for a mouse to trot across, and more invigorating than anything alcoholic would have been. Then I explored the place, carrying the storm lantern. There were the three sleeping bags, the crude stone table, some clothing in neat piles, the bottomless hole in the floor, the stack of turf, a cache of food, a keg of water with a spigot, some simple medical supplies running mostly to bandages, iodine, and aspirin, and the great careless clutter of tools. Among these were a couple of spades, several big powerful torches, another Coleman lantern, boxes of extra batteries, crowbars and spikes of various sizes, an old-fashioned barn lantern and a tin of kerosene, some well-used ropes and pulleys, a hatchet, hammers of different shapes, a wooden box crammed helter-skelter with bottles and glass jars full of liquids and powders that I didn't recognize, none of them labeled; and a few items like camel's-hair brushes and tweezers which made no sense to me at all.

For a moment, as I poured another mug of tea, I considered burning out the oak door at the lock with kerosene, for I knew that, once through it, I could handle the stone slab easily. But it might take all day to accomplish that. I had a hazy idea that oak burned very slowly. They'd see or smell the smoke. No, the spades were the answer: I would dig myself out.

The only logical place to try this was along the side in which the door had been placed, which I thought of as the front wall. For all I knew, the other walls abutted on parts of the ruins or were built slam against the hillside. My immediate task was to devise something with which to hide the signs of my work. Here was my second stroke of luck (the first being the presence of the tools)—that long heap of turf chunks, which ran straight back from the front wall, where the wettest bricks were stacked about three or four high, to just past the hole that Alanna called the loo, about eight or nine feet away, where the turf reached shoulder-high. The line of piled fuel was two feet thick and stood about a yard away from the side wall and parallel to it. I moved four rows of the damp peat a foot toward the door.

I gulped half my tea and, grasping one of the shovels, which had a pointed blade, I confidently put its tip on the floor where the turf had been, and slammed my foot down on its upper edge.

I almost broke my arch. That floor was truly harder than concrete.

I got the hatchet. With this I took a hearty swipe at the same point, which made my arm tingle from fingers to elbow. Grumbling with exasperation, I swatted it again. A small chip came out of the floor and lay there looking measly.

I swallowed some tea and brought over a spike and the heaviest hammer. These worked better. In ten minutes I had a hole about two inches deep. Then I made another a short distance away, and whacked down between them with the hatchet, dislodging three or four clods of tough old earth. I gathered the pitifully tiny debris in one hand and dumped it down the hole.

Two hours later I had discarded my jacket and sweater and still was sweating lavishly, and I had a square hole about one foot by one foot by eight inches deep. But I was reaching into earth now that crumbled more easily. I returned to the spade, after popping a lump of turf on the fire, and shortly reached a depth of more than a foot.

I sat on the cold floor and considered. I had planned to pile the turf back over my escape hatch when the trio returned, but I saw now that this would not do. I needed a platform of some sort on which I could arrange the sods, which could then be slid over the cavity in a few seconds. I made another search of the place; save for the wooden box, there was nothing wide enough, and if I removed the bottom of that, or a side, they would likely discover it at once. I looked at my suitcases, the only other things in the room that were in part flat. Opening the larger, I tore away the fabric that lined its lid. Inside was a sheet of dull gray metal. Praying that this was a lining too, and not the reverse of the plastic-covered top, I stuck the thinnest crowbar in along the edge and pried. With a little sigh of disapproval, my expensive bag seemed to disintegrate under my hands.

It had been a lining. It had loosened along three sides, buckling the plastic in with it, and I easily ripped it free of the last glued part. I closed and locked the case and turned it upside down, hoping that O'Flaherty would not decide to have his henchwoman search through it again.

Then I carried the thin metal oblong over to the place where I'd been dredging, and stacked turf on it as neatly as I could. I put this whole masking contraption beside the hole and went on digging, pouring the loose earth into the bottomless pit whenever I'd collected a spadeful. Once it occurred to me to test the depth of the loo—after all, I was digging scarcely three yards away from it on a direct line toward the front wall, and didn't want to burst through the floor into a long drop and oblivion. My ideas of the architecture of this place were absolutely nil. I waited until I'd dislodged a biggish hunk of rocklike earth, knelt above the hole, and dropped it in. Then I went to my belly and thrust my head down and listened.

I never heard it strike anything, though I listened for a full minute.

A cold grue came over me. Rising carefully, afraid for the moment that I'd fall into this dreadful pit, I went to search for something made of metal that would be expendable. I didn't dare sacrifice anything belonging to the Black Velvet Gang, for fear they'd miss it at once. I hunted through my suitcases and at last settled for my traveling clock. It was brand-new, but I could do without it, and I was in a fever of curiosity by now. I lay beside the opening with one of the torches in my hand. Turning it on, I aimed it straight down. The beam looked powerful enough to reach for a mile, yet the vent hole, which was hardly more than a foot and a half across, dwindled with distance till I could not make out anything; I think I could see for nearly a hundred feet, and then sight was baffled by remoteness. Holding the torch steady against the side of the shaft, I carefully dropped my clock into eternity.

After a second I saw and heard it strike the side, and then again more distantly. Then it was gone from sight. I leaned as far into the hole as I dared, held my breath and opened my mouth, and listened.

Finally there was a sound so tenuous, with so little substance to it, that even today I am not certain whether I heard or imagined it. It was the sound of something small and heavy striking water. I remained as I was, and gradually another sound came to me, as faint as the breathing of a sleeper in another room: it was the purling whisper of the Atlantic tide. I had not heard it since I had been shut into this prison last night, but there was the same steady rhythm and I did not believe I was imagining that. Alanna had been right. This terrible artery went clear down to the sea, somewhere near the foot of the cliffs, perhaps within them, into a cave or undercut of the rock.

I rose and went back to work, wondering.

The passage must have been natural. No medieval Irishman would have dug it out, even if he could. I was hazy in my notions of ancient sanitation, but I was sure that *nobody* had ever dug a seven-hundred-foot tunnel eighteen inches wide down through sandstone and shale to the waters below.

However, I had determined that some distance down, perhaps twenty or twenty-five feet, its walls changed color and form—above, it was circular; below, almost the shape of an eye—with a definite line of demarcation. So it was packed earth for that far, and then solid rock. And I was in no danger of tunneling down into a hideous drop.

I began to work even harder than before. My blouse was soaked, although the room must have cooled off considerably. I had got to a depth of a little more than two feet and was about to widen the hole in the direction of the wall, only a matter of inches away, when the spade clanked on stone.

At first I felt like howling with frustration; then I realized that two feet down was plenty for a tunnel. I might not be able to finish today (it was after one-thirty by then), but if they meant to keep me here for weeks, there was ample time. I widened the bottom of my excavation until I had exposed nearly a square foot of the stone. Then I knelt and looked at it in the glare of the torch. It was one of the flat flagstones that are even today quarried around Moher's cliffs for use as flooring, and there were marks on its surface that could be nothing but the scars of an iron dressing tool. I had uncovered, not the crust of the cliffs, but the old floor of the room.

I sat back and stared at the wall. That partition must go right down to this buried stone floor. I . . . I . . . oh!

But there was no use in stopping now. I had no other possible way out of this dungeon, and I had to continue my effort until I knew that there was no chance of escape in this direction. I picked up the spade again.

Another inch toward the wall and then I was hitting a third substance, not compressed dirt, not rock. I shifted to the hatchet, and whatever it was—a smooth little patch of stuff, brown with a tinge of dirty yellow to it—cracked and collapsed. I thought, *It's a pot, a bowl;* because beyond the break was dark emptiness. So carefully, using the blade of the hatchet as a sort of knife edge, I chiseled away the cementlike earth. A curious, familiar shape began to show. I was working away and sweat was in my eyes, and my brain had almost turned itself off, and I couldn't identify the shape. And then I pried off a piece of dirt as big as my fist, and saw what it was, and said "Ah!" very loudly and wheezily.

It was a skull, sitting upright and facing the outer wall.

It is humiliating to admit that for a space I believed that O'Flaherty's crew had already murdered one victim and interred him, or her, in the floor of their bedroom. Well, I was tired and in an agony of discomfort with aching muscles and soaking hair and clothes, and I could be forgiven the stupidity. The skull was very old, unquestionably. I had knocked in about a square inch of it at the left temple. I worked cautiously around it with hatchet and spike, trying not to think of it as somebody's head, until it came loose and rolled over at a chance touch of the tool. I picked it up gingerly and respectfully. It was large, the skull not only of an adult but of a very big adult at that. Numerous teeth were missing. The eye sockets stared at me, clogged with earth but observant.

"I have an Irish grandmother," I whispered to it. "I'm not as foreign as I look."

Where could I hide it in this barren room? I would not consider dropping it into that awful drain, to be knocked about and sunk in the ocean after centuries of lying cozily here, away from wind and weather. At last I put it back in the hole and pulled my camouflage stack of peat over it. I brushed up the crumbs of scattered dirt with my hands and disposed of them, made sure that no one could see my sheet of metal under the turf cakes, and, taking off my clothes, made a hasty toilet with a dampened towel. Then I stuck this back into my suitcase, put on fresh underwear and blouse, got into my damp skirt again, fed the half-perished fire, drank the rest of the now-cold tea, turned out the lantern, and lay down on the opened sleeping bag. It was mid-afternoon. I was exhausted. I was conscious of being inquisitive, anxious, and resentful; and queerly, almost recklessly excited, too. I pulled up the rug and went to sleep.

When the four of them came back—I'm including Balor, of course—I was so deeply in oblivion that I never heard a sound.

5

But they couldn't take me fist,
So I knocked the jailer down,
And I bade farewell to all
As I fled towards the town!
       —Whiskey in the Jar

A HAND ON MY SHOULDER WOKE ME, and I smelled bacon. For an instant I was back at O'Carmody's with high tea coming on. Then I stretched, felt my muscles shriek, opened my eyes, and saw the Dog Fox bending over me.

"Did you not sleep all night, then, you poor child?" he said quietly.

"Yes. Thank you." This was a different man I saw, concerned and seemingly penitent. I put out my hand to be helped to my feet, and it crossed my mind that this gesture that came so naturally would have seemed impossible last night. "Nice of you to ask," I mumbled.

"Come away a moment, will you? There's a particularly fine sunset, and you should have some air."

I slipped into my jacket and brogues, speechless. Alanna and Terence were busy at the fireplace, where food was cooking. O'Flaherty waited by the open doorway. I walked out into the most beautiful evening I'd seen in years.

"If you try to run, Balor will stop you." He shut the wooden door. That was Dog Fox himself again, the tough guy.

"I won't run. I'd hate to embarrass the hound, as Terence says."

"I rather thought you wouldn't, yet I had to tell you." Here was the other side, back already. Wondering, I waited. He said, "Let's go to the brink. The sea's marvelous."

I went by his side through the ruins, hardly noticing

73

them. The sun was touching the rim of the western ocean, and clouds like giant misshapen pearls, all soft silver and pink and lavender, were dotted about the darkening sky. The sea was the color of wet pitch and the sky was a kind of purple-blue fog hanging just above the clouds.

"Stop here," said O'Flaherty, unnecessarily, for we had reached an old, low, dry-stone wall at the rim of the cliff. I put one foot up on it and stared at the loveliness of the day's dying. The wind from the sea was cold and fresh. "Do you have 'em like this at home, Miss Kirk?" he asked me.

"No, oh no." I felt his eyes on me and turned. "You've changed, haven't you? Why?"

"I've thought about you all day."

I swear that my breath caught briefly, not with relief at what I expected him to say next, but of pleasure at the idea of his dreaming about me. My gaze wandered. "Oh?"

"I would have come in to speak to you, but the Blakes might have misunderstood."

"Oh?" I repeated, and then, since this was Ireland, "Is that the way of it?"

"Their minds are full of nothing but love-love-love, you understand," he said uncomfortably, "and, well, they'd have . . ."

"Suspected you of being human," I said. "God forbid. Are the Blakes recently married?"

"That's a cynical question. Three years and a bit."

"It wasn't meant for cynicism. Most people aren't as lucky as they are."

"That's true. In any event, I couldn't spare the time. But I wanted you to know that I believe you've told us the absolute truth."

"Why?"

"Because of the sort of girl you are."

"What sort? Quarrelsome, irritable, belligerent pain in the ear, wasn't it?"

He grinned. "I was bullying you to make you show your true colors. And aside from the fright, which I think is not common to you, you did show them. You're not a bad sort of girl." There was a lengthy pause while we both stared at the last wedge of orange sun. "Nervy, I mean. Lashins of courage."

"I wasn't so gutsy last night."

"For the fix you were in, and you not knowing who we

were, you behaved pretty well. That's all," he said, patting Balor's head absently. "Except I'm sorry we have to keep you for a while."

"But if you realize that I'm not in with Quinn, whatever it is that you think he's in, then—"

"In your place, *I* should go right away to the gardaí, Miss Kirk. I can't risk that. I have my people to protect. And you'll have gathered that what we're doing is not quite within the limits of the law." He thought almost audibly. "You'll also have guessed something of what we're doing."

"A little. Mostly I put it together in my sleep."

"What?"

"I woke up with it. I didn't think about it during the day. I was reading," I said, too quickly. "Joyce."

"What did you gather?"

"You're digging for something: there's the spades, the tools, what I think is a block and tackle for lifting the stones away, as well as all the mud you and Terence accumulated yesterday and again today. You mentioned relics, antiquities, treasure. It isn't a hard problem."

"I daresay. And this is government property, and we could be sent away for years. And now there's the kidnaping."

"You know I wouldn't make a complaint about that, don't you?"

"Why would you not?"

"I like the Blakes! They don't belong in jail, no matter what all this is about. And who'd take care of Balor?"

"I've thought of that," he said seriously. "The dog would die without me. There's no one I'd trust with him. Except perhaps yourself. He's taken a great fancy to you, and you to him, one can tell."

"If you're caught, I'll keep him for you."

He turned full around to me. "God bless the woman," he said, "and you would, too, wouldn't you? I may have to hold you to the promise." He looked out to sea again, where the waves were higher and blacker than ever, with scarlet crests. "Damn the luck of the night when I imagined that you were tied up with the likes of Quinn Griffin," he said viciously. Then, with an abrupt switch of tone, "It's been a pet day. I'm sorry I never allowed you out to enjoy it."

I pictured his face if he'd come in and found me

drenched with sweat, perhaps with the excavation imper-
fectly covered. I said, "The sunset makes up for it. This is
a wild, magical place."

"I'll have Alanna show you the castle. She knows more
about it than I do, though my own ancestors built the
original fortress. And Terence can tell you what we're
searching for, and how we know of it, for it's he that discovered the clues last year."

I sat on the stone wall with my back to the sea and the
ruins before me. From here you could see them almost *in
toto.* Directly before me was our little square building, its
back against a high rough hillock of grassy earth. To the
right, perhaps halfway to O'Brien's Tower from the Dog
Fox's den, rose what remained of the south wall of the
castle. This end was only clumps of broken stone, but
gradually as it marched inland this wall lifted until some
of the original battlements soared against the darkening
purple sky; that was where I'd first seen Alanna. Some inner structure had caved in and piled up against the wall,
making what looked like a fairly easy route to the top.
Left of our hiding place another thick, ivy-clad rampart
ran inland parallel with the south wall, but higher for the
most part and in seemingly better repair. Then came a
vast chaos of rubble and bare green slopes and portions of
walls like fangs thrusting up out of a living, wicked earth;
and another big crag of a wall facing us, and a long
spread of rolling grass till more wreckage of ancient
stones closed off the view to the northeast for a width of
perhaps forty yards and a height of about eight.

These ruins were really ruined. They were far more
shattered, more cruelly dismembered, than the well-
preserved remains of, say, Trim Castle or the Rock of
Cashel. These were overthrown, dismantled, four-fifths
demolished. Except for the few ravaged walls, the rock
shell that had once been a dwelling place and a mighty
fortress was little but vast low expanses of razed masonry
spread with thick crusts of dirt, dead lichens, and moss, all
permanently soaked by the incessant rains of winter and
the salt-laden lash of the sea wind.

And yet, the ruins were in their own fashion magnificent, a grand and monstrous spectacle that gave you little
chills as you stared at it and remembered in your blood
how splendid, how swaggeringly impregnable it must have
looked in its days of glory.

The landward side of the Cliffs of Moher is a long rip-pling hill covered with grass, descending to the modern road that runs south to north as the cliffs do. The ruins, therefore, were silhouetted against the twilight sky. Two or three embrasured windows survived, to gape full of purple firmament at us. With its terrible desolation, its blasted walls and destroyed beauty, there was nothing charming or soft about it; harshness was its keynote, even when spread with ivy or moss. In the fading day it rose, wholly sinister, above the land, like the malevolent ghost image of a castle. Poor little O'Brien's Tower stared out to the ocean blind and lifeless; this ruin *glared*, sullen, sen-tient.

I found myself shuddering. O'Flaherty was watching me. "A weasel jumped over my grave," I said. "What you're looking for—I infer that it's very old?"

"We think so, yes."

"Worth a lot?"

"We believe that. It may even dwarf the Tara Brooch and the Cross of Cong," he said, naming two of Ireland's archaeological treasures. "That's a surmise, but a sound one."

"But isn't there a what's-it, a treasure-trove law here? I know that if you find pirates' gold in America, you split it up somehow. The government doesn't take it all. You could still make a stack of money, and it would be legal."

"Divide it? Wisha, girl, we never even considered that!" He sounded shocked. I let the matter drop. Perhaps there was a primitive justice in what he said. If he and the Blakes did all the work, they doubtless deserved the spoils. Especially if the castle had once belonged to his own family. But I was a little disappointed, for I had begun to almost like the man.

"What about Quinn?" I asked.

"He's after what we're after. I'd rather not spoil a fine twilight by dragging his name into it again. Just one word, Miss Kirk—"

"For pity's sake, call me Grania, if we're going to be roommates."

"Grania, then. One word of advice. When you leave here, have nothing whatever to do with the man."

"Why?"

"Because," O'Flaherty said simply, "he is mad—bad and mad—all the way through to his bones." Then, before I could protest, "Will you look at that farthest cloud before it's changed?" said he. "The one there, coming up toward Hag's Head, that's shaped like a red grouse in flight, just going from violet to gray? You'll not see a perfect picture cloud like that one in the winter very often, at least not here in the West."

"It's lovely," I said truthfully, "it's all lovely. Thank you for bringing me out here."

"I owed it to you."

"Don't be grumpy, now that you've started being nice."

"I'm not grumpy," he said, and laughed shortly, the first time I'd heard him do so. "I'm dopey."

It took a moment for me to realize that he was talking about the Seven Dwarfs. I was going to retort, none too wittily, that I must be Snow White, but the dog Balor growled deep in his chest.

"Good Lord, what am I thinking of? We've not got so much as a sentinel out, and here it's going dark and I've stationed us right on the skyline! Come along," said O'Flaherty, gripping my arm hard, "we must get inside."

"Surely nobody is—"

"Will you come on!"

We went at a crouching run for the hidden room, Balor pacing us. I stumbled over a turned-up stone from the broken battlements and would have gone sprawling if the man had not held me up. Then we were at the door. O'Flaherty opened it a crack and hissed "Light!" and the lantern went out. He pushed me through the door and wrestled with the stone slab, which groaned horribly as it closed. Alanna was there with a torch and the big key to lock our inner portal.

"What happened, in the name of Cathbad the Druid?" said Terence, obviously shaken, as he relit the lamp.

"Nothing, but Balor heard or scented someone."

"He could have been growling at a flea," I said.

"Balor doesn't growl at fleas," said O'Flaherty harshly. "Only at ogres."

"He growled at *me* last night."

"He did not, Grania. He was saying hello to you. It was no more than the darkness that made you misinterpret him."

"It's 'Grania' now," said Terence. "Oho! Does she call you Dog or Tommy?"

"Dopey," I said.

"That's a new one," Alanna said.

Privately I decided that if he continued to be nice to me, I would start thinking of him as Tommy. But I disagreed with his ridiculous opinion of Quinn Griffin; and the idea that I would sit here meekly in this cell for weeks was intolerable. No, he must not be allowed to win me over with the gift of a pretty sunset.

I was still very tired, probably as much from the nervous commotion caused by all this melodrama as from the digging. I dozed off shortly after we'd had dinner, while Alanna sewed a torn pair of slacks and Terence sank himself into my copy of Yeats. Tommy—no, O'Flaherty—was already asleep, in all his clothes, lying on his back and snoring quietly.

It was about five in the morning when I woke. The fire was warm near my head and over its chocolate-hay odor I could smell their breakfast tea, but they had already left. I shuffled over to the door to find it, as I'd expected, locked. I felt better than I had in days, and eager to be at work. Pouring myself tea and (remembering yesterday's sweat bath) stripping off my blouse and skirt, I collected the tools and began digging again.

Three hours, with five-minute breaks to eat a bite now and then, brought my trench to the wall. I had been right: it went all the way down to the paving, a couple of feet below the dirt surface. I had now uncovered parts of two of the big flagstones that made up the old floor. There was the same ancient mortar between them that had been used to build the walls of the room, and it crumbled away under an experimental bang of my spike in great chunks of gray sandy powder and pebbles. It had deteriorated badly under its heavy layer of earth, while the steadfast rock endured as though it had been laid down yesterday.

Idly, to make myself believe I was accomplishing something, I chipped out a large quantity of mortar, until I had gone down about three inches between the flags. I gathered all my refuse and dropped it into the loo. I fed the fire and poured the last of the tea and ate some beef, and sat down on the cool floor in my bra and pants to stare and think.

There was something wrong here. I could not make sense of the construction. Granted that I was quite untutored in architecture; still, this *had* to be wrong. For below the stratum of flagstones was a second stratum—I could see plainly where two more of them were separated by mortar, the line of which ran at right angles to that of the top course. So the floor was made up of at least two depths of flagstones, each with mortar. Did that sound like a *floor?* Especially from the days when so many structures had been made in the dry-wall fashion, without mortar of any kind?

No, it sounded more like a *roof*.

Perhaps I was on top of another part of the castle, then. A dungeon or a crypt or a scullery. I concentrated on what I'd seen of the ruins last night. To my right as I faced the western wall there was a long, high rampart, but at the back of this building, not the front. I couldn't recall whether anything but grass lay along the seaward side. Maybe some rocks ... how ghastly to tunnel out through the wall and find myself under a ton of fallen masonry, or even in another prison. I wouldn't even consider that now. I'd just work.

It was growing chilly. I slipped on my skirt and blouse, and began again, this time digging away at the lowest mortar seam of the front wall. If I could remove about four of the stones, and there was daylight beyond them, or even earth, I'd be well on my way to freedom.

I heard the rock door sliding open, and in panic grasped the lid with its heap of turf and hauled it over the pit, thankful that I'd dressed again.

It was the Blakes. "Good morning, Miss Kirk," said Terence, cheerful as usual. "It's a soft day we're having." They were both dripping with rain. "We've just been seeing about the return of your motorcar."

"Return?" I said blankly.

"Dog thought it was going to attract unwelcome attention, sitting down there abandoned day after day. So we took it to the rental agency at Shannon Airport." He dug in his pockets. "You'd paid a lot more in advance than it cost you, as it turns out, so here's your change," he said, handing me a fistful of pound notes. "And under the seat I found these, which must be yours."

They were my lost cigarettes. I had never needed to walk out on that terrible brink at all. I might have stayed safe in my little fogged-up Ford all that night, and been in Lisdoonvarna at this minute. But no, O'Flaherty would have broken in the glass to get at me.

I said, "Keep them, I've stopped smoking." So my car

was gone. That was to be expected, and not to be held
against the Blakes, being the fault of the Dog Fox. "How
did you come back, afoot?"

"We own a vehicle, if one can call it that. Tucked away
a mile from here in an abandoned shed, because we
mustn't keep it too close. The ruins have to seem untenanted to the casual passer-by." Alanna in her soaked clothing
was already preparing more of the eternal tea.

"Oh," I said, "I'll do that. You dry off."

"Have you ever made Irish tea? It took Mother years to
teach me the whole trick. I'm all right, we're used to being
wet."

"Sometimes I think we've been sodden all our lives,"
said her husband. "If this weren't such a good cause, I
swear I'd have caught the father and mother of all colds
in the head long since, and my love would be in hospital;
but there's something about the idea of all that loot that
keeps one's carcass in great working order."

"O'Flaherty said that you'd tell me about it. All he
mentioned was that it's very old, and probably valuable."

"Beyond price, we hope," said Terence. "He said we
could confide in you, yes. Well, the thing is, we have no
concept of the nature of most of it. We're only half sure it
still exists, and I *think* we've judged fairly accurately
where it is, but I can't be certain. Other than that, we
know all about it."

I sat down on the table. There was a strong temptation
to glance across and see whether my excavation was well
hidden, but I had resisted it thus far and, with my back to
it, I could probably manage. "It sounds as if you're the
world's expert on whatever-it-is," I said lightly.

"Indeed I am." He had dried his hair and face, and now
tossed his towel to Alanna. "I found the first reference—
look here, may we call you Grania too, or does the O'Flaherty hold all your affections in thrall?"

"The O'Flaherty is a man I would happily see frying on
a greasy griddle," I said. "I'd like you to call me Grania,
though, both of you. You're really very nice people."

Alanna flashed me the widest smile this side of Quinn
Griffin's. Terence continued, squatting down before the
hearth to bake his spine. "Well, I first discovered in
O'Curry—do you know Eugene O'Curry, the nineteenth-
century Gaelic scholar? no reason you should—in his book
called *M.S. Material for Ancient Irish History,* I found a

reference to Dragon's Keep, and to one of its early-thirteenth-century owners, Bran Roe O'Conor, whose ancestors had been kings in Connaught. Bran Roe was a desperate fella for stealing things and amassing antiquities that nobody else was allowed to look at, do you know the sort? The vile hobbyists, the souvenir hunters on the broad scale, who plunder and murder and thieve so they can sit in a hidden room all alone and gloat. The late Hermann Göring was one of them, I believe. And someone stole the Mona Lisa once."

He began to pack a pipe, thinking. "I can't say why it took such hold on me, but it did. It may have been because I have O'Conors on my mother's side, and felt a bit sick to think that this Bran Roe might have been a relative. Or it may just be that, having visited Dragon's Keep twice, I was intrigued by the thought that it had once held such a hoard of fragile, precious, venerable things. At any rate, I went digging in books, and then in manuscripts. Dog told you where: Trinity College Library, and Marsh's, in Dublin; between them they must have over four hundred Irish manuscripts, some from as far back as the sixth century. I read in a lot of them—"

"You mean you can read ancient Irish?"

"Middle Irish. Oh, yes," he said carelessly, "it's a hobby of mine."

"May I ask, what are you? By profession, I mean."

"I'm an architect," said Terence.

"And an artist," Alanna added.

"The little woman there is an archaeologist, when she works at it, and Dog is—is O'Flaherty himself. So I found some absolutely brilliant stuff about Dragon's Keep, much of it predating Bran Roe. It quite gave me the itch to come see it again."

"I assume that this is Dragon's Keep we're in now," I said.

"Yes. I'm sorry, I thought you knew. This is a rather unorthodox outbuilding of the castle that we're inhabiting; for want of anything better, we call it the den."

"Dog Fox's den," I nodded. "That's how I classified it."

"Well, the material on Bran Roe bore out O'Curry. The man was a monster of greed and rapacity, and as rich as all those old devils were back then, with troops of gallowglasses at his command, or *buannadha* or whatever they called mercenaries before the fourteenth century; and he was perfectly capable of wiping out a village or a castle in order to lay his hands on one small nicky-noo that he wanted, such as a horse bit from the Iron Age with La Tène decorations, or a bronze goblet, or a golden bauble." He paused. "And from all that I could find out, Grania, no one ever saw any of his loot after he died, not from that day to this."

I gasped, I think. "Do you mean . . ." I said stupidly.

"I do indeed," said Terence Blake.

"My heavens," I said. It was inadequate, but it conveyed my emotions, because he laughed and slapped his thigh.

"Just what I said, sitting in that dim library—"

"You did not. You said, 'Mother of Laoghaire!' dramatically." That was Alanna, pouring tea.

"You were not there, love."

"You either said that, or quoted Oscar Wilde. You never said 'my heavens' in your whole life, Terence *a ghrá*."

"I accept the correction. But whatever I murmured, I sat back and the world spun round me for a minute, I attest to that. Afterwards I started on the books, which followed the manuscripts in time. Few of 'em said much about Bran Roe, except that his enemies the Sionnachs destroyed a fair bit of his castle in the year 1243, with him in it, and appropriated what was left and built onto it. This place had started out in life as one of the Ferocious O'Flaherty mote-and-bailey fortresses, built by an old scoundrel they called Felim Broc; and the O'Conors had taken it and erected a stone keep on its ruins, right here in O'Brien territory in the time of the last O'Brien kings of Munster, mind you! And now the Sionnachs completed it to *their* satisfaction, and lived here until Cromwell's jolly gunners swept up through County Clare and knocked it down around their ears in 1651. Since then it evidently hasn't been lived in, save by the occasional tinker or tramp, until we three came from Dublin in the early winter to try our luck."

"But surely the Sionnachs must have looted Bran Roe's treasure in their turn?" I said.

"I think not. Because none of his spoils have ever turned up anywhere, and some of them are *sui generis*, Grania; they'd never have sunk without trace, believe me."

"I thought you didn't know what they were?"

"I'll come to that. Regarding the Sionnachs, one of the old books, by Garret More O'Meadhra, says, 'The taking of Caisleán na Dragan'—that's Irish for Dragon's Keep— 'proved the beginning of the Sionnachs' downfall, for they grew poorer and of sickly visage one and all, until the survivors of this branch of the family lived huddled woefully together in the last of their strongholds, which was that same Dragon's Keep on the Cliffs of Moher. And at the last, they could not pay mercenaries to fight for them nor servants to wait upon them, and were only farmers who lived in a castle, so pitiful altogether that 'tis a wonder the men whom Cromwell had left in Ireland thought fit to besiege and destroy the place; but it is believed that they did it out of spite, for that Dragon's Keep was a splendid spectacle standing high above the ocean, and the Roundheads could never abide beauty."

"In other words, the Sionnachs took Dragon's Keep, and they never had a day's luck since."

"Grania, we'll make an Irish girl out of you yet," said Terence with approval. "You're right. Which suggests that they did *not* find Bran Roe's treasure store."

"Or found it and spent it."

"Some of the things would have been of no use—gold and silver can be melted down, jewels pried out of settings; but wood and iron are of no value, except as relics, and one item that was mentioned specifically in the manuscript that said most about the business, it would have been mainly iron or bronze and wood. And even the soulless Sionnachs would never have dared to destroy that."

"What was it?"

His grin was pure mischief, and he looked like a whiskery Puck conning the queen- of the fairies. "I don't think I'll tell you. Leave it for a surprise when we find it. It'll blow your head."

"He means blow your mind," Alanna said. "Love, that's not fair."

"It is. Poor Grania needs riddles and enigmas to keep her brains busy, since Dog's determined to hold her here. I'll say this, though—if the thing still exists, Grania, it's the only one left in the world."

"Oh," I said, my breath half taken away. "That's ... oh, you're right, don't tell me, I want to guess!"

"I said it," he laughed. "I knew it! You've the proper sort of soul. You must come in with us."

"I never did anything illegal in my life."

"Ah, but in such a magnificent cause! And let me tell you this, Grania," he went on, looking at me seriously, before I could ask him *Why magnificent?* "Whatever good and useful deeds most Irishmen have done throughout history have been illegal at the time. It's our heritage, it's in our blood. We are a law-abiding people whom the force of history has made into reluctant but enthusiastic lawbreakers. If we—"

"But is this a good and useful deed, what you're doing?"

He gaped at me. Alanna said, "Grania thinks that we intend melting the gold down and prying out the gems, since the Sionnachs likely did not," and Terence clapped his long hands together and shouted joyously, "Conchobar's teeth, girl! Did you truly believe that an archaeologist would be wearing her knees and knuckles away in the bitter winter alongside a couple of fellas who meant to destroy antiquities? Does my beloved wife strike you as that depraved a hellhag?"

"Don't be silly," I said, smiling at Alanna, whose round face was trying not to break up in laughter at her husband's larger-than-life outburst. "Of course I know that neither of you would. What about O'Flaherty?"

"Tommy least of all. He's devoted to Ireland, he'd give his life for her."

"He almost has, and more than once," added Terence.

Then what they were doing really wasn't all that criminal, except that they didn't mean to report their finds to the government. Tommy had been very emphatic on that point. Well, there was likely some not-too-lawless way of getting around the government. Perhaps Tommy had a hereditary right to this place; perhaps when the Republic was formed all these castles and manors had reverted to the original families. But no, Tommy had said that it belonged to the government. I was going to ask about it when Terence, who had lighted his pipe, went on with his story.

"Now when I'd collected everything I could find on the history of Bran Roe's place here, I put it in order and I went to the appropriate branch of the government, which I conceived to be the Commissioners of Public Works. I argued and cajoled and fought me bloody way, Grania, through about eighty-seven phalanxes of officialdom, dragging my facts behind me, and what did I achieve? Just sweet damn all! They paid me the courtesy of listening to me, disguising their thin superior smiles behind their hands, and then they said, one and all in succession they said, Ah, Mr. Blake, it *is* an interesting idea you have there, and while you are plainly quite crackers on the subject, we will not commit you as yet, you being the grand architect and all; though we will keep our eye on you, in case you become violent. The clots! The absolute hogheaded suet-brained bat-eyed scarlet-snouted pack of baboon-witted sods! Here was I"—he reached out and gathered his wife into a loving clasp and kissed her on top of her wet hair—"and dear little Alanna, who was with me through everything, and us bearing all classes of evidence and data and corroboration, and would they give us one bloody inch of belief? Ha!" he bellowed.

"Now be fair," said Alanna, rather smothered against his chest, "we didn't have any conclusive proof. All we had was a premise, a possibility, that was all. It's still all."

"Yet you believe in it, same as I."

"Yes, but—"

"But you're a couple of poets," I said, laughing. "It's true because you want it to be true. You're the last of the romantics."

"Not a bad thing to be, either, but I deny it hotly," said Terence, looking at me over Alanna's golden head. "It's practically what those dithering maunderers in Dublin told us. It's unworthy of you, Grania. You, with your sensitive spirit shining through those lovely eyes, and my wife will forgive me for that because you *have* lovely eyes, you should see the beauty of the conception. Think of it! Not simply an artifact or two, not even a Book of Kells or a Domnach Airgid, but an individually chosen collection of trophies from far down the ages, taken by a determined and powerful man at a period when looters were keepers, and when there were still plenty of relics available that hadn't been burnt or smashed by Normans or stolen by Vikings or—"

"Yes, but you don't *know.*"

"We don't *know* anything in this world. All may be illusion. But we *believe* certain things; and I believe that I have a fifty percent chance of being right. That's not a guess, damn it, or a wish. It's a mortal certainty."

"If the collection did exist, suppose the Sionnachs took it when they took the castle, and squandered what they could and dumped the rest into the sea? Who would know?"

"A man called Seán Ó Sionnach an Ghleanna, who wrote a manuscript of which part survives in Marsh's Library. He was one of the Sionnachs himself, and he told of the taking of Bran Roe's keep, and what they did with the people they captured—no, don't ask me—and of how they rebuilt it and added the barbican and the towers on the curtain wall. If they'd found the secret room, he would have splattered the news all over his parchment, because he was writing for future generations of his own family."

"But if there wasn't a hidden room?"

"Where do you think Bran Roe O'Conor would have kept a couple of tons of loot, in his airing cupboard?"

"What's that?"

"It's where you put your washed linen to dry. Biddy M'Graw's bustle, woman, have you no conception of the glory of this thing?"

"Yes, I do," I said. "I just want to know why you're so certain."

"So fifty percent certain," said Alanna, emerging for air. "Let me tell her, I can do it without roaring like a red bull." She set about effusing the fresh tea.

Terence said proudly to me, "Look at her, will you? Did you ever see anyone more domesticated? And yet she's the most gorgeous creature in the Republic, and a scientist of no mean ability; she's a complete contradiction, and she's my woman. I never consider it, but it astounds me."

The girl's face glowed with pleasure. I thought, as I had several times before, that they were the nicest pair, as a pair, whom I'd ever known, bar none. They were as radiant together as an enchanted couple in an old fairy tale: the prince and princess, treading a measure down life's ballroom, handsome in themselves but vastly more so because of their love. Tommy had been right to accuse me of cynicism when I'd doubted their three years of marriage; yet how often, dear Lord, do you find a perfect match in this contentious world? I think that a great part of the reason I was beginning to believe in their treasure was that they were two people to whom you longed for something wonderful to happen.

Later—not then, but afterwards—I realized that this was the first time in my captivity when I was not at least partially aware of an undercurrent of strong resentment at being held prisoner in this primitive place. Maybe it was because the Dog Fox was not there.

"Another possibility is this," said Alanna, handing me my tea. "Cromwell's men could have found it when they slighted the keep—that means, knocked the walls down. But there are pretty full records of *his* activities, and his generals' and his troops', and never a word of Bran Roe's hoard." She opened her eyes wide at me as the enthusiasm caught her, too. I envied her those eyes. They were of a darker green than my own, and they had little specks of sunshine within them, which seemed now to be dancing in her zest. "As an archaeologist, I've studied the matter in minute detail, Grania, and I think Terence is right. It's a good chance."

"How did O'Flaherty come into it?" I asked.

"We were at Clongers together. Joyce's old school. I've known him forever. When the all-wise government in its infinite opaqueness," said Terence, grinding his teeth, "determined that I was a certifiable lunatic, and Dog showed up out of nowhere, I hurled it all into his lap, research and dreams and all. He believed us thoroughly. It was he who decided we'd all turn criminal, organized this whole expedition, took on his shoulders our protection, and planned and financed everything. He's also worked about twice as hard as I have, being built out of bog oak and steel as he is. I often wake in the middle of the night and he's gone, out there digging in the rain and the wind. You mustn't judge him from his behavior to you. He simply feels that he must defend Alanna and me to the limit of his ability."

"Well, I forgive him that," I said, "but I think he might realize that he could trust me. You both do."

"We do. He begins to. Give him time. His life's made him fantastically cautious."

I could not ask them about Tommy's life, for that was his business, obviously. "How could you manage to leave your jobs for so many months?"

"I have a partner, and he knows about this and is all for it. He's doing double duty down in Dublin—that would make a smashing song title!—and I trust him entirely, as he's my mother's sister's son-in-law. And Alanna doesn't toil on any regular basis, only when there's a dig she's interested in."

And O'Flaherty, probably, was the sort of adventurer who could spare some months if there was a few hundred thousand to be picked up at the end of them. I sipped tea. "Sorry I've inadvertently caused you so much trouble," I said. "I never meant to hold you back and to clutter up your lives this way. But I was dragged into it by the hair."

"Our apologies are in order, Grania, not yours," said Terence.

And the door opened and O'Flaherty came in, scattering puddles all over the floor. "Where's Balor?" he said.

"I thought he was with you."

"He was. I suppose he's over on the brow of the hill keeping watch. Tea?"

"Buckets full."

"I'll have a noggin. It's a soft day."

"Getting softer by the minute when we arrived."

"It's so soft you could liquefy," said Alanna. She turned to me. "When the wind is just short of hurricane force, and you can't see a foot through the rain, we Irish always say it's a soft day."

"And many another outlandish thing we say, too," added her husband, "such as, 'Your man is not fit to bring guts to a bear,' and 'It's great gas to be after doin' that,' and all such low common phrases straight out of Rathmines. Ah, we picturesque Hibernians! Aren't you glad you came over to visit us?"

I cocked a very sarcastic eyebrow at him.

"She's too full of emotion for speech," he said, unabashed.

"This is good tea," said Tommy, after gulping an entire mug without breathing. "I'll eat in a bit. I need a rest." He went to his sleeping bag and lay down.

Terence put the iron key on the table. "We'll have a turn with the spades, love?" She nodded, and the two of them went out. I did not hear the rock door rumble into place. I stared at the key. Then I sat down by the fire and waited.

Out in that rain with two minutes' start they'd never catch me. Had Terence deliberately handed me the chance of escape? No, of course, he wouldn't lock the door with Tommy inside. It was pure circumstance.

I had given no parole. I was a prisoner with every right to escape. And I liked the Blakes, but I liked Quinn Griffin, too, in fact I wasn't sure that I didn't have a crush on him, and if I was to be here for weeks . . .

I looked at Tommy. His eyes were shut and his mouth slightly open, the only sign of weariness after heaven knows how many hours of toil in filthy weather. He seemed to be unconscious already, on top of the sleeping bag. I pulled on my Aran sweater. He had not stirred. I got into my jacket and zipped it up, opened a suitcase, found a huge orange and blue scarf and tied it around my head.

I could not see my handbag. As softly as I could move, I went around the small room, keeping half an eye on the jailer. My gloves and a couple of handkerchiefs were in my pocket; and there was the purse, forgotten against the hearth. I picked it up gently so its contents wouldn't clink. In it was all I'd need, my passport, money, travelers cheques, airline ticket. What was in the suitcases they could have; likely the Blakes would send it all to me eventually, for my address was in both bags. They'd speculate on the wrecked one for a minute or two, and then hunt and discover the beginning of my tunnel under the turf stack.

Holding my breath now, still not entirely aware that I was about to get away, because the opportunity had come so unexpectedly, I tiptoed to the door. Tommy did not move. I tried to think. I'd go straight to the road and to Lisdoonvarna, getting into a ditch or behind a hedgerow whenever I heard a car. I might have to hide, if they came close behind me, until it was night. I went back to the far wall and picked up one of their powerful torches. You don't catch me in the dark again, Dog Fox, I told him in my head.

I opened the oaken door. The rain sheeted in.

A hand came down so suddenly on my left arm that I squeaked with the shock, and Tommy said quietly, "Would you leave us then, Grania Kirk?" and in a despairing reflex of chagrin I whirled around and slammed out at him, saying "Oh damn you" or something like that.

I swear that I had forgotten I was holding the torch. I had never struck anyone in my life, certainly not with a weapon. I could not have hit any one of them on purpose, not to save myself from a year of this imprisonment. I simply reacted without thinking. I've gone over and over it since that day, and I know that I had no wish to hurt him. I think I meant only to show him that I wasn't afraid of him.

But the long heavy metal cylinder slammed him on the side of the head, and he fell away from me and banged against the wall and went over on his face like a man shot in the heart.

I dropped the torch and screeched. Then I was on my knees beside him, trying to roll him over, while the rain came hissing and smacking into the room and the turf fire blazed up in the gust of the wind. I got Tommy on his back and straightened him out; then I took a second to slam the door, not caring if the Blakes heard it or not. I pulled over his sleeping bag and put a couple of layers under his head. His eyes were rolled up so that crescents of white showed, and his breathing was awful, short and thick. I felt for his heart. I couldn't find it.

When I located a heartbeat at last, it seemed normal enough. At least it was strong. I hadn't killed him. Well, definitely I hadn't, or he wouldn't be breathing. I was in a rattle-headed panic. I smoothed his forehead and whimpered at him. And he opened his eyes.

"You're alive," I said.

He shut his eyes tight and kept them that way for a while. Then he opened them again and said, "Am I?"

"I think so." I stared around stupidly. "What can I get for you?"

"Nothing. Good as ever in a—what in hell's name did you hit me with?"

"I didn't mean to. I thought you'd catch my hand. Are you dying?"

He closed his eyes once more. "It feels like it, but I really think not."

He was going to be all right. I snatched up the torch, clicked it on and off to be sure it wasn't shattered, found my purse wet with rainwater, and stood up. "I'm sorry. I'm escaping," I said. "Can you hear me? I'm terribly sorry I hit you; I never meant it. Good-bye."

His hand reached toward me. It was such a feeble gesture for that strong man that my heart went out to him. I dropped to one knee and before I realized what I was doing I'd kissed him on the forehead. "Oh, Tommy," I said, "shall I get Terence for you?"

"I am not wounded unto death. I am just ... what do you mean, escaping?" His hand closed on my ankle. "For God's sake, Grania," said the dark velvet voice weakly.

"If you're certain you'll be all right," I said, and detached the fingers from my leg and stood back, "I'm going now. Good luck. And don't worry, I won't tell the gardai."

"I know that," he said.

"Good-bye," I told him again, and went out and shut the door behind me.

If you ever were pushed, with all your clothes on, under a cold shower turned up full force, you will know what that day felt like as I emerged into it. It took a while before I could open my eyes enough to see. And the Blakes were out working in this!

Getting my bearings, I started off toward O'Brien's Tower, but had gone only a few yards when Balor loomed up dolefully ahead of me, looking like a drenched pony who'd lost his saddle. I cuddled his enormous head. "Oh," I said, "oh, Balor, I'll miss you." Then I led him to the door and opened it to shove him in. I had a glimpse of Tommy, sitting up and touching his temple cautiously. Then I was alone again in that violet river of rain, and resolutely slogging my way toward Lisdoonvarna and warmth and safety and sanity.

6

Well indeed I'll go!
Don't ye know I'll go?
To me rightful darlin' laddie
Well indeed I'll go!
　　　　—The Jolly Tinker

THE TWO-MINUTE START FOR WHICH I'D HOPED stretched into five and then ten, and I still heard nothing except the pounding rain, and the soggy earth making a noise like sizzling bacon under my feet. I had not gone south to the lay-by after all, but cut straight across the open hill toward the main road. If this was not bog I was mushing through, it was next thing to it. My brogues were slippery with muck, both inside and out, and I had fallen twice. Yet I was free, and the taste on my lips was that of clean rain and not of bitter-sweet turf smoke.

I sloshed across a ditch full of water to my knees, and here was L54. I turned left and started off at a jog trot.

The going was far easier now. Not having to concentrate on my footing allowed me to think. And queerly enough, I began to feel small, lonely, dismal, and lost.

Had I genuinely hurt Tommy? He might be lying on his back at this moment, with a concussion or worse. He might have hemorrhaged inside his skull, and be dying, with only a poor helpless dog to watch him go.

Ah, the Weeping West of Ireland was saturating my thoughts! Tommy wasn't a man to be destroyed by a flashlight in a woman's hand.

The Blakes would never realize how much I liked them. Dear old one-eyed Balor would miss me, and wonder.

How the four of them had become my world, in only—how long? Thirty-six hours, give or take a little! They had constituted my first real adventure. And now that it was over, I was more alone than I'd been in Dublin or on the Ring of Kerry. The camaraderie of the group had already been reaching out to include me; not many strangers had ever been as nice to me as Terence and Alanna, and even Tommy O'Flaherty had started to treat me with gruff kindness.

The eternal sea wind blew, the cold rain fell as though from upturned barrels, and I padded along toward Lisdoonvarna, as miserable as I could be. A large red cow stared round-eyed at me from the shelter of a tree, as though she thought me brainless to be out there alone. I thought so too.

A big black-and-white bird, the size of a ringneck pheasant, burst spectacularly out of the hedgerow and flew across my path low and fast, to disappear in the rain.

I recollected that the Blakes had a car. I had no idea of where they kept it—about a mile away, Terence had said—or of what make it was. I'd have to avoid all cars. They would be after me by now. Would they believe I'd try for Limerick? Or Ennistymon; that would be far closer. No, they'd imagine that I'd head for Quinn Griffin. Which was just what I was doing. I'd have to get off the road if I heard a motor.

There *was* a noise behind me. Spooked, I dove for the cover of a stone wall, beyond which a brown donkey was pointedly ignoring me. Then I stopped, because what I heard was the lazy clop of horses' hoofs.

Slowly I came back to the road. Nobody on a horse, or riding behind one, was an enemy.

Through the thick curtains of "soft" weather came a couple of piebald ponies, with a man walking at the head of the left one, whistling tunefully, and ten or twelve mongrel hounds pattering alongside. I waved a reserved greeting to him. The ponies were pulling a big tinkers' caravan along the road.

I'd seen many of these vehicles in the South, but this was the largest and handsomest yet. It was dark red, green-framed, and painted all over with the fine fanciful half-primitive designs that the tinkers like: horse heads, white doves, yellow and blue flowers and geometrical patterns, shamrocks and horseshoes and ivy leaves. The rear wheels were half again as broad as the front, and all white with narrow scarlet stripes on the spokes. The caravan was shaped somewhat like a Conestoga wagon, with a flat bed and tall sides and the great half-round hood with a smokestack in the center that is typical of these anachronistic rigs. Strung out on long tethers behind it came half a dozen horses, all piebald but the first, a magnificent bay stallion.

The man, lean and dark in thick gray clothing and high boots, stopped when he saw me, and the ponies and dogs came to a halt, too. He stared at me, not impolitely but from the corners of his eyes, and when I realized that he was taking in some very peculiar details, such as long hair unbound and escaping from its scarf in soppy ropes, a very muddy maxiskirt, and a huge four-battery torch held like a weapon in my hand, I knew I wouldn't blame him for averting his gaze and tramping forward. But he cleared his throat and said civilly, "Would ye be needin' a ride out o' the wet, my lady?" as though I'd been standing there in a spotless farthingale and a wimple.

The girl who'd hidden in her Ford all across Ireland would have shaken her head and murmured a timid refusal. The girl who'd been kidnaped off the Cliffs of Moher in the dead of horrid night by the Dog Fox found herself made of tougher meat. "Oh, I would appreciate that *so* much!" she said.

"I'll just see that it's fit for ye inside, then," he said, and leaped up on the front seat, where another man was holding the ponies' reins. This one said something to him in a low voice, I think in Irish. He must have protested that I was none of their affair, that I looked hunted. The first man glared at him a moment and then with a motion as fiercely angry as any I ever saw, he gripped the driver by the back of the collar and hauled him off the seat and into the depths of the caravan. The last I saw of him were his legs, kicking frantically as they dragged across the wet planks.

I stood there dripping, and waited. Voices came to me, muffled and wrathful. Then there was the slam of a door opening, and the erstwhile driver flew out of the rear of the conveyance as though he'd been kicked in the stomach; which, for all I ever discovered, he may have been. He lit on his back under the feet of the bay, who merely glanced down at him as if this sort of thing happened every few minutes. An arm protruded from the doorway and a fist was shaken at him.

"Yer a very bad bit o' work entirely! With a sour face on ye as long as a hare's hind leg! Now ye can walk t' the

town, ye muzzy scut, and maybe that'll be after puttin'
some dacency in ye!" The arm withdrew and the door
crashed shut. The man sprawled there under the big horse,
looking half stunned. The other one appeared at the front
again. "Come up, my lady," he said gently, extending a
hand.

I walked through the incurious dogs and was lifted onto
the caravan. "Out then, Tadhg, and lend a hand with the
harses," he shouted, and a small boy popped into view,
pulling on an ancient macintosh and carefully avoiding my
eye. "Go right in, my lady," said the man, as I paused to
sleek some of the rain off my jacket and skirt. "Sure nav-
ver mind that bit o' moisture, it'll dry fine in the warm."

"Thank you," I said, and lifted the curtain and entered
through a door, which he closed softly behind me.

The inside of that caravan was stunning. I gaped
around and without even thinking I said aloud, "This is
the nicest home I've ever been in!" And I think it was.

Everywhere was clean and tidy brightness: nothing
seemed out of place except my dank and muddy self. Polished brass and copper glowed and mirrors, some cut into
mosaic patterns, glittered. Everything paintable was deco-
rated with flowers in clear primary colors. There was crisp
chintz and warm-looking wood and a great deal of handsome china. Four women, one with a baby in her arms,
sat in short-legged chairs in this small cheerful sanctuary
against the mad weather. They were dressed exactly like
everyone's family snapshots from the 1930's at home, and
they had the burned deep-red faces of their people. Two
of them at once stood up to make me welcome.

Trying not to drip on anything but the carpet, I moved
gingerly, at their soft-voiced insistence, to the side of the
small round stove, which was hot as hot might be. "Just
stand there, my lady," said one, a girl in her teens. "It's a
soft day altogether."

The oldest of the women—she might have been the
oldest woman in Ireland from the wrinkles of her face—
took the clay pipe from her mouth and made a noise that
I decided was a laugh. "Soft! It's a drencher. It's as wet as
a bowl o' watery stew!" It was one of the few sensible remarks I ever heard from anyone in that island concerning
the weather. I smiled at her. She returned the pipe to its
toothless home and puffed hard. The clay was about as
long as her nose, and what she was smoking in it smelt ex-

actly like turf. "Soft," she repeated, making it into the most objectionable-sounding four-letter word imaginable.

"Well, it is, Gram," said one of the women. "You stand easy, my lady, and when you've dried, there's salt bacon and ling and cabbage. Grania, do you pour tay for the lady."

I put my hand out to the girl and told her that my name was Grania, too. This brought forth a vast feminine babble of amazement and pleasure, and before I knew it the dreary rain was forgotten and my world was full of brightness and friendship. And the Cliffs of Moher sank behind me, defeated for then by all this homely sanity.

They were the kindest folk I ever met, even in Ireland. I remember thinking that they would have terrified me no more than a few days ago, when I would have run from their alien friendship. They looked after me as though I'd been one of their own, back from roaming abroad; they half undressed me and dried my scarf and coat, they cleaned my skirt and brogues (over my feeble objections) and propped the shoes near the stove; they poured strong tea and food into me until I was bulging. They did not seem in the least inquisitive, and certainly not faintly suspicious of this foreigner who'd burst in on them from the dank countryside. They were called Coffee, and belonged to one of the far-flung tinker tribes of that name.

And we talked. Heavens, how we talked! It was like a family reunion in Freeport. We talked of the weather: weather I had seen, weather they had seen; weather we'd been out in, weather we'd peered at from the safety of caves or empty houses or spinneys. We spoke of cities—one of them had been to London, and all knew Dublin well—and of the realtive merits of Waterford, Roscommon, and Clare. The girl, who was to be married in the spring, shyly exhibited her wedding dress. We played with the baby till it gurgled in joy.

Only once was a direct question put to me. The wrinkled woman, packing her pipe again, said, "What are ye doin' here in the oldest place?" which is an ancient name for Ireland. So I told them what I did for a living, and how my grandmother was Irish and still alive in America, and all about the making of television films; and the four of them hung on my words as if they were hearing tales of El Dorado, which in a sense I suppose they were. For the sake of returning their hospitality I talked myself hoarse. I believe I gave them conversation for a month; one or another of them may be telling her cronies even now about the famous American actress who became their dear friend and drank tea with them just as though she'd been plain Molly O'Hara out of Tralee.

It must have taken us four hours at the slow pace of the horses to reach Lidsoonvarna; it passed like twenty minutes.

But at last the man who walked before the caravan put his head in and said diffidently, "The town's just here, my lady." He cleared his throat, a constant habit with these folk of the roads who live outdoors in all weathers. "I wonder if ye'd be wantin' the gardai?"

Did I look so much a hunted fugitive, then? Likely . . . I said, "No, thank you, I'll go to the hotel. I know the O'Carmodys."

"We'll be forninst it in a bit," he said, and withdrew.

How could I show my appreciation without offending the Coffees? I took off a ring that I'd worn for a year or two, white gold set with two garnets, which is my birthstone. Being very wily and Irish, I offered it to the girl and said that since we shared the same name, it would bring good luck to both of us if she'd wear this on her wedding day. Even the ancient woman exclaimed in delight at the red stones, brushing aside my protest that they were only garnets. "Rubies they be, dearie," she said, touching them discreetly with the stem of her pipe, "rubies out o' the bowels o' the earth!" Then Grania must give me a present in exchange and finally decided on a little gewgaw she had pinned to her bosom, a copy of the fabulous Tara Brooch. I wear it to this day, in memory of those few delightfully sane hours in the midst of my Irish nightmare.

"Here's where we lave ye, then, my lady," said the man. I shook hands all round and hugged Grania, and departed in a tangled commotion of good wishes and thanks. The boy Tadhg slid over on the wet seat shyly as his father gave me a hand to the ground.

The rain had now slacked off to a raging downpour. I could not help asking him, "Why do you walk in this awful weather? Wouldn't it be a little more comfortable to ride?"

He smiled, "If them ponies don't be hauled by hand, my lady, they'll stop, and batin' nor screechin' won't keep the brutes from grazing, or maybe only standin' to think on things." He shrugged. "A man can get just so wet," he said philosophically, "whereafter he stays the same; and I'm used to it. Any road, I will not thrash my ponies, poor craturs, for their lot's hard enough. I'm content to pull them."

I shook hands with him and, remembering the formula, said, "God and Mary with you."

"God and Mary with you and Patrick, my lady."

I stood waving farewell till the whole lot—ponies, dogs, stallion, gay caravan, tramping men, and all—had vanished into the rain. Then I went into O'Carmody's place.

When I confronted the little fat man from a book by Dickens, it dawned on me that I had no prepared story whatever, that in fact I had no idea of what I meant to do next. So I simply said the first thing that came into my head. "I've lost my car and luggage, and I need a bath."

"Is it yourself, Miss Kirk? I thought you'd be in Donegal these forty-eight hours. Will Mr. Griffin know you're here, then?"

"Nobody but yourself knows. Can I have a bath?"

"Take a round dozen," he said, bounding forward to escort me to my old room. "Would you like tea? I'll have a pot on a tray for you before you unbutton your coat." Never a word of query about my missing property; I thought, that's hardly Irish, but it's a relief.

The tea came, accompanied by a pound or two of various edibles. I was not consciously hungry after the tinkers' hospitality, but found myself nibbling sausages and treacle bread and oatcakes. There is no sauce for the appetite like cold, rain-sodden adventure.

The bath was sheer heaven. I soaked in it, drowsily consuming tea and chips, which I'd set on a stool by the tub. When the water chilled after an hour or so, I got out, rubbed my skin into pinkness, and dressed again. I had managed not to think at all until then.

Well, I would have nothing to do with the police. I'd never intended to, despite Tommy's suspicions. Should I find Quinn and tell *him?*

I stared into the mirror at a suddenly bewildered girl. I didn't know. What if Tommy were right, and Quinn was a bad, mad man? He wasn't, but—

I would inquire about buses to Shannon. Then I'd de-

cide how much to tell Quinn. *You're only procrastinating.*
Yes, I am. However.

I put on my sweater and jacket, paid Mr. O'Carmody
for the food and tea (he would not take anything for the
bath), and turning from the desk, bumped into my broad
Quinn Griffin himself.

"You're back," he said, showering me with his smile.
"And without your bags and motorcar, too. What have
you been up to, Grania Kirk? Have you been consorting
with the Dread Women?"

So O'Carmody had told him already; probably had
hunted him up while I bathed, and been tipped well for his
thoughtfulness.

I had lived with devious ways and suspicions and inter-
rogations for a day and a half, and it must have become
second nature to me to pry and ferret, at least where this
tall handsome mystery man was concerned; for I smiled at
him and murmured. *"Où sont les neiges?"*

"D'antan," said he, blinking.

"It is a password, then," I said, and under the lightness
of the tone I could hear my voice tremble ever so slightly.

"How very intelligent you are. O'Carmody, bring us a
couple of soothing Irish coffees, do." His hand on my arm
steered me into the lounge, where horsehair sofas and ma-
hogany tables and steel engravings had been awaiting us
for a full century. Quinn's firm—yes, domineering—pressure was somehow not as pleasant as it had been before.
Perhaps I'd had my fill of take-charge guys. "Sit down,"
he said. "To be sure it's a password. How you learned it
I've no notion, though—"

"Every schoolchild in America knows it." I sank onto
the sofa. He'd kissed me here, and Alanna Blake had seen
us.

"My seven abiding curses on the verse, then, for a snare
and delusion. I found it in a book, and thought it was so
out of date it would be safe."

" 'Full fathom five my father lies' is pretty antiquated,
too," I said. It was the only Shakespeare that came read-
ily to my tongue, and it was misquoted. I thought of Terence, and Thomas the Rhymer.

"Does he now, your father?" murmured Quinn Griffin,
staring down at me. "There were four men went to sea in
a beautiful pea-green boat, and two came safe to land.

Maybe one of the two who didn't reach the shore was your father?"

"I don't know what you're talking about; my father's been dead for twenty years."

"Then why do you bring up his drowned state?"

"*Oh!*" I exploded, shoving myself to my feet and feeling my cheeks go red with anger. "Will you stop playing with poetry and tell me what's going on between you and the Dog Fox? I've met him, as you knew I would."

"And the Blakes," he said.

"Yes. A lovely couple."

"In a vile business."

"What business? Why vile?" The thought of Terence, let alone his wife, doing anything contemptible, that was ridiculous. The Irish coffee came and he pressed me onto the sofa again and gave me a glass. "Grania, I don't know whether to believe you completely, or to mark you down as one of the prettiest liars of all time." He sat beside me. The hand on my wrist may have been meant for solicitude, but came across as a threat. It said, I've caught *you* at least. Or was I reading menace into an ordinary gesture? I had come running to him for safety. . . . I began to feel ill-used. Then he smiled and said, "I'll assume you're innocent, else why would you come back? Grania, don't you truly know why they're out there?"

"I know what they told me." He looked his question and I heard myself say blithely, "They told me to beware of Quinn Griffin."

"They naturally would. Well. Grania, I must take you into my confidence, I see. They are engaged in the smuggling of drugs."

I have no idea how long it was before I could speak. Then I said, a little shrill, "Drugs? Why, that's just laughable."

"Not at all. There's enough money in it to tempt the jolliest of people. And O'Flaherty with his I.R.A. background never thought twice about getting into this game when he saw the chance."

"But they're not. They're doing something completely different."

"Put a name to it," he said sharply.

"They're hunting treasure," I said. It seemed such a childlike and innocent pastime compared with drug-running that I came right out with it, quite incautiously.

He chuckled. "Ah, away with that," he said in his blarneying voice, "they never made you believe that, Grania Kirk! What sort of treasure? In the Republic, of all places. Captain Kidd never got this far, my romantic American."

"They are. And you know it. They're digging all the time, and one doesn't dig for drugs!"

"Did you watch them at the digging?"

It was my turn to blink. "No, but—"

"What treasure?"

"I don't know. They never said."

"They've hoaxed you." He sat back, relaxing his grip, and drank the heavily laced coffee. "By God," he said softly, watching me, his beautiful eyes candid and full of mirth, "I thought you were in it with them, I truly did. And now I believe you're not. It was all a gigantic piece of coincidental idiocy."

"Thank you."

"Not your idiocy, mine. Look here," said Quinn, bending toward me, "I've wronged you, and I'm sorry. I can't tell you all the reasons why I thought what I did, but I can reassure you about the affair. O'Flaherty and his chums are not seeking pirate loot, but waiting to lay their hands on a drug cache worth more than half a million pounds."

"And are you after it, too?"

"Only in line of duty. Principally I'm after them. You see, Grania, I'm by way of being a special sort of policeman. And I shall take them as soon as the evidence is complete."

I stared at him aghast. What had I done? Exactly what I'd promised myself—and Tommy—that I would never do: I'd run to the law. "They simply cannot be smugglers, or have anything to do with drugs," I said. "I *know* this."

He held out a wallet that showed an official-looking card. I read part of it. Yes, he was of the police. But still he was wrong, he was entirely wrong, he had to be wrong about the drugs. "Both those men," he was saying, "and the woman, too, are baying on the track of a tremendous fortune. I only wonder that they didn't hurl you off the cliff as a simple precaution."

"I thought of that," I said. "But I never . . . no, no. It isn't possible."

"I'm afraid it's been a shock," he said tenderly, and put his arm over my shoulders. "I am so sorry that you had to be involved this way. But you're free of them now, and safe with me."

"Yes. I thought about you a lot," I said, hardly noticing what I was telling him. "When they had me locked up, I kept thinking of escaping, coming back to you." That was true. And now that I'd succeeded, and discovered that he was above suspicion himself, I ought to have been rejoicing. Why wasn't I?

Anyone can buy documents to prove to gullible people that he's a policeman or a detective or a veteran of the French Foreign Legion, if he's so inclined. But to believe that of Quinn on nothing more than the vague accusations of the Dog Fox would be credulous beyond words.

Anyone can splash a little muck on himself and say he's been digging for relics. But to believe that of Tommy on the unsupported word of Quinn Griffin would be brainless.

The two hated each other, and nothing had been proved on either side. Desperately I fastened on the hope that both were telling the truth about themselves, and that prejudice had blinded them to the truth about each other.

"Look here, Quinn," I said earnestly, "I *know* the Blakes. I'd believe almost anything of your Dog Fox, but Terence and Alanna are no more drug-traffickers than I am. It is *not* possible."

"With enough money in view, Grania, anything is possible to anyone," he said cynically. "That's the way of the world."

"No. I don't believe you. You're wrong."

The arm tightened across my shoulders. "I see a rougher side of life than you do, girl dear. When my men arrive from Dublin, I'll be able to substantiate my charges."

"Your men?"

"Two of us are not enough to take O'Flaherty and Blake. I've sent for half a dozen more. Can't risk losing him again," said Quinn, sounding like any Scotland Yard inspector on the old Warner Brothers back lot. "Oh yes, I've played against him before, and lost. I admit it. He's wily. Hence the name of Dog Fox."

"Otherwise known as Fu Manchu," I muttered. The minute Quinn had come up through the trapdoor waving a badge, I'd begun to smell grease paint. His manner had changed, there was a slight film of pomposity on the cheeks and the back had stiffened. Some men respond like that to their jobs; they lose the edge of humor and feel their importance the instant they stop being plain citizens. It didn't become Quinn Griffin. The charm was weakened as the power grew. I'd have been—well, *relieved*, if he'd whipped out that identification with a laugh and showed me the small print at the bottom saying "Made in Hong Kong for Fooling Your Friends." But he wouldn't, because he was a policeman.

"You're hurting me," I said. He took his arm away with a grunt of apology. "Hold this," I said, giving him my un-tasted Irish coffee so that he had both hands full, "I want to powder my nose."

"But it's—oh, I see. Of course," he nodded, smiling. "Hurry back."

I walked past my old room and on to the end of the hall, opened several doors, discovered the kitchen and went through it and out into the rear yard. A wet terrier barked at me once and then retreated into an outbuilding. Fumbling my scarf on as I moved through the muck, I came around the large low clay-colored inn to the town square. There was a bus parked not ten yards away. With one eye on the front door of O'Carmody's, I dashed across the street and banged at the door of the vehicle. The driver opened it suspiciously.

"Are you for the Cliffs of Moher?" He was aimed in the proper direction, but that meant nothing; after all, this was Ireland, where if you want to go north you will likely start off south by southwest. The destination marker still said "Lios Dúin Bhearna," which is Lisdoonvarna.

The driver blocked my way. "I am."

"Well, that's grand, can I buy a passage?" My skin was prickling with the dread of seeing Quinn Griffin emerge, and I was talking in imitation Irish, to speed things up.

"In this weather and afoot, miss, I'd not recommend it," said the man dubiously.

"Sure it's all right, I left my motorcar there," I said truthfully. "It's a pet day, I mean a soft day, isn't it? How much?" I began to fumble in my handbag, the big torch held under one arm.

"Have you any dangerous or offensive articles with ye?"

"Certainly not," I said indignantly.

"Nor any dogs or other animals?" he said.

I stared at him, almost snapped out that there were three chipmunks in my purse, and thought better of it. "No, sir. How much is the fare?"

He backed up with some reluctance, naming a small sum. I pressed it into his hand and shoved by him into the bus, which held an old man and two children, who all stared at me. I sat down on the far side, next to the dirtiest window, and held my breath. The driver watched me for a full minute, obviously longing to begin one of those interminable Irish conversations that center on the question of why on earth you should want to go wherever you're going. Then he examined his watch and slowly closed the door and hoisted himself into his seat.

I was, for the second time that day, running in great luck. I had come just at departure time.

As we groaned past the hotel, Quinn thrust his head and shoulders out of the open door and squinted at the bus. I sank down as far as I could. He did not move until we had turned the corner. He probably had not seen me. I began to breathe deeply.

My loyalties, which had been churning and shifting for many hours, had congealed at last. Against all reason, against whatever evidence the police might have, I believed in the Blakes. Yes, and I believed in Tommy O'Flaherty, the truculent mahogany-colored young man whom I had fled to find Quinn, and whom I may have injured badly or even killed; with all my heart I believed in him. He might be a lawbreaker—indeed, by his admission, he *was*—but not in the soulless fashion that Quinn had impugned him with. He was a hard man, but not evil. Quinn Griffin was simply wrong, monstrously wrong.

I was, of course, operating on sheer instinct. "And common sense," I said half aloud, as I tried to picture the delightful Blakes bargaining over a heap of opium, or whatever it might be.

And so I was with the Black Velvet Gang, and against the law of the land, even though that meant being against my handsome Quinn likewise. I was rushing back to my erstwhile jailers to warn them of the terrible charges that were laid to their door. I had shown my hand to a member of the police, whose former suspicions would now be confirmed. I had used trickery, deceit, and flight, to escape from Quinn and rejoin them.

I was an outlaw in a foreign country, and would doubtless end in some female prison alongside Alanna Blake. There were gardai coming from Dublin to see to that.

And I didn't care a damn.

7

I thought if me mother
Herself had been nigh,
She'd ha' buried me decent,
In case I should die . . .
     —The Kerry Recruit

AND NOW, THOUGH THE HIDEOUS MEMORY still haunts me
and I dread stirring it up afresh, I must write down how I
fought with the Dread Woman of Moher.

It seemed to me that that bus took nearly as much time
as the Coffees' caravan had to traverse the seven miles between Lisdoonvarna and the cliffs. It was a "local," I
think. Every few feet, the thing would barge off the main
road into the little hills to discover any possible passen-
gers. We had not been out of the town a quarter of an
hour before I was longing for the days of flying coaches,
or jaunting cars, or even donkeyback travel. We might run
out of petrol, at this rate, before we sighted the landward
roll of those bleak, haunted ramparts. And certainly we
would run out of daylight.

Well, we did. And with the early evening came a thun-
derstorm that reduced visibility to almost nothing, and the
clammy, cold little bus jounced its way through darkness
shot by an occasional streak of lightning. In Ireland, I
noticed (or imagined), even the lightning has a green tint
to it.

Cars passed us now and then, but I did not know what
sort Quinn drove, and so did not worry about them. Time
enough for that when we'd come to the cliffs.

Finally, as I was dozing in immense discomfort, the
driver bawled out that we were opposite Moher. I picked
up my bag and torch and stumbled from the bus, which
clattered off at once like a scared little dragon escaping a

witch. I sloshed through a puddle or two and found the road to the lay-by.

The wind from the ocean was alive with malice. It slashed at me and would not allow my scarf to stay on, so that my hair was soon wet through to my skull. It howled along that gentle slope like a mad thing, and I leaned into it and fought my way yard by yard, shuddering with a mixture of cold and fear. For some reason the entire affair now began to tumble about in my mind, with all its doubts and dangerous uncertainties; I told myself to stop anticipating, but I *would* repeat such futile questions as "What if Tommy is smuggling drugs?" and "How do you know the Blakes aren't simply good actors?" I couldn't answer them. I had to rely on my instincts, and go forward.

When I reached the lay-by and saw the dark Fiat 850 sitting there, I don't suppose I was really surprised, only frightened.

I clicked off the torch and thought wildly. It was either the Blakes'—improbable, for Terence had implied that theirs was less impressive transportation—or Quinn Griffin's, or some stranger's. If Quinn caught me he'd arrest me, no doubt of that. A stranger, another kook from America, determined to see the spectral site—that wasn't too far out, was it? But the little car was likely Quinn's.

I went around it toward the path that led to the ruins. The night was as black as a barrel of crows, and as noisy. My groping hand touched cold, wet metal and I moved farther out to skirt the car. A crackle of lightning with its thunder right on its heels showed me the bulk of the Fiat; I thought the door on the far side was open, so I bobbed down to avoid being seen.

"Is that you?" shouted a voice. *"Oo solly nedge?"*

With the grue running down my spine, I wasn't about to yell "Downtown!" I plunged ahead, past the car, sliding on the wet road and gasping through my open mouth. And the wide ray of another flashlight darted out to search and find me and hold me illuminated.

"Who are you?" called the voice angrily. It was not Quinn's. I turned around to face it, the light in my eyes, and in the irritation of partial relief shone my own torch straight back. The man and I stood there squinting resentfully at each other.

"Who are you?" I retorted.

He was a nondescript fellow in a macintosh and a

ginger mustache. He approached me, muttering. Then he asked, "What the devil are you doing here?" as though he'd owned the place.

"Poaching," I said. "What about you?"

"Poaching what?" Then abruptly he laughed. "Okay, I'm sorry." He dropped the beam below my face, and I did the same for him. "It's not a place you'd expect to meet a woman," he said more quietly. "I thought you were someone else."

"I often come here on soft nights," I said, "to sit on the cliffs and watch the storms. I'm an artist. It occurred to me that American tourists would like to have paintings of Moher to take home. Were you ever in New Orleans? They simply eat up the weird oils of Jackson Square by lamplight, and I think they ought to do the same here, you know?"

I could see him relax in the reflected light of our torches. For an impromptu explanation it was pretty fair, just unusual enough to be believable. "I've been there, yes. It isn't a bad idea. I'd take one of your cliff pictures myself if I liked your technique. Look, I'm really sorry I scared you."

"You didn't," I lied. "It's a funny place to meet anybody at night, though." Over to you, buddy.

"Not so odd to another artist," he said promptly. "See, my friend and I are photographers. Car there's crammed with camera stuff. We're going to make snapshots of Moher by moonlight, or by lightning if we can." That wasn't too bad, either, except that no professional photographer has used the term "snapshot" for a generation or two, and if I'd been him I'd have thrown away some more technical terms; likely he didn't know any, and had taken his cue from me. "Apologies again, ma'am," he said, nodding and smiling. "Are you going out on the view platform? It's supposed to be dangerous at night."

You're telling *me?* "No, I'm heading up to O'Brien's Tower. Good night," I said, dipping my torch in salute, and turned and walked steadily away. I glanced back and saw his light go off. I started up the path, going as fast as I could with the terrible east wind trying to knock me over. I'd use the flash till I reached the hull of the old tower, then go over the brink of the hill without it. He was certainly watching me to check my story out. He looked so unlike a policeman that I was sure he must be one, waiting there for Quinn Griffin. His accent was, I thought, Philadelphian. Imported cop? It seemed that I had very little time in which to warn Tommy and the Blakes.

The rain thinned out for a while, though the wind was rising. My feet slipped and my ankles kept turning on the mucky, uncertain ground. It was like walking up a tilted cow pasture that had been under water all week. Once I banged against an old wire fence on my right and fell over it; the flashlight rolled away and went out, and I groped desperately for several minutes before I discovered it. I stood up and turned it on, and stared down behind me at the lay-by. Dimly I saw that the ginger-mustached man was talking to someone who held a torch on him, and whom I couldn't distinguish, with the night and the rain.

They were closing in rapidly on us outlaws. The wretched bus had brought me here not a second sooner than necessary.

I dashed up toward the watchtower. When I'd come abreast of it, I doused my torch and looked back. Now I couldn't see the lay-by or any man-made glow, though a splash of lightning showed me the hillside and the ruins of O'Brien's old contribution to the cliffs. I faced toward Dragon's Keep, having taken my bearings, and walked as swiftly as I could over earth that I could not see.

I had gone perhaps twenty steps when a hummock threw me off balance and I staggered to my left, toward the brink. With a memory of my first terrible night on the cliffs, I lit the torch briefly to reorient myself. I was indeed heading off-route. I aimed at the unseen castle and extinguished the light once more. I went on, and now my path lay down the slope.

Then I was aware that just west of where I walked, there was either a noise or a movement. I cannot tell which it was, though that seems strange now, for every other detail of the next few moments is as clear to me as though it had been the climax of a movie I'd seen a hundred times. Reason tells me that in that wind, in that rain, in that blackness, I could scarcely have heard a sound quieter than a gunshot, or glimpsed anything that was not luminous. Yet the impression remains and will not die that I was conscious for a second or two of the beating of enormous wings approaching from over the Atlantic. Certainly *something* startled me badly, something more than an eerie premonition, for I turned seaward and threw up my arms across my face. Then I was struck heavily, a direct blow from the front, and dropped to my knees, clutching wildly at whatever it was that had attacked me.

One hand grasped wet slithery bulk and the other something like thin bone. Then I seemed all at once to be enveloped in a kind of living mantle, the consistency of which I cannot describe: there was the impression of leather, of porcupine quills, of fish skin . . . something beat fiercely at my breast and, less strongly, at my back. I must have shrieked with terror. Surely I heard the thing answer me with an ear-ripping cry in which, if there were syllables, they were those of ancient Gaelic.

Even before I felt the first iron talon carve into the jacket over my shoulder, I knew that I was fighting with one of the Dread Women of Moher. And there was no doubt in my mind at all that she had come out of the storm to kill me.

She was larger than I by far, though her frame was curiously light. Half corporeal body, half insubstantial phantasm? I felt her awful touch on my back, my calves, my stomach, and my face, all at once, as though she were poised in the rushing air and enveloping me as the dome of a jellyfish surrounds a condemned shrimp. Yet as big as she seemed, there was no vast weight anywhere on me. When I fell backward, I think it was as much from the roaring rainy wind as from the beating, whipping, volatile bulk of the attacker. Somehow I contorted myself up to my knees again in the slippery muck.

The weapon—dagger, claw, whatever it was—cut viciously at my shoulder, and I gave one despairing twist at the piece of her that I held in my right hand, feeling small bones collapse under my fingers, then released it and grabbed for the wrist that must be close to my collarbone. The grasp closed on greasy intangibility that writhed away, and I felt a sharp edge slice down my cheek, but no pain.

I remember as in a nightmare the noise we were making. It was indescribably horrible. I think I was as enraged as I was frightened. This being did not belong on God's green earth, not in the twentieth century. She had come out of the cesspool of past Time to assault me, and it was monstrously unfair. So we screamed at each other malevolently, and sought to destroy. And all the while there was a repulsive clacking sound in my ear, the source of which

I could not guess, and great gusts of the most evil smell that I had ever encountered, a fishy, carrion stench that nearly made me vomit.

Somehow my hands had found a purchase on a part of her body, and I drove them against her, groping with my fingers for some vital spot that I could rip into. Probably I was going, with primitive instinct, for her jugular; though I might have been seeking her cold and hating heart. The blade came down in a violent stab on the back of my wrist and my left hand began to tingle and go numb.

I was still fighting on my knees. I could feel a thrashing, ineffectual attack on my back, and it shot across my mind that she was flapping her leathery wings wildly there. The searching weapon just brushed my cheek and struck the lobe of one ear—that was the first real *pain* I had felt—and in a despairing frenzy I turned loose the slimy mass of whatever part of her I was holding, and clutched upward and caught a thick writhing thing that I took for a wrist, though what in heaven's name it must look like I could not imagine; it took both my hands to encircle it, and it must have had an incredible array of joints, for it twisted snakelike in my hands, and it was covered with a thatch that was both slimy and prickly. I dug in my fingers and at the same time was overbalanced by her violent movement and fell sideways onto one of her great flailing wings.

With a hoarse sound of rage, the Dread Woman cut mercilessly at my arm again. I felt the jacket rip under the driving blow. I gripped down with all the power of both my hands and twisted whatever awful thing I was clutching, and the clacking racket broke off, and a shudder convulsed the portion of her body that pressed against my chest. There was a perfect deluge of some repulsive oily substance over my face, making me retch; and then I was clawing with my nails at something that moved only in small, ineffective jerks.

I pushed frantically at her, and rolled backwards and scrambled to my feet in the stormy darkness. All I could hear over the rain and wind was my breath wheezing hideously through my open mouth. The whole world was full of the disgusting, sour, deathly reek. Then I felt my cheek begin to hurt as though it had been carved half off my face, and I burst into tears and backed away, whimpering and sobbing, until I fell over a log or something and nearly broke my spine.

There was no use looking for the torch; that had gone in the first moment of the attack, and I would never have located it without another to see by. Shakily I stood up, wondering in a dazed, half-interested fashion whether I was going to die, and the grandsire of all lightning flashes came out of the air and showed me the path to the castle. I glared at it as long as the afterglow lived, and then I ran along it without a thought of the long plunge to the sea, and by the time another bolt came, I was close to the ruins. I slowed to a shambling, drunken walk, and began to trip over things and fall with monotonous regularity. My face and hand were bursting with pain. I lost my way and believed that I must have left the keep far behind, and it would *not* lightning again, and I was crying and feeling so sorry for myself that I was on the point of dropping in my tracks and bleeding to death when my shins were barked on what some groping told me was the dry-stone wall above the cliffs.

How the ocean seemed to call me! Like a vast magnet pulling at a scrap of iron.

I faced about and marched forward until I came with a smash against the wall of the ruin. Edging my way along, I arrived by almost incredible luck at a big flat slab that moved sideways under the hard pressure of my palms. It was the sliding rock door of the hidden room.

I pushed it entirely over to the side and began to pound with both fists at the oak. For the longest time nothing happened. Then I realized that they would not open it unless I identified myself, so I shouted, "Please, it's Grania," over and over. I heard the big iron key grate in the lock, and the door swung inward upon more blackness. I staggered forward and put out my hands, and sodden, bloody, befouled, miserable with agony and terror, I said, "I've come home," and collapsed into the arms of the Dog Fox.

"It's never Grania," said the calm voice of Terence, "it smells like a swamp."

Alanna lit the big green Coleman lantern, as Terence locked the door. Tommy hoisted me up in his arms and, staring into my face, said huskily, "Oh, good God," and carried me over to a blanket before the fire, the blessed warm chocolate-smelling turf. The Blakes crowded around and Terence said, appalled, "Why, the child's all hacked and mangled! Love, she's in a wretched plight!"

"Get the medicine kit," said his wife, unfastening my jacket. "What happened?"

"It was one of the Dread Women." I lay there crying and shaking with relief and dismay. Now that I was inside, the whole episode with its ghastly implications of supernatural horror was really penetrating my consciousness.

"What? A *woman* did this?" shouted Tommy, bending over me.

"Not a real woman. A Harpy."

"Mythology. Part woman, part bird," said Alanna briskly. "Don't yammer at her, help me take these things off. Fetch some hot water and a towel. That cheek is a fright."

"I think it was her t-talons," I said.

"Might it have been a peregrine falcon?" hazarded Terence. "I've seen them—"

I produced what was nearly a laugh. I was hurting like one great open wound by that time. "The thing was bigger by far than I am," I said.

"Swan," he said promptly. "Mad swan."

I shook my head. "A swan doesn't have huge claws! It was a Dread Woman, and I killed her. I don't know how, but I did."

Alanna, having made me swallow a couple of pills to ease the pain, was cleaning me up with the wet towel, beginning with my face. "Grania, oh my dear," she said compassionately, "you'll have a scar on your right cheek."

"So long as they can hide it with cosmetics," I said, thinking of my profession. "I'm lucky to have a *face*."

"It should be stitched. We'll have to get you to a doctor."

"No," I said, startled at the thought and trying to sit up against hands that held me down. "No, fix it the best you can. No doctor. You mustn't go out. Neither must I."

"Why?" asked Terence.

"The gardai are on their way—at least two of them are on the cliffs now—they're after us."

"This is all too fast and numerous for me," said Terence, whose long expressive face showed his worry over my injuries. Tommy was saying almost nothing, but was divesting me in a businesslike manner of my ripped and tainted sweater.

"Throw it away," I said to him.

"Don't talk for a bit," said Alanna, sponging the rancid filth from my face and throat. "Oh, oh, oh," she said then, half to herself, "I don't like this. This is terrible. I don't even know what it *is*. And those gashes could be septic."

"It smells like dead fish," said Tommy, leaning over the two of us and scowling heavily. I could see the dark bruise on his forehead and temple. "Damn, damn, I should know what it is, and the facts churning in the back of my head," he said angrily. "Some bird. I've read of it often enough. It ejects an oil from its stomach through its nostrils."

"It was not a b-bird," I said. My teeth were chattering with the mounting pain. "Unless it was a pterodactyl."

"The pterodactyl was not a bird, and there aren't any left," said Terence. But I thought of those wings beating at my back, and the stabbing and unearthly screaming, and suddenly it seemed logical. The evil magic faded, replaced by a real and terrifying wonder.

"That's what they are," I said. "Pterodactyls. The Dread Women are pterodactyls. There are a few left, and they breed inside the Cliffs of Moher. And they seldom come out, don't you see, but when they do, the Irish—the farm folk—can't identify them, and they believe they're witch-women. If ever there was a real Harpy, it was the pterodactyl."

Only Alanna had heard of the Dread Women, apparently, for the men stared at each other with quizzical expressions. But the blond girl, now cleaning my cheek with soap and water, glanced up briefly and said, "Don't look supercilious, as though she were babbling. It's a very intelligent theory, it accounts for the Harpy legend occurring in so many corners of the world; and if a flying dinosaur didn't make these cuts, what was it? No mere falcon could have gashed this cheek and stabbed her wrist so badly, I can tell you that."

"Curse these females who always know better than we do," said Terence amiably. "Might it have been a skua?"

"Probably," said Tommy. "Only about two feet long, but vicious birds they are."

"This was *big*," I said firmly, wincing away as Alanna sluiced soapy water into my open cheek.

"Peroxide," she ordered.

"Oughtn't we to have sulfa or something in this medicine chest?"

"Tommy, you're in the Dark Ages. Sulfa was World War Two. This will hurt, Grania," she said, rather unnecessarily I thought, and carefully poured liquid from a bottle that tore through my whole head like flame. I gave a yelp and clutched Tommy's hand to keep from writhing.

"Good girl! Now I'm going to put on a pressure bandage, which ought to stop the bleeding in about five minutes. Luckily the cheek isn't a very vascular area."

"Imagine that," I said weakly. "What's vascular?"

"It isn't crammed with blood vessels, I mean. There," she said, having padded my face with something that felt as tight as tree bark, "now let's see to the rest of you. This blouse must come off and be washed. You two louts go over in the corner."

I kept firm hold of Tommy's hand. "I do wear a bra," I said through clenched teeth, hoping that the torment of the wound would soon be eased. "We're all grownups here. You can see a lot more on a beach. And I have to grip something, or bite a bullet." Terence retired, nevertheless, taking my jacket to tidy; but Tommy's fingers bit into my own harder than ever as Alanna took inventory and cleaned.

She murmured half aloud: "Back of left wrist, fairly deep-looking stab . . . left ear torn . . . cuts on right arm and shoulder, not too bad . . . bit of a slice on the other cheek . . ." and ludicrously I was reminded of a makeup man ticking off a list of Injuries to Be Simulated for a battle scene. "Grania, are you hurt below the waist?"

"No, just bruised from falling over every r-rock in County Clare," I said to her, smiling into Tommy's sober face. It was a strange moment in which to realize that I had come back to Dragon's Keep because of Tommy—not because of the Blakes, no, however fond of them I might be; but because of the mysterious, cool, insulting, overbearing and beautifully strong man who was called Dog Fox, and for no other reason in the world. And the motive behind that was so obvious that it did not occur to me then at all. I knew only that I had run from the law and safety in order to hold his hand and look into his eyes.

Oh, and to warn him! As Alanna worked over me, removing the blood and slime and putrid matter that was smeared on me, splashing antiseptic in the lacerations and dressing them, I told him what had happened in Lisdoon-

varna, and how I'd let it out that they were after treasure;
and how Quinn Griffin had not believed this; and what he
had believed. "There's one of his people, an American, out
there now, I met him," I finished, "and another man, I
suppose it's Quinn, and they're coming for us this minute,
no doubt."

"No doubt." Still sitting beside me and holding my hand
as firmly as if I'd been dangling over that awful precipice
a hundred feet beyond our walls, Tommy frowned heavily
for a minute and then said, "I don't understand all this
about drugs. What the devil has he in his mind?"

"Your man is a queer one, right enough," said Terence
in the background, affecting Tommy's accent, "and there's
no readin' his brains, not for a sane soul, this side the
grave."

"I'm so sorry I mentioned the treasure," I said. "I was
confused—"

"Never mind that, Grania," said Tommy carelessly, as if
I'd apologized for treading on his foot. "Understand this,
though, my dear, since you've thrown in with us: Griffin is
no more a policeman than I am, matter a damn what
cards and badges he exhibited. I'm Irish, as you'll doubtless remind me shortly, and I do sometimes exaggerate
when I talk, as many of the men in this island are prone
to do. But I tell you this solemn and plain, my dear, and
it's as true as the sun; and that is that Quinn Griffin is a
paranoid maniac, as well as one of the worst men alive."

I think I hardly noticed what he was saying, except for
the fact that he had called me "my dear" twice in the same
speech. I said "Ouch!" as Alanna swabbed my torn ear
lobe, and then, "Where's Balor?" for I'd just become
aware that the big dog was missing.

"Out rummaging somewhere. He's been gone for
hours."

"I think he's searching for you, Grania," said the blond
girl. She found a fresh blouse in one of my suitcases and
helped me into it. "Too bad he couldn't have shown up
when you were brawling with your Harpy. Now let's see
to that cheek."

She took off the pressure bandage. "Hold still one minute longer, and I'll try to minimize the scarring, *gradh
geal mochroidhe*," she said, lapsing into Irish. "Somebody
cut me about five strips of the half-inch surgical plaster.
With clean hands, please! I'm going to improvise on this

slash, since I daren't sew it up, Grania." She carefully pulled the skin edges together and secured them with the tape, and laid a fresh dressing over the cheek. "I'll change this bandage every day," she told me as she finished, "and in about ten days, supposing we haven't taken you to a doctor before then, the strips will come off. Then dry dressings for a while. And we'll all pray hard."

Tommy arose. "I'm going to have a look outside. I want to see what Griffin's up to. And what you were actually fighting."

"Take a gun," I said automatically.

"We have no firearms," said Terence. "What do you think we are, girl? Drug-runners?"

"No. That's why I came back, don't you see?"

"I see perfectly well why you came back," he said, smiling. And I believe that he did, bless him.

"Come along," said Tommy to him, shrugging into heavy clothing. "If there's two of them, there'd best be two of us."

"Three," said Alanna, and "Four," said I, to an immediate chorus of protest. But I, who was appalled at the idea of being left alone, said that I was quite able to walk in spite of having been nearly torn in two by the vulture-woman; and when they shouted at me, I stood in front of the door and wouldn't budge, nor admit that I was indeed shaky in the legs. So they put my torn jacket on me again, with an old tweed cap of Terence's to keep the rain from my wet hair, and we all went out together into the unrelenting storm.

"It's a soft night," I said mechanically.

"It's a cruel night entirely," said Tommy, the wind whipping his words away like dead leaves. "It'd blow the teeth from a shark's jaw."

Alanna and her husband took hands, and it seemed natural for Tommy and me to do the same. We went toward O'Brien's Tower, with a pair of big torches lighting our way. Before we had cleared the site of the ruins, dear old Balor had joined us, quiet and unobtrusive, as though he'd only run off for a moment to chase a hare. I put my free hand on his head and he leaned into me heavily. We went up the slope.

It was very good to be back, and not to be alone in this eerie world any longer. Even so, I found that I was canting my body away from the cliffs as I walked. They had already sent one of their own against me, and might send another.

At the crest, as I was thinking that we had passed the place where I'd fought her, and had seen no carcass within the range of our lights, the one-eyed wolfhound left my side and vanished quickly ahead of us, looking as intent as only a questing dog can. Without saying a word, we all quickened our pace. Then it was there before us at the edge of the torch beams, and Balor, black with the rain, standing over it looking down.

"Stay back, don't come nearer," said Tommy, and let go my hand to go forward with Terence.

"Oh, curse the man, does he think we're inferior beings?" snapped Alanna angrily. She went to them and stared down. Then she turned away and hung her head and moaned, trying not to be sick.

After the Dread Woman, it would take a worse sight than I could imagine to turn me ill. I walked down the grade and stood beside Tommy. No one spoke for what seemed a long time. Then he said, "Could this have been your Harpy?" while Balor rumbled in his throat.

The man lay on his back and stared up into the glare of the torches. I could not take my gaze from his own, although that would not have mattered to him.

It was the fellow with the ginger mustache, and he had been shot through the center of his face and was dead forever.

8

O'er hills, dales, and rocks,
They all set out so jovially in search of the Fox!
Tally-ho, hark away, boys, away!
                                            —Reynard the Fox

THE NEXT THING I REMEMBER is Balor growling ominously, and both torches going out on the instant.

"Take the girls back," said Tommy, and my hand was seized by Terence's long fingers and I was led off through the pounding rain and charcoal dark; I heard Tommy murmur, "Balor, seek!" and then we were out of earshot.

"What will he do now?" I asked in a trembling, husky voice.

"He will find Griffin," said Terence, "and I hope that he will beat hell out of him before we turn him over to authority. This is monstrous. Murder! Murder, by God!"

"Why do you think it's Griffin? Did you recognize that man?"

"No. Lord knows who he was."

"He was the man I spoke to on the lay-by."

"Connachar's eyelids!" he exclaimed. Even this horror could not eliminate his hoary expletives, they came so naturally to his lips. "That's rough on you, Grania."

"He was from Philadelphia, and was waiting to meet Quinn, because he gave me a version of the password. That's all I know about him."

"You can be bloody sure that Griffin is at the bottom of this," said Terence coldly, and the change in his uniformly good-natured tone was somehow more impressive than Tommy's solemn, biased assurances of Quinn's villainy.

"But that man was shot by someone," I said, beginning to hold back, "and Tommy's out here with no gun!"

"Trust the Dog Fox, Grania. He was born and bred in the I.R.A. I've seen him do fantastic things against automatic carbines, and him armed with half a brick. A weapon is only as deadly as the man who's using it. Watch this rough bit of ground here." I could, of course, see nothing whatever. "I imagine it wasn't that poor dead chap whom you were fighting a while back?" he asked diffidently.

"Oh, don't you suppose I'd know it if a *man* attacked me?"

"In the storm, I thought perhaps not. And he could have hacked you up with that knife."

"What knife?"

"The big clasp knife in his right hand."

"I didn't see it. But it wasn't a human being that I fought." I remembered the putrid stench of the thing, like that of something emerging from an old grave, and shuddered. After a moment we came to the den.

Terence let us in and by the dim glow of the fire took a hand of each of us and said quietly, "Stay here, loves, whatever happens. We'll be back all safe, you'll see."

"How will you find Tommy?" I asked him.

"The curlew's cry," he said, and pursed his mouth and gave a kind of mellow, two-part birdcall, like the notes of a flute. Then he'd kissed his wife and was gone.

Alanna lit the lamp, her face white as a shroud. "At least," she said, trying to smile, "it's a chance to really clean you up." She stripped me to the buff, for I was feeble by then and my fingers were all weak and fluttery, and she gave me a sponge bath in front of the stoked fire. "Your left eye's turning black," she said. "Whatever the beast was, it came too close by half to gouging out that one. Oh, Grania," she said, starting to cry, "what *did* we do to you when we abducted you into this damnable bedlam?"

"I came back myself," I said. "I wouldn't be anywhere else in the world. I'd come back again. I'd come back again!"

So we wept together, and somewhat relieved the ferment of terror and perplexity that had engulfed us.

When she'd seen to all my least hurts and made sure that the dressings on the bad ones were still secure, she washed my hair in a bucket of hot soapy water and put me, protesting, to bed in one of the sleeping bags. Then she brewed us some powerful tea and we lay there, holding hands for comfort, and waited.

By and by I started to chuckle, just this side of hysteria. "What is it?" she said, alarmed.

"I was remembering that only a few days ago, I hadn't a legitimate care in the world, and was feeling so sorry for myself that I truly didn't care if I lived or died. And now I'm in the worst trouble of my life, and I hurt like mad, and I feel far better than I have since I was five."

She shook her head, smiling. "You belong with us. You're absolutely certifiable. Tell me about your life, Grania Kirk."

So I explained my profession for the second time that day; only Alanna asked me questions, being a friend and privileged, and another half an hour went by while we waited for our men.

"You really have to go to a doctor in the morning for that cheek," she said. "You mustn't be scarred, not an actress! I don't care what's at stake. We're only here on a wild chance, anyway, however sure of himself Terence may be."

"Don't even think of it," I said firmly. "There's always plastic surgery, if the miserable thing's too ugly. It's not your fault that I was pounced on by a heathen spirit. After all, I asked for it. I came here to meet one."

"You did what?"

I explained as well as I could about Grandmother and the Dread Women, and my nerves driving me up all those overcrowded walls until I had fled to Moher to die. "That's it," I said, amazed at the conviction with which I'd stated it, but recognizing that it must be fact. "I came here to die. It was a weaselly way of committing suicide. I expected to be killed by the Dread Women. Because I believed in them as deeply—at least the six-year-old child in my heart did—as I believed in anything. And I was right."

"And you were right," said Alanna slowly, and we both shuddered in the lamplight, in our ancient, lonely room at the center of the storm. "I'm awfully glad that you weren't killed, Grania."

"Well, I wasn't looking for death by then, so I fought it."

"You'd have fought it as bravely whenever it had come at you. You're not the sort to die easily, whatever you once thought."

I stared at her for a moment. Then I nodded. It was true. I loved life too well. "Why did I come here, then?"

"The toughest of us need escape sometimes."

"Yes. Is it a malady of our times—overwork, over-worry, suffer the strain of living, then try to get away from it all?"

"Maybe it's a basic disease of our times, or maybe of humanity in general. Or of life?" she said, cocking her head in reflection. "I wonder if Balor occasionally longs to 'get away from it all'?"

"Home to the puppy farm," I said. "You know, Alanna, looking back from the vantage point of forty-eight hours, it's hard to understand my attitude. I'm in television, about as cynical and tough-minded a business as you can find. I honestly don't believe in fairy tales."

"Did Grandmother?"

"A little, I think."

"Then so does Grania, a little."

"Her stories," I said, "her best ones, had just enough down-to-earth gory detail to make them stick in the memory. Every banshee and giant and fairy king from Cork to Coleraine once thronged these cliffs for me. Then I found out they existed. Then I heard from Grandmother that only the goriest of the evil spirits were really supposed to focus here. And then I came." I rubbed my eyes. "It's as if you discovered on the soundest evidence that there actually *was* an Oz, a Looking-Glass Country, a Toad Hall. No matter how old you'd grown, you'd want to visit, wouldn't you? But what if you also heard that the only inhabitants were the Wicked Witch of the West, or the Jabberwock and the Bandersnatch, or the gangs of ferrets and weasels? Wouldn't it be pretty sick of you to want to go anyway?" I thought of something else. "Quinn said I came because I felt a kinship with lonely monsters."

"Perhaps *he* does," she snapped. "Not you. You came because you were nervous and tired and you needed to fight something, and you were caught in a bind where there was nothing to fight but phantoms. You can't turn and rend success, can you?"

I have never discovered any better explanation for my flight to the Cliffs of Moher than that one, given me by a kind and lovely woman who was waiting to see whether her husband, the center of her universe, would return to her or not.

We were silent for a long while. She said, "I wonder if it was a pterodactyl?" and we both giggled. " 'When the gods wish to punish us, they answer our prayers.' That's from Terry's sainted Oscar. If he finds out that you came looking for the Dread Women, you may be sure he'll repeat that to you."

And then we heard the key in the lock, and our breath stopped until both men had come in, Balor at their heels.

Alanna flew to Terence, and Tommy came straight to me to sit down, his sodden clothes squishing, and say with great urgency, taking my hands in both of his, "Are you all right then?"

"I'm marvelous," I whispered. "I've never been so happy in my life." There was suddenly no doubt in me whatever that Thomas O'Flaherty, late of the I.R.A., was the first soul with whom I had fallen, wholly and unquestionably, in love; and never mind those adolescent crushes that had wound up with that stupid actor, for this was a *man*.

Soon we were all drinking tea and eating boiled eggs together, in a tight crescent in front of the fire, with Balor steaming very wet and doggy-smelling at our feet. "We nearly had him," said Tommy bitterly. "We were on the edge of the lay-by when his bloody motorcar started up and flew away into the storm. There's a Fiat still down there."

Alanna said, "What about the dead man?"

"Gone. Slung into the sea while I was up over the hill searching, with the hound at fault due to the downpour."

"Tommy read the spoor," said Terence, and I was reminded irresistibly of some Victorian hunter bragging about his peerless native guide, so that I had to smother an inappropriate laugh by thinking of the poor murdered man who'd spoken to me only a few minutes before he'd died; which turned my emotions around with a jolt, and the tears fell into my scalding tea. Terrence went on. "Whoever killed him—"

"Griffin," said Tommy harshly.

"Griffin, then, had come back and dragged the corpse to the cliff rim and shoved it over. He went through deep mud, and the signs hadn't had time to wash out." Terence surveyed us gravely. "This destroys our work, you know. We must report it, and then we shan't be able to come back, not for a year or two at least. I've thought it out: we claim that we're touring the country, and had motor trouble in the storm and sought refuge in—"

"That's a very poor glass of water," said Tommy, fierce and idiomatic. "We'll do no such raving thing. We can't prove a single fact against Griffin, or even against parties unknown. We can't prove there was a corpse. All we can prove is that we're blathering idiots. The work here is too absolutely vital to throw over for any such quixotic gesture."

"We can't ignore murder," said Terence.

"We cannot. But we have sweet damn all to tell the gardai, now haven't we?"

"Right," Terence agreed after a pause. "Wait, though; the Fiat."

"Hired. Under a false name, without question."

"So it's up to us to watch out for Griffin, then? To play polis, or avenging angels?"

"Entirely. This isn't finished. It is for us, yes, if we choose to report a vanishing body, an abandoned car, and an unknown murderer. Then we can leave, and Griffin can go on with whatever he's doing, quite unhindered; and the hoard of Bran Roe O'Conor can lie where it is for another century or so . . . or forever. Because we'll *never* be able to come back."

"You've the right of it," said Alanna. "We're all in danger, though."

"So we have been from the start, to judge by what the man Griffin said to Grania today. Don't you see, he's got something big in his fist, concerning drugs—hereabouts, of all the filthy luck—and he thinks we're onto it. He might have potted us all like so many mallards on a turlough, if Grania hadn't forewarned us." He laid a hand on my damp hair and smoothed it, rather absently. "I know that man. He'd have shot the lot of us on the bare suspicion that we had wind of his plans. I'm amazed that he's not done it already. Didn't I see him at work in Belfast!"

I closed my eyes under his casual caress. I heard Terence say, "The poor child is half dead with fatigue and loss of blood," and I was going to deny that; but it seemed a nice idea to lean against Tommy for just a jiffy before opening my eyes again, and when his arms came round me and their voices mixed softly together and I felt myself being slid down into the sleeping bag's fleecy depths, it was too much effort to speak, and I would rest briefly before I explained to them how wide awake I was. . . .

I slept, Tommy told me afterward, for fourteen hours and twenty minutes.

"How are you, Grania?"

"Fine," I said through a dry mouth, rubbing grit from my eyes. "I dreamed I was hot, terribly hot."

"You had some fever, not bad. It came and went quickly. We were afraid those cuts were infected, but I think now they're not."

I accepted a thick wedge of fresh-baked soda bread paved with butter. "We located your purse and the torch last night," said Tommy. "Your scarf's been blown to County Kildare by this time. I never got round to telling you before you fell asleep."

"Did you find the Dread Woman?" I asked, the bread halfway to my lips, and saw his gaze drop. "What was it?" I demanded.

"We were right; it was a bird. Either it had been caught in the updraft over the cliffs and rammed into you accidentally, or it was rabid and meant to attack you. I tend to believe it was a mistake. The creature was blinded by lightning, or confused in the storm."

"But a bird! It was so enormous."

"It had the longest wing span of any bird I ever saw, nearly a dozen feet. And a body the size of a big goose. Great thick bill, hooked, very horny. . . ."

"What was it?"

"The Japanese call them *bakadori*, the Americans 'gooney birds.' If you're dazzled by my knowledge, well, ornithology's a hobby of mine." He pushed the bread to my mouth, and I took a bite. "It weighed fifteen or twenty pounds, my dear; small wonder that it gave you such a combat. Heavy enough to knock you over, and that beak—it wasn't talons, by the way, that scratched you up, but the bill. They have only webbed feet, the claws are negligible. They follow ships for the garbage that's thrown overside, and God help the sailor who falls into the water then; they'll slash the life out of him under the impression that he's edible." After a pause he said, "They're white and black. Rather pretty. I'm sorry."

"There's something you're not telling me." I recognized that, for I was growing to know my man.

He stared at me. "I feel rotten for you. That's all. It's such a stupidly unnecessary coincidence that you should have been there when the creature came in on the storm.

I've never even seen one in these latitudes. Which means that I've never even seen one at all before." He got up to fetch me a drink. "They fly all around the world, literally, Grania, without touching land except to breed."

"And I had to kill it. The first thing I've killed, if you don't count bugs."

"Never regret that. Once the two of you had slammed together, you had to defend yourself! You broke its neck—an easy death enough."

"I know. But I feel sorry for it. Are they really rare?"

"Oh, no. But they don't visit us much. Their usual beat is the tropics to the Antarctic. That stuff you were sprayed with, that should have told me at once what bird it was precisely, but I couldn't think well. It's an oil they bring up from digested fish. They spit it, and shoot it through long tubular nostrils that lie along the bill. Filthy stuff."

"Was it really beautiful?"

He said judiciously, "All life is beautiful, if you see it in the right light, I think. Naturally I exclude Quinn Griffin."

I pulled out a handkerchief and blew my nose. "You've told me what people call it, Tommy," I said, "but you haven't told me what it *is*. I thought gooney birds were fat little petrels."

"It's a member of the petrel order."

"Why aren't you telling me its name?"

He rubbed his jaw. "Look here," he said almost angrily, "are you superstitious?"

"No. Yes, I suppose I am. I thought it was a kind of black goddess of the sea, didn't I?"

"It was, rather. It was what they call a wandering albatross."

"Oh my," I said faintly. "The Ancient Mariner."

"Bags of bad luck it's supposed to bring the one who does it in. Yes. A lot of sheep-headed nonsense. I will not stand for it, do you hear me? You are not to worry yourself over a thing that was unavoidable!" he shouted.

"All right, darling," I said meekly.

"And another item: you are not to look into a mirror until I tell you to do so, have you got that straight?" he went on ferociously. "I will not have a weeping, sniveling female tearing her hair under my feet for days and days simply because her face is temporarily destroyed by bruises and bandages and a black eye you could see from the top of Nelson's Column, supposing the same hadn't long since been blown down! Is that understood?"

"Yes, darling."

"Not that *I* mind staring at it," he said, "but you wouldn't like it much yourself."

"No, dear."

"I'd kill the sow-faced cod that raised his brows at the state of it, mind you, but—"

"Yes, dearest."

He stopped blustering. It had been nine-tenths joking, anyway. He stared at me for a moment. "Why do you persist in calling me those things?" he asked, as if I had genuinely amazed him.

"I don't know. I'm probably grateful to you for helping to patch me up. I'm probably coming around to the old show-biz custom of calling the slightest acquaintance 'dearie.' I'm probably head over heels in love with you."

"Oh," he said blankly, "is that the way of it? Which?"

"Choose one. What happened to the albatross?" I asked seriously.

"I put it to sleep in its ocean."

"I'm glad."

He watched me with his head cocked. "So you were safe away, and then decided to come back to us, Grania girl. I never thanked you for that. May you be the better for it! Which I doubt. We're between the great waves of the law and the vicious rocks of Griffin's mob. It'll be no picnic."

"As though I cared," I said, sipping tea.

"What a swine I've been to you," he said, "and then you to rejoin us, with kind words and warnings and all. I'm not sure that I understand it."

"Yes, you do," I said, and put my arms around him and kissed him. And the ferocious O'Flaherty, being as I'd guessed a conventional and modest Irishman, blushed deep red under his tan.

"But you don't know the first thing about me," he said, sounding as bewildered as a boy. I thought *Twenty-six and never been kissed?* with some dismay.

"Certainly I do. You're a lawless I.R.A. gunman, running drugs and kidnaping women on the side, and pretending to dig for some silly treasure on the edge of the worst place in the world. That's enough for me. I always wanted a man who Did Things."

"You are teasing me," he said, "and I'm enjoying it. The universe is upside down. I'll wake presently in Clongers, with one of the masters bellowing at me for oversleeping."

Then he kissed me, for a much longer space of time, and I was relieved to find that he was far from amateur at it.

"Grania," he said finally.

"Yes?"

"Where have I seen you before last Thursday?"

I spluttered with laughter. "On television. I'm an actress."

"Then I was right. In black and white I saw you once, but more shame to me, I don't recall—"

"In Ireland, likely on a PanAm commercial," I told him. "And it was in glorious color, but you have a cheap set."

"I have no set whatever. It was in a pub. Do you do nothing but commercials? Not that they don't involve acting. I wouldn't like to insult you at this point."

"I do a lot of different jobs, but I don't think you get most of the programs on the Irish systems."

"We have the I.T.V. and the R.T.E.," he said, "and of course there's the bloody B.B.C."

"Yes, well, I did three PanAm commercials and a cosmetics ad that you might have caught a few times."

"Is it an interesting life?"

"Sometimes. I had a little too much of it; that's why I came to Ireland. I was on my way to Donegal. Ancestors, relatives, you know. Would you kiss me again, Dog Fox?"

He did. "You know," he said, just as I'd started to notice that I was out of breath, "you're the first American I've ever heard pronounce that right."

"What? I wasn't pronouncing anything."

"Donegal."

"I learned a great poem when I was four. Grandmother taught it to me, and I never forgot it. It was the first piece I recited in public, and I'm afraid I haven't shut up since. Would you like to hear it?" He nodded. I said, "Mister M'Call from Donegal eats potatoes skins and all."

He laughed. "Something Granny brought from home, no doubt. Look, my girl. I must go out there and help my people."

"Tell me how I can help, too."

"There's one chore you can't do, and that is to dig. You're to recuperate for at least a week."

"I couldn't accomplish much with this," I admitted, waving my left arm. The wrist was stiff and painful.

"You can help Balor keep guard. Is your daytime vision any good?"

"Perfect. I simply can't see through an Irish night."

"Then you will be invaluable. I'll show you a place where you can sit and watch the whole countryside—it's a fine day, by the by—and that will allow the three of us to kill ourselves with toil in safety. Grania," he said, taking my fingers in his a little hesitantly, "you do believe us? About what we're doing?"

"Certainly."

"You're quite mad," he said with approval, getting to his feet. "Lock the door behind you when you come out, and bring me the key."

I finished my brunch in a glow of happiness. I am ashamed to say that I had nearly forgotten the fact that a man had been shot to death last night only a couple of minutes' walk from where I sat. While I lingered by this cozy turf fire, all that had happened outside seemed unreal, a procession of damp and horrible illusions moving behind a curtain of dismal, half-remembered gray rain. And when I had bundled myself up like an invalid and ventured outdoors into the loveliest of sunny spring afternoons, with only the crashing surf sound left from the past days, it was impossible to believe that this was the land of those nightmares.

Alanna and Terence greeted me, their clothing splashed with dark mud. They were standing beside a black, raw hole in the earth, some ten or twelve feet across. "We were telling himself," said the girl, thumbing down this excavation, "that the Fiat is gone. No other news. How are you?"

"Up to a tour of the site?" asked Terence.

"Yes," I said, "and then I'm supposed to be a sentry."

"I know. Come along. Oh, Alanna love," he said, "give Dog a hand with the pick, there's a good child. I'll be back in a few hours to assist."

"Overbearing swine," said his wife happily, and disappeared into the pit.

"Now," said Terence, taking me solicitously by the arm,

"we are facing east. The enormous area directly before us was the main building of the castle."

"It looks a little neglected," I said, inadequately.

"Well put. This was a feudal-period hall keep; that is, the castle proper was erected around a huge oblong hall and another big room called a 'solar' under which were the cellars and storerooms and the dungeon, if there was one. None of these Irish castles ever followed the classic English patterns exactly, but I worked out the location of what should have been the treasure room by elimination of impossibilities. I had two probable situations for it, and we took the easy one first. After something more than a month we broke into it. An old storage place, full of rotted casks and trash. I wept. Then we began on this one."

"How did you ever begin to guess such a thing?"

"Oh, knowledge of some hundreds of plans, and all that. The entrance to such a room would have been cleverly camouflaged, incredibly cleverly; and after a vast amount of surveying and plotting and elimination, I was sure that the portal would have been behind the biggest fireplace in the hall itself. That was an excellent deduction that led to the storeroom. Only the builders could tell us why they hid that."

"Could it have been the—"

"No. Not large enough, no sign of anything of any value ever having been there. . . . I grubbed over the floor, I assure you. Come over to the south a bit." We walked up and down a hump of beaten grass. We were just up-coast of the northern wall of the keep, which began fairly high, perhaps thirty feet, and ran rapidly downward as it went inland, like a rough giant's stairway, its top all jagged, till it petered out in a mass of crumpled masonry; the whole thing was heavily ivy-covered and rather forbidding.

"Down at the far end where you're looking is our first dig, but you won't recognize it as such," said Terence, pointing. "We spent two full days ripping our muscles to hide it."

"Why?"

"Evidence. The careless visitor mustn't suspect any present inhabitants."

"What about that hole you're making now?"

"There's a screen for it, a model of cleverness that I thought up. It's made to look like a large fallen stone that's overgrown with ivy, but it's actually a wire frame of the bloody weed that Alanna can lift by herself."

"And how did you decide on its position?" I asked him.

"Briefly, the O'Conors who built it—perhaps Bran Roe's father and uncles, or even Bran Roe himself—certainly not so far back as his grandfather—situated it here for a good reason. You see it faced directly inland. Down there was the great doorway of the castle. Its backside was comfortably toward the sea, from which no attackers could come. That's how the old . . ." he trailed to a silence. Then he said, "I shall *have* to start at the beginning. D'you mind a lecture?"

"Not at all."

"Sometime after 1171, when the Normans finally came to Ireland in force, the O'Flahertys threw up a mote-and-bailey fortress here, quite possibly on the foundation of a prehistoric burial mound. The place does go back farther into time than these mere modern walls would suggest. Don't giggle. The mote-and-bailey was nothing much but a great mound of earth, flat on top, crowned with a wooden tower and surrounded by a ditch. Next to it was a broader, lower court, also with a ditch, and connected to the high mound by a gangway. The commander lived on the big one, the mote, and his garrison in sheds on the lower one, the bailey. Both of these areas were palisaded with heavy timber. Very, very simple, and quite effective in awing the simple country folk, especially if the owner was able to enlist a dozen Welsh archers, the marksmen of their day."

We were walking up rolling ground to where the crest would give us a view of Route L54 running parallel with the cliffs. Terence went on. "The mote was likely here on our right, the bailey about where we are now. The mote was, I imagine, about thirty feet high. I think the ditch would have been very deep and filled with water from a spring that still flows over south there.

"The O'Flahertys either abandoned it or were chased out or destroyed by the O'Conors; no history on that, alas. The O'Conors, at any rate, took possession early in the thirteenth century and tore down the mote to build their stone castle."

"Why wouldn't they have built on the mote? All that height—"

"Smart girl. Too much tonnage, though. They had to

found the keep on the solid rock, or it would have sunk and tottered and fallen of its own weight. They spread the earth of the mote to the south there, where you see that small hill, and perhaps between here and the Lisdoonvarna road. Here, look at it from here. You can follow its lines even where the walls have gone. It was a massive keep, built on a rectangular plan and originally, I think, about seventy feet high, its interior measuring fifty-five by forty, with the longer dimension running east to west and the gate facing the land."

I could see now that the few walls of any height had been part of the castle proper, and pieced out in my head how it must have looked; I think I pictured something out of *Ivanhoe*.

"Come this way," Terence said. "About here would have been the main doorway, you see—indeed, the only doorway. Looking inland, fierce and rude. Beyond it was a forebuilding, likely timber in the O'Conors' time, later a real stone barbican erected by the Sionnachs. Between forework and gateway tower, a drawbridge, with a moat beneath. The moat's been filled in over the centuries but you can still trace it.

"Around the keep itself was a huge yard called the ward, and in it would have been various smaller buildings, the stables, forge, and so on. This was enclosed by high curtain walls of stone, perhaps following the outer limits of the old mote-and-bailey thing; there are two chunks of the outer walls left standing, the one over south there where you first met my wife and she was chilly to you, the other there," he said, turning to our left and pointing out to the northward where perhaps forty yards of wall seemed nearly intact. "Otherwise it's just shattered, strewn rocks like big mossy dominoes after a game. That north corner, though, that's a lovely survival and I wish we had time to clean away the vegetation and examine it properly. There's a sallyport beyond what you can see from here; that's almost certainly a Sionnach addition—ah, that's by the way, you want to know about the keep itself. Unless you'd like a closer look at the wall?"

I stared at all that was left of what had once been considered, no doubt, an impregnable barrier. Thorny undergrowth and ivy protected it from near examination; the stones were dark where they could be seen, and the whole angle gave off a dismal, forbidding aura. "No, thanks," I said.

"But doesn't it make you think, rather, of the magic vegetation that protected Sleeping Beauty's home?"

"Terence, if that lichen-crusted rampart protects anything, it must be the Sleeping Toad."

He laughed. "All right, to the keep, then. The perimeter of the whole thing measures about twelve hundred feet, but that includes the cliff edge where they naturally didn't need to build a curtain wall. The back of the keep was open to the ocean, so they had nothing to worry about there except for your Dread Women. Oh, dear," he said, his face lengthening, "I am sorry, girl dear. That was tactless of me."

"It's all right. I still believe in them, by the way, despite the bird you found."

He pulled at his lip. "I wonder," he said, and then went on before I could ask him what. "At any rate, Grania, the keep itself: likely two stories, though just possibly three, and erected for one purpose, to keep the occupants safe while overawing the countryside. The walls were twelve feet thick, all around—not the outer defenses, but the castle walls themselves. They were hollow, you know, made of the native limestone coursed a bit roughly, and filled with a core of hammer-dressed rubble and mortar. The great stones of the outside and the inside were bonded with ground oystershell and the blood of oxen. They must have thought it unconquerable on this height, with such views of both sea and land to give them warning, and these incredible walls all about them.

"Notice that the windows we can see are all quite narrow and small. They may have been larger on the upper stories, but I doubt it. There is also no ornamentation whatever. Everything is plain, functional, austere—it was a keep indeed. It would keep the world away."

"Naturally, it didn't."

"Nothing ever does," I said.

"No. . . . Do you have the general picture now?"

"I think so. The keep here, around it the courtyard, then the curtain walls except where the cliff made them unnecessary. The whole terrible beast of an overbearing colossus glaring inland to scare the peasantry."

"Not so much the peasants, who weren't any threat, but the O'Briens, who held this land for many miles, and the

Normans when they came by. Yes, you have it. Now, do you know the least thing about mural passages and chambers?"

"Not the least."

"All right. Here come the clues I dealt with. In just about every castle of this period, we find staircases, rooms, and passageways; even latrines and sleeping rooms and access tunnels to the defensive windows—all in the walls. D'you comprehend? *In* the walls. Hence, 'mural' passages and chambers. Not to glance at staircases and treasure rooms. Ah, no! Not the one we're looking for. But likely, all but certainly, there's where we'd find the small dark highway to it—within the thickness of a wall."

"Right," I said. "I see your point. I didn't know all that old Warner Brothers hidden-room gimmickry was true. I thought it was invented by someone for Lorre, or I ought to say Lon Chaney."

"Some day we must discuss the merits of the great Irishman Cagney as Chaney," said Terence, and came back to the subject with obvious difficulty. "Now: they would not use many of these mural tunnelings and stairways in the walls that were open to attack, because they'd weaken them and they wouldn't stand bombardment so well. I mean from flung stones and the like, not cannon. So do you begin to see what I guessed, when my fireplace idea proved a delusion?"

"That the stairs down to the undergound strongbox would be in the west wall that faced the ocean."

"It was just that easy. So we probed, measured, traced out what plan the interior may have had, and settled for that place you saw down at the opposite end of the seaward wall from our den. And in a few days or weeks, I forget how long precisely, opened up what I am confident is it. The thing itself. The opening. The gates of an archaeologist's heaven, as it were."

"I do hope you're on the right track this time."

"We are," he said firmly.

I looked across the ruins, dark and brooding against the sun. "And it was Cromwell who finally smashed it."

"It was. The Sionnachs held it, one way and another, for nearly four hundred years. Then the Roundheads came up the coast and stone by stone they knocked it down with no remorse, with their customary zeal for obliterating anything royal, anything bigger or finer or more beautiful than their grubby selves. The vandalous apes," said Terence through his teeth.

"I don't think it could have been exactly beautiful, surely?" I said.

"Well, it may have been too functional for that. There was nothing we ever found to suggest the magical loveliness of some of the old Norman castles, I grant you. But—but regal. Bold, splendid in its strength; not a romantic building, certainly, but damnably impressive. Not a decent thing to level it so. No."

"Did they do *all* this damage? There seems so little point in it."

"What you see here, I suppose, is the end result of many centuries of decay, carelessness, invasion, rebellion, civil war, clan war, the troubles ... the weather and the tourists."

I clucked my tongue sympathetically. Terence added, "And the neglect of the Commissioners of Public Works! Under the National Monuments Act they've accepted a lashin of castles for state care, but not Dragon's Keep! Too badly in disrepair, they say. Lir's sainted kiddies! We, the Irish, began to build castles about the year 1318. This place predates that. Yet the O'Conors built it, maybe with the help of a kidnaped Norman architect or two, I couldn't say—but the Irish O'Conors built it before the Irish were even *building* castles! Yet it's not in decent enough shape for the bloody government to—oh, well." He grinned. "One of my hobbyhorses. Sorry, love. Here's where you sit to play lookout for us." He indicated a heap of pretty clean stone rubble. "This is what remains of the forebuilding that sheltered the castle gateway. Balor will be around somewhere; I'll whistle him up."

I took off my jacket and spread it on one of the big flat stones, from which I could if necessary dive quickly into cover; and together the one-eyed wolfhound and I kept our silent watch and ward against the faceless, unknown enemy.

Unknown, for I had decided that Tommy was wrong about Quinn. Quinn, for sure, was quite wrong about Tommy, too. They had simply got muddled about each other at some point in the past; and Quinn, being assigned to this filthy drug affair and seeing Tommy, had jumped to as inaccurate a conclusion as had my dear O'Flaherty. If either of them could have looked at the matter for two minutes without all that prejudice, they'd have realized that there must be some third party, large or small, causing all the trouble. Quinn would not have shot his own man (who'd given me Quinn's password), nor had Tommy disconnected the battery wires of my car. The smuggling crew were out there somewhere, while the two decent men warred against each other.

I would not comment on the matter at all any more, and it would all come out in the wash ... "or the rain," I said to Balor, though the clouds today were fluffy and innocent.

The nicest people can be so utterly wrongheaded about the strangest things. I recollected how Grandmother was always asserting that Herbert Hoover had been a tool of the anarchists.

Very little happened that afternoon. A dozen cars passed along the road, one Fiat among them but of the wrong color; there were bicycles and sheep and cows and solitary dogs; several men on foot, farmers apparently, appeared and disappeared near the eastern horizon; and a tinkers' caravan trundled by just before dusk, reminding me of my friends the Coffees. At last the curlew's cry summoned Balor and me to supper.

As I walked toward the open oak door of the den, I noticed where a heap of big broken half-dressed rock was piled against the old wall. That was precisely where my tunnel would have come out, provided I'd been able to finish it. So much for all that back-spraining labor.

And so began some days of the most extraordinary activity—or I should say "inactivity," for I moved about very little, being stiff and achy. I continued as lookout for the gang, and hour followed hour and I watched carefully, and nothing happened except the inevitable changes in the weather. Always I could hear the tumult of the ocean, though in that time I never once walked to the brink to look down at it.

Once a day Tommy kissed me a brisk good-morning, and once a day an all-too-brief good-night; no more. And except for the casual use of *dears* and *a ghrás*, no love talk, though I was starved for it. Nor would I begin it, for this was old Ireland. And he did have an enormous burden on his mind, not to mention, I suppose, a permanent throb of dull pain in his overworked frame.

"You must give Tommy time," Alanna said to me

rather abruptly one evening, in the middle of a conversation about fashion.

"Is it that obvious?"

"It is. You see, it's never really happened to him before, I believe, and he's terribly confused. He's so used to looking on himself as lone and self-sufficient—"

"Like a good dog fox," I said. "I thought it was simply common Irish reticence."

"How can you watch Terence for two minutes and even dream of such a phrase as 'common Irish reticence'?"

I laughed. "Your husband is a law to himself."

"This is very, very serious with you, isn't it, Grania?"

I nodded. "I don't think I ever truly knew what it was before this time, either."

"Then be patient. When we're out from beneath Griffin's shadow, Tommy will be a different man."

"I'm quite content for now with the present man," I said. I watched Alanna filling her bastable oven, a big black three-legged iron pot that hung from two iron arms within the chimney, with the ingredients for stew: mutton, potatoes, onions, water, and seasonings. She swung it over the fire, and with the tongs laid some red-hot sods of turf on the flat lid. This oven was the same in which she baked our marvelous soda bread and roasted our meat; I had long since decided that the first thing I was going to demand for my kitchen, when I had one, was a bastable oven. "I wish . . ." I said.

"What, dear?"

"I wish I dared to ask Tommy about himself. About what his life's been like. I don't even know what he does for a living!"

"He'd take a very high view of your asking him about it."

"What does that mean?"

"Am I being incomprehensibly Irish again? He'd like you to question him, I feel certain. He's very much under the glamour, I can tell, but still he can't sit down and reel off his history without being asked, now can he?"

"I'd have asked days ago if I hadn't been scared of seeming too brazenly inquisitive."

"Have you always been this shy?" she asked frankly.

"And is that why I'm not married yet? Lord, no. I—well, I don't know how to *be* with him, that's all. There are things so foreign about him. I don't mean Irish, though that must enter into it. I mean, I've known almost nobody in my adult life but actors. And I'm sick to death of actors. I was even sick of myself until this howling adventure came along." I touched the bandage on my cheek, and the wound underneath gave a twinge. "Actors are too self-centered, or at least self-conscious, to make good husbands and wives. That's how I was feeling, especially after my own actor absconded. I've discovered that I can be myself for days on end now, without sliding into a part that someone's written for me. But Tommy . . ."

"Yes?"

"He's so complete, so undivided; a whole, mature man, you know? Thoroughly the Dog Fox. Nobody wrote any speech for him to say, ever. And I'm not used to that, I guess. You take Quinn Griffin. After two evenings I was getting interested. Then the third time we met, I saw him, suddenly, as an actor. His charm is an actor's, he's *thinking* about charming you as he does it. When he admits to being a policeman, then he has to become a traditional motion-picture policeman, stern and serious and unintentionally too firm with you. Nearly everyone I know is like that."

"That's dreadful," she said. "It's a real professional hazard, isn't it? Do you think Terence is acting?"

I sat back and laughed at the idea. "Not for an instant. Terence Blake is as naturally full of flair and gusto as he can be. If you saw him in a flick you'd think it was a well-done bravura performance. Listening to him day after day, you realize that all the larger-than-life gestures and expressions are as normally Terence as his decency and love. Yet I wouldn't have realized that if I hadn't had Tommy and Quinn to compare him with. Quinn may be sincere, but he's an actor, he does what he *thinks* he should do in any given case. Terence does what he *wants* to do, what he must always have done, to get through this world in the nicest possible way. Tommy—there's a shade of difference here—Tommy does what he *is*. I don't mean—"

"I see what you mean. Terry's flamboyant; if he squelched his exuberance, then he'd be playing himself false."

"Yes. He's a gorgeous man. And Tommy has the same sort of respect for himself that Terence has, and so he's different." I told her about the Black Velvet simile that had occurred to me even before I'd known either of the men well. "They can both be counted on," I said, and almost added "unless it's by the government," but luckily didn't say it aloud. "I want so much for Tommy to believe that I can be counted on, too," I said lamely. "So I don't know exactly how to act, because I'm an actress and—"

"You haven't been acting for days," said Alanna sharply. "Stop running yourself down to no purpose, Grania. You only have the residue of a few years' work to be rid of, dear. As to being reliable, Tommy hardly ranks you as a possible enemy any longer. From the time when you staggered in out of the night, vilely coated with blood and excrement, and announced that you'd come home, he's thought of you as one of us."

"Yes, but he hasn't kissed me in a while, except hello and good-bye, and I wonder if he likes what I am. Which is a plain old Freeport girl with some patches of cynical veneer left from television. And if he doesn't . . ."

"Then you won't change. Because I think you're as true to yourself basically as he is."

"But if I ask him questions about himself, he may think I'm a nosy American!"

"You silly sweet," she said, patting my hand as we heard the men coming back from their nightly prowl down the cliffs, "he might also think that you're a woman in love with him."

I looked at Tommy as he walked in, shedding his coat and smiling at me across the little rock room. Yes, it was true that he wasn't as colorful as Terence, or, for that matter, Quinn Griffin; but to say that he was not colorful would have been immensely unjust. The rich leathered brown of his face was that of good things, of the earth and of tough wood—like the earth, he could smile on you and take care of you; like wood, he could shelter and support you when necessary. And if there was a curious streak of larceny in him, well, neither is the earth without a flaw, nor do we love it less for that. His brown colors suited him. A Tommy pale and white would have been a Tommy whom I couldn't even imagine.

Often they worked till full dark and even beyond. This evening, though, a vicious-looking bank of clouds coming up out of the Atlantic had made them stop the digging earlier than usual, so that, even after the customary camouflage job, which involved rather more labor than moving Terence's ivy screen, we were given a longer time indoors than we usually had in which to lounge and talk around the fire. (Whatever progress was made each day had to be hidden before Tommy would allow a night's rest. This sometimes entailed moving a few of the largest stones with block and tackle, and always meant a more thorough dirtying of the hands than the actual work had caused. In the really vile weather of the winter, Alanna had told me, she and Terence had once or twice voted to leave the dislodged earth lying there all raw, but Tommy had bullied them into tidying it—"himself, naturally, doing most of the real work"—into its natural condition of what they referred to as "semi-picturesque decay.")

While we waited for the Irish stew to be done, and while we ate, the men kept up a passionate discussion they'd started that morning, something about the bardic schools as a factor in the life of the Irish nation, terribly obscure to me and shot with quotations in Gaelic. At last, replete, I pillowed my head on Balor's side and said loudly, "What was it like?"

"What was what like?" said the O'Flaherty. Expectantly, I thought.

"Being in the I.R.A."

"I've been wondering how long—" began Terence, and stopped, looking astounded, with his wife's elbow jammed in his ribs.

"Messy," said Tommy to me. "And very stupid."

"Tell me about it," I said. "I'm bored with your ancient bardic schools. I don't even know what one is—and please don't explain. Tell me how you got into an outlawed army in the first place."

"Born into it, you could say. The da fought with them in the troubles, when he was about as tall as your shoulder."

"Who did?"

"My father. The da. He married very late, long afterwards, and I was the only child. He'd stuck with the organization. I thought they were like Robin Hood's men, you see, from the stories he'd tell. I never have been a political creature, and so the worst of the bigotry escaped me. In school holidays I used to go up to what we called the Black North (Ulster, you know?) and do mad things with a gang of other I.R.A. brats of my generation, like smuggling butter, and parts for motorcars, and drunken pigs; and then give the money to the Official wing. How the devil should we ever have thought it was Marxist? How did we know what Marxist *was?* To us, hell, we were working for Ireland's freedom. Plaguing the Orangemen. Hurrah, me boys, hurrah! What a pack of fools," he said bitterly.

"Go on. Why drunken pigs?"

"A pig with a skinful of stout makes no noise, but happily ambles along wherever he's driven. There was a lot more of that in the old days, before the trade war with Britain ended, but even in my time it was profitable enough. So was taking in cigarettes and poteen. Robin Hood," he said, shaking his head, "shepherding tiddly pigs."

"Go on."

"Well now," he said, looking almost bashful, "I, ah, well, I somehow got the notion that I was Errol Flynn, playing in Sherwood Forest. And when I'd taken my degree at Clongers along of Terry here, naturally I went back North to oppose the Sheriff of Nottingham, who was played by the British government."

I saw Alanna glance at me. Her expression said, "What were you saying about actors?" mischievously.

Tommy said, "That was the time of the nonviolent civil rights campaign. It was still a frolic to me, you understand; any boy who loved Ireland—and oh Lord but we're taught to love Ireland!—might as easily have found himself involved in the patriot game, with his father always egging him on to duplicate old glories."

"What a pack of fools, indeed," said Terence quietly. "I was one, too, you remember."

"Never so moldy patriotic as I," said Tommy. "You had the sense to cut when you saw what was going to happen. I stayed till one day, instead of playing pranks on policemen, I found myself running guns over the border. Then even my thick wits grew aware of what I was actually accomplishing. I am not a man for real violence. I reverence life too much for that. And there I was dodging back and forth between one nation and another—though they ought to be united, Grania, you must believe that—and carrying deadly weapons, old submachine guns and new .303 rifles, to men who were already beginning to use them. So I quit in disgust, quit cold.

"Before that, though, I'd worked with Quinn Griffin at

Belfast. We were in a few street brawls together, but thank God I never shot a man."

"You did take out a peeler very neatly with a brick, one day that I recall," said Terence.

"He was using his baton on a woman," said Tommy.

"I wasn't criticizing you, old fellow," Terence objected. "I was merely pointing out that you hadn't been precisely a pacifist. And there were carbines pointing down your throat when you did it. That's where he picked up the nickname," he said to me, "in the North. The Orange chaps pinned it on him because he was such an artful dodger, always one wide leap ahead of them."

"Griffin and I began as comrades," said Tommy, "and then, when the whole country heated up and we started to see our doings all over the front pages of foreign papers, he panicked and sold us out to the British. Quinn Griffin is the ancient curse of Ireland—and may God have mercy on us for that streak of depravity—he is an informer."

"There are decent men in Cork and Dublin today," agreed Terence, "who would kill him on sight."

"Well, there are some citizens who'd like to do the same for me," said Tommy, grinning slightly.

"The polis in the Narth is still after him, Grania," said Terence broadly.

"I meant the hotheaded gentry of the Provos. The idealistic terrorists, Grania, the Provisional wing of the I.R.A. I've no manner of use for what they're doing, and they think I ought to be gunned down for quitting them. But schoolboy harassment is one thing and wanton murder is another."

"Then you're in danger, even aside from what you're doing in Dragon's Keep," I said breathlessly.

He looked at me square. His calm face showed the almost frightening strength that I had sensed in him the first night we'd met. He said in a reasonable tone, "Grania, *a rúin*, is there a soul in all this world who is not in danger? Only a good young milk cow in her pasture lives in comparative security."

"By the Black Stone of Tara, but that's well said," Terence cried.

"You wouldn't want me to emigrate to America to avoid a few enemies?" Tommy asked.

"No," I told him. I would not have him recast himself for me, not a scintilla; especially I would never ask him to moderate his wholly admirable courage. I thought of a rather stupid slogan that had enjoyed a fad back home a few years ago, and before I realized what I was doing, I'd altered it and voiced it. "Love means never saying 'I want you to change something about yourself.'" Tommy looked startled, and I think I flushed, but the Blakes applauded, and Terence said, "Dog, if you let this splendid wench get away from you, our friendship is at an end!"

"What does *a rúin* mean?" I asked, and he told me "my treasure" as casually as could be.

"And speaking of that," said Terence, "it should not be many days before we break through to it."

"If it's there," said Alanna.

"It is," said Terence.

I said "Oh!" a few times, and coaxed them to tell me more of what they expected to find, but they would not spoil the surprise for me, they said. Then Tommy talked some more about partition, and how difficult it was to understand it totally even if you were born Irish, and Terence said *especially* if you were born Irish; and they tried by turns to educate me in the historical subtleties and the layers upon layers of fierce antagonisms among the factions in the North, some of them dating back more than eight hundred years.

When my head was spinning, Tommy threw up his hands and exclaimed, "Ah, what's the use? Try to interpret the two Irelands for a stranger and you only see that you don't comprehend them yourself! I'll tell you one thing, girl dear, and that's this: If I believed that violence would unite us at last, I'd be up there today fighting in the streets of Belfast; but the problem won't be solved in our time."

"Of course it will," said Terence. "It must be solved, though not by violence. The 1970's can surely finish what primitive old 1921 began. The six counties will soon be ours."

"You are an optimistic romanticist."

"You're another. How often have you said that nothing's insoluble to this age?"

"How do we solve Quinn Griffin?" asked Tommy glumly.

"I'd solve him briskly enough if I had a good revolver," said Terence, in a most uncharacteristic remark. "What's become of him, then?"

"Grania put the wind up him, appearing and vanishing as she did. He may wonder if there aren't half a dozen more of us hiding here. And then there's the chap he killed; that will have scared him, too. But if there's enough money in it," said Tommy, "wager your shirt that he'll be back in the neighborhood before orchids bloom in the Burren. Meanwhile, we will stop trying to riddle out his purposes, and go on with the business in hand." He glanced around the lamplit room. "Living in Ali Baba's cave," he said, shaking his head, "and blithely digging like so many children for a fortune in jewels and gold, while murderers prowl all about us! If that isn't an Irish trick, what ever is?"

9

My heart is always trembling
From the clear daylight of dawn . . .
　　　　　—The Rocks of Bawn

THE CLEAN COLD BREEZES OF SPRING came in upon the
land, even though I'd slain the bird that brings the wind.

One afternoon Alanna ran up to my rubble heap in
great excitement, to tell me that they had opened the passageway leading into the earth. "You must come down
with us, definitely! We must all be there. Watch, Balor,"
she said, and we left the wolfhound gravely scanning the
countryside, and hurried toward the work site, stumbling
over rocks and sliding on grassy slopes. "This looks like it,
Grania," she said, panting a little.

"Oh, I hope so."

"Did Terence describe the vice to you?"

"Whose?"

"Whose what? Oh," she said, turning to match my grin,
"I see. A vice is a winding staircase down through the center of a mural wall, actually in the wall, as most of the
stairs and a lot of semi-secret passages and rooms always
were."

"In the wall that fronted on the ocean, in this case," I
said.

"You did get the lecture tour. But he didn't say we'd
been cleaning out a vice?"

"I'd have remembered." I jumped a lichened stone, and
said, "He did mention stairs, yes. I suppose I thought of a
straight flight."

"No, it's a spiral. It was blocked with earth and fallen
pieces of wall, blocked with centuries of settling—cracking
open a pyramid would be child's play in comparison. But
now we've done it. The lads got one last stone up and out

with the block and tackle, and all at once the vice is cleared."

Until we were all but on top of the thing, I could see nothing that indicated all their digging and moving about of the broken fabric of this once-mighty fortress: thanks to Tommy's zeal for neatness, the ruins looked as timeless, as untouched as ever. But we skirted the towering end of the north wall and there, in what had been the twelve-foot-thick wall that faced the sea, was the black, ragged hole. Tommy and Terence were squatting beside it, staring intently into its depths with the aid of two torches. A Coleman lantern had already been lit, too.

"You're here, then," said Terence. His lean face had the vacant expression of a man who had just been slugged on the back of the neck. "Well," he said; "well. I suppose we can go down." The pending finish of his dream, which might be either triumphant or disastrous, had almost petrified him. "Who first?" he said. "Dog?"

"This was your scheme from the beginning, Terry. Your honor."

"Blessed Sir Boyle Roche bring us luck, then," said he, and stood and blinked and grinned, and started downward *larghissimo*, carrying the Coleman, which trembled in his hand. His wife followed him, then I, then Tommy.

Around a central pillar, the steps with their slightly hollowed treads descended, turning round and round toward our right. Tommy said quietly in my ear that this was a hopeful sign. "It's usually the other direction, you see," he murmured, "down to the left," and something terribly masculine and technical about the defenders not having the pillar in the way of their broadswords when they were swatting at any attackers. "This way," he told me, excitement throbbing in his low voice, "it means that the garrison wasn't expected to be defending whatever's below, and therefore—"

"Kindly shove a sock in your gob," said Terence from ahead, his voice echoing weirdly. "Don't you realize that I'm praying?" And then, in a moment, "This is as far as we'd come, Grania. From here it's virgin ground."

"You mean you dug it out this deep?" I said, surprised. "We must be forty feet down!"

"About thirteen," whispered Tommy. "When the wall collapsed above, when Cromwell's bullyboys destroyed the keep, one gigantic piece of the dressed stone from the wall's surface got wedged across here. See the gouges? And the mortar and rubble core of the wall avalanched down, along with other stones and plenty of dirt, and filled it in above. Of course, even then, in 1651, nobody had been up or down these steps for about four centuries. If we're right."

"Oh, *do* shut up!" said Terence.

Around the center pillar we went, gingerly, kicking the litter of that ancient collapse out of our way; accompanied by the reverberations of our footfalls, into the earth, the dark crudely cut rock on either hand exuding a dank chill that bit into the flesh as wickedly as a gale from the sea. The steps, each one a narrow arc of a circle, rose behind us toward a daylight that now I could scarcely remember. I have said that depths frighten me far more than heights. I suppose that descent took us no more than a minute, cautious and snaillike though our pace was. It seemed an hour. The damnable staircase would have been a terror anywhere: here, a few yards from the Cliffs of Moher, it was utterly horrible.

Being enclosed in the ground, in caves or even deep cellars, has always made me feel like the narrator in Poe's story of premature burial. And the age and location of these steps gave me goose flesh. Bran Roe himself at the bottom, sword in hand and eyes blazing with the green fire of the Irish district of Hell, would hardly have astonished me, I thought.

But here we were at the foot, and the place was untenanted; not even the sound of a rat broke the silence that we held when we had come down, only the subdued hiss of the big Coleman.

It was a great square vaulted chamber, far larger than I had expected. Two enormous fireplaces, even blacker than the walls although their fires had gone out so long ago, were set into the right side, which was the southern wall. In the center of the filthy floor, shapeless red-brown smears marked where some iron apparatus, likely a brazier, had stood and rusted into crumbs through the long centuries. Similar marks in the nearer fireplace must have been the firedogs that supported a grate.

And there was nothing else, nothing else at all.

After a while Terence began to walk slowly around the walls, holding the lantern high. My heart went out to him, even more than to the others, for it was primarily his grand vision that had evaporated in the bone-cracking chill of this huge and empty crypt. I watched him circle the place, the radiance moving with him. There were scattered mounds of unidentifiable rubbish here and there, which he kicked moodily, sending up little fogs of gray and red dust that hung in the air behind him. At last he came back to us.

"Well," he said conversationally, "we're down to bedrock in more ways than one, eh? This is the bottom of the keep. It was this that the O'Conors dug down to and exposed, in order to erect their walls that were never to sink again. Well below ground, but right on the top of the cliff rock. Down to the bedrock of my theory, too, aren't we? With the sense of nadir, or lowest point."

He held the lantern over his head, looking anywhere but at us. "Wilde says, 'There is no sin except stupidity,' and I'm the sinner of all time. Do you know what this place is? Do you realize what we have been killing ourselves to reach, all through the filthy winter, in every sort of loathsome weather, breaking our hands and our backs like a gang of slaves, grubbing our youth and health away on these putrid cliffs when we might have been sitting in pubs and singing? I'll tell you what it damned well is! It's the BLOODY KITCHENS!"

The full-throated roar died away in frightening echoes, like the angry ghosts of medieval cooks and scullions shouting at us with Terence's voice. No one moved. I think Alanna was crying; I know I was. Then Tommy put his hands on his friend's shoulders and shook him gently. "Well, then, there's nothing for it but to come back next year and try again," he said. "The stuff is here somewhere, old fella, and do you know what I'm going to tell you? We are going to find it. Let there be no nonsense about that. It is practically in our hands this minute. This gory livid bleeding green setback is not going to stop us."

Terence said, "You sound like Greenstreet at the end of that Bogart flick, still going after the falcon," and his voice was uncertain, the rage gone.

"Why not? Is perseverance out of date? We cannot give up because of one little miscalculation."

"He's right," said Alanna, "darling, he's right."

"He is," I said, "and I'm not giving up either. I'll be back with you in the autumn."

Tommy turned a great grin on me. "You will so! I

knew it. Terry, we have months and months to scheme out where the hidden room may lie. And we've narrowed the possibilities considerably with these—"

"These two rotten maggoty mistakes of mine."

"These grand archaeological discoveries," said Tommy.

"Ah, let's get out and have a cup of tea and stop breathing cold wet dust!" said Terence with the anguish in his throat again. "I tell you I am perished in this refrigerator of a ruin!"

"All right," said Tommy, "but don't be discouraged, that's all."

Terence laughed, about as mirthfully as a man impaled on a stalagmite. I blew my nose, and we began to climb the staircase, Tommy first.

Then I heard the wolfhound barking, as faint and far as a dog in dreams.

We came up fast and crouched at ground level, and Tommy whistled. Balor was there in seconds, wagging his hindquarters and woofing quietly. "The den," said Tommy, and we all ran for it, doubled over as though we were surrounded by enemies with rifles. For all I knew, we were. The dog was not a beast to howl because he missed us, or to bay a passing cat; he took his job more seriously than most humans do. We got ourselves into the little turf-scented room, slid the tall rock panel shut, locked the door, relighted our hot lantern, and stared at one another.

"He's back, then, or his friends."

"Or early tourists. It's a fine day for viewing the cliffs."

"Yes. It's nearly teatime," said Alanna, "and we needn't go out again today. You won't investigate? There's no need."

"No, love, there's no need," Terence reassured her. "And it's hours and hours till teatime, but if you want to pretend it's dark out there, I'm with you. I've had enough of the bloody Cliffs of sanguinary Moher for one long day."

I was about to say that surely we weren't *really* going to be shot at or anything but recalled the man with the ginger mustache, and kept my silliness to myself.

"I'm not certain that there's no need," said the O'Flaherty slowly, poking up the fire. His broad back looked rigid with the tension that so often possessed him, that tautness that was not strung nerves, but a vigorous intelligence constantly at work. Like a fox, indeed, I thought for the twentieth time; ready at any instant to hunt or be hunted, and not a bit worried about it. "If Griffin's affairs are about to terminate, I want to be there. Whatever they are. We've no chance of bringing him to justice unless—"

"Not in daylight," said Terence, and whether by accident or design, he leaned against the locked oaken door. "He's armed, Tommy, and you aren't. And that's that."

Tommy watched him. Then he smiled. "Right. We'll wait till first dark. Now forget about him. What's to be done concerning the hoard of Bran Roe O'Conor?"

"I would speak my mind," said Terence evenly, "but there are ladies present." He gave a groan of disgust. "It was mad, the whole idea was quite mad. Seeking on purpose for something ancient, with solid facts to get on with, is not the Irish way, and was sure to bring no luck at all!"

"What on earth do you mean?" I asked him, as Alanna and I began to put together a meal. "What is the Irish way?"

"Why, don't look for a prehistoric necklace like the Gorget of Gleninsheen in graves or beneath cairns—go hunting rabbits and you can see it in the rocks, lying there under the open sky winking at you. Don't dig below a dolmen for the priceless Book of Kells—glance into a ditch you're leaping, and there it will be. Never set out on a systematic search with instructions for locating the Tara Brooch—wait another minute and a little tinker girl will pluck it out of the sand of the shore for you. Sure never mark out a sensible plan for ascertaining the whereabouts of the golden Killymoon Hoard—a man footing turf in a bog in Tyrone will turn it up for you. And as for the Ardagh Chalice, Lord! If you hang about looking careless, a boy who's digging potatoes will stumble on it in a thorn bush! This toil we've been expending is all balderdash. How they've found everything of value in this ridiculous island is by accident! We were doomed from the start. Bran Roe's collection of nicky-noos will be discovered when we're dead and gone, by some ruddy farmer picking shamrocks for the American trade!"

"You are simply being a nattering, disappointed ass," Tommy said.

"Yes, curse you, I am. But can you argue with me?"

"I can. We have come too far to quit," said my man, filling his pipe leisurely. "We've opened up two rooms that nobody's ever seen since the seventeenth century. We can open a third or a fourth if we must. With what we know now, we can lay out a far better plan of the keep, and make more well-founded calculations."

"Well-founded brandy butter and apple fluff," Terence exclaimed. "I'm for Dublin in the morning, I tell you. I am choked to the craw with this miserable castle and these foul cliffs and the bloodshed and mysteries and the eternal cold and wet. The blight of the madman O'Conor is on the place. Not to mention the curse of the Dread Women, whom I begin to believe in."

"When does the tourist season begin in earnest?" asked Tommy, as though he hadn't heard him.

"Two or three weeks," said Alanna, "such as it is, with the Ulster troubles and all."

"Well, I'm not leaving. I am not beaten yet, no, not even for this year. I'm going to stop here till the first gapers arrive, for at some moment between now and then, Quinn Griffin will make his move, and I shall be here to ... to quietly protest it," said Tommy. "And while I'm waiting, I shall be digging."

Terence ran his fingers wildly through his vast Dundrearies and wailed. Then he smacked his palm with a fist and said, "So shall I, naturally," and snorted with amusement at himself. "You, love?"

Alanna looked at him soberly. "We agree that Bran Roe was insane, don't we?"

"Oh, I think that's taken for granted; at least in his special field he was a bloody March hare."

"Then there's one conceivability that never occurred to me until you called him a madman just now," said the blond girl slowly, "and that is that when Bran Roe was attacked by the Sionnachs and saw that his garrison would fall—"

"I've already considered, it," said Tommy, abrupt. "I don't believe it happened."

"What?" Terence demanded. "What are you both suggesting?"

"She's thinking that the O'Conor himself may have dumped his loot into the sea, to keep it from the Sionnachs."

Terence sat down on the edge of the rock table, his legs gone to jelly. "The one possibility that never entered my mind," he said. "Ah, but doesn't *that* throw a gloom over the business!"

"I do not believe it happened," said Tommy again, even while I was taking it in and beginning to shake with the ague of disappointment myself, in sympathy with Terence. "I'll tell you why: the things he collected by force of arms were probably his whole life to him, since we know he had neither wife nor child; and he would not destroy them unless he was certain that he was going to die. And how did he die? Unexpectedly. He was in one of the brattices— Grania, that was a kind of temporary, overhanging enclosure, made of timber, and in this case it jutted out above the gateway—and he was supervising the defense from there. To be specific, he was watching his lads pour molten lead down through the murdering hole on the attackers. And he didn't have the slightest apprehension of losing his keep, much less his life, because *he was winning.* So he never had a chance to jettison his treasure."

"If he was mad, then that's just wishful thinking, Dog. We don't know that he wasn't being defeated, either."

"We do. You remember the Sionnach scribe's manuscript as well as I. The brattice caught fire, from the melted lead or perhaps from a fire bomb hurled by the besieging force, and he was trapped there and burned to death. And only then, while his people were in confusion and trying to save him, were the Sionnachs able to get a battering-ram on the gate and knock it down, which was the start of the castle's overthrow."

Terence considered. "I'll accept it. I will. But if he was mad . . ."

"I think he was only mad about art and antiquities. He was viciously cruel, but how many powerful lords were the same in those days? He took whatever he could, with no sense of the rights of others, but who didn't? No, no," said Tommy decisively, "he was not mad. I offer in evidence the fact that he hid his strong room so cleverly that it stayed a secret for seven hundred years, and even we three—we four, now—haven't been able to locate it."

"You're truly sure that the Sionnachs didn't find it?" I said.

"Absolutely. They did discover his ordinary wealth, you see," Terence told me, "his store of noble metals—which would not have been coinage, of course, but chunks of gold and silver weighed out in ounces—in a repository in the wall of his bedroom. It was cleverly concealed behind a garderobe."

"A loo," said Alanna helpfully.

"A latrine," said Tommy. "It was a neat idea, though not unique. There was a passage from the seat to the treasury. The secret of that was tortured out of Bran Roe's steward. But he knew nothing of the real hoard, or he'd have told them that, too."

"Why?"

"The man was four days dying," said Terence, "and however loyal he may have been, his master was already dead and gone, leaving the steward very little reason to withhold any secret through a hundred hours of ghastly pain."

I said "Oh" with a gasp.

Then we had our tea, broiled lamb chops and onions and fried eggs, with brown bread and jam.

Tommy lit another pipe afterwards and said, "Grania, I've been considering, and I think it's time and past time that you left us."

"Why should she?" said both Blakes together.

"You're afraid for me, but you mustn't be," I told him. "I came in of my own free will, and when I knew that the police were after us, too."

"*Cad tá ort*, woman? The gardai are no more interested in us than my old aunt's donkey! Why would they have held off all these days, do you think? I tell you, Griffin is not on the side of the law," Tommy said. He took both my hands in his own hard fingers. "It is he that's out there, planning to do for all of us, and I will not keep you in such jeopardy any longer. Tomorrow Alanna will drive you to Shannon—or perhaps you'd wait in Tipperary?"

"It's a long way to Tipperary, so I'm staying here," I half sang at him. "I won't leave till you four leave," including the wolfhound, of course.

"You will do as I say."

"Try and make me."

"Woman," he said in that dark voice, "I am chief here."

"This is my tenth day at Moher. I've been kidnaped, jailed, and hunted through the rain," I said, ticking them off on my fingers. "I've escaped from both sides in your crazy mixed-up feud, I've talked to a man five minutes before he was killed, and I've fought with a gigantic bird or devil on the edge of the most frightful cliff in the world. I am likely scarred for life," I went on, touching the bandage on my cheek, "and I am very fond of all of you. So you can't ship me off to a town while you lurk in these ruins without even a pistol among you. As often as you do, I'll come back. I'm justified in that, eight times over!"

"Is there no reasoning with you?"

"Absolutely not."

He threw up his arms in a gesture of resignation that I had never seen outside of the late-late reruns. It was worthy of Terence himself. Balor got to his feet and stared at his master uncertainly. "Then you'll stay," Tommy said. "I suppose I do owe it to you. But we'll be so careful of you—Alanna, you, too—that you'll think you're two porcelain dolls!"

"Dog," said Terence, "where the devil is that sheaf of notes?" He and Alanna, ignoring Tommy's outburst, had been dredging around in the clutter along the south wall.

"What do you want out of it?"

"The thing from O'Curry."

"You know it by heart," said Tommy.

"I want to *look* at it, and consumin' to your impudence," snapped his friend. "Where have you hidden it?"

"I haven't seen it in months."

"Here it is," said Alanna, handing a dozen sheets of grimy paper to her husband. "It was under the brushes in my bone-hunter's box."

He snatched them with a grunt of thanks and shuffled through them. Tommy grinned and said, "Determined you are indeed."

"It's yourself has persuaded me to stick! By the fingers of Turlough O'Carolan, where is that bit? Here it is." He began to read aloud in Irish.

When he paused, I said, "That sounds almost like poetry."

"It's a song," said Terence absently.

"A song? Your information comes from a song?"

"The original evidence, yes. Why not?"

"Are you telling me that you've been out here all winter on the strength of a *song?*"

Terence sat down on one of the sleeping bags and began to lecture me. He reminded me of his research in the Dublin libraries, looking happier by the minute as he went along; it occurred to me that Terence Blake had a large helping of the pedagogic instinct, and might, if he ever wanted to leave architecture, become a very good teacher. (I mentioned this to him later, and he was delighted at the idea, which, oddly, had never presented itself to him.) He cited the manuscript fragment by Seán Ó Sionnach an Ghleanna, and the book by Garret More O'Meadhra, and others. He waved his fine hands expressively and declaimed.

"But none of them said anything of the treasure," I protested.

"Of course they didn't, or Dragon's Keep would have been overrun with fortune hunters long ago."

"Then you *are* saying that your only source for the presumable hoard is a song in a book."

"Ailill's eyebrows, child! It isn't just 'a song in a book'—it's a piece of oral history, composed by the bard of the Dragon himself."

"Who?"

"Bran Roe was called the Dragon," said Alanna. "Hence, Dragon's Keep."

"It was used figuratively," Tommy put in from behind a fragrant cloud of pipesmoke, "meaning a warrior or chief, as well as one of your scaly green maidennapers."

"Well," I said, "if this bard didn't write it down—"

"I will explain the Poet in Irish History to you," said Terence patiently.

"At another time," said Tommy. "Just grasp this for now, Grania: fifteen hundred, a thousand, even seven hundred years ago, there were poets in Ireland who made the historians of the rest of Europe seem like boys scribbling rumors on fences with chalk. And research shows plainer every year that they were accurate in their stories, if they did paint the lily a trifle. I can't give you an example you'd appreciate, because you've never had a course in our history."

"Troy," said Alanna. "You know how Schliemann and Dörpfeld proved that the Iliad and the Odyssey were basically fact, instead of the pure fiction they'd always been considered?"

"I've read something about that, yes."

"The Irish bards were roughly equivalent to Homer. The more we learn from archaeology, the more we realize how much reality there is in the old epics and other verse."

"The man who wrote your song in his book—O'Curry? When was that?" I asked.

"Nineteenth century," said Terence.

"So it had been sung, but not written, for six hundred years before that?"

"Yes. O'Curry collected two partial versions of it in the Aran Islands, which are just up the coast a bit."

"It's really a valid source, Grania," said his wife. "Homer probably got the Iliad from some such originals. When people can't read or write, they preserve their songs of history scrupulously."

"You *are* an archaeologist," I said slowly, remembering, "and I don't know anything about this sort of stuff; but a song seems like pretty flimsy evidence to send the three of you here in the winter to dig out a lot of medieval kitchens and bathrooms or whatever. And why wouldn't the Sionnachs have known the song, and believed it, and hunted for such a unique collection of valuable things?"

"The song was made in memory of Bran Roe by his bard, who had gone to the Arans before his master's death, and missed the attack and the wholesale executions. He'd have sung it there, where the chances were that it wouldn't have penetrated the mainland very deeply if at all, because the Aran people kept to themselves very clannishly. Then the generations of islanders would have gone on singing it as part of their oral tradition. Maybe an occasional adventurous soul might have sneaked over the water to hunt for the lost, but history would tell us if he'd discovered it. The song isn't known even in Aran today, so far as we could discover. O'Curry caught it just in time."

"Thanks to the radio and the gramophone," said Terence sourly, "wonders of the ages, that kind of thing has died out." He shuffled the papers. "Here," he said, "listen to this if you've got two ears on you." And he began to read aloud.

"Hand to me again the harp of my young days,
  The glorious-throated music-tree on which I played for
    the Dragon,
  And I will tell once more of his mighty deeds,
  Before the Man of Hunger, the *Far Goila*, has taken me;
  Before I, the last who lives that saw him in his prime,
  Am laid in death below the rocks of this island.
  I will tell you of the crown of Macha Mhong Ruadh,
  The ravening warrior-queen of Uladh in the north,

Made of gold and crystal, which the Dragon took
By force of arms from MacConn of Munster. . . .

And so on and so on, this nicky-noo and that one—"
"It doesn't say that!" I exclaimed.
"Well, not precisely, but that's the gist of it."
"I know about Queen Macha," I said, "from Grand-
mother."
"Good. What I'm looking for is down here somewhere—
ah:

"And when the Dragon had returned from Clusin
Bringing his spoil, the silver chessboard of Cormac,
That great king who fell at Bellach Mughna so long ago,
Muise! Four hundred years past lacking but sixty
Of the death of my strong master himself—

Now there's one of the points, Grania," said Terence, in-
terrupting himself, "that proves to me beyond the whisper
of a doubt that this bard was one of the old school, who
had thousands of dates and facts on the point of his
tongue, and that he was Bran Roe's man, not the bard of
some other chief styled 'the Dragon,' and that this song is
the genuine article. Because Cormac was slain in the year
903, and O'Conor in 1243. Three hundred and forty years
to the minute, you might say."
"Go on," I said, rather breathless. I had been thinking
*A song, for heaven's sake, they're here because of some
silly old song;* and now he'd handed me a clue with which
Basil Rathbone could have skewered a doubting Nigel
Bruce to the wall.

"Then said the Dragon to me, his trusted confidant of so
    long time,
That he had gathered all the treasures that it pleased him
    so to do,
And he would seal them up now in the place he had
    made ready for them,
Set sentinels to watch, and hide the compartment
From every prying eye of living man. And, that I need
    not die
For knowledge of that site, he'd send me o'er the waves
Till all was finished as he long had planned.
Hear this: in the matter of the treasure-hoard
He would trust no lips save his own to keep the secret,

Not mine nor his brother's nor those who with their
    skilled hands formed the lair
Which held the harvest of so many battles. . . .

Then the song tells that the bard went to Aran, and lived
there in marvelous comfort and luxury with the local roy-
alty (flattering them so they'd keep his song alive, I suppose) until word came of the siege of the castle—'that
great fortress on the heights above the black and haunted
walls of Thomond' which again nails it down, because Moher was called the Wall of Thomond, see?—and then of
its overthrow. So he stopped where he was, and likely died
there in his old age."

"He had no idea of the location of the hiding place, of
course," said Alanna. "That's why Bran Roe sent him
away, so he wouldn't have to kill him as he must have
killed the men who made the strong room for him."

"And perhaps his own brother, too," added Tommy,
"unless he'd shipped *him* off somewhere. And that's why
we're pretty certain that no one looted the stuff. O'Conor
made sure of that for his lifetime at least."

I was thinking hard, while Terence scowled over the
sheets of paper, searching for hints that he might have
missed. "He sealed the things up," I said, "and put sentinels to watch. What does that mean? If he didn't even
trust his poet, who seems to have been a valued friend,
then why sentinels?"

"No ideas from this corner," mumbled Terence.

"They may have been old pagan idols, or magic sym-
bols," said Alanna. "Bran Roe wasn't, I'd suspect, much of
a Christian."

"Like hex signs," I said. "I understand. Well, if the bard
didn't know where the loot was, he couldn't very well pass
along any clues, could he?"

"Only inadvertently, if he actually knew something that
he didn't know he knew," said Tommy lucidly. "Sentinels
to *watch*. That doesn't sound like magical pentagrams or
. . . to watch? Well, perhaps idols, yes. What is a hex sign,
Grania?"

Before I could tell him that, "Listen!" said Terence suddenly from where he stood beside the door. "Did you hear
it?"

"What?"

He hushed us with his hands, cocked his head almost

against the oak. He said quietly, "Something out there, like a scraping—"

Then we all caught it, the only sound short of thunder that you could ever hear from the outer world when the door was shut: the tentative sliding of the rock gate in its groove. I made a motion to turn off the lamp, but Tommy shook his head at me. I saw that the iron key was upright in its hole; still, light could be leaking out around it. We all held our breath, I think. I put my arms around Balor, soothing him. The rumbling sound of the doorway's camouflaging barrier came again. Now it must be entirely out of the way. Someone had found our den.

I thought of the gardai, the government men under Quinn Griffin, and a pack of faceless smugglers and drug addicts. Six of one, half a dozen of the others. I thought of curious German or American tourists, more comforting thought by far. I—

Come out, O'Flaherty!

At first I believed that I had imagined it, the whisper that penetrated our little room as inexorably, as impersonally, as a ferret sliding into a rabbit's burrow.

Thomas O'Flaherty! Come out, O'Flaherty!

Oh, merciful God, I hadn't fancied it, it was there, a real, hoarse, carrying husk of a sound that put the chills into my spine. I actually clutched at Balor now, I was so frightened. You're being a baby, I told myself; and held him tightly.

Come out, Dog Fox!

Tommy looked over at me and gave a tight little nod of triumph. I knew what he was saying. It was Quinn. And yet I could not identify the voice at all. A whisper is sexless, without identity.

Come out, said the thing, and I felt it looking at me, a sound that was equipped with eyes. The wolfhound shook me off and padded over to glare at the keyhole with his ears back and the blind eye staring, and I knew that the voice could no more see me than could that milky ball of Balor's, and still I felt naked and alone in the stone room with the seeing whisper of evil. *Come out, man, I've no wish to hurt you*, it said; *my word on it, Dog Fox*. This time I caught the exact lilt of Quinn Griffin's speech, and all doubt was gone.

And in that moment I finally began to realize the truth, which was that only a few days ago I had been kissed by a handsome, cold-blooded murderer. Just as Tommy had said. I was an abysmal fool not to have recognized it before now. For everything that he had claimed to know about Quinn was in that whisper—treachery, arrogance, cruelty, and yes, lunacy. It filled our clean little room with its depravity, it was no more to be believed than the voice of the serpent in the garden; even our turf fire seemed to shrink a little at its sound, and I had a strong urge to wipe my fingers across my face, as if I were standing under the drip of dirty water from a leak in some foul gutter above us.

Tommy came on tiptoe and looked at Alanna's wristwatch. He grimaced. It would still be full day out there. He picked up a crowbar from the heap of tools and hefted it and stared uncertainly at the door. Terence shook his head violently.

The door was tried, first stealthily, then hard in anger. *Last chance, O'Flaherty*, said the whisper. *Come out and talk. We can make an agreement, man dear!* Then, after a pause, *Wouldn't the British love to know that the Dog Fox is alive and kickin'!*

And somehow that empty, gratuitous threat took all the horror out of the thing, and left us standing there with only a man outside, a bad man, certainly, but no longer a half-known force of darkness; only a man standing in the sunlight. I saw Tommy and Terence exchange grins, and with their relaxation I knew that they must have been at least touched by the eeriness that had petrified me.

Last chance, said the whisper sharply.

Terence made a motion as though biting and then tossing some object. Tommy shook his head and shrugged. I think they were wondering whether Quinn might have a grenade. They both moved away from the door, Balor following at a hand signal. I pulled Alanna back until we stood in front of the long reserve stack of turf.

The silence lengthened. At last Tommy went to the fire and poured a mug of tea. "He's gone," he said quietly. "He'd never have the patience to stand there three minutes without making a sound." He handed me the mug and poured another for himself. "If it had been dark," he said, half to us, half to his own conscience, "by the Lord I'd have gone out to him!"

"You would not," said Terence.

"I would so. He was right at the door, bending or

maybe kneeling. I could have caught him flatfooted. I could have laid open his head with that bar."

"What will he do now?"

"I can tell you as true as though I were seeing him do it. He'll be away now, running for his motorcar. It's his way. He's bold before any action, he's in great control of himself, he can outwait a pillar box if he must. Then when things hum he's in fine style for a bit, excited and very quick and competent. But if he's balked, if things don't go according to plan, it frightens him. A kind of gibbering madness may come on him for what seems no reason. He'll quit, he'll run. It was at such a time that he went to the British in Ulster to sell us out."

"He may not be quite that consistent," said Terence uneasily. "After all, Dog, all he got from us was silence."

"Where he expected a fight or a surrender. It will have torn hell out of his ego." Tommy pulled at his ear thoughtfully. "He must have been out there when we came in, and seen the working of the doors."

"Likely he's watched that before," said Terence. "Balor must have warned us today when Griffin's car turned off to the lay-by. He couldn't have come in sight of this place before we were snug and dry inside. No, he's known about the den for a while."

"The hound is trustworthy," Tommy agreed. "I think you're right. Griffin's spotted us, entering or leaving, before this. Which means that he's grown very edgy and peevish about waiting any longer, which means further that his game is coming to a head, and he daren't linger."

"All classes of ill luck to him, then," murmured Terence. "Shall we simply forget him and have a decent evening!"

Easier said than managed, I thought, as I realized that I was still trembling with fright. I pictured that tall, broad, elegant man with his engulfing smile waiting by the door, an automatic pistol in his hand and death in his heart. And I remembered him saying, ages ago in Limerick, "If you're playing with me, it will be the worse for you," and the raw rage in his jewel-blue eyes, which I'd persuaded myself had been my own imagination.

What an absolute fool a lonely woman can be! I sincerely thanked God that I was no longer lonely; and went to sit on the hard floor beside Tommy and lay my bandaged cheek against his shoulder and hope—futilely, as it turned out—that he would stay here in the scent and warmth of the turf fire and not leave me behind to endure the bullying of my own imagination when the darkness had fallen.

10

"HOW MUCH DAYLIGHT HAVE WE NOW?" Tommy asked Alanna for the third or fourth time.

"About an hour."

He got up and prowled. "Hell take this stone-jugful of claustrophobia, then. Come out and view the ocean, Grania girl," said he. I got up obediently and put on my jacket.

"No got out there, bwana," said Terence, who sometimes seemed to have been weaned, like so many Irishmen, on American movies. "Big juju. Bad man have little stick that spits fire, you rash and sod-headed hero."

"You can't risk Grania, either," said Alanna. "I have an intuition that Griffin hates her most of all, because she tore herself out of his arms to come with us."

"He's gone, I tell you. Balor," said Tommy, opening the inner door on the day, "seek!" The dog bounded away. "We will go only to the cliff wall, and leave the door open."

"Keep a couple of throwing rocks handy, at least," said Terence.

"Fair enough." He took me by the arm and we walked out to the low dry-stone wall, which we had not visited since my second evening there. "It's Sunday, isn't it? It feels like Sunday. Lovely hush on things," he said, staring out to the west. It was a beautiful day, nearly cloudless, with a hard blue sky and a yellow-white glare where the sun was dropping. There was no great excess of wind, but the tall waves boomed and sucked at the foot of the precipice. As Balor had given no warning, we did not even glance behind us.

"Do you know what you're looking at, Grania? I mean,

what that is, and that?" He pointed to the coast south of us. "Just on the horizon there, that's County Kerry, the end of the Dingle Peninsula. Up there, the farthest north you can make out, is Connemara. But closer, those land masses there, six miles or so northwest, those are the three Aran Islands. Where the old bard died. A rugged, bare sort of place. I'd like to take you there one day. If you'd care to see it."

"I'd love to. And Slieve League. I understand it's the highest sea cliff in the world."

"What ass told you that?"

"Well, Quinn Griffin."

Tommy made a noise between a snort and a cough. "That one should have gone to the wall years ago. He can't even tell the truth about geography. Any schoolboy knows that the highest sea cliffs in this country are in County Mayo, on Achill Island; but I doubt if even they are the tallest in the world. Slieve League's impressive, though. I'll take you there." He thought. "And to Tory Island. That's where the original Balor lived, and you'd like to see that."

"When was that?"

He chuckled. "Prehistory or myth, take your choice; there's no knowing in this land which is which. Balor of the Magical Eye—he had but the one, you see, that's where the hound gets his name—was either a Fomorian chief or a giant. It's a nice sort of name for a dog, anyway. He was born with that eye, in case you've wondered; it was no horrible accident that took it from him."

"He's a dear, gentle beast."

"Gentle is it! If I gave him the command to attack, you'd see how gentle he is."

"I believe you're a little jealous of Balor and me."

"How do you make that out?"

"He's never taken to anyone but you, entirely, until I came along. I think that causes you a slight pang. It's alright; it proves you're human. It's even endearing."

He stared out to sea, thinking. "You're right. I wasn't aware of it, but you're right. How bloody mean of me that is."

"No, you can't insult yourself in front of me." I faced him. "Thomas O'Flaherty, I'm in love with you."

"Why?" he said, turning to me.

"Because I am. Because of what you are."

"What's that?"

"A man. What we used to call a natural man. Yourself."

He said, "I've given you sweet nothing on which to base that, *mo-húirnin.* I woke up a day or two ago and realized that I'd been barely civil to you, and me eaten up with love, too, so that my head spins with it." He was not touching me or even looking straight at me now, but I could feel the electric tension of his body in the air all around my own. "I haven't wanted anything in this world but to take you in my arms and spend a solid week trying to tell you and show you how very much I love you, Grania Kirk. Do you know why I haven't?"

"You've had too much to cope with, and you knew I'd keep."

"My God, was I that sure of myself, to know you'd wait day in and day out?"

"If you weren't sure of me, you wouldn't have waited. And that's a compliment, after all. You knew—when you'd kissed me—that I was in love with you. You had no need to cope with that at once. If you'd thought I wouldn't wait, you'd have been insulting me."

"Why?"

"Thinking I kissed just any man with that much fervor," I said frankly.

"I forget precisely how much fervor that was," he said, and took me with both hands on my waist and kissed me on the mouth long and gently, then long and heartily. Finally, with my head on his shoulder as I caught my breath, he murmured, "I have had all I could handle, Grania, in the way of emotions and plans and hopes and fears and working till I was sick with fatigue, but that's no reason to let the most important matter of all slide along without doing anything about it. I will not do it any more, mind you. I intend to annoy you with my attentions at all odd hours. I do love you."

"Why?"

"Don't give me back my own questions. For yourself. Ah, you said that first." He kissed my cheek, the one that wasn't bandaged. "It's true, though, and it's about all you can say, isn't it?"

"Sort of," I said. "Inadequate ... but all words are. I love you, O'Flaherty darling."

"Are you sure? Think well," he said; "to love, with a fella like me, means to want to marry."

"I'll marry you." I touched his lips with my fingers. "When you ask me, I'll marry you. You aren't getting away."

"But could you ever learn to spell my name properly? I mean my real name, O'Flaherty in the Irish?"

"How do you spell it?"

Smiling, he spelled it out. He had to repeat it twice, but I had it then. "Ó Flaithbheartaigh," I said. "Good grief."

"Could you bear it?"

"I intend to."

He looked out at the ocean again. "I can't excuse myself on and on, dearest, but I have had a thing on my soul that's been more a worry to me than that dead man or Griffin's drug nonsense or anything. And it was dear old Terry."

"In what way?" I put my hand on his arm, for he was troubled.

"I began to realize, oh, days and days ago, before you came it was, that we were on a wrong track with that vice. The staircase. I couldn't talk to him about it, or spoil his pleasure in the fine discovery, even if it wasn't the treasure room—which I was almost certain it wasn't. But I had to go on alongside him, for I might have been wrong." He sighed inaudibly. "I wasn't."

"How did you know?"

"The steps. Those stones had been hollowed down by too much traffic for it to have been a secret place. Centuries of feet, right through the tenancy of the late Sionnach clan. Terry would have seen it too in a minute if he hadn't been so eager. And there was always the bare possibility that I *was* mistaken, that the steps had been moved there from some other place. Damn it! I will help him find his treasure if it takes years. You understand that."

"Your treasure too."

"Oh, everyone's, of course. But the thing is his child from the first."

"But you'll all share in the profits."

He stared at me. "What?"

"Except the government," I added ruefully, hating to bring it up on the heels of our love chatter; but he had to know how I felt. "I know you have no intention of letting the government take a treasure-trove split, Tommy; you told me you'd never even considered it. I wish you would. Whatever claim you may have from the mote-and-bailey times, when your ferocious O'Flahertys held this place, it does seem—"

"You wish I was a shade more scrupulous in my dealings," he said. "You would like me to inform Dublin of our progress. You have a reservation about loving me, for I have this callous, greedy streak, is that it?"

"No! Don't be angry, please. It's your business, it's your decision. I came into it very late. I've no right—"

"You have no right," he said heavily. "I think, from what you said a few evenings back about never asking a man to change himself, that that's a true statement of your deepest feelings. So you will take on yourself no right. Very well. Shall we leave it at that?"

Then he took me by the arm and, whistling for Balor, marched me back to the stone room.

I felt worse than I had since I'd left the television studios behind me.

He and Terence read and reread the manuscript until Alanna, on his asking her, said it was nine o'clock. "Time to scout," he said. "I rather expect Griffin back tonight." Picking up his crowbar, he came over and kissed me. It was a brief touch, but it was a kiss. I cheered up a little. Tommy turned off the Coleman. "Balor and I will go looking. If we find him, I'm going to bring him here and sweat the truth out of him." He was at the door, a dimly seen figure in the low firelight. "Do not come after me, Terry, old fella," he said, "I don't want the women alone. Understood?"

"Right."

Tommy was gone, and Terence locked the door behind him. Neither had slid the rock into place; that would have been pointless. Terence flapped out a sleeping bag and lay down on it near the entrance, fully clothed. "Let's try for some sleep. It may be a long night," he said quietly.

I sat by the hearth, chin on knees, and my heart thumping badly, listening for the muffled noise of a shot. Alanna kissed us both and stretched out beside her husband. We waited, each of us knowing that the others were wide awake, while Tommy O'Flaherty prowled through the dark Irish night on his self-imposed mission of justice. For the sake of my peace of mind, I tried to avoid thinking about his danger by coordinating my various impressions of the man, attempting to bring his code of honor—obviously a high one, involving as it did the single-handed capture of a murderer against whom there was no evidence beyond our unsupported word that there *had* been a corpse—into harmony with his unlawful search for a treasure that would enrich his friends and himself at the expense of the Republic.

Supposing it were simple vindictiveness that had sent him out after Quinn Griffin, then the facts made up a consistent whole. But that whole was a false one. Unless I was the worst judge of character who ever came out of Freeport, Tommy O'Flaherty was a good man.

Barring the single flaw, the determination to lay hands on that ancient booty: which was just the sort of flaw I'd have expected in a devil-may-care adventurer who'd grown up in the I.R.A. thinking that he was Errol Flynn.

But Tommy wasn't devil-may-care. He was steady, solid, very thoughtful of others . . . and here I was at the start of the circle again, as always happened, and nowhere to go but back along the same impossible path.

Perhaps they didn't like their government, and believed it unworthy of owning archaeological wealth. No, that wasn't so, for what the government owned in that sense was also a possession of the people. And it was the Ulster authorities whom Tommy had fought, not those of the Republic.

"You love him, anyway," I told myself, whispering in the thick dusk of our den, "so accept any slight imperfections (such as a crooked streak) and be happy."

Which, by and large, I believe I would have been, if he hadn't been searching for a gunman along the Cliffs of Moher, after a cool good-bye kiss which after the embrace of early evening was little more than an insult.

The two tiny strips of silver on my watch said that it was past ten. I lay down and concentrated on falling asleep. I had seldom been more awake. A dread for the Dog Fox began to beat in my breast until I thought it would rouse the others; I could tell that by now Terence, worn out from his excitements and disappointments, was deep in dreams, and Alanna always slept easily.

What sort of weakling was I, to hide here while my darling Irishman faced his dangers alone? I wasn't an invalid, my left wrist was a little stiff but that was all; the only bandage *I* still wore was the one on my cheek. I was fairly tough—hadn't I laid out Tommy with a flashlight?—and there would be a quarter-moon if clouds hadn't come up, so I'd be able to see well enough.

Tommy would be furious if I went out. He'd forbidden even Terence to leave.

If Quinn had him at bay, and was just about to shoot him, and I crept silently up with my faithful torch and took aim at the back of his head . . .

Scenario by Sam Peckinpah, I thought scornfully, Grania Kirk played by Ernest Borgnine. Yet the idea would not go away. I recollected a series episode I'd done in which I'd come on stage in the nick of time to zonk the villain spectacularly with a portable record player. I couldn't remember whether I'd been the Rebellious Girl or the Freaked-Out Genius. I tried vainly to concentrate on that momentous problem. All my television world was a dull blur in the back of my head. I kept seeing Tommy on the brink, the black ocean thundering below, Balor perhaps shot, Griffin moving forward with his smile and his gun.

It must be nearly morning. I looked at my watch. Ten-forty.

This was intolerable.

I rose and pulled on my beat-up Aran sweater, which I had sewed into a semblance of its former glory a few days before; I remembered, incongruously, that it had come from the same place as Terence's old song of the Dragon. I found the big torch by the fire-flicker. I tiptoed past the Blakes, Alanna's golden head pillowed on her husband's chest, and as noiselessly as possible unlocked the door.

Now here was a true danger. I couldn't lock them in and Tommy out, taking the key with me. Nor could I leave them defenseless behind an unfastened door. I trailed back to the fire and sat down to brood on this. I was not departing because of intelligent thought, but because of fear for Tommy; I knew that, and accepted it as a necessary idiocy. Also I was full of incompleteness, due to our half-argument which had made me mope.

But I must protect the Blakes, even if I had to sit here and go out of my mind.

I sat there, and I went out of my mind.

At four minutes after eleven, when Tommy had been gone two hours and must be presumed to be in trouble, I took a wrench, what Terence would have called a spanner, a quite formidable weapon, and put it down beside him. I laid his right hand over the handle and tried to curl his fingers around it, so if he woke suddenly his grip would tighten as he felt it there. He grunted and moved, then settled down once more. I lifted the tea kettle from its old iron hook over the fire and found a jar which had held marmalade and which we used as a water glass. Opening the door cautiously upon a cool, almost calm night, I slipped out and pulled it within a foot of closing again. Reaching into the room, I set the jar as near as I could to the door, and balanced the kettle atop it. Then I shut the oak door, with its key inside.

Anyone opening the door would knock the kettle and jar down, making a racket. And Terence, I hoped, would be on his feet with the spanner ready when the intruder recovered from his surprise. It was the best I could do for the Blakes. I *had* to go out and find Tommy. They'd understand that.

Besides, Griffin, if he came back, would assume the door was locked. . . .

I tore my thoughts away from all that, to concentrate on my surroundings. After sitting wide-eyed in our darkened den for a couple of hours, I found the outdoors startling in its visibility. The quarter-moon rode high in a nearly cloudless indigo vault. The ruins of Dragon's Keep off to my right were menacingly plain to see, the ivy sprawled black against the deep olive stones. I could distinguish a multitude of stars, which was rare for me in that island. I decided that I must be seeing them by reflected moonshine, which was as whimsical a notion as I was going to have for a long, long time.

The ocean was talking to me in a quieter, more personal tone than usual. I walked over to the dry-stone wall and looked down: the rolling swell of the dark waters was much lower than I had seen it before. I thought of my poor dead albatross and shuddered. At last the wind had died in its memory.

I listened intently, turning in a slow circle, and there was no sign of Tommy; and then I heard a curlew cry to the east of the ruins. That was their signal, but he wouldn't be calling for Terence—did Balor respond to the fluted double-note, too? It came again, much nearer. Then a bird flew straight over my head with a powerful, steady beating of wings, and the cry came back to me from the sea. It had been a real curlew.

I walked northward and then inland, meaning to climb the ruin of the castle's forebuilding, from which I'd kept watch during the last week, and scan the country for movement or light or whatever I might see. For all I knew, Tommy in his single-minded pursuit could have been halfway to Lisdoonvarna by that time. But I had to move, to accomplish something.

There was little reason in anything I had done or planned to do. Cool Reason is not a native Irish goddess, and I became more Irish every day. Which is really a poor excuse for myself, wandering around in the night endangering us all, simply because I was in love with the O'Flaherty and wanted to be with him whether it was sensible or not.

I did feel better now that I was outside. Moving across the ground toward the keep, I felt myself in the same world as Tommy, not snugged off in a windowless medieval blockhouse with my imagination roaring at full blast.

There were night sounds all around—predominantly the ocean, of course, like the deep sustained drone of a bagpipe behind the reed chanter's notes that were nocturnal birds and insects and the small secret noises that come from the Irish earth in the dark hours and that may be, for all I know, the forgotten fairies and their kin making revelry in the great labyrinthine halls of their underground palaces. I walked as silently as I could, listening hard for human sounds.

That turned out to be unnecessary. I had passed the tall piece of ivied masonry that was the keep's north wall and nearly reached my goal on the rubbled slope when I heard the whistling, and even if I hadn't been straining my ears I couldn't have missed it, for it was loud and cheerful and it easily overrode the other night noises. It came from the landward side of the hill, straight toward me. It was a man, and he was whistling the reel with the lovely name of "The Mooncoin" and doing it very well, with trills and an enormous amount of breath for a man who was climbing a stiff grade. A big man, then? With a big chest?

It couldn't be Tommy acting so incautiously, though his lungs would have been equal to the job. Unless—the thought flicked through my mind like the bitter crack of some demon's lash—unless he had found Quinn and killed him, and was joyous over it. Unless he *was* all of a piece, and wholly immoral.

That idea was into my head and out in the space of one heartbeat. That was nonsense.

I turned and leaped down the open fall of the land, dodged a patch of rock-strewn ground, dashed across a spread of grass all black-green under the moon, and went to earth behind the northern wall of the keep, about twenty-five or thirty feet from the eastern end where the Blakes and Tommy had dug their first tunnel to the empty storeroom. I was, that is, actually within the keep itself, though only stumps and peaks and rotten tusks of stone rose from the earth to mark where most of the walls had stood. I lay on my face in tall dew-soaked grass growing out of earth that was more puddle than dirt, until I could no longer breathe; then I propped myself on my elbows and waited, shivering, watching down along the shadows of the ragged limestone barricade, while my sweater and long skirt sopped up all the cold water beneath me.

I knew whom I was waiting for.

The whistling was clearer; he had crested the rise and was coming down in my direction. How I wanted to run! But he would have heard and seen me at once, and his legs were longer and stronger than mine.

There was an odd fraction of time in which I experienced the queer sensation of having suddenly splintered, so that part of me was watching in dismay as another part tried to run and a third told it not to, and a fourth cocked an ear toward the approaching enemy and a fifth shrieked mutely for Tommy and Balor to appear and a sixth kept saying monotonously over and over in my mother's voice that the ground was too wet to lie here long. . . .

I was as near to schizophrenia in that instant as I'll ever be. The pieces of Grania came together with a brisk snap and I was me again, clutching my great silver torch (which I hadn't used yet) and listening as the man's shoes crunched over broken rock and then squished onto boggy soil and the whistle went on and on and at last stopped in the middle of a trill, as the footsteps halted too, and there was absolute stillness and I heard him sniff. And sniff, and be silent, and blow his nose and inhale sharply. He was standing so close to me, with the chin-high wall between us, that I could hear the cloth rustle as he stuffed his handkerchief back into his pocket. There was no wind moving at all. He said, softly as though to himself, "Violets."

There was surprise, and pleasure, and a perfectly loathsome wickedness in the sound of the single word. I don't think that the finest actor I ever knew could have managed to put so much into those three innocent syllables.

I could have bitten my tongue bloody with the anger at myself that shook me then. If I hadn't freshened my scent that afternoon out of sheer vanity, he would have passed me by, he would never have known that I was out in the night. The man had the nose of a damned bloodhound.

"Grania," said the voice, a little louder and with the malevolence gone, "where are you, girl dear? Come here. It's Quinn."

I know it's Quinn, you hateful brute.

"Afraid? Away with that, you surely don't think I believe you're in it with them? They've fooled you, Grania love, that's all; they've told you lies about me and you're afraid. That's without sense. Would *I* harm you? I am the law, Grania."

In your twisted mind, I thought, *you are indeed. What you want is what's right to you, whether God and man approve or not.* I lay there in the grass and felt tears of fury and (yes) pity for him running down my cheeks among the splashes of dew.

There was a small snick of noise. A shaft of yellow-white light prowled vividly over the tops of the stones above me, then along the ground within the keep but past me toward the center. "Grania, where are you? You must not hide, girl, you must let me send you safe to the town." He chuckled, such a normal healthy sound that it startled me. "Between you and me and Jack Mum, I've a dozen men on the cliffs at this minute. We're going to take the Dog Fox and his pack. There may be shooting. Let me send you out of it first, Grania, my *peely cuit bán*, my dear silly innocent Grania."

I tried to burrow deeper into earth that despite its liquid content would not accept me further. The bean of his flashlight shot here and there, but evidently the wall was too high for him to lean over far enough to get it onto me. The masonry was so badly shattered here, I saw, that only the outer shell of the wall and part of its rubble-mortar core remained standing. A good push might send it all down on him. But he'd hear me moving.

"This is beyond reason," he said. "I order you to come here. You know fine that I can nose you out if I must."

Well, I was sure he couldn't do that, anyway; a man may have a phenomenal sense of smell, but he cannot follow a trail of scent as though he were a questing animal. Griffin was bluffing. If I lay quiet long enough, he would think that I'd gone, that only my violet fragrance hung in the air.

I began to pray that this would happen.

Then he stepped over a ridge of weed-grown wreckage about six yards down the landward side of my wall and his light shot forward and pinned me like a frozen rabbit crouched in her form.

"Ah, there you are," he said jovially. "What a ridiculous sight you do look, Grania love. Especially when one remembers you in that rose gown. Let me help you up." He started toward me.

There was a lump of ice in my middle the size of a football, and I wasn't aware that my mind was working in any way whatever; but if I'd thought out the plan for an hour I couldn't have improved it, because there is just so much you can do in such circumstances. I clicked on my own torch and aimed it directly into his eyes, using the extreme limit of my peripheral vision with my head tilted to one side so that his light wouldn't blind me. I shoved up to my feet slowly, obviously reluctant to move, the torch held hip-high. He came toward me with that marvelous grace of movement, squinting into the brilliance.

"No need for two, dear girl, put that out," he said easily, reaching for me as he came. I held the beam steady on his face till the last possible microsecond. Then I snapped off my torch and swung it up as hard as I could, smashing it into his own and sending it flying with a crunch and tinkle of bent metal and broken glass that sounded like two instantaneously dead flashlights to me. At once I brought the long tube slashing down again in a desperate sweep at his face, but he'd jerked his head back and I thought I only grazed his chin. Hurling it at him sidearm, I leaped as far and fast as I could to my right, shot past him like a scared cat scrambling away over slick mud, swarmed up the rampart of cold, wet, moss-skinned stone where it was down to waist level, panic snapping at my heels, and jumped into space and lit running, hearing some part of the keep's wall rock and then fall in my wake. I had a fine start on him, with luck both torches were broken, and it might be eight or ten seconds before he could see by moonlight as well as I, in spite of his possible Irish owl vision.

There had been a single bawl of rage behind me. Now I ran in silence, my own footfalls obscuring the sound of his—if, indeed, he was coming for me yet.

I reached the corner of the north and west walls, and saw the big black hole, the vice that led down to the ancient kitchens of Dragon's keep. I stopped here to listen, holding my panting to the minimum, looking over my shoulder, gauging the time it would take me to reach the den. Then I heard him coming down the ruin toward me, swearing and hurrying, very close though I couldn't see him. And as I wavered, a taut sort of rabbity fascination holding me there, I saw his head and shoulders in silhouette against the stars, all but within reach. Without any drive now but stark fear, I dived into the open pit beside me, slid and went down on the second step with a jolt that seemed to crack my kneecaps, scrambled up and groped wildly for the central pillar, found its dank rough surface at my right side, and plunged downward as fast as I could go, down into an empty burrow that had no second exit.

The clever, clever prey pouncing directly into the trap, all of its own volition.

Yet I could never have beaten him to the den. I'd had no choice.

My feet accustomed themselves, after two more falls, to the shortness of the worn stone treads and the distances and angles of the spiraling descent. The blackness was pure and absolute. The horror of my first night on Moher, when I had almost walked into the sea, returned; yet because I knew who was on my heels, it was somehow easier to bear than that ghastly experience had been. And I knew where I was going, while Quinn did not. I recognized that my brains were still functioning, even if they were almost gelid with dread.

Down, down, how far was it? I began to wait for the sickening, jarring moment when you reach the bottom of a flight of steps and don't know it and go down and there *is* no down; when it came at last, I felt that I would vomit with the suddenness of it, though there was no pain at all.

I recovered and stood as still as possible, taking my bearings in the blind midnight of that terrible great crypt. I had stood here only a few hours ago, looking at the double fireplace on my right. But had I moved out into the room then, turning one way or the other before looking at them and at the emptiness and the rust marks on the floor and hearth, the small heaps of metallic rubbish and lumber dust? Or had I remained where I was now, at the very foot of the staircase?

The fireplaces were the only shelters here, such as they were. If Quinn had seen me vanish into the stairwell, he would follow me down, there was no doubt of that. His blood was up, as Tommy might have said; the hunt had only begun for him. I had to hide as deep as I could in one of those hearths, and trust that my wrecking of both torches had been thorough enough that he'd have no illumination. Then he'd have to grope around the walls in the dark, and—

Dear God, I must do better than that! Even if he hadn't found and investigated this cellar in the last few hours, and he probably hadn't, my own scant knowledge of them wasn't much advantage. He'd track me by sound and get me if it took all night.

Or perhaps not. He might be afraid to descend that jet-black shaft, for he was superstitious to an unknown but positive degree; he might assume the existence of another entrance, or a warren of rooms down here in which I could safely lose myself. He might anticipate being trapped himself—couldn't I have been the bait for a trap? He might simply wait up there for me to come out. And if he waited till daylight, Tommy would find him, and Balor, and Terence.

I heard a faint noise from above. Bats? No, the enemy, approaching with more care than I had taken.

I walked straight forward across the black room, my arms stretched out before me, aiming a little to my right so that I'd come first to the wall with the fireplaces. My heavy brogues, however careful I tried to be, went clump clump on the dirt-gritty old stones, where once, I imagined, a thick mat of rushes must have been laid fresh every week or two. Echoes from all sides, from the vaulted ceiling above, grunted clumpclumpclump back at me. I was not exactly impersonating the spirit of silence; but he *knew* I was down here, and I must hurry.

I touched cold stone and halted. Were the hearths to right or left? I took a chance on left, and marched that way, my fingers trailing lightly along the wall. After twenty or thirty steps I hesitated: was I going away from them, to the blank far side of the gigantic room? I turned my head, instinctively I suppose, for certainly I could have seen through an aquarium full of India ink more clearly than through the Stygian gloom, and stood irresolute. The echoes dulled and I heard Quinn on the steps. With a violent start, I fled on in the direction I'd been headed. And the wall was abruptly not there.

I stepped back and felt for it, touched it, slid my hand along till it turned a smooth old curve of rock and went at a right angle into the wall. I had found one of the fireplaces. The westernmost one of the pair, in which firedogs and grate had died and left their rusty traces.

I ducked my head—I could not recall how high the things were—and moved onto the hearthstone, keeping one hand on the near wall. I did not penetrate the depths at once, though, but turned and thrust my head out again, staring sightlessly in what I assumed to be the direction of the stairs. And *ahh God!* I saw the faintest flicker of a light touching the rounded column of the vice.

I heard myself gasp from the horror of it, and put my fingers across my mouth so as not to betray myself with a panicky howl. He had another torch. Perhaps one of those pen-sized pocket things.

No. This was no beam, but a shimmer that touched the stone faintly and had no solid core to it, as if a yellow-blue flame were reflecting from some tiny blaze.

That was it precisely. He was carrying a cigarette lighter. He came into view, holding it above his head and studying the treads of the stairs as he came. I remember that I wondered why a man who did not smoke would carry a lighter.

He stopped where I had stopped and glanced around. I could see him plain, but I knew that he couldn't detect me from that distance.

"Well, Grania Kirk," he said, and the roof muttered Kirkirkirk down to us. Abruptly he swore and clicked out his lighter; it must have grown too hot for comfort.

And then he began to speak into the dark, his voice pitched a little higher than usual, and he told me what he would do when he caught me, and what I was, and what—well, I shall not put down the things he said then. They were sick, vile, and even the echoes came back warped and blurred, as though the old kitchen ghosts disdained that sort of language. It was not imaginative profanity of the Irish kind, but the obscenities of the American or English gutter that he was using. I realized that he had been so enraged at my attack and escape, perhaps most at the violent swipe I'd taken at the great irresistible Griffin, that for the moment he had lost all grip on himself.

The foulness of the words splashed at me like the putrescent filth that the albatross had spewed out. He was turning this ancient chamber into a sewer. I had never felt more defiled. I put my hands tight over my ears, then snatched them away—I dared not deprive myself of the only useful sense I had left in this black hole. Even Quinn's besmirching words must be endured rather than that. They went on and on amid the racketing echoes.

I had to stop him. It was not a sensible wish, the words could not harm me and I stood in peril of my life if he caught me, but somehow I must make him shut up, now, *now*, or I would be violently ill and betray myself to his knife, or gun, or hands.

Because the lips that were forming those repulsive sounds had kissed my lips not so many days before.

Simultaneously, while I felt my gorge stir in my throat and try to rise, I realized two things: first, that I could not locate him by the noises he was making, which seemed to come from everywhere because of the vast vault and the jumbled echoes, and so neither could he find me by ear; second, that I had no weapons except my carcass, which his outweighed by nearly two to one, and my talent. Which was acting.

I could act at him. And he was mad, quite mad, and perhaps I might work on that madness.

So I screamed.

It was a very protracted scream, comprising all the theatrical screams I'd ever heard; once I had begun it I could not seem to end it, and I found myself for some reason backing deeper into the cave of the fireplace, till my head knocked on a projecting shelf and I stopped moving; then I realized the danger of hysteria, and let the shriek dwindle away into a gurgle.

The enclosure had acted as a megaphone, funneling the

cry out and intensifying it until it hit the great vaulted chamber like the skirling of all the old banshees who ever existed. I crept forward and listened to it clamor and yell and pile up on itself in a shrill hullabaloo that whirled and whipped the dead dank air of the underground kitchen into a maeslstrom of sound. I could not recognize my own tones in it. Gripping the vertical edge of the fireplace, I peered out, waiting. The hideous chorus finally came to its close.

There was absolute stillness.

I could hear, then, the blood pumping in my ears, the harshness of my breathing. For the first time I was aware of the discomforts of my body, the thick wet skirt flopping against my bare legs, the sweat ice-cold on my face, the dew-soaked hair swirled close around my throat, and the dull pain of knees and shins where I'd barked them on the stair.

Quinn snapped on his lighter again. I could see him by its spectral glimmer, his head cocked and the blue eyes glaring impotently out across the room. I doubt that his vision carried farther than eight or ten feet, or that he could even see the suggestion of the nearest wall, let alone the fireplaces. He turned his face from side to side, and the expression was one of rising fear.

"Do not do that again," he said quietly. But his voice quavered.

I'd got to him! I had, I had!

A less experienced actress, I think, would have repeated the screech and so diminished its effect. This time I laughed. Terence's mention of Sydney Greenstreet that afternoon must have put the beginning of it into my head, for I started with that marvelous chuckling basso grunt of his: *huh ... huh huh ... hah!* My voice has plenty of range and flexibility and I used it; I went on and did Lorre's crazy giggle, and a couple of cinematic variations, and ended with a full-bellied ho-ho-ho laugh that would have done credit to Alan Hale playing Little John.

My stalker peered around as the reverberations bounded wildly, and his eyeballs were almost lying on his cheeks. I saw something in his face then that seemed to explain Quinn Griffin to me, through and through. When he had a grip on himself, he could be a charming and obviously intelligent man. But there was a child alive in the man, a child he had never managed to be rid of; and that was the source of his insanity, for the child, as some few are, was born twisted and bad—as though it had quoted Milton's Satan in the womb, "Evil, be thou my good"—and when the child took control, its monstrous egocentricity dominated the man. Which would also account for the almost childlike terror which Tommy had said overcame Quinn after violent action.

That's likely far too simplified to be exactly true, and psychiatrists would sneer at it. But I know that it was a hateful, terrified child who yelped, dropped the hot lighter, wrapped his hand in a handkerchief, picked the lighter up still burning, and came out into the room, saying in a whine, "Please, stop that, don't do that," again and again.

In his other hand he now held an automatic pistol.

I retreated. By ill chance he was heading almost directly for me. Instead of buying myself time, I seemed to have shortened it.

Frantically I groped at the walls of the fireplace, finding that projection I'd hit a minute before; it was a stone, or perhaps brick, bracket, solid, extending all along the back, angling outward toward me till it ended just above my head. I felt at its edge and part of the flat top. This was what is called a smoke shelf, and recalling our old hearth at home on Market Street in Freeport, I realized that in front of the smoke shelf, in the throat of the fireplace, there should be a damper (had they been invented, back then?), above which would be the smoke chamber and then the flue of the chimney.

Stupidly, I had never even considered the fact that (1) existence of fireplace = (2) existence of chimney.

And chimneys, provided they aren't too broad, can be climbed.

The damper, if there had been one, had long since rusted to red scrapings along with the iron pothooks, crane, firedogs, pokers, grate, chains, turnspits, and whatever else had once been in daily use in this huge cavity at the heart of the kitchen. I gripped the smoke shelf and tried to pull myself upward, as though I were chinning myself. Grit and sharp fragments bit into my fingertips and the heels of my hands. I lifted my body a foot or so off the hearth and then slipped loose, thrashing wildly with my legs, and fell with a thump.

On the instant, Quinn Griffin fired. The shot was a slamming grinding crash, as though one of those brutal crushing machines had compressed an automobile into a three-inch cube. The succeeding imitations of shots came back like a dying machine gun, and frayed away into tatters of flat horrible sound. I bit something, and thought it was my heart, but it was only my tongue.

He must have fired at random. The darkness was absolute within the fireplace. As swiftly as my hands would work, I unbuckled my belt and stepped out of my heavy wool maxiskirt, slung it onto the shelf, untied my brogues and shed them, pushed them up with the skirt, and tried the chinning stunt again. Without the sodden drag of the green cloth and thick shoes, I swung up easily enough and after some flailing hooked a foot over the smoke shelf and huddled onto it, shuddering. Squatting there, I shoved my bundle of skirt and belt and brogues to the back of the ledge, and tried standing up. It was all right: I could stand tall without bumping my skull. I was in the flue.

I heard a voice say, quite muffled, "I'll kill you, I'll kill you!" and knew that it was still the child who sought me, the malignant child who must destroy what it feared. I had frightened all the intelligence out of him by then, I believe. To any balanced adult, my shriekings and cacklings would have been laughable.

But if the idiot child came into the fireplace, he would see me, or at least my naked legs, standing up here as plain as day; and the child had a deadly weapon in his fist. I pawed out desperately to one side and the other, found the wall of the chimney on my left (I was facing toward the room), edged carefully sideways and touched the opposite wall, and calculated that they were at least six feet apart. If the damn thing was square, I was finished. You can't climb a six-foot-square channel when you're only five feet nine.

Another shot made me jerk back in panic. God knows at what Griffin thought he was firing.

I slapped the stones behind me to get my bearings, put both hands forward and discovered that from front to back the flue was no more than a yard deep. I had never done any mountain climbing, but I knew that if you set your back against one wall and your feet on the other, you could ascend a crevice fairly easily. I kicked out with one green-socked foot and could not find anything solid. That startled me so badly that I had a moment of nauseating vertigo, and clutched the stone flue at my back with both sweaty palms. Again I reached out a hand cautiously and touched the wall in front of my chest; knelt slowly, dragging my fingers down the rough damp surface until at about knee level it suddenly vanished. Then I knew that the front of the smoke chamber merely slanted forward at that height, to end a few feet out at the opening of the fireplace.

I lifted one knee breast-high and put out my foot and felt it flatten out comfortably against a good solid wall.

I heard Quinn calling to me, loud and plaintive and far too shrill for any fleck of rationality to be left. I looked down and saw what I took to be the reflection of his lighter's flame. I squashed my back firmly against the wall and swung up my other leg and, braced firmly in the chimney, I hung there some eight feet above the great hearth. I took a long deep breath, which must have been the first one in a quarter of an hour, and stepped upward with my left foot and then with my right and inched my shoulders up, wriggling and twisting, until I had risen a little higher. And there I stuck. I could not summon either the energy or the funk to force my body onward. I seemed to have used up my adrenalin.

J'y suis, j'y reste.

After the small rattlings and scufflings of my climb, the silence now was so thick that it matched the blackness in its intensity. Whatever I had or had not seen below me, it was gone now. I was in Poe's untenanted burial chamber once more.

Trembling from the strain of shoving at the walls with all the force of my legs and shoulders while gripping for support with my fingers, I tried to relax. I might have to remain in this ghastly position for hours. The bare thought tensed me again. Deliberately I began to loosen the muscles from taut neck downward. I found that I could prop myself in the chimney with only the power of my thighs, and gradually managed to do so without the sudden nervous jerks of calves and back that made my stomach turn over.

The odors of antiquity far below ground level—dust and damp, ageless stone and unmoving air—pervaded the flue. At least Quinn's phenomenal nose would do him no good here.

Nothing happened.

My socks grew damp, then really wet, from the rough

rock on the soles. Somewhere above me, in the ravaged walls of the keep, there was a path that rainwater could take to reach the clogged chimney and thence the kitchens. No wonder everything of iron had rusted. I remembered our snug, dry den; *that* was construction. I imagined that Cromwell's men had spared it because it was plain and hardly noticeable, set into its hillock. There was a temptation to think about the den rather than the death who was seeking for me.

I looked at my watch. Somewhere, in one of the hectic spasms of my flight, I had smashed the crystal to shards, and one of the luminous hands was missing; the other glowed helplessly at me out of the enveloping night.

How would I know when morning came?

Oh, well. I was prepared to stay where I was until the middle of next week if necessary, so long as Quinn Griffin was prowling the kitchen.

Where was he? I could hear nothing. Had my ridiculous impersonation of the Phantom of Dragon's Keep driven him aboveground? Possibly. How was I to know?

I shifted restlessly. I was not to know. The only thing I dared do was stay right where I was.

My legs ached, not badly yet, but with irritable promise of pain to come.

I looked at the pitiful hand of my broken watch again, holding it before my nose, solely in order to see *something*.

Think about items of interest. Rescue the mind from itself. Think of Tommy. Is he all right, is he safe, is he alive? That isn't the way to stay sane. What about Terence's old song, written by the bard of Bran Roe O'Conor? Hunt for clues to the treasure.

The treasure seemed as remote and unimportant as Studio D in New York with its monitor screens, yapped camera cues, frantic casting directors, control booth, actors and producers wrapping up the show. . . .

Unquestionably the Black Velvet Gang were all dreamers, and their treasure a will-o'-the-wisp.

My knees hurt.

What did the song say? "He would seal them up . . . set sentinels to watch . . . hide the compartment from every prying eye . . ."

I was jolted, really physically jarred, as an idea struck me—yes, struck, was not formed by my own intellect but occurred to me in the same way that an accident occurs to one from outside the body. And it was so obvious a thought that not only could I take no credit for it, I actually felt ashamed that I had not reasoned it out hours before.

It was just then that Quinn Griffin walked into the fireplace below me.

I stared down between my legs at him, aghast and trembling so hard that I could hear my teeth rattle. He stood there, holding his flickering lighter over his head, and looked around the hearth, the "angel of the darker drink" himself, ten feet straight down from his terrified quarry.

I clenched my jaws and stopped breathing. He stepped back, he was turning, and a thought came to him and he pivoted and lifted the lighter and went to his toes to stare at the smoke shelf. He knew fireplaces, too. I waited in clammy dread for him to spot my cast-off skirt and shoes, or to raise his head a short distance and see me watching him, spread helpless, ridiculous, totally vulnerable in the chimney.

He turned and walked out of the fireplace.

I will never know how he came to overlook the clothes. Either they merged with other dark lumps of shadow, or he was peering higher where he'd expected me to be standing, or the flame had by then distorted his vision.

"Grania, you *briochtóg*," I heard him mutter, "where in hell's name have you got to?"

The child finally suppressed, he was recovered, in command again, but he still meant to kill me. I exhaled. My legs twinged severely. I did not move at all.

It was only a matter of time until the cramps and stiffness became so bad that I would lose control of my legs and fall, paralyzed, down on the hearth. The racket would be awful. I tried to console myself by recognizing that I would likely break my neck in the drop.

Quinn exclaimed angrily. He must have been standing right outside. I heard a click, then a series of clicks. He said, "Lord save us!" under his breath, an uncharacteristic remark; then he suddenly shouted, wordlessly, furiously, and I heard metal clink twice on stone below me.

By the time the echoes were fading, I had comprehended it: his lighter had burnt away all its fuel, and in a rage he had flung it into the fireplace.

I thought that through the last reverberations I caught the sound of footsteps quietly moving away. My legs were going from raw agony to numbness, well before I'd anticipated it. If I didn't move soon, I would be immobilized in this flue, unable to move down except by a dangerous lurch and sprawl. I had to chance his hearing me. I had to.

I *must.*

I could not. I couldn't get my legs to budge, I couldn't draw one back and place the foot lower on the wall and slide gradually toward the smoke shelf, I tried and tried, almost shrieking with the mortal fright of my position, I could not, I could not do it, I would never be able to descend, but I must, but I could not, but I *must.*

I pulled one dead limb away from its place and the other began to buckle, and my hands ground themselves into the rock behind as I kicked violently and hopelessly forward and attained another foothold. I was beaten; it had been the last effort I could possibly make.

Quinn Griffin had won, then. I would lie on the hearth with my spine snapped and die hideously of pain and thirst while Tommy and the Blakes worried about me and Quinn stalked them in turn, the odds against him cut down.

I was sliding slowly, slowly down the back wall. I have no idea how I did it. The way I was jammed into that horrible chimney, incapacitated from the hips down, it was obviously impossible for me to stir. Yet I did.

My knees were, from the little I could feel of them, on a level with my face. It was time to lower the feet again.

My curled toes were sending muffled messages of cramp along pinched nerves to my brain.

Slap, crunch, I'd done it.

I did not fall.

I was going to win.

Merciful God, I was going to get out!

After another period of snail's progress I had lowered my body, with the sweater riding up and the skin tearing itself to strings on that rough stone, and my backbone apparently cutting right through the flesh, till it was time to drop my legs again; and when I did, one heel jerked forward into space because there was nothing there, and that was nearly the end of me. I had reached the forward angle of the front wall of the smoke chamber. Forcing my other foot into firm contact with the solid stone and shoving my back from head to hip the other way, I groped down with my poor moribund leg and heard, rather than felt, the shelf smack soggily against the sole of my mushy sock.

I stood there, like some silly stork, for a number of uncountable seconds or minutes, and at last, with a prayer, lowered the second leg. I swayed forward without volition, saving myself from a face-grinding smash at the last instant by throwing out my hands. Then I was paralyzed once more, and leaned there over the unseen hearth, resting my forehead on cold dank hardness, listening to my breath whistle and whimper in my throat.

I'd made it.

By that time my brains must have been as petrified as my legs, for I have no memory of the next movements. I came to myself lying flat on my back along the smoke shelf, with needles sticking everywhere, suffering the twinges and shooting pangs of the circulation restoring itself to my much-abused body. Eventually I began to notice the terrible coldness and the black silence, and realized that I was better. There was gnawing fire in my back, and my legs would not feel like walking for weeks, but I was alive, in one bleeding piece, and I had beaten Quinn Griffin.

If he was gone.

I sat up, groaning with the intense discomfort of motion, swung my legs over the edge and almost dropped to the hearth, recalling in the last possible flick of time that my skirt and brogues were crammed against the back of the shelf. If I hadn't stopped myself with a frantic twitch, I'd have had to go back to the den half-naked, for nothing could have forced my wretched muscles to lift me off the floor of the fireplace one more time. I groped and found the wet garment, one shoe and at last the other; thought of the two-yard drop, rolled onto my face and shoved my lower half into space. Wriggling as a wounded earthworm might, I went back and down until I was supporting myself on my forearms. Then I gave one final heroic heave, and fell a couple of feet and struck the flat; and wobbled and stood on two legs that felt like pillars of sodden spaghetti threaded with dry ice. But I stood. I was back in the world again. Pain had even made me forget to be afraid of being so far below the surface of the earth.

I clambered, floundering a great deal, into my skirt, and

buckled the belt with sore, shaking fingers. I put on one brogue and couldn't find the other. After I'd hunted all over the hearth, I put my hand up to the shelf, halfheartedly, and discovered it perched on the edge where I'd dropped it. I stepped into it and without tying it, fumbled my way out of the fireplace.

If Quinn had been there and flashed a light on my face, I don't believe I'd have had the energy to retreat into that dismal cavern; I'd have stood helpless and let him murder me. But he was not there.

I listened, my mouth hanging open, for a count of twenty, and there was no sound but the pulse thumping away again in my ears. Taking a bearing as best I could in the godforsaken blackness, I started toward the vice and the upper air.

I made it without a hitch. In three minutes I felt the blessed salt air on my face, and the light of the lowering quarter-moon seemed as marvelous and clear as sunrise.

I halted just before coming out of the shadow of the pit. Any sensible madman, I reminded myself, would be waiting to ambush me out there. Should I wait for Tommy, or more likely Balor, to discover me? Then I heard the O'Flaherty saying in my retentive memory, "He'll be gone—it's his way—he's bold and then he's frightened, and runs away." Surely his neurosis, his superstitious belief in the walkers of the night, would have him on the way home by now?

If he was waiting, I couldn't help it. I had no reserves of patience or bravery left. I walked out into the moonlight and stood there. Nothing moved but a flight of wakeful birds. I was alone.

The wind was calm, but there was another storm coming. I heard its muted thunder over below the western horizon.

11

Too late, too late are they!
—Roddy McCorley

I KNOCKED GENTLY, put my mouth close to the keyhole and said, "It's Grania." I thought I heard Balor woof, muffled, but not for sure; then the key turned and the oak swung inward. I limped into the dark little box. "Well," I said, with a fleeting realization that I was being redundant, "I'm home."

The rock panel slid shut behind me. The door was locked, I was in solid blackness once more, and I thought, for the first time, *What if it's Quinn?* and my flesh crawled; but the wet nose of the great hound pressed into my palm and I knew it was all right. Alanna pumped and lit the Coleman and Tommy took me by the shoulders and glared into my face.

"I'm back no more than two minutes, and in that time I've aged ten years. I knocked over the tea-kettle contraption and nearly gave Terry a stroke. Where in hell have you been?"

"In the kitchens."

They all three said, "What!"

"Look," I said, all at once so weary that even my relief at Tommy's safety seemed diluted, "my back needs iodine, and I have to rest."

Terence guessed, "You've met your man the albatross again?"

"What happened?" said Tommy.

Alanna pushed at them and said, "Lie down with your faces to the wall, both of you, while I see to her," and brought her medicine kit to the low fire while I pulled my sweater inside out over my head, noticing that there was blood on the wool. I stepped out of my skirt and kicked off the brogues, and gave myself like a flabby rag doll into her hands. She laid me face down on the traveling rug and sponged my wincing back. "Oh, not nearly so bad," she said cheerfully. "It won't even need bandaging, you've only scratched off a square yard of skin. . . . What *were* you doing, and why in the kitchens?"

"Hiding from Quinn. He's crazy," I said, "you were right. And he has a gun. He shot at me twice."

"Griffin did this?" she asked.

"Did what?" demanded Tommy.

"No, I did that climbing the chimney to hide from him."

"Scratched up her back, that's all," said Alanna, as Tommy continued to mutter. "It's nothing at all. Never mind it. Did he go away, then?"

"Yes, after his lighter ran out of steam. He'd been using it as a torch."

"How much sense does this make to you, Dog?" Terence asked.

"Not any more than enough, I tell you," said Tommy with gloomy resignation. "Modesty alone prevents me from turning and shaking the facts out of her."

"This won't feel as bad as a sunburn by tomorrow," Alanna said, beginning to paint me with stinging antiseptic.

"Shins, too," I said, "and knees, and my palms." I brought a hand into sight and discovered with mild surprise that, though dented badly, it was scarcely bloody. "It did hurt," I said, defensive.

Tommy began audibly grinding his teeth. "Grania, in chronological order, in short words, in simple declarative sentences, will you tell me what happened?" he said tightly.

So I did. Alanna rolled me over and inspected my knees, which looked as if I'd been rollerskating all evening on the sidewalk with a pack of rough little boys. When I'd finished my story, Tommy said, "You are very brave, and very resourceful, and very determined, and very silly."

"Thanks," I said. "I know."

"He did not touch you, then?"

"No, though he would have, and killed me, undoubtedly, if I hadn't broken that torch. He wasn't being at all careful, because—well, I guess he never thought I'd have the nerve to attack him first."

"So you accept my statement that the man is—"

"A March hare," I said. "Yes. I saw it, I heard it."

"Good. Then tomorrow you go to Tipperary."

I swallowed two capsules that Alanna gave me, and laughed, a somewhat rickety sound. I knew that with the warmth and safety I had rapidly grown drowsy, and that these were going to put me under in a hurry. "You won't send me away," I said. "Not now."

"Why will I not? You cannot follow orders, you risk your life and mine for a bloody whim—"

"It isn't a whim to want to help."

"How? By clawing his eyes out?"

"You don't have to be sarcastic. I couldn't stand the thought of you out there alone."

He said something under his breath, I think in Gaelic.

"You won't send me away," I repeated.

"Why will I not?"

"The booty," I said, my words slurring a little now. "The store of Bran Roe."

"What of it?"

"I can tell you where it is. And I think . . . think I can tell you with . . ."

"With what?" Tommy asked, as my voice trickled away. "Alanna, has she fainted? Is she hurt worse than you're telling me?"

"No. She's exhausted. Let her sleep."

"No," I said. "I'm okay." I wasn't, though. I could not keep my eyes open, and Alanna was going to have to put me to bed, I was slipping off into—

"Oh!" I said, jerking awake. "With assurance. I can tell you with assurance that it hasn't been disturbed since the Dragon put it there." I remembered a similar line from "Little Boy Blue." I murmured, "Since the Dragon kissed them and put them there. . . ." Then, in the middle of what I must tritely describe as a thunderstruck silence on the part of my audience, I fell sound asleep.

They were wonderful. Even after a full winter of misery, exploded hopes, and near-abandonment of the whole expedition; even though (as Terence told me later) they believed that I actually was onto the actual location of their goal; even though they were suddenly festering with bewilderment, curiosity, and anticipation—they did not waken me. Alanna finished dressing my minor wounds, put my prettiest pajamas on me, and somehow maneuvered me into a sleeping bag.

They talked a while, I imagine, quietly among themselves, and likely had a final cup of their eternal tea, and then lay down themselves to toss and turn and speculate.

I slept like a stone for a while, and then gradually began to have scraps and flickers of dream; mainly acted out in partial darkness, and leaving only a residue of uneasiness behind, as though I'd been told not to remember something but was trying to do so nonetheless. I think I woke once or twice, but so briefly and hazily that not much registered on my mind except faint noises from far away. Then I found myself in the middle of a full roaring nightmare.

It began with a song that Grandmother used to sing to me, one called "The Pride of Ulster," about Red Macha the legendary queen of the North. I was walking in the ruins of the keep, with the song on the sound track, as it were, in a man's deep voice. It was light, but not daylight. I would describe it as manipulated lighting, in the argot of my profession. The mutilated shell of the keep stood out against deep-green backgrounds of indeterminate character, its horrid and magnificent walls very pale and mostly stripped of their mantles of ivy, lichen, and moss. The ground was strewn with dressed rocks and stone slabs, and these seemed to be moving slyly behind my back as I walked, though I was afraid to glance over my shoulder at them. I was waiting for something to happen.

The singing faded away, and I heard the wheels of some vehicle coming toward me from the direction of O'Brien's Tower. Then Quinn Griffin took my arm and said urgently, "We'd best take you away out of this, my love, there's another of the troubles coming."

We were back from the scene, standing together out on the brink, and up over the crest from the south came an enormous golden chariot drawn by two matched stallions and driven by a monumental figure of a woman. A spotlight held on them as they plunged down toward the keep. Quinn murmured in my ear, "Macha Mhong Ruadh, 300 B.C., the first Irish queen. Now we'll see action."

She was magnificent. Disdaining a charioteer, she drove her team herself with one hand, while in the other she brandished a long silver-and-gold spear with flames licking up along its length. On her rein arm she wore a round shield studded with crystal and garnets. She was dressed in long robes of royal purple and white, and between her breasts hung a gigantic emerald; but no diadem or crown confined the great flying mass of vivid red hair that streamed on the wind behind her. The coats of the stallions were of the same color as her hair, as though dyed with claret.

Her face was long and full and startling white, with impatience and pride and fury in it. Her eyes were also large emeralds, which did not surprise me.

Opening her mouth, she gave a piercing cry of defiance. At this cue, the Dread Women began to fly in at her from beyond the keep. And Red Macha charged into the ruins—which were considerably more extensive now than I'd realized, covering several acres—with her flame-spear raised in her hand, and spitted first one and then another as they swooped toward her. They evaporated as she struck them, with wails of rage.

"Grandmother told me about this," I said to Quinn. He put his arm around me. "Wait," he said, "she never knew what came after."

The Harpies lifted away from the queen, who clattered the fiery lance against her shield with vexation. In a vast flock they wheeled in the air and dived behind one of the towering crenelated battlements. Red Macha whipped her chariot round and galloped straight toward it. And along the top appeared the heads of many dark-faced men.

Quinn pressed me close. "They are the villains," he said; "they are the merciless I.R.A. boyos."

"You were one once," I said. We were like two people talking at a drive-in. The spectacular charge continued.

"I was not," said Quinn indignantly. "Another lie of the Dog Fox. I was always with the police."

"Tommy says you're crazy."

He smiled broadly. "Grania, hasn't it occurred to you that madmen always believe others to be mad, and themselves sane? Just think of the Dog Fox in that light. If he's thwarted, might not his calm strength become the fanatic power of a maniac? He's admitted his insatiable greed. Isn't that the beginning of a dirty kind of insanity?"

I nodded. "But why did you chase me in the kitchen?"

"To steal a kiss," he said primly. That seemed to make sense. I looked at the I.R.A. men. They had begun to shoot at Queen Macha, and some were throwing gelignite bombs that exploded beneath her chariot wheels. "Armalite rifles," said Quinn, "M-1 rifles, .303 rifles. Semi-automatic carbines. Yet the Marxist Official wing opposes violence. Here he comes now."

Like the hero appearing on the battlements to lead his band to victory, Tommy sprang into sight high over the queen's head. She shook her lance at him. The bombs detonated around them, and Tommy leaped down the fifty-foot wall and caught her by the waist to pull her from the chariot.

"He wants her crown," said Quinn with disgust. "That's grave robbing. All your friends are grave robbers."

"She's not wearing a crown."

"See what I mean?" he said. "The man's mad."

Tommy was in the chariot now; he had flung the tall woman to the ground and his men were bombarding her with bullets and shells, all of which seemed to miss. She lay there, her face contorted with hate, as he drove her matched pair in a tight circle and came directly toward us. I suddenly realized that I wasn't watching the performance, I was in it; I screamed. Quinn faded away, laughing. And then, amid a perfect pandemonium of explosions, the mighty Cliffs of Moher came folding in across the scene like theater curtains closing, cutting off my view, and I struggled and thrashed and woke up.

Tommy was saying my name repeatedly. His arms were around me and his cheek on mine. I went dead quiet until I'd shaken the effects of the dream, and all of a sudden there was another burst of gelignite bombs and rapid firing, and I shrieked.

"It's all right, Grania, you're only—"

"That was no dream."

"That was thunder."

I drew back a little in the dark, and then pressed myself into his embrace. "I thought it was you and the I.R.A."

"It sounds more like a battle of the Red Branch knights," he said. "Listen and you'll hear the crash of swords and axes and the rending of slashed mail. It's a peevish morning out there."

"Is it morning already?"

"Only about three. Plenty of time for sleep yet."

"I had a nightmare," I said. "All made up of you and Quinn and Terry's song about Red Macha's gold-and-crystal crown, and Grandmother's stories, and the Dread

Women." I thought. "Quinn said that you were a grave robber."

He chuckled almost silently. "Bank robber would be more to the point, but the bank closed more than seven hundred years ago."

It was safe in his arms. "I don't want another dream like that."

"I shouldn't worry. It's a quick storm and it's passing now. If only you wouldn't go roaming about on your own, you wouldn't collect material for nightmares. Promise you won't do it again."

"I promise," I said. I breathed a few times and fell asleep in his arms, and did not dream again.

When I woke the next time they were ready to feed me breakfast, with Balor's head on my knees and his one eye watching my every motion. They talked about the weather (which was marvelous again), and inquired after my injuries (which were insignificant), and told me that there was no sign of Quinn Griffin or his hypothetical men (which was fine with me). Once Terence caught my eye, grinned, and said, "Was there ever such a woman for coming home in a sorry condition?" Then as I began to sip at my scalding tea, he said casually, "About the treasure."

"Yes?"

"You believe you know where it is?"

"Oh, yes."

"Then you were not delirious last night?"

"Oh, no."

"Do you think you have the strength to, ah, give us a hint of its location, then?"

"Oh, yes."

"Please do," he said affably. I have never seen such powerful emotion held in such check.

"Well," I said, "what did you tell me this place was originally? I mean our den here."

"An outbuilding of the keep."

"A 'rather unorthodox' one, you said. What was it used for?"

"We don't really know," he said a little blankly. "Perhaps as a hideaway for the owner in case of treachery—supposing he had to go to ground for a while—"

"Even I know better than that. No water supply. And it

was hardly hidden, sitting here between the keep and the outside curtain walls; and it wasn't made for defense."

"She's right," said Tommy. He looked at me. "The oak door is nineteenth century, we know that from its hardware and the key."

"How did you acquire that, by the way?"

"Found it inside, a bit rusty, on a hook above the door. Someone, tinkers or a hermit or some fella wanting privacy for reasons of his own, hung the door about a hundred years ago. The stone slab is much older, probably of Bran Roe's time, and a neat piece of engineering, too; but if you're thinking that *this* was the storehouse, I'm afraid—"

"No," I said, "it was camouflage. I only wondered what Bran Roe might have given as an excuse for building it. A guest house for traveling princes? Granary? Storeroom? Stable? Extra bedroom where he could hide when he felt solitary?"

"We aren't to guess that for certain, I suppose," said Alanna.

"Anyway," I went on, "I'll bet it was smugglers that found it and gave it a lockable door. Remember the spikes on the cliff, that you told me were put there for smugglers to hang their rope ladders on? They could have used this as a temporary storeroom."

"Good thought. They did favor this part of the coast for smuggling in velvet and French wine and brandy, and *smaichtín crón*, which was a kind of tobacco they could show a great profit on."

"Ah, but concerning the man O'Conor," said Terence with patience, "you said 'camouflage,' I think, Grania?"

"Yes. Also, I believe he may have wanted a place to just come and sit alone and dream about the marvelous trinkets he'd squirreled away, so very close by."

"Where?" said the three all together.

"Down there," I said, pointing at the floor. "Right under us."

There was some silence. I drank my tea. "How do you make that out?" Tommy asked dubiously.

"Have you looked into the loo with a bright light?"

"Yes, when we first came. You can't see the bottom."

"You don't need to. Starting at our floor level, it's earth packed solid, just like this"—I thumped the ground beside the hearth—"for at least twenty feet down; then the hole, which that far is absolutely round, goes into an elliptical shape, or is the word I want 'oval'? Like a partly closed eye, anyway. And at that point the material changes from earth to what I think must be rock."

"I don't remember that," said Terence.

"Why is it significant?" asked Tommy.

"Anything is significant in this game," said Terence, and, picking up a torch, went over to the fearsome hole and stared into it. "I can't see ... yes, by Tara's bloody harp, you're right! Why the devil didn't we spot that? We all looked down there."

"You were only looking for the bottom," I said. "You weren't searching for proof that there's another room under this one. You had your minds focused on the keep itself for Bran Roe's depository." I finished my tea. "If you hadn't, you'd have wondered instantly why anyone had ever made a stone room with a twenty-foot-thick floor."

Tommy in his turn was peering down into the heart of the cliffs. "I stood here and dropped a stone," he said slowly, "and watched it out of sight, but I never saw that shape-change at all. I see why, of course; you have to squint like mad to detect it. Still, why does that tell you there's a room below us? It may be a natural formation."

"It is, as long as it's elliptical, but where it turns into a circle, it becomes man-made."

"There are perfect circles in nature," he objected.

"You're more than usually pigheaded this morning, O'Flaherty," said Terence, who was fairly sizzling with excitement. "Now think: suppose this packed earth, right up to this floor, were a normal accretion that's settled, by whatever process earth does settle on rock, over the centuries. Maybe over a million years. That does happen, doesn't it, love? Land levels often rise?"

"Yes, certainly," said Alanna. "Or this may have been where they put the earth that they displaced in digging out the underground parts of the keep, the kitchen and so forth."

"But why would they have kept the damned crack in the rock open?" shouted Terence. "They'd have had to go to a lot of bother for no reason. Put a log in the hole, pack their earth around it, pull out the log at the right time and position it higher, pack the ground very tight so that it wouldn't crumble inward—or if it was simply dirt that built up over an immensely long period, as I was saying, then why would that hole stay open above the fault? And so absolutely flaming *round*?"

"There could be explanations," said Tommy stubbornly. "Is that your evidence, Grania?"

"No. It's only one of the things that struck me last night, while I was in that chimney trying to tear my mind away from discomfort and death."

Before I could go on, Alanna snapped her fingers. "Wait a minute! I know what it means."

"What?" said everyone.

"What was Dragon's Keep erected on top of?"

"The O'Flaherty mote-and-bailey fortress."

"Which would have been—the mote anyway—a mound of very solidly packed earth, which they partially leveled and then dug into to reach the rock for their own foundations. That's what this earth floor is: twenty feet of old O'Flaherty mote." She looked at me and said, "Sorry, dear."

"Would they have kept that hole open when they built up the mote? What for?"

"Not to use as a loo, that's certain," said Terence. "Might it have once been a spring of water? Drying up later—"

"No," I said positively, "because the bottom of it opens into the Atlantic Ocean. I dropped my alarm clock into it and heard it strike the water, and then I heard the waves."

I was observed dubiously. "That would be nearly seven hundred feet down," said Tommy, "and you wouldn't hear anything smaller than an elephant fall in the sea from this distance."

"Acoustics," I said. "Alone in a tight room, with the noise funneling up. I did."

"At any rate, the earth-to-rock thing is a mystery, but it doesn't prove the existence of a room below us—rather disproves it, on the whole, I'd say."

"Obstinate," I said. "Want to hear the rest of it?"

"Go on."

"Well, there I was in the chimney, conscious of nothing around me but rock, and it crossed my mind that if I went tunneling almost directly west, I'd come to the den, only I'd be yards and yards below it; then I remembered the earth that became rock over in that sanitary convenience. I thought the rock was a little higher than the floor of the kitchens, but couldn't be sure because I hadn't measured either place."

"Where the circle becomes an eye *is* higher than the kitchen floor, yes. Likely the rock shelves upward toward the sea, because near that dry-stone wall it's only inches from the surface. They must have gone into the rock when they made that kitchen floor flat."

"Okay, okay, whatever. Anyway," I said, impatient to get to my surprise, "I thought of the loo, and how improbable it would be for them to make this building on top of solid earth and then dig out a narrow shaft that would meet a natural cleft in the rock. And I remembered what else I'd found, and suddenly I had it."

They all stared at me like kids watching a magician who's already produced one dead rabbit, and is reaching into the hat again. None of them spoke. I would now show them.

"I realized, for one thing, what the sentinels—*who* the sentinels were that Bran Roe set to guard his accumulation."

"Who? How? That is," said Terence, "how did you guess who?"

Still doubtful? I thought, grinning to myself. "Well," I said, "because I found one."

"Woman, go on!" shouted Tommy, which made Balor sit up and cock his head. "You're dragging this out to tantalize us!"

"I'm not. I'm trying to take one point at a time. Wait a second." I got up and went behind the turf stack and with some minor creaking of muscles I tugged the long-undisturbed sheet of thin metal aside, its load of sods wobbling as my excavation appeared below. I picked up the ancient skull, carried it over, and put it into the hands of my short-tempered love.

"One of O'Conor's workmen, I'd guess," I said as nonchalantly as I could. "Dead men tell no tales. I found it between the floor of this room and the roof of the treasure room." Then, as he gaped at me and at the skull by turns, I asked Alanna for another mug of tea.

It was my moment, the total justification of the outsider.

Terence was the first to recognize that, and rewarded me in typical Terencian fashion. He went to one knee, took my hand in his, and touched it to his brow. "Lady witch," he said gravely, "I salute you. I don't even need to *see* the said roof; if you tell me it's there I believe you. You are completely magical."

"It was nothing," I said. "One tongue of bat to two newts' tails does the trick every time."

"My God," said Tommy. He rose slowly and walked behind the peat stack, carrying the skull; Alanna followed him with the Coleman lantern. Terence offered me his arm, which I accepted, and escorted me like some *grande dame* to the others, who were looking, mute, at the big squarish cavity I'd dug. "When?" asked Tommy finally.

"The first two days you kept me locked in. I was tunneling out to freedom. And then when I'd gone to Lisdoonvarna and come back, and so many things started to happen, I pretty much forgot about it. Till last night." I pointed out the second layer of flagstones. "Does that make sense as a floor?"

"No," said Alanna, "nor as a ceiling either, but no Irish castle ever conformed in every way to the usual Norman—oh," she exclaimed, turning to me with the golden flecks swimming in her dark-green irises like so many irrepressible little fairy fish, "oh, Grania, you're right, it must be the secret room!"

"You found the skull in there?" Tommy asked.

"Yes, facing out toward the ocean."

"To protect the place from sea gods, I suppose, and your Dread Women." He stared around as though seeing this room for the first time. "There must be others buried all along the walls to ward off thieves approaching from inland, too. Sometimes they'd bury the head of a relative or any enemy, or even one of their own great heroes, to protect a site, though I thought the practice had died out by O'Conor's time." He looked at Terence. "Flint," he said.

"Right," said Terence.

"Flint?" I said.

They both said, "Captain Flint," and Tommy chuckled grimly. "Who went ashore with six fine tall lads, and came back alone . . . *Treasure Island*, my dear. Flint slew his half-dozen, but O'Conor must have done better, or rather worse, by a damned sight. This was a big man, too," he said, hefting the skull. "I wonder if they were his own mercenaries, or farmers recruited by force from the countryside? I wonder if he had half of them kill the others, and then one by one——".

"Don't," I said, shuddering. It had happened seven centuries ago, but the skull made it very immediate to me.

"He was a monster," said Alanna.

"By his own lights, merely practical," said Tommy.

"In the name of my sanity," said Terence, "let's bring the picks and spades!"

"Caution," said Tommy, "self-control, and brainwork first. Council of war. 'Twas impatience killed the silver cat." He turned to me. "You know what convinces me? Not the loo, nor the skull, nor the double rock floor; because the first O'Conors may have built this place and done all those things for some obscure reason. But the man who put two feet of packed earth on a perfectly serviceable floor and brought it up to ground level was after one thing only—concealment. And why make a place seem less well-made than it is, as though he'd stuck four walls down on the ground and let it go at that? *There* is your great and final fact, which indicates something fantastic below."

"Caution, self-control, and blather," exclaimed Terence. "I was convinced by the skull. What sort of plan do we need? Clear away the earth from these two stones, lift them, raise the two beneath and——"

"And what? What manner of construction lies beneath them? Timber beams, wickerwork? Is the ceiling of the crypt flat, or vaulted? Will you drop a ton or two of stone onto all those precious, fragile trinkets?"

"Curse and swear, Lord Kildare!" grumbled Terence, and ran his fingers nervously through his whiskers. "How do we tell?"

"We sit down and think it out calmly, while Grania gets dressed," said the O'Flaherty.

While I scrambled as hastily as I could into jeans and a plaid wool shirt, and got my brogues on all warm and dry from being by the fire, they argued back and forth, drawing quick little diagrams in pencil on the backs of the sheets of their old song, appealing to me, who knew perhaps a thousandth part of what they knew on the subject, falling into silences and bursting out of them to talk all at once. The skull sat on the rock table and stared into the heart of the glowing turf with its grotesque look of comprehension. Balor went to sleep on my feet.

"One more thing they never let me get out of my mouth," I said quietly to the dog, "and that was the song. The old bard referred to 'the lair which held the harvest of so many battles,' and that made me think of us calling this 'the den.' But I won't bother them with trifles. Let 'em argue about stone corbels and skewbacks till they—"

" 'Lair' was likely mere coincidence," said Terence, who had heard me after all. "The bard couldn't have known anything. Unless Bran Roe called it that habitually."

"I thought it was a case of supernatural finger pointing," I said.

"But listen," Alanna was saying for the third or fourth time, "there must have been some provision for an entrance."

"Why? Bran Roe never expected to see his nicky-noos again. 'Set sentinels . . . and hide the compartment from every prying eye of living man,' remember? That must have included his own. Look about this place, darling: where would he have hidden an entrance?"

"Why, in the same place we decided on in the keep," said Tommy. "Behind the fireplace!"

Terence flung himself at the hearth with a shout of expectation. Ignoring the gentle heat, he thrust his body into the opening and banged on the stone of the rear wall. Then he emerged, sucking at his knuckles. "We'll have to begin with it, at any rate," he said. "You can see, now it's been mentioned, that there's really nowhere else possible." His gesture encompassed the whole tiny room.

"Except the loo." Tommy padded over to it, and came back. "No, he could never have got his shoulders into it. Let's try the fireplace."

At the same-moment he and I glanced at the skull and then at each other. "He does seem to be suggesting that, doesn't he?" I said.

"If you care to be mystical, or fanciful, he does." Tommy grinned. "Have I congratulated you on your achievement, Grania Kirk?"

"No. Not a word. But supposition isn't achievement."

He took both my hands in his; the pressure was warm and hard, and I remembered him holding me tight last night from the storm and the nightmare. "I feel in my bones that it's achievement. I am sorry, *croidhe-shearc*," he said, the dark eyes fixed on mine. "I would have thanked you eventually."

"You might even do it now."

He threw back his head and laughed. I did not remember hearing him do that before. It was a lovely sound. "Forgive me, Grania! Under this sullen exterior beats a heart of pure lard, and a brain of the same. I congratulate you. I thank you in behalf of all of us, and of the ghost of poor old Bran Roe O'Conor. I tell you, the only intelligent deed I've done all winter was to kidnap a girl with a real head on her shoulders, and the nerve to try digging herself out right under my nose." I was afraid for a second that he was going to kneel as Terence had, but he took me into his embrace and kissed me hard on the lips. When he drew back, I followed him and kissed him in my turn.

"Why do you thank her for O'Conor, though?" asked Terence, whose mind could not have been wrenched far from his objective at that point by anything less than the collapse of Moher itself. "He hid it from all mankind forever, and she's unriddled the secret. His spirit must be howling madly."

"I'm not so sure. Why did he leave that fault down there to show so plain, if it wasn't for a clue to those to come? No, we'll talk about that later," Tommy said, going to the tool clutter. "Now we dig and prize our fireplace to bits. Is anyone hungry, before we begin?"

"No," we all said.

"Good. Charge, Terence, charge! On, ladies, on! There's one long day of work ahead. Oh, damn," he said, straightening, "there's Griffin, too, I'd forgotten him. I shall have to reconnoiter."

"Forget him, Dog."

"And forget the drugs, and the poor devil who fed the fishes last week?" asked Tommy mildly.

"Report him when we're done here," suggested Terence.

"Much good that might do."

"You're right," I said.

Amazed at myself, I paused with my mouth agape and thought, or tried to think, clearly. Here I was, encouraging my man to go searching once more for an armed killer—*why?* For an instant, I didn't know. Then it came over me, the bursting of knowledge, of intuition perhaps, that the Zen people call a *satori:* a sensation of having been bathed in a great illumination of truth.

How very dull I had been about Tommy. How incredibly unaware I had been, in the main, of life itself.

There was only one way to take a man like Thomas O'Flaherty, and that was on his own terms; I had said as much to them the other evening when I'd denied wanting to change him. And I *would* take him, Lord knows I loved him as I'd never loved anyone else, I *did* want to be his wife, or his woman, or whatever he wanted me to be, so long as I need not change radically myself. And that meant that if his conscience told him to charge off into danger, then I must accept it as right and proper for him to do it, and I must not argue, I must not spill my quick terrors on him, I must back him to the limit. Even when he appeared to be suicidally wrongheaded, his actions had been determined by long and dangerous experience, and were not made in gusts of emotion. However quick he might be off the mark, there was a coolness in this man that showed in the stance, the constant easy readiness, the firm line of the lips and the slightly narrowed eyes, that let you know he was in absolute command of himself. To worry about him simply because I didn't understand how he dared to go after a vicious enemy without so much as a slingshot in his pocket, to disobey him and put myself in jeopardy as I had done last night only because I did not basically trust his judgment, was a flat betrayal of him. I must not do that any more. Neither in deed nor in word nor in thought should I ever again shake my silly, inexperienced head *No,* not when I knew that Tommy in his knowledge of the world and of himself had decided *Yes.*

Perfect love, I hoped with all my soul, would eventually cast out fear.

Otherwise, I didn't love him enough, and ought to be out on L54 thumbing a ride to Shannon Airport.

In the two or three seconds that all this fresh wisdom took to register on my consciousness, Tommy had stepped across to me and tipped up my face with his fingers. "You mustn't cry, girl dear, I shall be safe as houses; I'll have the hound with me."

"I'm crying for the man who died out there that awful night," I said. It was true, it was the other part of my complex and shattering *satori.* "You see, I—I think my profession has separated me from living. It's sort of numbed me to reality, I mean. And I never realized it till now. I've hardly thought of him from that night till now. He wasn't really a man who was *dead,* do you see?"

"Not too clearly," said Terence, scowling.

"Yes," said Alanna.

Tommy did not speak, but watched my face, fingertips on my cheek.

"I've spent nearly all my life in front of cameras, or watching screens, or listening to stories. Flesh and blood don't really fly when the lead hits, you know, it's just the ketchup and the foam rubber spraying out at the sound of the blank cartridge. I believed in the albatross because that was me who was killing it, poor thing; and I mourned it. But the man with the ginger mustache was just an actor, walking around somewhere again now, in another studio, playing another part. I might meet him at lunch in the commissary. I mean, damn it, I *knew* he was dead, but I didn't *know* it. And that's—that's simply horrible! That isn't human! I'm about as involved in m-mankind as I am in the—the manufacture of shoe polish."

"You're protecting yourself against unnecessary hurt," said Tommy with much gentleness.

"Oh, that's for a Jane Austen maiden! I'm supposed to be a woman! I met that fellow, I talked with him; no matter who or what he was, he treated me in a friendly way; and he was shot afterwards and I didn't even *think* about him! What kind of human being does that? I'm sorry," I said, blowing my nose, "but it struck me hard when you said that about him being in the sea. And it never did before. And I'm ashamed, and—and I shall do better. And I'm worried about you; honestly, if you say you'll be all right, I believe you."

He smiled at me. "What a woman it is," he said slowly, shaking his head. "What giant steps she can take when she wishes."

"I'm ashamed of myself."

"I, conversely, am very proud of you."

"I can't imagine why."

"Because, Grania, if a clod be washed away by the sea, you will know that you are the less, or however those wonderful words go. You are aware."

"It seems to me that I've attained the awareness a dozen years later than I should have."

"But a hundred years before most people ever do," he said, without cynicism, and with a kind of sorrow.

"Well, well," said Terence, "what is it Wilde says? 'The heroic cannot be the common, nor the common the heroic. Congratulate yourself that you have done something strange and extravagant and broken the monotony'—and turned out to be even more uncommon than I've always thought you, Grania Kirk."

"Yes," said Tommy, kissing me lightly, "that for me, too, my love. Now, Balor." He unlocked the door, slid back the rock, and vanished with his dog into blazing sunlight.

"We can improve our time by moving the fire off the hearth," said Alanna, as though nothing out of the way had happened. "Where shall we put it?"

"On my aluminum sheet," I said, and went to haul it from beneath the turf sods. We heaped the glowing stuff carefully onto it, using a flat spade, and set it where the thin smoke would still be drawn eventually into the chimney, where it would not bother us. Alanna took off her fancy boots, which she never wore when she was working, and put on brogues; and we all rolled up our sleeves and set to work on the black, warm rocks behind the hearth. These were joined with mortar, too, but of a different type, much harder than that I had chipped out from between the old flagstones; or perhaps it had been tempered, if mortar can be, by the heat. Terence whanged away with chisel and hammer until he had two of the big blocks loose in their sockets. Then we drank tea and I took my turn, and then Alanna, and Terence again, till Tommy returned.

"No sign anywhere since the rain. But a curious change." he said, scratching his ear. "The old smugglers' spikes, that we were talking of not long ago, have been pulled up, at least four of them have, down there on the platform."

"That's vandalism!" cried Alanna.

"Yes. They're lying there loose, he hasn't thrown them in the ocean; I give him that. But there are two shiny new steel pitons, huge ones, driven in solidly in their place, as well as two tall rods, quite thick, the purpose of which I can't conceive."

"Any rope?" asked Terence.

"Not yet. That's to come, I imagine. At least we know his matters are afoot. The pitons and rods weren't there yesterday."

"Drugs," said Terence slowly, "half a million pounds' worth, that's what he told Grania. Smuggling. Yes. I suppose we can put most of it together now."

"What's he going to do?" I asked.

"Either meet a boat, possibly a curragh and certainly a small boat, which is bringing drugs here; or else he's to deliver the drugs to men coming from the sea."

"Then shouldn't we inform the gardai now?" I asked.

"I suppose we should. I know we should. Oh, damn the wretch! Why couldn't he have waited two more days?" Tommy cried. "Curse the ocean and blast the wind! Why could they not have kept up their bluster a while longer? That's the reason he's been waiting, of course; to descend those cliffs with a high sea running would be suicidal, and the water's been boisterous every day till now."

"Couldn't we tell the gardai and then come back here and lock ourselves in. . . ."

"I hate to take the chance," Tommy said, "but if—well, let's give it today. By all means, today. We may be only hours away from the stuff. If Griffin hasn't made his play by tomorrow morning, we'll go into Ennistymon and enlist the law. And then we'll all get fluttery-eyed drunk." He wooled Balor's shaggy ears. "The dog shall be our sentry. Grania, love, take him to the crest overlooking the platform, no farther than O'Brien's Tower, and tell him 'watch.' Not 'guard,' mind you, but 'watch.' Then if anyone comes, he'll let us know."

I went out with the wolfhound into the cool, bright spring air. It was so lovely, with the calls of cuckoos and plover echoing from landward answered by shearwaters and gulls sailing above the water, and the salt air full of a thick new-grass fragrance, that the little cell behind me suddenly seemed confining and unnatural; but when I had brought Balor to where he could survey the lay-by and the cliffs, and ordered him to play guardian for us, I hurried back through the marvelous day and popped into our den once more, leaving the entrance open.

The men were lifting out one of the loose blocks, a dressed stone hunk of perhaps a hundred pounds. I went over and said to Alanna, "Did Quinn really think that you three were mixed up in this drug horror, or was he projecting? If it entails his meeting someone from out there . . ."

"Who knows what he believes? He didn't take you seriously when you said we were treasure hunting."

"Ouch!" said Terence, as together he and Tommy set the big rough cube down carefully on one of his feet. He went hopping around the room, growling; and that was the last time I thought of Quinn for a while.

" 'Indeed your dancin' days are done,' " quoth Tommy unfeelingly. He bent into the fireplace with a torch. "Packed earth," he said. "Let's take out a few more rocks and then dig back a bit."

"He wouldn't have stuffed up an entrance with dirt."

"He would so. I begin to understand the old Dragon. Give me a hand, Terry, if you can stand quietly now."

Muttering something about unsympathetic oafs, Terence helped him to remove two more blocks of stone, which they ranged beside the turf stack. Tommy went to the door and sniffed the air as Balor might have done, and then packed a pipe and lit it as I in my turn whacked out some mortar with the chisel.

"Away with that," he said to me. "I've the crawling of the flesh that says we don't have much time." He pushed me aside and, the pipe smoking away between his teeth, began to slam at the cement with the transverse edge of a pickax. I retreated as the lumps and sharp grains sprayed back viciously.

"I should have brewed fresh tea while we had the fire in there," said Alanna, making do with a cup of water.

In less than half an hour they had taken out six blocks and had a cavity in the rear wall the size and shape of a low doorway, backed by black soil. Tommy went at this with his pickax, now the point and now the edge, and shortly, as I was gazing vacantly at the tool whipping in quick arcs and thinking that he handled it as a lesser man would handle a riding crop, it crashed through the earth barricade and sank to the shaft head. He tipped it and hauled it toward him and a great lump of compressed soil fell out on the hearth like a boulder, without breaking. He snatched up the torch and shone it briefly, then laughed. "Lumber!" Before Terence could come within reach, Tommy had the pickax flailing again, and cleared most of the black layer away, showing us a wall of venerable, time-stained wood.

He whirled round and literally leaped at me, picked me up and twirled me around with my hair brushing the ceiling, and cried out in a voice I'd never heard him use before, an exultant Minotaur's bellow, "Grania, pulse of me life, you did it! You gave us the Dragon's stronghold cupped in your two hands, you magnificent girl! Here," he said, setting me down and dragging me across to the hearth, "I think even Terry'll admit you've earned the right to tear down the last bulkhead yourself."

"With what?" I asked helplessly.

"Your fingers, don't you see? Look where the thing sags and buckles!"

I looked. Then experimentally I put my palms flat against the old, old wood and shoved. I could feel the panels move inward. They did not seem to be very thick; not as thick as beams, certainly.

And Tommy had removed all that stone-hard earth with such precision that, except for the first blow that had made a hole the size of a knot, the wood behind it was hardly scratched. Yet I sensed that the entire fabric of this partition was so rotten after its centuries of contact with the soil, after intermittent periods of heat and then of creeping moisture, that it was indeed ready to cave in.

I couldn't resist asking him if he'd learned the trick as a laborer, and he said No, that this winter had accustomed both Terence and himself to the accurate swinging of a pick. I still considered it an astonishing feat of coordination.

His hands came to my waist while I set myself and pushed harder. Then, as the thing collapsed with a decayed creaking—crumbled and withered and even powdered here and there as it came sliding and shattering down—Tommy hauled me backwards with a strong, smooth jerk that took me out of harm's way.

Our little stone room began to fill with the dust and the myriad particles of the wreckage I had made. We all hacked and choked, and Alanna called to us from the open door to come and breathe till it settled; but Tommy in the grip of his joy moved straight forward and plucked up the torch and flashed it on. As even Terence came to the doorway, eyes watering, I heard Tommy laughing and coughing and shouting all at once, as if he had been holding his natural exuberance in tight check for months, and only now could let it explode.

Where my man could go, I could at least try to follow. I walked toward him through a filthy fog of dirt, rottenness, and stinging dust-atoms of stone, earth, wood, and mortar. It seemed so great an eruption, I knew that something besides the barricade of blighted wood had gone down to ruin.

Tommy was standing on the debris within the new-made opening, flicking his torch from side to side. I shoved him a little and stood beside him. His arm came down on my shoulders, shaking with excitement. "Look," he said hoarsely, "look here. Another sentinel, by the Lord!"

A dead man sat against a stone wall opposite, some four feet in front of us. This was no skeleton, however, but a dark-brown mummy, with wisps of what had once been cloth lying here and there on his shriveled frame. His head rested on his chest—mercifully, for I would not have liked to look into his face—and his legs were sprawled out at an angle that had held him upright, as he shrank and turned to bones clad in human leather, through the centuries. Beside him sat a lovely bronze lamp, its oil burnt away or evaporated these seven hundred years; as well as a big, broad-mouthed, keg-shaped baked clay vessel of some sort and a tool that looked like a trowel.

Tommy went to one knee before him. "Will you look at this," he said, his tone thickly reverential. "Great God! What a man this was. And what a man he served, who could call such loyalty forth!" Tommy always seemed to go all nineteenth-century in his speech when he was emotionally touched.

"What is it?" asked Terence behind me, spluttering with the dry rot and grit in his throat. "What is it, man dear?"

"One of Bran Roe's *gall-óglaich*," said Tommy, using the Irish word that meant foreign warriors who enlisted as mercenaries under the ancient kings and chiefs of the island. "A gallowglass, half Scot and half Viking from the size and the yellow hair of him."

"I thought Vikings were short men?" I said.

"When your grand old Gráinne Ni Mháille went to England to visit Elizabeth," Terence said, rubbing his eyes, "her bodyguard were the biggest men that London had ever seen; and they were Scotch-Viking gallowglasses. So much for the tiny-Viking slanders. Maybe it was the mixed blood."

"Look here, you three," said Tommy. "This is a thing to tell your children. This was the bravery that our world's lost somewhere. Talk about the Spartans at Thermopylae!"

I bent over beside him. In the white torchlight I saw his hand go out and lightly touch the white-and-green-stone ornamented hilt of a dagger whose blade was buried in the shrunken chest. "No, not murdered," said Tommy softly. "He did it himself. See where he tried once and just missed the heart, so that he had to work it loose and stab again. Bran Roe left him here to plaster up the inside of the wooden barricade—that's what made most of this dust, the old plaster—with a mortar tub and a trowel, and the light that flickered in this priceless bit of bronze here ... and a dagger to close his eyes when the work was done." Tommy looked round at me. "I hope the Dragon shook him by the hand before the last boards went up. I rather think he did. Do you *see*, darling? This was voluntary. The man knew all along that when he'd walled himself in, he would do this. Remember it if you ever hear anyone sneer at the paid soldiers of the past."

The draft of the chimney behind us was gradually sucking up those particles of dust that were not heavy enough to fall on the hearth and floor; the air was clearing. I stared, half mesmerized, at the dagger's hilt. "Why mortar? When there was timber and earth and stone too?"

"O'Conor may have thought to protect his treasures from more than man," Terence said. "From air, for instance, and the corrupting elements in it like salt and smoke. They weren't so ignorant in the thirteenth century that they couldn't observe how certain things deteriorate in certain atmospheres. Bran Roe seems to have made his storehouse into something very like a vacuum bottle. Mad he may well have been, but not unintelligent."

"Mad he was not," said Tommy harshly. "Do you not see that yet?"

"But to wall a man up alive," I said.

"A man who went on working till he'd done his job. This man had been paid all his life for risking his life, and it's plain that he gave it freely when the time came. See that ax fornenst the wall? He could have cut down Bran Roe with that in a snap of the fingers, and why would the Dragon have let him keep it by him if there'd been the least possible doubt of his loyalty? The man was—well, a Spartan. Bran Roe had long since bought his death. Look at the belt here, that's gold on the links. This will have been the captain of the gallowglasses himself."

"If O'Conor asked for volunteers to die," said Terence grudgingly, "this fella'd be first to step out. Dog's right, this was a high honor."

"God rest him," said Alanna.

"I think it more likely he's swilling mead in Valhalla this minute." Tommy picked up the beautiful old lamp and handed it to her. "Here's the first of the loot. Three or four thousand years old. . . . Bronze Age, I think?"

"Yes. Oh yes, yes," said the archaeologist. There was scarcely any breath behind the words. I knew that this little lamp had made the hard winter worth while for her already.

"Bran Roe saw to it that his captain went out in style," said Tommy with approval. "Now fetch a lantern and we'll go on."

The Blakes left us alone with the gallowglass. I was thinking that it might be him and his men who, according to Grandmother, marched forever along the Cliffs of Moher. Tommy turned the torch to our left; against the wall of mortared rock leaned the hideous battle-ax, of the single-bladed short-hafted design of that in the Tower of London's execution room. Tommy picked it up and swung it experimentally. He set it beside the mummy. "Sure you were a tough one to use *that*," he said. The flash sought right, and there a narrow flight of steps descended, flat stone unhollowed by treading feet. "Pride of place is yours now, Grania. This is your triumph. Go first."

"No, Terence must."

"As you like." The beam went shooting around the tiny chamber that had been here so close to us all the while. "Months and months out in the weather," Tommy murmured ruefully. "All the cold-bit fingers and raw noses and ears. I may never play the guitar again. And this waiting for us behind our own den, within that innocent hillock all covered with icy grass that backs the place up! Where *were* you, girl, all through the winter of our discomfort?"

"Reeking with perspiration under the studio lights," I said.

"What a world of misery you'd have saved all four of us had you come to Ireland in November. It was thoughtless of you." He clicked off his torch and sought me in the gloom and kissed me hard. "I forgive you," he said.

"I love you," I told him, momentarily taken by such a wave of shyness that it came out in the tiniest whisper. Then the Blakes were there with our Coleman. Terence was persuaded, rather easily, to take the lead, and down we went.

It was probably the only time I'd ever gone under the earth without being frightened.

Despite the large opening we had made, with its resultant inward rush of ventilation, the atmosphere was still attenuated and smelled of antiquity—air, you might say, in its extreme dotage; yet there was no stench here of mold or damp as in the kitchens, and we could breathe with little discomfort. It was a genuine strongroom we were approaching, its shell three- or four-plied with all the materials that could protect it short of metal. The vice turned to our left, opposite to the horrible staircase I'd traversed the night before. I tensed and held back at the remembrance, just long enough for Tommy to bump into me and Terence and his wife to move out of sight. I turned and was about to offer my man a quick kiss when from below us there rose a cry of such fearful consternation that we stared at each other in the lantern gleam for one breath, then leaped down the steps.

I remember shouting, "What is it?" at the top of my voice, as though the Blakes had been a hundred feet ahead.

Then I was right on them, almost knocked over Alanna, and was caught by Tommy from behind and saved from blundering right into Terence, who stood transfixed at the threshold of the treasure room.

There before us was a vast chaos of torn wickerwork, great oak beams and dark timbers with jagged ends, shattered flagstones, and unidentifiable litter. The Dragon had protected his hoard too thoroughly. At some time in those seven hundred years of waiting silence, the roof had fallen in of its own awful weight; and several tons of carefully placed building components had smashed down upon the delicate, brittle beauty that Bran Roe O'Conor had gleaned from all the past ages of his island.

12

Castles are sacked in war,
Chieftains are scattered far;
Love is a fixéd star. . . .
                    —Eileen Aroon

I COULD FIND NOTHING TO SAY. The entrance before us, a low arched narrow opening, was jammed to eye level with the wreckage; I saw that Terence had gone so white that even his sunburn had paled. Tommy said quietly, "It's to be borne, old lad; it can't be helped."

"I will not have it," said Terence loudly. "I will not accept this, do you hear me? It's a mistake. We're shocked too soon. Damn it, the treasure room is beyond this. It's merely a passage." He went to his toes and shoved the lantern in over a beam. "Dog!" he shouted. "Give me the torch, man!"

"It's above," said Tommy.

"Then get it!" He was absolutely squeaking with agitation.

"But you—"

"Will you in the name of everything sacred bring me the torch!"

Tommy went up the vice obediently, me at his heels. "What is it?" I asked. "What does he see, or expect to see?"

"Perhaps only a part of the roof went. Wisha, girl, *I* don't know!"

"I hope nothing was near the door, then," I said.

"There was. I saw something of silver on the floor."

"Oh," I said helplessly. We went past the captain of gallowglasses and into the den. Tommy had his head bent, searching for his torch, so that I was the first to see the wolfhound, standing in the sunlight outside the open door

213

looking at us. Recollecting Quinn Griffin with a start,
"Balor," I said.

Tommy walked toward him at once, the dog backing up
until he was out of sight. "Take them the torch," Tommy
said, and was gone too.

I found it in the fireplace and went scurrying downward, shying away from the dead man. Terence had set
the lantern on the lowest step and was waiting for me,
looking as though he were about to burst into flame with
impatience. "Tommy says there's silver on the floor," I
told them.

He snatched the torch and went tall again, pushing his
arm into the darkness above the broken timber. I do not
think he'd heard me, but Alanna had. She knelt and pulled
something out, something that was not damaged, that had
been protected by beams and wicker which had fallen
obliquely and been wedged tight just in time to shelter it.
It was a large square slab of silver, less than an inch thick,
with some Gaelic lettering graven into an otherwise plain
surface. She stood up, holding it, and turned it over. She
gave a long sigh. "Grania," she said, "the song. This is the
chessboard of King Cormac."

"Who died in the year 903," I said, staring at the marvelously incised piece of ash-colored metal. The surface
was blocked off in the usual alternating squares, the dark
ones indicated by a finely cut hatching. The border and
the sides were engraved with the intricate interlacing rib-
bon design that you see in the old illuminated Irish books.
"This must be worth half a museumful of anonymous relics."

"Almost. Show it to Tommy."

"Tommy's out after Balor. Terence must see it," I said.

She gave the wonderwork into my hands; it must have
weighed twenty pounds or more. "Terence is transfixed
with something. He'll come out of it in his own time.
Show this to Tommy!"

I went up the steps, holding the board in both hands.
The middle part of the climb was in total blackness, but I
was growing used to going up and down medieval vices in
the dark. Luckily there was some light at the top, so that I
did not fall over the mummy.

Tommy was not back. I hadn't expected him to be.
Cradling the weighty board in the crook of an elbow, I
marched briskly out into the afternoon. Nobody had told

me not to follow him. (I didn't realize that Alanna, as bemused in her fashion as Terence, had not even registered what I'd told her about Tommy and Balor.) I would not encumber him or try to dissuade him—I'd learned that lesson—but I would be near or with him until he ordered me away.

Besides, it might be early tourists. It was heavenly weather for them. The only clouds I saw were a low pale line of the western rim of ocean. The cliffs were a bright clear black all the way down to Hag's Head, crested by the spring green of the grass, and a cow or two browsed about a mile away under the warm sun. I came almost to O'Brien's Tower before I saw Tommy crouched beside the path ahead, his fingers tight in the shag of Balor's shoulder. Bending low, I joined him.

"I expected you," he said. "I was resigned to it. What's that you're lugging about?"

"Cormac's chessboard."

He squinted. All he said was "Is that the way of it indeed?" but there was an undertone of absolute awe in the casual phrase. And was there a terrible, hungry greed, too? I tried to think that there was not.

At any rate, I could tell that he was even more impressed than Alanna, the professional antiquary. "Well," he said, "it shines like a bloody searchlight, doesn't it? That will give us away if the man turns." He took it from me to lay it on the grass. Then he stripped off his shirt and wrapped it around the beautiful slab. "We'll keep it by us, since you've brought it. There may be other visitors on the cliffs today. And I'm damned if I don't feel better when you're with me, if only for moral support."

"If only so you know I'm not making trouble somewhere," I said.

He nodded, then pointed. "See him?"

I looked at the platform. There was a man out there by the edge, working at something on his hands and knees. He had several lumps of stuff beside him that I could not make out. A small blue car sat on the lay-by.

"It's Quinn," I said.

"It is. He must have miles of rope there."

"Is that what the orange heaps are, rope?"

"Mountain-climbing ropes, I'd think." The man in the distance got to his feet and walked toward the edge. "Oh," said Tommy half aloud, "that's it. A windlass. That was what the new rods were for; he's anchored it to the rock with them. The pitons—wait a bit now—that's not just a rope, it's a rope ladder. What the devil? Can't the man shin down a rope and climb it again, but he must have rungs, too? A mere six hundred and fifty feet? He's gone soft."

"Could you?" I asked him, appalled at the idea.

"I could not. No man could. I'm joking. Badly. Because I'm keyed up. No, I thought he'd have a confederate to go down in a sling, when I saw the windlass. He must be alone. Would you care to bring Terence to me? No, steady," he said, pressing me as I moved, "he's facing this way. Lie flat, dear. He's putting the end of the ladder over. There's plenty of time, if he means to go down now. It isn't as though he's going to take an electric lift up and down that brute of a cliff, *whoosh.* Lashins of time yet. I give the devil his due, when there's money to be got, he's hell's own nerveless boy. I should not be exactly itchin' to crawl down the face of that drop myself. Stay low, will you? He's paying out the ladder and looking our way. Ah, you're nervous about *me* though, are you, Quinn boy?" And then the O'Flaherty began to sing, random fragments of old songs, in a rich whispering rumble. I had never heard him sing before. It was gorgeous, and made the skin creep on my arms.

"'A little rest, and then the world is full of work to do,'" he sang, his hands gentling both my head and Balor's. "'Alas and well may Erin weep, that Connaught lies in slumber deep' ... hmmm ... 'And later times saw deeds as brave, for glory guards—' ah, there, in spite of all his careful rolling of it, was a twist; now if he'd chucked it over all anyhow, that might have snarled in the middle of the drop and—"

"Tommy, can't I look?"

"Be cautious, my dear, that sorrel mop of yours shines in the sun as if you'd oiled it."

"That's because it's dirty," I said humbly, lifting my head.

"So is my hand," he said, keeping it where it was in my hair, the fingers moving lightly on my scalp. "See, he's got it straightened out and o-o-over she goes! That wasn't meant, that length got away from him. 'Perhaps she'd take it into her head for to wed with an Irishman,'" he sang softly, not looking at me. "'Now I'm the boy can squeeze her rough, and I'll tell ye what I'll do—I'll court her like an Irishman, with the brogue and the blarney too is me plan. . . .' "

I thought, if he would go on singing, and the breeze blow so cool and light on my sun-warm face, I could lie here all afternoon.

Eventually Quinn had his rope ladder all paid out, its top, Tommy told me, secured by the steel pitons; he then went to the windlass and attached one end of the single rope to it with great care and much fiddling around that I could not understand at this distance. He took a small khaki bundle in his arms and dropped it over the edge of the cliff a yard or so from the ladder. He stepped on the orange rope as it shot forth like a striking snake, and bent and lifted it and ran it out swiftly through his hands.

"He's wearing gloves," said Tommy, reading my thought. "This rope's to haul up the stuff he's come for. Heavy, there must be a lot of it, or he'd not need the windlass."

"Wouldn't the rope be very heavy, too, that much of it?"

"I suppose so. But the stuff will be heavier still. We know now it's coming to him, not being sent out."

"Or he wouldn't have dropped this rope now'?"

"Right. That was some class of a sling on the tip of it."

"Should I go for Terence?" I could not imagine why he or his wife hadn't come out to find us by now; we'd been here for at least ten minutes.

"Wait. Griffin has a bit of his eye on this part of the country. Don't underestimate the enemy, Grania, he's a survivor too."

"He wasn't so much of a one last night."

"This is daylight, and we won't scare him with a scream."

The second rope was over now, tugging at the windlass. Quinn took off his jacket—he was dressed in a business suit, with a white shirt and black-and-white shoes, of all strange costumes for this work—and laid it neatly on the rock. He walked to the head of his ladder and turned and let himself down over the brink of the platform and in a moment had vanished.

"I am damned," said Tommy blankly. He sprang to his feet and ran over to the cliff edge on our right, though he could not have seen Quinn from there. Then he came back. "Get up, the pair of you," he said. "The brazen cheek of the man! But we have him."

"Terence—"

"Will be along shortly, but we won't need him. Your man has made us the present of himself. There is no boat anywhere on this ocean that I can see, and Griffin is alone."

We were running down the headlong path to the lay-by, Balor in the ditch beside us looking happy to be stretching his legs. Tommy, bare to the waist, carried the wrapped chessboard under his arm. "You know what I think?" he said over his shoulder. "I think what he's after has been down there all winter, and him dying for one day of quiet wind and low surf. He hasn't been waiting for a curragh to deliver it. He was waiting for the climbing weather."

"But where has it been?"

"In the old smugglers' cave!"

It was logical enough: the cave, wherever it might be, must be sheltered from the highest tides, or men of the lawless old times could never have used it to store their secret imports of Chinese silk and French cognac.

Tommy ran over to the Morris Mini and opened the door, scanned the interior, rooted in the glove box, and came to me with a grin. "No weapons there, but the swine's not so crafty as he thinks." He showed me the car keys in his palm.

We went down onto the platform and Tommy inspected the windlass as though he'd been given untold amounts of free time. I was in an agony of apprehension. The windlass stood about ten feet from the rim. It was a simple contraption of wood and metal, with a fairly thick barrel, or roller, and a crank on each end of the axle, outside the vertical posts. Tommy pointed out in a conversational tone the gear, whose cogs could catch and hold the cylinder if the cranks were let go.

I gestured madly at the rope ladder.

"He's a third down by now. His caution's deserted him in his haste. He must imagine we're afraid to come out in the daylight. Let's see if he's left anything in his coat." I watched him pick it up, search it, then inspect the lining. "Expensive. He does himself well, does Quinn Griffin. This rope is nylon, too."

"The ladder's nylon, the single rope is Perlon," said Quinn.

I sucked in my breath with a rasping screak. We twisted our necks and looked at the enemy, Tommy as discomfited as I. Quinn had lifted himself till his chest leaned on the edge of the rock, and he held the automatic in his hand pointed directly at me. "There's three hundred quid's worth of rope here, not to mention the rungs and the hammock and all. Pity it has to go into the sea when this is finished. Now just draw your weapons slowly and toss them over—not in my direction, please. I can't fail to blow that bitch apart at this range. These are, naturally, expanding bullets."

"So much for bravado and vain pride," said Tommy with a deep breath, looking at me. "Well, the fact is, I have no weapon, nor does Grania."

"I'll give you the usual count of three," said Quinn.

Tommy set the shirt-wrapped silver board on the platform at his feet, pulled out all the pockets of his trousers, and turned in a circle with his hands up. Quinn looked at me; I revolved likewise. "I'll be blowed," said Quinn.

"You've been away from the game too long, you bloody fool; you've lost your touch."

"I agree," said Tommy quietly. "I was blaming you for the same fault. I was wrong. I deserved to lose. Down, Balor." The wolfhound lay obediently beside the windlass. "How did you know I was here?"

"I saw the beast while I was lugging the ropes down. I knew he'd fetch you. And I was prepared to wait till nightfall if necessary."

"I underestimated you," said Tommy frankly.

"You've done that before, haven't you?" Quinn climbed carefully over the lip of the rock and moved down a couple of yards toward his right, the gun still aimed at me. "What's in the shirt?"

"The first of what we've been digging for. It's a silver chessboard."

"How silly of me to ask," said Quinn sarcastically. "What else would it be but a silver chessboard! Come here, Grania."

I stared at him. Tommy said, "She will not."

"I'd as soon shoot her as you," said Quinn, "and I don't think you want to lose her. I've tasted that mouth myself. Come here, you poisonous young hag."

I walked to him; he twisted me around to face Tommy. If I'd thrown my weight backwards, I would have toppled him over, but I would have gone with him and I knew I'd never have the stomach for that—probably not even to save Tommy. It is not something that a sane person can do, to commit suicide in such a terrifying way. I could have stopped a bullet meant for Tommy, I'm sure of that, but I could not have jumped off that dreadful height backward to save every friend I had in the world. I was by no means frozen with fear, but I was sick with it, and stood there hoping that I wasn't going to throw up and disgrace our side.

"Now, show me what you have," said Quinn to Tommy, holding me by one arm and digging the automatic into my ribs.

Tommy unfolded the shirt, picked up the slab and laid it on the platform, and after flapping his shirt to show it was empty, put it on and buttoned it. Quinn Griffin must have gazed at the silver object for half a minute across my shoulder before he finally said, "So you told me the truth, they *were* digging for treasure. And they found it." He did not try to disguise his avarice. "Dog Fox, I thought—" and his greed clotted in his throat. He knew that he was looking at the promise of more money than even he had ever imagined he could have, drugs and all.

"You thought I was after your cocaine or whatever it is, down there in the old smugglers' cave," said Tommy quietly.

I felt Quinn jerk with surprise. "That too?"

"Half a million pounds' worth of drugs, in polyethylene bags packed into an aluminum barrel," said Tommy, throwing it off as if it were some incidental fact of little importance. "I'm not sure what the powder is, but it tastes like hell."

I gaped at him. He looked blandly back at both of us.

"*Two* barrels!" shouted Quinn. "There were two of them, you fool! What of the other?"

"Good Lord," said Tommy, his eyes widening, "two? I swear I found only the one. Missed the second entirely. I'd no notion how much the stuff was worth till you told Grania—stop that!" he blazed out, as Griffin swung me around so roughly that I almost lost my balance. "She didn't know about it, nor the Blakes either; only about the treasure in the ruins."

Balor was on his feet, growling angrily. Tommy caught hold of his collar. Quinn was raging, shaking me to and fro and waving the gun at Tommy. "How did you get it up?" he yelled. "That sea's been a bloody maelstrom all winter!"

"Not *all* the time. There was nothing much to it, so long as a fella could handle a curragh," said Tommy. "There was no need to go up and down the cliffs."

Quinn began to swear.

"Don't offend Miss Kirk," said Tommy.

"Offend her, is it? I'll chuck her off this rock into hell if I like!"

"And lose everything?" Tommy shook his head and smiled. "I doubt it, Griffin."

Quinn subsided. "You're just bloody enough of a half-wit knight-errant to do something lunatic," he said and produced a sound that was meant, I suppose, for a laugh. "Go over there and sit down," he told me, gesturing to a place some distance from where Tommy stood. "I must think." I stumbled away, stupefied, cowed and forlorn, and collapsed on the cool stone.

I had begun to take it in. Tommy had known of the drugs all along. He had even had half of them hidden somewhere, likely in Dragon's Keep, perhaps in the storeroom they'd unearthed; and long before I set foot in Ireland. The implications were obvious.

I could feel the tears trickling down my cheeks. I turned my head away, toward O'Brien's Tower, and tried to wonder where Terence and Alanna were, but it was like trying to concentrate on poetry in the dentist's chair.

"I was going to send you down for the goods—it's heroin, incidentally—while I waited here with the wench," said Griffin. "Then I was going to shoot you both and kick you into the water."

"Obviously," said Tommy.

"It seems you have a certain advantage."

"I do."

"Of course you don't trust me—"

"Well, no," said Tommy, smiling.

"And I don't trust you."

"Wise of you. So we must both be careful," agreed Tommy in a positively lighthearted tone. "Keep our distance, don't turn our backs, all that."

"Right. Alliance. What about the Blakes and this Kirk witch?"

Tommy chuckled. I think it was a more horrid sound to

me than Quinn Griffin's obscene tirade in the kitchens. "Bloody Monday?" he said. "I've not made up my mind."

Quinn whooped and slapped his thigh. "By God, and to think how I went about telling people that you'd gone all buttery! Lost your nerve and taken to singing in pubs for a living! Dog Fox, my apologies." He laughed as if it were a huge joke. "Partners, then—with the reservation that mutual faith is, well, not to be expected at once."

"As you say."

Quinn was silent. Then: "You must go down for the rest of it, you know, old lad. I can't do it. I'd load the sling and send it up and then you'd drop me, ladder and all, into the Atlantic."

"I would so." I heard Tommy muttering to Balor, and the hound came padding over to me and thrust his face against my shoulder. I put an arm around him and snuggled my face into his shag. I knew perfectly well, if I knew anything for sure in all the world, that Tommy would die rather than injure the Blakes or me. That much was for Quinn's benefit. He had to play along, it was life and death that he appear to make a deal. But he had known about the drugs; there was no explaining that away, when he could reel out how they were wrapped and barreled and how they tasted. And he had kept this fact secret from us, for which there was no explanation except that he was avaricious and less principled than I had believed possible.

Love doesn't die that suddenly, I suppose; but love can certainly turn on you in an instant and curdle your heart's blood.

"I can't manage the ladder in brogues," said Tommy. "Chuck me those gaudy slippers of yours."

"Don't sneer, they're made for friction climbing and they cost me three fivers." Shortly I heard the soft black-and-white shoes, which I had taken for ordinary sneakers, thump on the rock. "Keep that hoop thing in your fist or over your arm when you go down," Quinn said. "If you don't have it to draw the other rope to you, you may find the sling entirely out of reach when you hit bottom, and it's a long way up and down again."

"You think of everything, don't you?" asked Tommy mildly. "Well, I'm ready. Two words in your ear, Griffin."

"Yes?"

"I hold the trump for the time. I want my half of everything, and I'll kill you like a toad if I see you thinking about crossing me. It was I who took that curragh into the winter sea and risked my neck for that keg. It's I who's going down this rotten spider-thread ladder. And but for me, you wouldn't have had a smell of that bloody hoard of jewels and gold up yonder. Kill me and you lose half the heroin, and maybe all the loot in the keep, because Blake has the door secured and won't budge without me. Deal fair with me, for once in your life, and we can divide about three million pounds between us."

He dragged out the enormous figure in a drawl that must have made Quinn's mouth slaver. The man said thickly, "And?"

"And if you're fit to mind mice at a crossroad, which I think you are, then you'll keep your hands off Kirk here, and the Blakes too if they should come down. Because we've got to talk this out very thoroughly before we commit ourselves to—what's the phrase? 'Termination with extreme prejudice.' "

"Want to save her for one more night?" Quinn brayed with laughter. "Look here, though, damn it, if Blake has a gun—"

"I'd have brought it with me."

"Oh. Naturally."

"Now who isn't thinking?" jeered Tommy in his turn. "Now who's out of practise?"

"All right, I'll preserve your slut, Dog Fox. Start, for God's sake, man, I want to know that the other keg's all snug down there. Oh, I forgot: catch this. Hang it on your belt. You'll need it to dry your hands now and then."

I heard Tommy walking toward the edge. Almost involuntarily I turned to look at him. He pivoted on the brink of the drop and as he went over it backwards, he caught my glance and deliberately winked with the eye that Quinn from his angle could not see.

Against all common sense I began to hope again. Then I thought, he's simply telling me that he won't let me be killed. As though I'd have minded.

He was gone.

Quinn sat down comfortably at the very brink. The gun was trained on my breast; indeed, I don't believe it had ever moved from me during his whole conversation. "Ah," he said, grinning, "alone at last. You lanky young swine."

I said nothing, but kept my hand tucked under Balor's

collar. I could sense that the dog was unhappy about the whole affair, and that he did not care much for Quinn either.

"You put the wind up me good and proper last night, didn't you? Where in hell did you go? My light burned out or I'd have had you."

"I was up the chimney," I said.

He nodded. "And me right below you at the end?"

"Yes."

"If I'd known! If only I'd known. Look here," he said, "what about the Blakes? Are they really in the dark on what he's got hidden up there?"

"I'm sure they are. They wouldn't touch anything as foul as drugs. Neither would I."

"Still the moralistic little innocent, are we? You poor bloody fool," he said, "if you'd come with me when I asked you, instead of dashing away to that crew again, it'd be you and me now, instead of me and the old Dog Fox."

"Did you shoot the man on the cliffs that night?"

He lifted his brows at that. "I? Shoot a man?" Then he laughed. "Of course I did. The idiot heard you howling up there. I told him not to interfere, but he defied me, he shook me off and went after you. I could tell that you were in trouble," said Quinn Griffin, giving me that incredible, sunny, wholesome smile of his, "and I wanted you dead."

I watched him, and as often as I'd seen the villain at the end of a drama expose the profound extent of his dark evil, I was shaken by this reality. For he looked as attractive, as dashing and romantic and, well, as *nice* as he had that first evening in Limerick. "Why?" I asked.

"Because you were a nuisance. Because you were an unknown quality, and I didn't know how hand-in-glove with O'Flaherty you might be, and because I simply wanted you dead," he told me.

"Because I preferred Tommy to you, and dared to run away from you back to him, when I might have had the honor of—"

"*Yerra* never mind that, and shut your stupid mouth," he said.

And last night, I thought, *you wanted me dead for sure, after I'd had the gall to slash at you with my torch. Lese majesty!* "You must have the ego of a—of a wolverine," I said. "To kill a man for trying to help a woman in trouble."

"Oh, I didn't need him any longer, any road," Quinn said easily. "And I couldn't use a man who'd disobey me, now could I? Shall I tell you the tale, I wonder?"

Then he looked at me expectantly. He *wanted* to explain the whole thing to me. I had never believed that anyone did that, not truly, not in life. That was a playwright's transparent device to enlighten the audience. It used to grate on me to play one of those scenes. But it appeared that some men did do it, out of a terrible need to brag or taunt or excuse themselves. And I realized that except for Tommy, who was going, Quinn thought, to join him, and myself, who was shortly, Quinn thought, to die, there was not a soul in the world to whom he could confide his cleverness, his power, his savagery, of all of which he was doubtless very proud. I recollected a director telling me once that he'd never met a bully who didn't believe himself to be a good guy; even Iago probably considered himself the hero, and would have loved to tell somebody all about it, no matter what he said in the end of the play.

"Go ahead," I said, taking a firmer hold on the restless Balor, who was trying to move off and look for his master.

"There were four men went to sea in a curragh," said Quinn Griffin, in almost the identical words he had used to me in Lisdoonvarna; "two Americans and two men from Aran. They were carrying about six stone of the finest heroin down the coast from the Aran Islands to the beach beyond Hag's Head. The weather was flawless, it was night, and the rowers knew this coast like their own palms. And then the weather turned treacherous on them."

"Were you one of them?"

"Catch me in a curragh!" he said. "That's for madmen like the Dog Fox. Did you ever step into one of the blasted tar-covered grapefruit rinds? No, I was at Hag's Head with a pal. The storm swept down without warning, and as one of the rowers knew of the smugglers' cave, they came in there and snugged the stuff away. It was in two aluminium kegs, about three stone, that's forty-odd pounds, in each. Well over a million dollars, my sleek young wench, even before it's cut with lactose; perhaps ten or twelve times that, afterwards. I stick with thinking of it as a half a million pounds' worth, to allow for error and small catastrophes, but it will likely bring me more. ... It had come from Marseilles, where there are laboratories that process the raw opium. It was on its way to the States. My pal and I with the two Americans were going to get it there. Your customs are just jam when it's Ireland a man's coming from, I tell you. Nothing's ever smuggled out of Ireland but shamrocks and souvenir chunks of turf."

"Then you weren't going to sell it here."

"Who'd buy it in this country?" he jeered. He leaned sidelong and looked down the cliffs. He seemed to have no fear of heights whatever. "That's a tough little bastard," he said, ungrudgingly. "He's three hundred feet down already. Well! They cached the goods in the cave, nicely above high tide. Even heavy spray would do no harm, you see, for the kegs were secured to the rock with wire cables that were already there. The men started downcoast in a rising sea, and the bloody curragh turned over near Hag's Head. Two men got to shore. One lived, one was stoved to bits and died on the strand.

"Then I took care of the fourth, and my pal went off to America to enlist two others."

"You took care of the fourth," I said. "You killed him. Why? Because he was there?"

Quinn laughed. "I like that," he said, showing me all his teeth. "The slogan of the mountaineer, isn't it? No. He had a broken arm and we were in a hurry, so I bashed his head in with a rock. Besides, he'd told me where the stuff was, and he was only a hired islander. My pal—shall I call him O'Kelly, a fine Celtic name?—was to send me two people from New York, from the Irish-American 'family' that's buying the goods. You know the password I gave him. Incidentally," he said, "I *do* believe you stumbled on that by accident, didn't you?"

"Yes. I never told you anything but the truth; I'm a bad liar."

"You once said that you wanted to powder your nose, I recall."

"I simply didn't mention that I wanted to do it in Dragon's Keep."

He dropped his weapon into his lap and applauded with what appeared to be genuine admiration. "What a pity it can't be you instead of the Dog Fox! The added dimension of fun and games. Ah, that's only wanting jam on it. There's bags of women to be had when one's a millionaire. Tell me, how did you come by whatever's under that bandage?"

"I was fighting with one of the Dread Women of Moher. That's when your—your *victim* wanted to help me."

He sat up straighter and glared at me, brows furrowed. "What do you mean? That's a story to frighten babies."

"I have the scar to show for the story, then." I reached up and pulled the dressing free of my cheek.

I had not seen the wound yet, of course, so when he produced the most overdramatic shudder this side of a sitcom, I was quite startled. "You never fought with a Dread Woman, now did you?" he asked, wheedling. "You admit you lie poorly. What was it? The truth now."

"I never saw it, but it felt and smelled and sounded like a Harpy, like something that should have been dead two thousand years ago."

"Lord almighty!" he exclaimed, and looked away. It was not the mere sight of a healing wound that shook this multiple killer, but the idea of the supernatural. Even in the sunlight. "That oaf always said they were real," he muttered.

"Who?"

"My father. How did you get away from it?"

"Tommy was there." I didn't say where.

Quinn leaned backward and stared down the cliffside. At last he said, "That's a man," and shook his head. Without intention, I had brought the child in him to life again. I wondered whether I should scream and point out to sea; he would whirl round and I would dart forward and shove. . . .

That was impossible. And while I was desperately trying to think of a way to follow up the slight advantage, he picked the gun off his lap and aimed it at me once more. I watched him as I peeled the strips of adhesive tape from my cheek one by one. It had been a week and surely that was time enough; besides, what did it matter? I was half convinced that I was going to die today, along with Tommy and the Blakes, so what was a scar?

"You know," he said calmly after a little while, "I almost got you that first night. Pity I didn't. You're the trollop who's done me at every turn. But for you, I'd never have lost my temper and shot Moran. If you hadn't stuck

your long nose into things last night and lured me into
that filthy cellar, I'd have shot O'Flaherty through the
head as he came back to your digs, and got the Blakes
when they rushed out after the noise."

"You were stalking Tommy?"

"I saw him and the brute there, what's his name, Balor,
down on the road. I was cutting up through the ruin to sit
outside that rock door of yours till he'd had Blake open it,
and then pot them both, and that little blond epithet, too.
And you, I was going to throw you off the cliff. Alive."
He chuckled. "I may do that yet, if I can convince the
Dog Fox. Though I wouldn't have known about the heroin
he'd stolen—nor that loot he's uncovered, come to think
of it—well, well, Grania my dear! I do have you to thank
for that. I hadn't looked at it that way before. All I knew
was that you were the skinny green-eyed brat who was always getting in the way. Making me wonder how much
you knew, so that I had to follow you to Lisdoonvarna.
All those references to snow and dope and Moher and re-
wards. ... Perhaps, after all. God sent you as a gift for
me." The horrid aspect of this blasphemy was that he was
not joking.

"It was you who disabled my Ford." I hadn't remembered that incident for days.

"It was. I didn't want to toss you over in daylight, and I
had to get back to Lisdoonvarna quite urgently, so I
thought I'd stick you here till I could return. If O'Flaherty
took you in, fine, I'd be certain where you stood; if he left
you alone, I'd do you properly. I saw you speak with the
Blake woman, though I wasn't close enough to hear you.
That's when I hared back and unwired the car."

"But didn't it occur to you that if they left me out here
alone, it meant that I was a perfectly innocent tourist?"

"Oh, I couldn't take chances on that," he said carelessly.
The man was monstrous.

"But if I'd known the first thing about cars, I could
have fixed it at once."

"I assumed that you didn't. You're a woman, after all."

"And you are a male chauvinist pig," I said loudly and
angrily. It was irrational, but that remark made him as
despicable to me as his cold-blooded egocentricity. To
have branded me absolutely ignorant because of my sex!

"What exactly does that curious phrase mean?"

"Oh, never mind," I said crossly. "So it was you I heard

on the platform here, just before Tommy showed up and captured me."

"Right. I went to Lisdoonvarna and called the Limerick hotel to see whether anyone using the O'Kelly name had registered there yet. No luck. So I came back to get rid of you. A shade too late for that night." He stretched, then brought the gun back to its position. "Eventually he sent Moran, alone, and the two of us were to take half the goods to New York. Then the 'family' was to send over two others for the second part. I never much cared for that idea. This is *my* haul. *My* money's invested in it. It's just as well that I did shoot Moran! The Dog Fox and I will make an unbeatable pair."

"You mean to kill him as soon as you've got everything," I said. "Why lie? Out of habit?"

"I'm not sure I'll put paid to him, no," said Quinn. "He's extraordinarily competent in many ways. I need one good man with me for the negotiations that are coming up. Besides," he said, "the two of us will stand that bloody New York of yours on its ear before we're done. It's never dealt with fellas like us, I tell you that. And the treasure! I think Amsterdam's the place to sell that. I need him. Yes. The stuff is too full of possibilities to simply melt down for a few quid. How much more is there?"

"We don't know yet. We only started finding it this afternoon."

"Much digging left? I loathe manual labor."

"I don't know."

"O'Flaherty will tell me," he said equably. "Any notion how old that chessboard is, love?"

"One thousand and seventy-odd years."

He whistled, and asked me how I knew.

"Oh, leave me alone," I said despondently, fingering my cheek, where the gash felt hideous. I wanted to think about Tommy.

Quinn Griffin smiled and leaned out to look down again. "Your man's coming up already. I hope he's found the keg all safe. It *must* have been there. I can't see anything but the Dog Fox; the cliff goes out a bit down there, and you can't see the base beyond the part that juts. Suppose you give that windlass a turn or two." He gestured with the automatic.

I stood and told Balor "Down," and went to the apparatus. "How do you work it?"

"Just push on the crank nearest you."

I tried, first listlessly, then with what strength I could muster. It turned slowly and the rope began to wind around the cylinder. After a minute or so, Quinn said impatiently, "Let be. He can do it when he's here."

I sat down.

It was impossible for me to think straight. I felt that I was going to be murdered, unless Tommy could prevent it somehow; and even if he did, I was not sure that I had the nervous stamina to go on living through the months and months that I knew I would need in order to recover from loving him. My whole life was in that hard brown man who was climbing up the face of the Cliffs of Moher.

Balor crept over to me on his belly and licked my face. It was the last straw. I began to cry again. I hated to do it in front of Quinn, to give him satisfaction, but I could not help it. I turned partway around and sat facing O'Brien's Tower, stroking Balor and blubbering.

And then it occurred to me. *Where were the Blakes?*

I glanced at my wrist, forgetting that my watch had been smashed and that I'd sent it to its long rest, down the loo, this morning. We might have been out here half an hour, an hour, even longer.

Could they have seen us, guessed the situation, slipped off down the slope for their car? Were they on the road now from Ennistymon with the gardai?

Did the gardai have guns? Was there such a thing as a rifle in Ireland, besides those of the I.R.A.? That, I thought in a bloody-minded fashion, was the only way that Quinn might be picked off from a distance, before he'd had the chance to shoot Tommy and me.

I prayed, and hugged Balor, and wept, and my brains were no more use to me than a bowl of mush. Less. I could have thrown a bowl at the maniac's head.

I looked at the heavy chessboard. I had the power to throw it certainly, at least to skim it at him over a short distance. But I have neither the arm nor the eye for throwing.

If Balor knew an Irish order for *Sic 'em*, it was useless to me, for I didn't know it myself. Tommy had said that he would attack on command, but he'd also said, that first night down here, that the dog would not harm me even if he were told to do so. Besides, I would not hazard Balor's life.

I had to wait for Tommy.

Tommy.

Think, don't feel, I said to myself.

What had he known before, for sure? That the drugs were worth at least half a million pounds; Quinn had told him that, via myself. That they were in the old cave; he said he'd guessed that on our way down here, and he could have, too, what with the ropes and windlass.

How about the polyethylene bags, the aluminum barrels?

No way, I thought, unless he'd already seen them for himself.

Or could he have surmised their existence? Could his entire offhand performance have been *just that*?

I found my mind clearing, as though a thick sour fog was blowing away in the rising wind from the sea. Had I been reacting so very extravagantly to a rather fine piece of my own craft?

He had been so convincing. . . .

Was Miss Grania Kirk of television such a snob that she'd credit no one outside the profession with being capable of playing a part for two or three minutes?

Oh Lord, Grania Kirk was indeed.

I remembered Tommy's bafflement on the night I'd told him of Quinn's talk about drugs. I could have sworn that was genuine.

Of the two episodes, one had to have been a piece of acting. Everything I knew, all that my intuition told me about the man, shrieked that today's was the performance. But I couldn't fathom how he'd known what sort of containers were down there. Maybe that was simple ignorance on my part. Maybe all opium—no, heroin—was shipped clandestinely in plastic-lined metal barrels? For all I could tell, every man alive knew that, just as every man alive apparently knew how to start a disabled car.

Quinn said something; I have no idea what it was. I was arguing myself out of the smog of suspicion into the clean air of trust. Doubt lingered, I couldn't rid myself of the knowledge that Tommy's prime motive for this painful winter on the cliffs was avarice, but the longer I thought, the more I convinced myself that my man had only taken a shot in the dark, and bought us some time.

And what could I do to help him make use of it?

"Quinn, dear," I said with some difficulty, eyes downcast.

"Here he is," said Quinn, and I jumped and looked up and Tommy was clambering onto the platform. He blinked at me, then at Quinn, as though he were not quite seeing us plain.

"Well," he said at last.

When it seemed that he was never going to add anything to that single word, Quinn said angrily, "Was it there, man?"

"Oh," Tommy said, "oh, yes, it's all right. It's in the sling." He shook himself all over. His shirt was blackened with sweat and spray, his trousers were soaked. I thought he was paler than normal. "That's the devil's own height," he said. "Look here, Griffin, when I secured the keg and shoved it off, it sank like a stone, sling and all."

Quinn burst into a laugh. "It's Perlon, I told you! The rope's Perlon. It stretches nearly a third of its length if you throw enough weight on it. Made for climbing, you see. It'll be right as a gold guinea, you watch. Put your back into one of the cranks, Dog Fox; we can't stand here all the day, and a wind rising."

"Give me a hand, then. I'm killed with the climbing." He walked slowly toward the machine, and I thought, he's not acting now, he's nearly reached his limit.

"You're being clever," said Quinn, grinning mischievously.

"Blast you! Damn you for the fool of all time! How can I haul that up by myself? After that climb? Tuck your bloody gun into your bloody pocket and give me a hand," shouted the O'Flaherty. "If you have anything in your head over and above those baby-blue eyes and the odd cobweb, use it! You know the contacts to sell the stuff, and I have half of it salted away. We need each other."

Quinn motioned me off to a safe distance, and thrusting his automatic into the front of his belt, took his stand on the opposite side of the windlass, facing the ocean. "Ready."

"Ready."

They began to crank together. Slowly the orange rope built up in layers on the cylinder. I wondered what I could do to help Tommy. I couldn't stand here being nothing but a burden to him. If I could distract Quinn so that Tommy could attack him—ordinarily I would have been sure that he could handle the man, but fatigue showed so plainly in his face and the movements of his arms, I was filled with doubt.

I picked up the silver chessboard, trying to make it seem an idle gesture, and turned it over and stared at the old letters engraved on the bottom. Terence would be able to read those runes easily, but they were a total mystery to me. I began to walk slowly away from the sea, my head bent over the heavy slab.

"Grania," Quinn grunted, hauling on the windlass, not even glancing at me, "if you take two more steps, you're a dead kipper."

"I'm sorry, I wasn't thinking," I said in a sulky voice.

"You were not," said Tommy. "Sit down."

I sat cross-legged where I was, the board on my lap. Balor tried to approach his master, was ordered off gruffly, and came slouching to me, bewildered and forlorn. I patted his neck.

We were about fifteen feet from the brink of the cliff.

The reeling in of the rope took longer, it seemed, than Tommy's climb had done. Eventually, though, the cranking began to look easier, and as the now-huge bulk of the wet rope was about to reach the crosspiece, which would have put an end to the machine's usefulness, the khaki sling came edging into view, bulging and still sodden with sea water.

The windlass was cogged. Quinn came around it and went to the rim, his gun again in his hand and his back turned only partway toward us. He bent and lifted the booty onto the platform. Tommy walked over to me. I handed him the precious ash-gray slab, staring into his eyes, trying to communicate my idea without making a sound, twitching a muscle.

It was the only weapon on the length and the breadth of that grisly stone deck. Many people would argue that, flawless and unique, historically priceless, it was worth more than were our two lives. To employ it as a club or missile would be a fantastic gamble.

And somewhere, far down in my soul, I think I was still unsure that Tommy, with all that fortune in sight, would really want to use a weapon against his old comrade-in-arms Quinn Griffin.

He took it from my hands.

13

And the poor old dog was drowned. . . .
—The Irish Rover

TOMMY SWUNG ON HIS HEEL, evidently examining the chessboard anew. Quinn faced toward him, the ugly muzzle of the gun rising. "You wouldn't be thinking, now that the stuff's home and dry—"

"Is that to be the rule from now on? Is that the way of it?" demanded the O'Flaherty. "Neither of us dares move?"

"For a while," said Quinn, studying him. "It's all where you can touch it now, Dog Fox; but *I* have only the half of the powder here."

"My face is hurting," I said, touching the scar. Quinn's eyes flicked to me at once. Tommy lowered the chessboard, dangling its unwieldy mass in his right hand. "It must mean that the Dread Women are near," I suggested.

Griffin's mouth opened, he swore savagely, his head snapped upward as he scanned the hill where O'Brien's Tower sat with its blind blank windows full of sky. The gun pointed at Tommy.

I drew a breath and, aiming a rigid arm out to sea, I emitted the loudest scream I could summon. Probably the oldest trick in the world for distracting someone's attention.

The reason that the oldest tricks in the world *are* the oldest is because they often work.

That wound on my cheek had been troubling Griffin, I believe, ever since I'd mentioned the Harpy fight. It had set his nerves on edge just enough to make him subject to suggestion. He jerked his face toward the ocean, for no more than a second or two.

Tommy raised his arm straight from the shoulder with enormous energy and slung the relic in a swift, vicious, underhand heave. I was aware in a fragmented way, among so many other things, of the board spinning, revolving in the air, like a shallow tinfoiled box thrown by a boy.

As it left his hand, he snapped out "Attack!" and Balor, who must have been yearning in his faithful doggy heart for this instant, surged up and forward. I do not remember whether he barked or howled or went silently for Quinn's throat, but his very motion was like a great roar.

Quinn Griffin fired twice before he was struck in the chest by the metal projectile. I suppose he must have been staggering backward even before the wolfhound hit him, but all I can see in the part of my memory where I unwillingly retain that terrible sight is the tall man, the silver slab crashing edgeways against the center of his white shirt, then the enormous grizzled dog obscuring everything as he slammed into Quinn, and after that the sudden disappearance of every element of the horrible tableau, dog and man and chessboard and the brown sling with its burden of an aluminum keg full of slow death.

I was up, running three or four long steps, throwing myself prone at the brink. I was not conscious of Tommy at all. I could hear only the diminishing shriek of the falling man. I stared downward, narrowing my eyes against the sun's glare on the blue water. I was in agony for the hound. No life could survive that plunge down the black cliff. Yet I must watch.

The combined force of hurtling slab and dog had carried them out in an arc past the narrow ledges, and they were dropping straight toward the water when I looked. The loaded hammock swung just below and beside me, quite safe, if anyone gave a damn.

I could see them plain at first. The dog seemed to have fastened his teeth in Quinn's neck, or face, and in a reflex of hideous pain Quinn had gripped Balor in an embrace like a parody of affection. I never saw the silver chessboard again; likely it was held tightly between them.

They revolved in air, so that for a moment the man was uppermost, then the dog, then the man. They grew tinier as I watched, and tinier still.

I heard Quinn screaming all the way down, seemingly without pause. At the last, it was a thread of sound broken by the mewing of startled gulls. They struck the surface of the ocean and were for a long instant the center of

an expanding, opening flower of white spray. Then this began to dissipate and die on the gently moving breast of the
waters.

But I was sure, I was almost sure, that I could see a
line moving directly inward toward the unseen base of the
cliffs, a line like a wake behind an infinitesimal dot.

"He's alive," I said.

Tommy was on one knee beside me. "No," he said, "no,
dearest, he could not be."

"The dog is alive," I said, insisting, talking to Tommy
or to God. "He was on top when they hit."

"You couldn't tell that from here. They are both dead,"
said Tommy, and then in that maddening kismet-phrase
that the Irish overwork, "It can't be helped."

I struggled to my feet and put my arms around him and
held him in a bear grip, saying that he was alive, Balor
was alive; and then that Tommy was alive and how glad,
how inexpressibly happy I was for that.

"You saved both our lives," he said into my hair, which
was blowing all over his face. Then he winced a little.

I drew back and saw that he was bleeding. "Oh," I said
stupidly, "oh, you were shot." Somehow I'd assumed that
Griffin had missed.

"Not badly. He fired too fast." He showed me the left
arm, where a bullet had furrowed down the heel of his
hand and left a slice diagonally across the muscles of his
forearm. It was welling scarlet. "It's nothing, truly," he
said.

I took him at his word. Under any other circumstances,
I'd have fussed all over him. But there was Balor.
"Tommy, I tell you he's alive, I saw him go, I saw them hit
and Quinn was underneath. He's alive. Quinn broke his
fall."

"Broke a six-hundred-and-fifty-foot fall?" He shook his
head, and there was naked sorrow in the dark face. "It
couldn't be done."

"I saw him swimming toward the cave!" I stared at his
wounded hand. He couldn't climb with that, he might have
got down to the sea but he'd never have come up again. I
said it without thinking: "I'm going down for him." Then,
in the pause afterward, I realized that it was true.

"You're not." He was sopping the blood into a dirty
handkerchief, examining the wound.

"I can do it. We'll drop the sling and if he's at the cave,

I can put him in it and you and Terence can haul him up." I sat on the rock and pulled off my brogues. "Give me those fancy tennies," I said. "The climbing shoes."

Tommy peered at me as though I'd gone crazy. "Grania, you know I'd do anything for the dog, but he's gone, he's dead. You haven't been down there. I have. You've no conception of the height."

I picked up Quinn Griffin's automatic pistol; he'd dropped it as he went back and over. I handed it to Tommy. "Is it still loaded?" He did something to it and nodded. "Fix it so I can shoot if I have to."

"Why?"

"If Balor is too badly hurt," I said, and my flesh crawled, "I won't be able to lift him. Or if it was Griffin who swam to the cave, I'll want protection."

"I tell you that you cannot go down, Grania. I won't allow it."

"Oh, *Dog Fox!*" I said angrily. "You'd go if you weren't injured."

"I would not. I know better than to think—"

"Stop wasting time! Give me the shoes and the gun!" Suddenly I was yelling at him, and I must have looked like a witch myself, with red scar and flying hair and contorted face. "You'd go, or Terry, but he's not here and seconds count! Hurry! Please *hurry!*"

He handed me the gun. "This is the safety," he said, tapping it. "If you need to fire, move it this way and pull the trigger." He sat down, almost sprawling with weariness or shock, and began unlacing the black-and-white shoes. I put the gun in the deep pocket of my shirt, and pulled on the soft, thin-soled footgear as Tommy watched me. "You have rather large feet," he said, "they fit you well."

"Do you like me less because I have big feet?" We were abruptly speaking idly, irrelevantly; the whole time that was coming now could not be dwelt on.

"Of course not, you're a tall woman. I meant that they suited you, not that the shoes fit. I would not have my girl teetering around on useless, miniature feet. You are really going down, then?"

"I am."

"Do you climb? Are you used to heights?"

"I never climbed, but heights don't frighten me. What can you tell me about it, to help?"

"Oh," he said, thinking, and unbuckling his belt, gave

me a little powdery cloth sack on a thong. "Hang this at your waist, it's full of chalk, it's to dry your hands on. Never look down, no matter how long you think you've been traveling. The gulls may come in to investigate you, but don't be frightened, just shout at them and they'll go away." He snapped his left hand irritably, so that the bright blood flew off to splash on the rock. "Damn it," he said, "what am I thinking of, to allow you—"

"You aren't allowing me, O'Flaherty," I said, standing up and testing the shoes, which felt like part of my feet, they were so light and flexible. "Nobody allows me. I'm going down so that I can sleep at night for the rest of my life."

"I know," he said. "And so that I can sleep. You're a marvel. Here, give us a hand."

Together we dragged up the sling and put it on the platform. I rolled the squat silvery keg of metal free of the soaking folds of cloth and was about to send it off the edge when he grabbed it.

"What are you doing? Would you have it picked up somewhere by some innocent soul? Or rot open and murder a million fish?"

"What will *you* do with it?"

"It must go to the authorities," he said. "There's another one down in the cave, but leave it, the gardai can fetch it later. We'll let the ropes be, they can use them ... what is it?"

"Nothing. I was only remembering what a terrific actor you can be when it's necessary."

He grinned. "I rather thought I'd given you a couple of bad minutes," he said, and that was all. He didn't reproach me for my lack of faith by so much as a lifted eyebrow. I believe he enjoyed knowing that he'd managed to fool a professional. "Here, put this ring on your wrist."

The steel hoop, which slipped over my hand easily, was attached to a four-foot length of Perlon, the other end of which had been fixed to a second ring that encircled the sling rope. "It keeps this within reach," he said, shaking out the soggy folds of khaki, "while you're negotiating the ladder. Then you can pull it to you when you're at the cave, if it's necessary."

"It will be. He's alive."

"You're an absolute single-minded donkey, you know," said Tommy sadly. He kissed me briefly and hard. "I love

you very much. Stand back a little now." I did so, thinking
that I *was* a fool but was stuck with it, and he pushed the
empty bundle over the edge, went to the windlass, and began to let the rope down as quickly as possible, having re-
versed the cog so that it wouldn't catch. I took the ring off
my wrist, which was being tugged back and forth, and
held it in both hands. The rope paid out with infinite slug-
gishness.

"How did you guess what the heroin was packed in?"

"Oh, that was a hopelessly inexcusable wild stab, I suppose, and if Griffin had been capable of thinking clearly
for a few seconds, he'd have known I was bluffing, for
how else would you take all that valuable powder to sea in
a small boat, if not in plastic bags within airtight, water-
tight aluminium barrels? How else could it have been
packed, to stay dry in a sea cave all winter? It was our
good luck that I said 'a barrel' and not 'barrels.' The rest
followed beautifully. I nearly ruined everything by saying
that the stuff tasted like bitter almonds, but stopped short
of that because I wasn't really sure; we were running in
great luck, my dear."

"You were using your brains, you mean. I never think
that fast."

"You underrate yourself consistently, Grania. The
chessboard was your idea, as well as the marvelous scream
at the imaginary Fury. I'd decided to send Balor at him
and follow myself, for I knew he never meant you, or the
dog, or any of us, to leave this place alive. I was all he
could safely watch at one time, till he'd found the rest of
his rotten narcotic. But the chessboard, that was genius. *I*
never considered it till you handed it to me."

"It was too valuable, too incomparable a thing to lose
like that," I said softly.

"Better it than the lot of us, Blakes and all. And better
at the bottom of the Atlantic than defiled by Griffin's
hands."

The rope was out.

"All right, my dearest girl," he said, putting his good
arm around me and hugging me, "time to go." It was a
measure of the man that, being convinced of my serious-
ness, he put no further objections in the way. "I'll run up
to the den, splash some antiseptic on this gash, and try to
find Terry. If he and Alanna are gone, for the gardai I
suppose, I'll do my best on the windlass alone. When

you've got Balor in the hammock, fire two shots. I'll bring him up."

"And one shot," I began.

"I shall know what that means, too."

"See you in a while," I said, and kissed him and went to the head of the ladder. I lay down on my stomach and wriggled backward, holding Tommy's hand tightly with one of mine, and felt my legs slide over into space; I bent in the middle and groped and got a good firm purchase on a rung with both feet, and eased back and down and before I knew it was holding the ropes instead of my darling's hand, and there was black stone in front of my face and a wind at my back and nothing else in the whole world at all.

At first it was not bad. I remember wondering whether my nerves had taken all the punishment they could absorb, whether I was beyond caring what happened to me, out of pure exhaustion of mind through fear and horror; for I was quite cool, indeed, quite cold, descending rung by rung as if I were going to touch ground in a few feet, as if I were only scrambling down out of an apple tree. Then I began to think about that, and recognized that whatever had happened to me, I was still in command; I meant to go to the bottom of the cliffs and rescue the wolfhound and get back to Tommy, that was that, and I need not search for explanations of why I was proceeding so well. I recollected the afternoon I'd traveled with the tinkers to Lisdoonvarna, and how I'd realized in the caravan that I'd been turned by hazards and afflictions into a very different girl from the timid miss who'd been creeping mousily around Ireland. And I'd been toughened up immoderately since *then*.

If I hadn't been so aware of how I'd wronged Tommy in my thoughts such a short time ago, I'd have been pretty proud of myself.

How far had I come?

Mustn't look down. Could I look up? No. Watch the rock. Pride goeth before a fall.

Don't even think that word!

The big ring was on my left elbow, and the single line out there kept tugging at it lightly, suggesting a sentient thing that would like to pull me off into space if it dared. I veered my mind away from fancies like that. This precipice was haunted enough without inventing ghosts.

I'd laid the Dread Women to my own satisfaction, at any rate, if not to poor mad Quinn's. He had really believed in them.

Never mind, Quinn was dead and gone.

I was descending a dead man's ladder, with dead man's shoes on my feet, a dead man's gun in my pocket.

Enough! My palms were sweating.

I stopped, toes nudging the dark stone, and hooked an arm around the nylon rope and rubbed my hands across the dry chalk sack. I took a long breath and began to go down once more.

The breeze pushed gently at my back. I had forgotten to look to the west, where much earlier I had noticed a line of low clouds. Were they building up?

What I needed to polish off this whole adventure was a brisk squall of wind and rain.

Why had I thought about the Dread Women? Now they came back to me, or rather, one did: I felt her brush at my mind and then I clearly saw a terrible image, lasting no more than three or four seconds, of myself like a fly on the face of Moher and a great ragged-winged creature coming in toward me from the sea, talons set like a diving falcon's. I was beginning to think in pictures, an occupational hazard of mine. I tried to wrench my thoughts from this one and so naturally it stuck; and like a sequence from some film by Bergman I saw the Harpy's plunge, my cringe against the rock wall, then an instant repetition of it, and another, one after another, the same bit of action—perhaps seventy-two frames, I said to myself idiotically—over and over and over with no variation or letup, that damned zoom shot from the POV of God till I thought if it didn't end at once I would go out of my head.

All this while, I went down step by step, the reach of my legs adjusted now to the precise distance between rungs, my hands steady on the ropes. The cliff had been slanting slightly outward from the perpendicular; now it suddenly moved inward, and the ladder, instead of resting against the wall, dangled in air. I had to be careful not to thrust my foot too far forward, lest I miss the rung and—well, I wouldn't fall, but a misstep would scare the assurance out of me, and make this descent more of a nightmare than it needed to be. There was a fierce desire to look down, to make sure I would plant each foot properly. I lost the steady mechanical rhythm of my step and now every advance meant groping and patting with the sole so that I wouldn't flounder down too far or put my weight lopsided on a crosspiece.

I realized that I was rid of the recurring flick of the Dread Woman, and concentrated on the ladder so that the maddening, unfinished scene wouldn't return. Then I was close to the sheer rock again, and got back into the right cadence and moved downward briskly.

After some time I halted to dry my hands, and stood for a moment on one of the treads, wheezing and gaping at the wall before me. This journey to the ocean was almost as hard on the legs as my chimney climb and perch of last night. Shooting pains were becoming a way of life.

I tried to relax my body, and found it surprisingly easy to do. Somewhere far inside my consciousness I had been thinking that bad tension was inevitable. Now I discovered that I'd been wrong. Deciding that a rest would help me, and in spite of the urgency I felt about Balor, I stood stock-still with my arms entwined in the ropes and caught my breath. The gulls were calling ceaselessly in a querulous chorus. Without thinking, I looked down, and below me a multitude of the creatures poised hanging in the air, as motionless as a school of fishes floating in clear water.

I closed my eyes, sick of the sight of layered black rock and a little afraid of continuing to look down, for fear I should start to think of this as going into a depth (as if the ocean were the floor of some unimaginable cellar) rather than descending from a height.

Closed eyes, however, were no good at all. I instantly became aware of movement, a motion that I could not define—whether the ladder and I were swaying gently back and forth in the wind, or the cliffs were moving in and out before me, I knew that there was no such thing as a dead calm to be had. I opened my eyes. I could detect no motion. I shut them, and it was there. But the cliffs could not move; they were not part of some titanic creature, but only . . .

Only the Cliffs of Moher. Yes. Oh yes. If any mountain on earth deserves the use of that curious phrase "the living rock," they do. And here was I, a midge creeping down their flanks, and if they took it into their uncanny thoughts to shake me off, they would do it.

I had been safer in my emotions watching the reduplicated episode of the Dread Woman. I unwound my arms and holding the ropes as casually as possible, I leaned backward and rested like a sailor in the high sheets, spine straight, heels down and head tilted upward.

I couldn't tell how far I had come, because of the bulge of the cliff, but it looked to be a very long distance to the top of the wall. And I had no vertigo whatever. Should I look down again? No.

I thought of Tommy, and smiled. I tried to remember how many stairs there are in the Washington Monument. To estimate the number of rungs I'd put above me by now. To relax, rest, rest.

I nearly let go of the ropes.

Collecting myself, I started again, pleased that I could be at such ease here. Only my legs ached, and my palms were wishing that I'd put on Quinn's gloves.

The dread for Balor, the gnawing worry about Tommy's wound, they must have been there in my mind, as well as horror at Quinn's terrible death, and sorrow for the drowned silver chessboard of Cormac; but until I was aware that the sea was very close, I thought only of the descent, of one crosspiece and the next, without end, limitlessly going down down down.

Then I felt a curious pain in my eyes, and blinked until it faded. They had apparently been drying up and shrinking in the sockets from my unblinking stare at the rock. So much for Grania Kirk's superb ease and control.

Now it must be safe to glance down. I felt the lightest of salt sprays on my face, tasted it, and heard the sliding, talkative waters. So I looked down. It was all right, for I was only about the height of a bungalow from the surface. But two things appalled me and made me flinch: the cave was nowhere to be seen, and directly below me was Quinn Griffin. He was floating on his back, his arms flung out at full length above his head, and there was a large brown bird perched on his chest watching me.

I had never seen one like it before. It resembled a mean-tempered gull. Trying not to see Quinn's face, I shouted at the brute, which grudgingly lifted itself and flew off with one harsh, contemptuous yell in my direction. I am grateful that I did not then know that it was a skua, which is vicious and can knock a man down with one swipe of a wing. After my recent experience with that other seabird the albatross, I think, had I known the skua's nature, that I might have panicked and fallen straight onto it.

Facing inward again, I went down the ladder for perhaps a dozen feet, past a slight overhang, and abruptly there was darkness before me, blacker than the rock wall. It was the smugglers' cave. I glanced down and gauged my distance, swung round to the left and dropped onto a ledge like the pouting lower lip of this small, deep stone mouth; and righted myself, with the splashing of the low surf on my ankles. I believe it was almost exactly high tide. Without thinking one way or the other about anything, the corpse or the dog or the ocean, I started into the cavern, and got the greatest shock of the whole event, perhaps of my life. Something jerked at my arm and yanked me back and sideways.

I screamed.

Quinn Griffin had come out of the sea and laid his hand on my elbow—

Well, he hadn't. It was the ring on the Perlon rope, to which I'd grown so accustomed that I'd forgotten it. The sling was under water, and creating a drag.

That was all there was behind the single sharpest fright of that miserable, dangerous hour.

I shook my head, wiped clammy sweat with the back of an almost useless hand, looked into the hole whose floor slanted sharply up and in till shadows hid it, and shouted Balor's name.

At the third call he came out to me, as I had been convinced that he would: limping, a look of bewilderment in his one good eye, and apparently sore all over, but alive, whole and alive, our dear old dog waiting patiently down here in the dark for us to come for him!

I fell on my knees and embraced him, and he licked my nose tentatively, then with a burst of joy. He put his paws on my shoulders and barked, with a great lapse of his usual manners, right in my face. He was sodden and shivering, but he was alive.

Disengaging myself with difficulty, I took off the hoop and hauled on the rope until, after I'd heaped up some yards of it, the end with the sling appeared. I got this onto the rock beside us. It was made of some sort of thin, tough cloth, attached to the orange rope with four or five bands of webbing, and after I had sloshed and wrung the water from it, was very light for all its bulk. Balor sat and stood alternately beside me, wagging his tail at half speed.

Then the body began to come in.

I did my best not to see it, but with each low wave it crept nearer, the arms at full stretch toward me, the head thrown back and the mouth open. Soon I was shuddering as frequently as the soaked Balor. It was only a dead body, it was not the evil, pitiful man any longer, but the time was gone when I could have shrugged it off as a hideous prop dummy of straw and wax. This was Quinn Griffin.

The skua had been at him, and the beautiful sparkling eyes were not fine and handsome any longer.

"It's all right," I kept saying to Balor as I worked, spreading the khaki out into a hammock for him, "it's all right, he can't hurt us now." The dog, sensible as ever, ignored him.

When I had the sling ready, I looked at Balor and knew that he should be dried a little; but there was nothing except my plaid shirt. That must do, for his need was greater than mine. A wet shirt wasn't going to give me a cold, but the shock and drenching might well bring on pneumonia for him. So I stripped it off and after sleeking his coat down repeatedly with my palms, as I used to do with my Irish setters after a rain, to splash away as much water as possible, I toweled him briskly until the shirt was wetter than he. I put it on again, and, smelling remarkably doggy and salty at the same time, induced him to step onto the middle of the sling and lie down.

It was time for the signal. First I petted Balor and made much of him, so that he wouldn't be too greatly startled; then I went to get the automatic, where I'd laid it just inside the mouth of the cave. It was then I first noticed the stench. Whether it had grown until it now could overpower the pervasive salt tang in the air, or whether I'd simply been too occupied to notice it before, I don't know. But it was there, a noxious odor leaking out of the depths of the smugglers' hole.

I cannot adequately describe it. If you can imagine a deep burrow in which a family of some sort of carnivorous beasts have been living for generations, never coming out and certainly never cleaning the place up at all, and if your nose will stand for you conceiving what such a lair

would smell like, you may have it. Something between a
fish market, a slaughterhouse, and a hyena's den.

The wonder was that Balor had not come out of that
place with the charnel stink in his coat. Perhaps he was
too wet.

I backed off from it, having half meant to step inside to
look for the second barrel of heroin, but absolutely op-
posed to doing so now. I aimed the automatic out to sea
and tried to pull the trigger. Nothing happened. I'd forgotten about the safety. I fiddled with it, got it off after a
couple of false starts, and shot twice, the echoes booming
and crashing over the water and in the unknown, reeking
depths of the cavern behind me. Balor pricked his ears but
did not move. Oh, *good* dog.

Inadvertently I glanced at the corpse as I waited, and
just then a swell pushed it partly out of the water at me,
and I disgraced myself with a choked-off scream, huddling
down beside Balor. The loose coils of rope began to rise.
Resolutely I put aside horror, dropped the gun into my
pocket, and gave the great wolfhound a last pat on the
neck. I stood up until it was time, then brought the material together at the top so that he was hidden in its folds
and the straps of webbing tightened without twisting or
sliding out of place. When the rope was taut I watched,
talking to him all the time, but the shapeless bundle did
not move. If Tommy were alone on the windlass with his
one good arm, he might not be able to lift Balor at all;
the beast weighed about a hundred and twenty pounds.

In that case, I would just have to wait here until
Tommy had found help. I prayed that Quinn Griffin would
sink, or be washed somewhere else.

The Perlon was very tight, as I discovered when I
touched it. Could it be caught above, on some sharp spur
of rock? No, it was stretching, stretching till it almost
twanged; Quinn had said that it would lengthen, under
enough pull, by a third.

Balor stirred restlessly in his khaki bag. I raised my
voice and told him that he was a splendid dog, the best of
all possible dogs, that we loved him and would see him
safe home, that he had been given his life by a miracle
and could not possibly lose it now, that he would lie very
still whatever happened. . . .

There was an upheaval within the cloth, and then quiet.
I think he had turned around and lain down in an easier

position. Then the sling was moving along the wet stone, inch by painful inch. It bumped once and lifted into the air, swung out and back and moved upward.

Watching it, I moved to the ladder and went up two or three rungs. I had decided against holding the hoop, for fear of being tugged off my perch. Then I heard a noise that was not the grumbling and licking and swoosh of the ocean. It came from behind me—no, from in *front* of me, in the depths of the cave. It was a dry, dry rustling sound, a stirring and shifting of something alive in there. I stared at the opening for a moment and then climbed rapidly half a dozen rungs. From the corner of my eye I could see Quinn's corpse just touching the rim of rock before the cave. Then I had ascended to the jut of the overhang, and saw and heard nothing further from below.

I risked my balance to lean out and shove the big lump of the sling free as best I could. There were a bad few seconds when it seemed to be caught under the rock, but then it came loose and rose without a jerk. Whoever was on the windlass was going slowly but steadily. I climbed, not knowing that I climbed, all attention focused on the dog in the bag.

Nothing was important in the universe but the dog. There was no body moving smoothly in and out, in and out, on the water beneath. There was no mephitic grotto housing seabirds or pterodactyls or Dread Women. There was no loving man above me either. There was the dog, the dog who must be saved.

The straps were firm, the rope held; the fasteners were solidly placed, and I watched and talked, saying "Easy, quiet, good dog, easy, easy," to let him know that I was with him, and all the while I prayed for him not to panic, but to come safe to the top.

I should have known that Balor would do as he had been told. He never budged, but lay there, his body spread over the support of three of the webbing bands, unable to see anything except, perhaps, a loop or slit of blue sky at the top when the folds of cloth gaped for a moment.

There seemed no such thing as time. At least, I don't recollect thinking at any point, *We must be halfway*, or *How long?* or anything save *Please, God, let him be saved; let him lie quiet and be saved*.

The rise of the sling was constant. Tommy had found

someone to help, the Blakes or tourists or a farmer or tinkers.

The rope and the sling held, there was no ghastly instant when a hook tore loose or a band snapped, and if the Perlon frayed I never saw it; but we went up, up, the magnificent dog and I, and although my legs must have shrieked in agony, their message did not reach my brain. Without fright, without glancing up or down, I climbed, I went clear to the crest of the Cliffs of Moher and did not even know when I was at the platform until my wrist was caught and I cried out and clutched for the eternal rope that was no longer there, but Alanna said "Hush, dear," and dragged me over the brink, as Tommy and a man I had never seen before took hold of the bundle and pulled it to safety alongside me.

I watched them unhook and unwrap and bring Balor into the sunlight, and he blinked at Tommy with his good eye and whined.

"Hello, old fella," Tommy said huskily. Then the hound stood up and stretched and rammed his head into Tommy's middle, and the O'Flaherty went to his knees and, looking over the gray head at me, said, "He'd have died if it hadn't been for you. He'd have died alone."

I crawled across a yard of the rock—my legs were totally numb—and Tommy lifted me and held me tightly. His eyes were running with tears. "Thank you, Grania Kirk," he said.

"I told you he was alive," I said, "and he was."

"It wasn't possible," he said, "but here he is, and yes, *a ghrá,* you told me so."

"I did." I hugged him hard, as hard as my flaccid muscles would permit. "Oh, darling," I said, "I'm back!"

"Keen as ever," said Terence, who had come around the windlass with a fourth man and was standing beside us. "No addleheaded babblings about dreadful heights and dizziness, just the straightforward statement that she's back. Gentlemen, may I introduce Miss Grania Kirk, an American lady, who has the nerves of an ingot and the bravery of Finn Mac Coul himself."

I smiled weakly and shook hands with the two policemen.

14

We'll join our hands in wedlock bands—
I'm speakin' to ye now!
    —Maid of the Sweet Brown Knowe

A GREAT DEAL HAD BEEN HAPPENING while I was on my rescue mission.

When I'd disappeared below the first overhang and Tommy had been satisfied that I could manage the rope ladder, he'd gone up to the den to discover the Blakes toiling away, oblivious to everything including time, at clearing the entrance to the treasure room of Bran Roe O'Conor. They were thunderstruck to hear that we had been gone for nearly two hours, that Tommy had been wounded and Griffin killed, and that I was descending the Great Wall of Thomond after a dog who was certainly dead.

"I thought the two of you were just upstairs, you know," said Alanna. "I thought you'd been gone ten minutes." No one is less aware of the world than a scientist at work.

"I never thought of you at all," Terence admitted.

They fixed Tommy's wound hurriedly; it was, as he'd said, only a shallow but gushing furrow down the hand and arm; then they rushed to the platform. In Quinn's blue car, Alanna roared off to Ennistymon to bring help, while Tommy and Terence waited for my signal shots. These sounded just as she returned with the politely skeptical gardai. While those two gentlemen, with an occasional spelling by Terence, cranked Balor up the cliff, Tommy told them everything that he knew of Quinn Griffin, both now and when he had been with the I.R.A. in Ulster.

"An informer, was he?" said one of them, who was not working on the windlass at the time. "Small loss then, sir, if I may speak such ill of the dead and he at one time a friend of yours." He began to loosen the metal straps of the squat aluminum keg.

"A man who's dead isn't worth hating," said Tommy soberly, "except of course for King Billy and Cromwell; but I could find it in my heart to hate that man down there in the sea."

"I know what you mean, sir," said the garda. He got the keg open and undid the top parcel of shiny white, crystalline powder, touched a finger to it and to his tongue, and made a face. "They couldn't sell that to *me*," he said. "What is it again?"

"Heroin," said Tommy. "At least he told us it was."

"You wouldn't have a notion where it came from, would you?"

"I would not."

"Pity. Perhaps the young lady down there will know?"

"If Griffin confided in her." He explained who I was—evidently he'd left that out before, for this is the way Alanna told it to me—and how I had come to give Griffin the password by accident.

"On the television, is she?" said the garda, giving Tommy a peculiar look. "Is that the way of it?"

"It is," said Tommy.

"And what did you say this is worth, in round numbers, again?"

"Griffin claimed half a million pounds."

"God and Mary with us! I wouldn't give you a tanner for the lot," said the garda, and shut the keg up. "Well, you understand there will be all classes of questions asked about this, by one authority and another."

"Naturally."

"I wonder if I might take just a note of your identifications?"

Terence and Alanna gave him that information. He lifted his brows at their affiliations. "There would be persons in Dublin who would know you, then."

Terence, grunting at the windlass, said a name. Rather carelessly, Alanna told me with a smile. It was not just a name, but a Name.

"Indeed," said the officer. "You would not be making sport of me, sir?"

"No," said Terence, "I have too much respect for your position for joking. I'll come in to Ennistymon with you, and we can speak to him on the telephone. I designed his house for him."

"You understand that I would never in this world doubt you myself, but there are certain regulations. And hero—hero— and drugs, that is, and a dead man, and him lost in the sea and all, it is sobering business."

"Perfectly understood," said Tommy.

Again the garda shot him an odd look, but said nothing, and went to take his turn at a crank, evidently forgetting to obtain Tommy's credentials.

When I had emerged from the horrible spaces below the platform, and Alanna was massaging my calves and thighs to ease the astonishing pain of them, I repeated to the police what Quinn had told me while we'd waited for Tommy. I also remembered to hand over his automatic to them.

"Not much to go on," said the younger, "but there's a name or two, at any rate, and certain places and passwords. Well now. You're a brave young lady, Miss Kirk. And I've seen you on the I.T.V. or the R.T.E., I'm sure of it. Your face is most familiar. How do you like Ireland?"

"Very much indeed," I said shakily. I was in the midst of all sorts of reactions to my climb, as well as to the forces of the law. I seemed to have been a fugitive for half my life in this place.

"Do you plan to be in the country for a bit yet?"

"Oh, for a very long time," I told him, not catching Tommy's eye.

"You'll be with these gentlemen and this lady?"

"I will."

"That's grand." He faced Tommy with an abrupt movement. "I know you," he said, and my heart gave a thump of fear. "I've been studying on it, and I know who you are. Fox, Fox—"

"Right," said Tommy, as I felt my insides flop.

"O'Fox! Tommy O'Fox!" said the garda jubilantly.

"That's meself," said he broadly. I stared, but now *he* would not catch *my* eye.

"Sure I've sat this far from you," said the man, measuring with his hands, "many's the night. I hope that isn't going to interfere with your craft," he said, pointing at Tommy's bound hand.

"Not a bit of it, it's not all that bad as it looks," said Tommy.

"I'm happy to hear it. You're the best, you're one of the very best." The garda burst suddenly, ludicrously into song. " 'The gray dawn had crept o'er the stillness of morning, the dewdrops they glistened like icicled breath!' "

I gawked at him.

"Damn the tune else I'd ever start off with," said Tommy incomprehensibly.

"Nobody brings the tears to a man's eyes like you do with 'Lay Him o'er the Hillside,' sir. Here, Joe! This gentleman here is Tommy O'Fox!" the garda shouted at his mate, who was about four feet away from him. "I for one'ld be proud to say I'd shaken your hand if I might." Tommy, looking embarrassed, shook hands with both of them, "And me to be demanding that Mr. Blake go into town and prove who you all are," said the young fellow scornfully. "Sure the duties of a chap's job should not blind him to all decency. Ridiculous! Of course you needn't leave here till your archaeo-what's-it is done, Mr. O'Fox."

"But you'll need—"

"Do I not know you better than me own wife if I happened to have one!" It was the first Irish bull I'd ever encountered, and I had to cough to cover a chuckle. I had never really believed in them. "Isn't your word as good as Kevin Barry's himself, by God!" His gaunt scarlet face was full of pleasure. "Never worry your mind over this bit of a muddle," he said confidently. "Just come in at your leisure and sign the statement and it'll be grand."

"That's good of you."

"It's the least I could do for yourself and the son of your father, Mr. O'Fox. What was his sainted name again? I'm bad on names."

"Hugh O'Flaherty."

"Red Hugh O'Flaherty?" said the second garda, who had not been overly impressed before. Tommy nodded. "This is like meetin' a piece of history," said the man with awe. "Tim's right, sir, there's no need for you to be bothered by the red tape. We'll see to it."

"Very good of you both," said Tommy. They shook hands all round again, including mine, and the younger one picked up the keg of heroin and balanced it on his shoulder. He saluted.

"We'll take the man Griffin's motorcar to Ennistymon, then," he said. "Have you the keys? Thanks. It's probably stolen, if the truth were known. There was no good in that one. Great luck to you all with the digging yonder." They left us, and Tommy and I at last stared at each other.

"O'Fox?" I said.

"It's a County Meath name."

"But what was that all about? Red Hugh?"

"The da was large in the Troubles, for all he only came up to your shoulder. He's in the history books. I told you. As for me, a man must earn a living somehow, mustn't he? I changed my name so I wouldn't be trading on the old fella's reputation, but word got about."

"You're a musician?" I said. "I thought you were—"

"You thought I was the sort to lounge idly on the da's bags of money."

"I did *not!*"

He laughed. "You thought I was an adventurer. I know. When you could never get down to asking what I did, I knew. Ex-I.R.A. runner, for hire as troubleshooter, spy, or what-have-you."

"What do you play? Why, you're really in my own line of work," I said happily.

"I tinker with a guitar, and I mumble sometimes."

"Oh, he's a folk singer," said Alanna. "He does the pubs and someday I think he'll be doing the concert halls. He's very good."

"As the peeler said, one of the best," added Terence.

"You're prejudiced, there are hundreds as good as I, and better. And shall we take the dog up now and put him by the fire?" Tommy's voice had a blush in it. "And see what we can do about the wreckage in the crypt?" He picked up Quinn's coat and gloves, and the climbing shoes that I'd discarded; he glanced at the windlass and ropes. "Safe enough to leave them as they are," he muttered. "No tourist's going to climb down *that* for a lark." He collected the old iron smuggler's spikes from where they had lain at some distance, and thrust them into his pockets for safekeeping.

"Where's the chessboard of Cormac?" asked Terence suddenly, staring around.

"In the ocean below these foul cliffs," said Tommy shortly.

"Oh." The long face looked stunned for only a moment. Then Terence said, "Well, so long as you three aren't!" and turned toward the keep. Of all the selfless statements that I have ever heard of, I believe that this was the most splendid. Poor Terence had not even glimpsed that incredible relic. Yet he never spoke of it in my hearing again, or seemed to grieve. So far as I know, he never even asked Tommy how its loss had come about.

We started for our den. Alanna asked why on earth Quinn hadn't recognized that Tommy was bluffing about having found the heroin, for even she could have guessed how it would have been packed.

"I can't say, of course," he told her, "but I think that at bottom he was simply lonely. Something human in him, or sane if you like, wanted a partner, a friend. I used to believe that the most isolated creature in the world was the informer; but an informer who's gotten himself into the dirtiest business going, well, he must be far more alone, especially when he's as intelligent as that man was. He longed to think that I was on his own level and ready to join him."

"A friend would have helped him to fight off the Dread Women," I said, clambering over the tilted flags above the platform. I told them how Quinn had been as credulous as I had once been about those sick horrors.

Terence looked at my slashed cheek. "I shall always wonder, I suppose, if that *was* an albatross you fought."

"Who's credulous?" asked Tommy.

"I am. I examined that bird carefully. There were teeth marks on its neck. Grania never bit it. I think it rammed into Balor and he killed it. You know he'd never savage a dead bird."

Tommy frowned. "You never told me that. It's odd."

"Another thing. The way Grania described what she fought reminded me of something in Yeats, something that Wilde once quoted—"

"Of course."

"Curse you. It was about the pooka. I looked it up, to refresh my memory, in Grania's Yeats. 'Like all spirits, he is only half in the world of form.' Now doesn't that sound like the thing Grania told us of?"

"It's perfect," I said. "It felt partly intangible." I gave a quick, irrepressible shiver. "Another thing—"

"I take a very poor view of this sort of superstitious chatter," said Tommy. "You've had enough nightmares for one long year."

"Wait, though. Did you smell anything in the cave, the smugglers' cave, when you were getting the barrel?"

"No. Only the salt air."

"Well, I smelled the most horrible stench, except for what the albatross or whatever spat on me, that I've ever encountered. Not at first, but just before I went up with Balor. And I heard a dry, leathery, rustling sound, like something disturbed in its sleep, something made of wings and bones and gristle."

"Imagination," he said shortly.

"No! I was thinking of nothing but the hound." I put my hand on Balor's head where he tramped wearily beside me. "I wasn't scared, except of Quinn's body. I was *busy*, damn it. I wasn't looking for Harpies."

"I always did like the pterodactyl theory," said Alanna.

"I, conversely, hold for the Dread Women," said Terence. "I'm serious. There are more things in heaven and—"

"Shut up," said Tommy. "That's not Wilde, that's Shakespeare."

"Nonetheless," said Terence quietly, "I shall always wonder."

"Me too," I said.

Then we were at the den, which stood open and inviting after so much hellishness in the outer world. I made certain that Tommy closed both doors.

"And there is this fact," said Terence. "You are the dearest friend a man ever had, Tommy, and vastly superior to me in many ways; but by Garad of the Black Knee, you haven't an ounce of Celtic psychic power in you, and this girl carries it in her bones. I believe she smelled the Women in their lair and you did not, because the stench, shall we say, was only half in the world of form. There let the matter rest."

"Amen," said Tommy. "Build up the fire for the hound."

We did so, and he made Balor lie down almost on top of the smoking turf, and gave him a bowl of warm tinned broth with whiskey in it, the dog's favorite treat. While Balor was lapping this, Tommy ran his fingers all over the damp body, probing and testing, and told us that he would be lame for a few days, but was not permanently injured.

"Why did you tell me that he wouldn't attack me?" I asked, curious.

"When?"

"The first night."

"Oh, yes. He wouldn't. He will attack only men. I trained him so."

"You trained him as an attack dog?"

"Only for cases of dire necessity. Today was the first."

"And the last," I said.

"He is your dog now, of course."

"Ours."

"Yours. You'll see. Well," he said, rising and rubbing his hands together, "will we just see to that small problem below? Now that we're sealed into our snug old world again? Do we need tools, you Blakes?"

"No. We're almost through. It's a very slender passageway we're opening, Dog, a niggardly little tunnel; the archaeologist here won't let me move much for fear of bringing it all down. But I think we can manage to negotiate it. Maybe you're too broad," said Terence, his brows creased, "I'm not sure. But it won't be long, at any rate, till at least the Kirk child here will be able to wriggle through."

"If the Kirk child has any strength left after climbing the cliff," said Alanna. She touched my cheek just below the scar. "Dear Grania," she said, "it will need plastic surgery. You look like a veteran gallowglass yourself."

"That's okay," I said, "as long as I don't have to see it until I'm stronger."

"Would you like to sleep a while?" asked Tommy.

"Try to make me lie down, with the hoard waiting!"

We each took a lantern or a torch this time, and trooped down the staircase to the chaos of the lower entrance, the ancient stonework of the vice absolutely glowing with the blaze of light. At first I saw no change in the cascaded beams, wicker, and debris. Then Alanna pointed out where the two of them had pushed gingerly, shored up, drawn out, and nudged ever so gently aside until they had penetrated that hugger-mugger complexity with a winding burrow that looked like an underpass for elves. I was the narrowest of shoulder and hip, but I doubted that I could get through it without bringing down half a ton of wreckage on my back.

"And we thought we'd done that in ten minutes. . . . Don't worry," said Alanna when I'd mentioned dubiously that it seemed very cramped in there, "the jumble isn't as bad as it looks. It's the harmless heaps of plaster and broken rock, really, that make it appear so impenetrable. The only danger is that a timber will slide down and drop some of those slabs on us—"

"That's a relief," said Tommy. "Only a slab or two! My God!"

"It's had a long time to settle and wedge into place, and I *have* done a little work of this sort before," she said tartly. "The tunnel's quite safe if nobody bangs an elbow or a foot into one of the supporting members."

"Supporting members of a disjointed anarchy of precarious havoc," said Tommy, who had set down his lantern and was moving from side to side scanning the caved-in mess. "Look here, I know you two are wild to see what's safe in there, if anything is, but shooting through the midst of it like hares into a warren is, well, it's a ticket to Hy Brazil."

"Where?" I asked.

"That's one of our mythical places where the living don't go," he said, standing on his toes. "I wish I were a foot taller. What can you see over this bloody barricade?"

"About a third of the roof's come down. All the ruin is on this side of the chamber, I think," said Terence. "You can see where they extended the loo upward from the natural crevice to the den above, using wickerwork packed with a sort of mortar that probably was mixed with earth and bullocks' blood. It's almost like a baked clay pipe. I still don't grasp the reason."

"I do," said Tommy.

"I bet I could get through this," I said, grunting, as I knelt and peered into the crude tunnel. "Why don't I try it?" And Tommy began to object strongly; and with no forethought, I compacted myself as much as I could and started in.

It was inexcusable. I had no right whatever to jeopardize the treasure, the dubious stability of the broken structure, or my own life, which no longer belonged exclusively to me. I can say in my defense only that I felt invulnerable. I had traversed the Cliffs of Moher, and an eighteen-inch-high gallery under tottery beams and tilted flagstones was as comfy by contrast as my own bathroom at home in New York. I didn't even think of the fact that many a mountain climber and steeplejack has come to grief in his tub. I simply went in.

Alanna told me afterwards that Tommy had made a grab for my legs, but missed, due to my first impulsive scuttling rush. After that he didn't dare try to reach me, for fear of the enormous weight above.

I crept forward, or perhaps "wormed" is the only accurate word, keeping to the center of the tunnel and using my elbows and hands to haul myself forward. The Blakes had both been in here and there was plenty of room for me. I had gone about three yards, I think, when I found the thing narrowing. I stopped. My forearms rested on sharp stone rubble. There was a long solid-looking timber aslant the path. Beyond it I could make out shadowy forms, some pillars and cubes, some intricately shaped and unidentifiable to me. I had left my torch on the floor beside Tommy's lantern, but there was plenty of light sharding through the debris from the Colemans, by which to view the room when I got out of this shaft. All that I was interested in at the moment was passing the big beam, for, so far as I could tell, it was the final obstacle.

I squinted at the upper end. It rested on a twisted mass of wickerwork. The other end lay on the flagged floor. I could see nothing that was supported by this beam.

"Hey," I said.

"Yes?" said Terence eagerly.

"We can do it. Stand away," I said, "in case."

"In case of *what*?" demanded the O'Flaherty.

"Of a slight setback." I was not being stupidly funny in the face of peril. I was merely aware that now the gods of the island were with me for good and all, and that I could not be hurt or endangered any more.

I got both arms under the canted beam and propped my elbows close to each other and, ignoring the babble of questions behind me, lifted. It was an excruciatingly painful movement, and for a few seconds I felt every muscle of my body contract in protest. Then I gave a great heave and the timber moved sluggishly away from me and slid down the other side of the heap of wicker and smashed on the floor, and I waited calmly as the brief echoes faded and the dust rose.

Nothing else fell. I'd been right, the oak beam had lain on the verge of the wreckage without anything being balanced on it. The Blakes had been within one minute of victory when Tommy had arrived to drag them away.

I crawled over the beam and got to my feet. "Come on in," I said, "it's all right."

The Blakes came first, pushing the lanterns before them, and then Tommy with two big torches stuck in his hip pockets and his shoulders brushing the sides of the tunnel now and again, but without catastrophe.

And we were standing together, the four of us almost shoulder to shoulder, and what was left of Bran Roe's treasure house lay before us.

There was a silence that you could have rubbed between your fingers. It lengthened and thickened until it began to choke the breath back into my throat.

There were things there, many things untouched by the fall of the roof and undamaged by the passing of the centuries: there was the warm old glow of thick gold and the sharp-soft half-eternal radiance of jewels, the sheen of untarnished silver and the dull gray of curiously shaped iron, the black tall splash among them of some unbelievably ancient pagan idol carved in a hard close-grained wood; at least a half of the wonderful collection that the Dragon had amassed with untold bloodshed and committed to the earth. But after a glance or two, I could look only at one object that stood in the exact center of the stone chamber, a thing so astonishing in its dramatic impact that instinctively knew it to be the secret they had kept from me for a surprise, the only one of its kind in the world. It was the largest article in the room, but that was not why my eyes were drawn to it. It was alive. It stood there as proud and fierce and alone as though the place had been empty around it. I thought then—or perhaps afterwards, I'm not sure—that what remained of this hidden cache, gleaming and gorgeous and stupefying in its glory, was really no more than a great three-dimensional tapestry encircling the central piece for backdrop.

Yet it was not so beautiful as most of the other articles; not filigreed with delicate gold, nor wrought through years of craft and toil to the impossible perfection of (to name only one of the items that surrounded it) a fragile chaplet of precious metals and gemstones that must have graced the head of a young king's daughter in the olden time. No, it was a thing of use, of grim and merciless use even, and the life in it was still and terrifying. And it held my gaze for longer than I can guess, until at last the men began to speak. Of course they spoke of it.

They did not at first know that they were talking, because when I asked them later what they had said, they denied that they had made a sound until I'd broken the silence myself. The words were Gaelic, and after two or three attempts from me to reproduce the syllables as I recalled them, they decided that Terence had said, *"Cathcharbad,"* and Tommy had said, shaking his head vigorously, *"Cárr draoidheachta!"*

Which meant "A battle chariot" and "A magic chariot!"

But that was afterward. For now, I knew only that they were husking away in incomprehensible Irish. I said, "This is what you wouldn't tell me about. The last one in the world."

"What?" said Tommy blankly. I repeated it. He rubbed his forehead and scowled and asked Terence what I was yammering about, and Terence started violently and asked me if I'd said something, and I said it again and he grinned suddenly and nodded. "I wanted it to be a surprise. I never dreamed . . . I never imagined at all. . . ."

"What?"

"That it would be so perfect. God," Terence said reverently, "how can we ever repay this sight? What do we do to earn it?"

"Nothing," said Alanna softly, "nothing but accept it. It's a gift of God."

All three crossed themselves. I saw that, for the second time that day, there were tears in Tommy's eyes. His hand sought mine and squeezed it hard. "My dear," he said, "oh my dear girl, have you the least conception—do you know—but you can't." He blinked his wet lids, quite unashamed of the emotion. "Listen to me, Grania, *cuisle mo chroidhe*, we four blessed blundering fools are the first to set eyes on this vehicle in more than seven hundred years, yes; and it is the only Irish chariot known to exist today—known again, only by the four of us here—and just that much is very amazing and wonderful and all such bloody sentimental rot. But if the song of the bard is right, and it's been right about everything else, then this is the very scythe chariot of Macha Mhong Ruadh, the warrior-queen: the first Celtic queen of Ireland, who ruled our land in gory justice long, long ago."

It did not surprise me. I had dreamed of it the night before, and though I'd constructed the dream from Grandmother's stories, still I felt that this reality buried here

below my bed must have influenced me in some dark, enig-
matic way. "Yes," I said quietly, "about 300 B.C., I know.
I think I read it somewhere." Quinn had said it to me in
the dream, but I wasn't so far under the mystic spell of
Red Macha that I would believe *that* had been supernatu-
rally given to me. Ghosts are surely not interested in
dates.

Tommy turned away from the chariot for the first time
and stared into my eyes. His whole frame was trembling
like a plucked guitar string. "Yes, three hundred years before Christ," he said hoarsely, the dramatic, romantic
words tumbling out helter-skelter, "that great proud red-
haired woman went roaring over the land in this rig here,
in the van of her armies. Into battle and safe out of it, her
spear adrip with the life of a dozen enemies, her gold-
clasped purple cloak streaming behind her, her embossed
silver shield dented by javelins and sword hacks, the scythes
on those wheels there crimson with blood, and the twin
red horses all blackened with the sweat of their charging!
Dar Crom! Can you see her? One of the immortal women
of this country, one of the great women of all time. Macha the Red! I tell you, Grania, this is a holy relic to sur-
pass anything! The Stone of Scone's a pebble and the
crown jewels of England a bunch of glass that was polished yesterday, compared with this. I wouldn't trade it
for a dozen certified barges of Cleopatra, with Julius Cae-
sar's helmet thrown in!"

"Oh," said Terence, managing to grin, "perhaps it isn't
all that fantastic; but it is ... well, incredible. Incredible
that it stands here before us. Oh yes," he said, gripping his
long hands together tightly, "oh yes, incredible. And the
queen herself more than two thousand years dead."

Alanna stepped toward it a couple of paces. I became
aware that none of us had moved since we'd seen it. I
went forward myself, drawing Tommy with me, he almost
reluctant, it seemed, to approach. Terence hung back, too.
You would have thought it was the Grail itself.

Alanna said to me. "It's the most priceless archaeological discovery you can imagine, and we owe it to you."

"Don't be silly. I only happened to find a skull and look
down the john."

"After we'd been digging mole holes all winter. Do you
know, it's already settled half a dozen problems for me

alone, and will put an end to scientific arguments that have gone on for generations?"

"Really?" I said.

"Wait till Pól Boudakyn, the only reliable authority on Celtic chariots I know, sees this. He will—why, he will—" She couldn't express the delight with which Mr. Boudakyn would view the thing, but could only make small motions of astonishment with her hands.

"Really?" I said again. All I could see was a big chariot, nothing like the golden one in my dream. It was mainly bronze and iron and venerable wood, with two enormous wheels from whose hubs thrust out vicious, rusty scythes. Including the pole, which ended in double yokes for the horses, it was about a dozen feet long. There were iron tires on the bog-oak wheels (I owe the technical details of this description to Alanna), the struts of the frame on which the rider and her charioteer had stood were also of the flint-hard wood, and the half-circle side screens, which in most chariots are presumed to have been simple wicker-work paneled onto a bent-ash frame, were made of beaten bronze, these at least so marvelously wrought that the story of it having belonged to a queen was wholly credible.

"Curse your archaeological problems, darling," said Terence. "Only feel the glamour of the thing! A chariot! An Irish chariot, Queen Macha's mighty battle chariot! Do you think we dare touch it?"

"No," said Alanna sharply. "Don't even walk around it. Don't blow the dust off it. The wood may be as rotten as your great-grandfather's eyeteeth. We'll bring a corps of people from Dublin and—"

"Yes, yes, I know. Your artifact preservers," said Tommy.

"Well, would you be after wanting to see the whole thing collapse into a pile of motes, redsnout?" cried Alanna angrily, more Irish in her speech than I'd ever heard her. "That would be the grand class of thing to do after twenty-three hundred years, would it not?"

"Smart boy wanted," said Tommy deep in his chest, and laughed. "It's only that I can't equate the aura of this great, great magical beast of a war chariot with the cautious sable brushes and gum arabic of eighteen bespectacled scholars. I know it's necessary, Alanna, I know you'll save it forever, but I cannot see both pictures at once, not yet; and here it is, and I want to fondle it, or—Christ! or go to my knees in veneration."

"That would be proper, yes," said Terence, "veneration would be the thing."

"I'm a liar," said Tommy suddenly, and very sober. "I think I would wish to see it crumble away this minute."

"What?" shouted Terence.

"Look at it, man. Remember that first instant when we saw it, when even Grania, who knew nothing whatever about it, was gripped by the most mind-shivering silence and awe that I've ever encountered, a stillness that would have made you believe the world had peacefully stopped revolving and everything on it had fallen asleep. What were we all thinking? 'Oh, God, that I should have lived to see this.' There's a kind of rightness to that, here, and for we who solved Bran Roe's riddle." He inhaled hugely. "But in a year's time, or whenever it's been pasted and glued and polished and solidified so that it can be moved, they'll take it down and set it in the National Museum, and a cult and a popular mythology will grow up around it, and fools will say to their poor kids, 'That was Dervorgilla's carriage,' and 'See where Queen Maeve herself sat'—*sat!*—and all the folk who must stick tags on things in order to appreciate 'em, who can't take in a thing that's simply a lovely, unique thing in itself, will gape and photograph and . . . ah, I'm mean and jealous," he said, breaking off and looking as though he wanted to spit. "No matter what they say about it, it will sit there perfect and beautiful and terrible, and *it* will know."

"And *we* will know," added Terence.

"And God will know," I said.

"And so will thousands of others," snapped Alanna. "Tommy, you're simply being a dog fox in the manger."

"Stingy," said Tommy agreeably. "I said that I knew it. But remember the first glimpse. Remember *now*. If it fell into dust, we four would carry this instant of wonder to our graves, the last of mankind to gaze on the war chariot of Macha Mhong Ruadh as it was in the days of her glory. The glamour of it! Allow me my snatch of covetous greed. I would mourn as heartily as you if it died with a crash before us here. It's only a wild, poetic idea. I'll make a song of it, and forget it."

"If we'd found it in the tomb of the queen," said Ter-

ence slowly, "or some secret place where her heirs had put
it, I'd leave it there. Wall it in, heap up a cairn over it. Or
else feel like a looter of graves. But O'Conor set it here
for us to find."

"Oho," said Tommy, "you're beginning to understand
him, too."

"Yes, a little. This is his time capsule for the future,
isn't it?"

"I believe it is," said Tommy. "He scoured the island
for everything he could get wind of that had survived the
ancient times. He squirreled it away, not to gloat over, but
to preserve for whoever could find it, as a memorial to us
of what fine brave men and women we descended from.
Think of the bard's song: everything in it once belonged
to somebody big in war or statehood, or—"

"That's not scientifically accurate," said Alanna. "It's
only a matter of a century or so since men began thinking
of salvaging the past to show to the future. Before that
they lived for their times, and the devil with those to
come."

"What about the pyramids?" demanded Terence hotly.

"Pride. Self-aggrandizement."

"Isn't this much the same? 'Look what we could do, a
thousand years before you were born.' And even that's
putting it at its lowest point, and hardly fair to the
Dragon. The chariot, now," said Tommy earnestly. "It
must surely have been the only one extant in O'Conor's
day. They'd all been junked and lost and broken up centuries before. But he knew that MacConn of Munster had
this one, by some miracle, as well as Queen Macha's gold
and crystal crown—that must be somewhere here too, by
the way—so he went and beat hell out of MacConn, and
brought the old chariot here to save it, knowing that otherwise it was bound to be destroyed eventually in some
fool brawl between local chieftains. He was a conserva-
tionist. His methods were of his time—"

"Of the blood, bloody," murmured Terence.

"But his consuming idea was far in advance of 1243."

"Why don't you believe any longer that he was simply a
selfish swine?" asked Alanna. "You have for a long time."

"The clue of the loo, Watson, which can't be explained
except as a deliberate pointer. There was no overwhelming
desire in the thirteenth-century mind to have a sanitary fa-
cility going down to the sea, whatever that den up there

was supposed to be for. And he could have disguised the jointure where the eye shape turns round, oh, easily, easily. But he went to immense trouble to make it as it was, just as he took the greatest pains to erect the arched roof of this chamber beneath hand-hewn beams and that double layer of flagstones, with these stone pillars and the wicker-mortar-rock vault that was the strongest he knew of, to shut out moth and rust and thieves and everything else he could. Yet he left the one clue for those who would be intelligent enough to read it, and therefore presumably smart enough to value these—these unparalleled curiosities."

Tommy drew breath and looked from one of us to the other. "But beyond that," said my man, "the whole ambience of the place has been talking to me quietly for some time. The song of Bran Roe's minstrel has been humming in my head. I think *he* knew why his master was sealing this up and setting sentinels. Because that song is a tribute, a sensitive piece of homage to the Dragon, who was dead; and the bards were educated men, sophisticated men even, who may have complimented dead masters for war and drinking and all classes of villainy, but not for hoggish mean-mindedness."

"I think you're right," said Terence. "Look at this place. It's like a museum, by Saint Gobnat of the Bees! Look at the chaplet on its pedestal. Look at that silver hand set out on—oh, dear heaven!"

"What is it?" I asked, jolted by his cry.

"The song never mentioned that," he said, more to Tommy than to me. And his voice shook uncontrollably. "Dog, do you think it might be . . ."

"King Nuada's silver hand? That Creidné fashioned for him?"

"Do you honestly suppose that in a million years it *might* be?"

"What are they talking about?" I asked Alanna. "They can be so cryptic that it makes my teeth ache."

"King Nuada Airgead Lam of a vanished race you've never heard of, dear, had a silver hand made to replace one that was chopped off in battle. That was at least three thousand years ago, and no, I doubt very much that this one is it; but I admit that nothing would astonish me much after this chariot."

Terence turned his back firmly on the silver hand,

which was a rather horrifying thing as it rested on its fingertips in a mound of dusty purple velvet, and he faced the chariot once more. "What I was saying, friends, was that since Bran Roe set this here for us, I agree that it must go to the Dublin museum. It never belonged in the dark and cold at all, it's a thing of flashing sunlight and bracing open plains and great movement and noise. But a museum's as near as it can ever come again to its destiny, so we'll trust Alanna and her crew of archaeolaters to get it there intact. Perhaps if enough people admire it and give it their wonder, it will be all right."

He moved to the chaplet that I had noticed earlier, and picked it up gently. "This makes the Tara Brooch look like a Woolworth gimcrack. And how many such incalculable treasures surround us? And how many fabulous nicky-noos are crushed and mangled under that ton of roof yonder? And still, you know, loves, I can't take my mind from the chariot. The very last Irish chariot in the world. I don't think that I could be happier if I'd found a pair of passenger pigeons sitting on a big clutch of eggs." And now his eyes were wet, too, and the question that had been quivering on my tongue for a quarter of an hour could no longer be stifled.

"You're going to sell it to the National Museum in Dublin?"

"Yes, it will naturally go to the Irish Antiquities Division."

"What do you mean, 'sell,' Grania?" That was Alanna, blond brows lifted. "One doesn't sell relics, dear, one donates them."

"Sell?" repeated Terence, apparently waking up. "*Sell?*"

"Oh, Lord," said Tommy, and groaned.

Of course the chariot was too fragile and too enormous to be smuggled out; besides, I recollected, the gardai knew that we were dredging up Dragon's Keep. "Then I suppose the smaller pieces," I began.

"Wait a moment. Are you suggesting that we *sell* these relics of our country's past, these monuments to our glorious history?" blurted Terence, gazing at me as though he had just discovered that I was Quinn Griffin's partner. "You would have us make a vile profit from the priceless antiquities of Ireland?"

"No, no," said Tommy, "it's all right, Terry lad, she—"

"They tell us at every turn that Americans are insane

about money," said Terence, "but this is impossible! That you, Grania, the nicest, the most decent woman I've ever known except for my wife, should even glance at the possibility, should urge—"

"I'm not urging! I only thought—"

"It's a mistake," said Tommy, catching hold of his friend's shirt and shaking him. "Stop nattering and listen. She's been under the delusion that we were out for ourselves in the whole affair, and that's my fault because I said something to her that made her believe it."

"But how could you think that of us, Grania?" asked Alanna, bewildered.

"I didn't. I mean, I did, but I couldn't believe it, only Tommy said—"

"I said, in a spurt of idiotic rage, because I was hurt that she'd think it of me, that we were going to keep the loot ourselves. Or at least I implied it."

"Tommy, how could you?" Alanna said.

"I'm Irish! I've got a whacking great temper! And I'm proud, and easy hurt. I thought she ought to know me better. After all, I'd kidnaped and insulted her. I'd called her names and accused her of being everything from spy to slut—how could she put all that together with my I.R.A. background and suspect me for a moment of being covetous? I'm the clod of the world," Tommy said bitterly, looking at the floor. "You, Grania, with your actor's memory, tell 'em what I said."

I thought. "I said there must be a treasure-trove law in Ireland, but that they'd let you have some of whatever you found; and you said, 'Divide it? Wisha, girl, we never even considered that!'"

"You see?" he asked the Blakes. "Perfectly logical for her to take it we were out for ourselves. Then— was it only yesterday, at the wall out there? You tried to persuade me to turn honest, and I was shocked to realize that all along you'd been believing me to be a common crook. What did I say then?"

"'You wish I was more scrupulous, you'd like me to inform Dublin of our progress.' I said I had no right to butt into your business, and you said, 'I think that's a true statement of your deepest feelings. You will take on yourself no such right. Shall we leave it at that?' And you got mad and dragged me inside and wouldn't talk to me, so eventually I chased after you to make up, I guess."

"Dog," said Terence, making the name into about six syllables.

"Oh, Tommy!" said Alanna.

"I was stabbed to the soul to hear she'd been regarding me as a paragon of wickedness. Then when I'd got over that, there was never a flick of time to free her of the notion. Something was going on at every turn. And I forgot all about it!" He pulled at his ear. "There was pride, too. I thought you should have figured it out for yourself."

"I should have," I said miserably.

"You let her believe we were crooks," said Terence. "Greedy swine like Griffin."

"I didn't believe it," I said, "or at least I never understood it, it didn't fit. I kept making excuses for you. I thought you probably deserved the treasure because Tommy's family had once owned this land."

"Oh, you poor child," said Alanna, embracing me. "What a hell you must have been dragging through all this time. And that brute there, pretending to be in love with you and allowing you to suffer."

"In the name of sanity," bellowed Tommy, with the echoes crashing all around us, "I never even remembered the clot-headed conversation until now! I tell you I forgot!" He stared at me and said more calmly, "I suppose I wanted you to try to change me, despite your views on the subject. I want you to know that you have the right, if you love me. There's a limit to the hands-off rule. If I saw *you* contemplating something unworthy, I'd soon let you know my feelings."

"You're right," I admitted. "Then the three of you actually endured all this—months and months of ghastly cold and wet and wind on these haunted cliffs, work harder than you'd have on a chain gang, and the risk of prison—all for Ireland and nothing for you but some satisfaction?"

"Of course," said Tommy.

"Certainly," said Terence.

"Yes, dear," said Alanna.

"Oh, gosh," said silly young Grania Kirk.

I thought. "Then the only illegal act you were committing," I said, "was to dig in a ruin? Why did you ever need to kidnap me, then? Why didn't you call the gardai when Quinn murdered that man Moran?"

"For the reasons I gave you," said Tommy patiently. "We had no proof of the murder, we dared not trust you at first, and digging in a government-protected castle is not that much of a venial sin. There is a very tough law against it, and Terry's references to Mountjoy Jail weren't all joking by any means."

"But now?" I asked, rather fearful.

"Well, we're not certain. But there is a man at the National Museum," said Terence, "who wanted to believe me. He could not go to Public Works and demand that they listen, of course; but he said privately, behind bolted doors and over a teacup of sherry, that if we were to come up here and find something on our own he'd back us to the hilt and see to it that we were granted a finder's fee."

"You wouldn't touch that," I said.

"That's true, we wouldn't. You don't take money for following a dream." This would have sounded ridiculous from an American, pompous and theatrical; from Terence it was simply a fact. "The chap was very skittery about it, up and down and back and forth, and said twice that if we were caught with nothing but a lot of holes in the ground, then he'd never heard of us and we might rot in prison for all of him. But he was really a good enough sort of fella, only timorous, you know, and he absolutely yearned to believe in the idea. When he hears of this"—he swept a hand around at the trove—"he will, I think, announce that we were acting under his orders. If he doesn't, well, we'll see. I'm not especially worried about it now."

I looked at each of them in turn. "Can you forgive me?" I asked.

They glanced at one another. Then Tommy said carefully, "I imagine that you will be wanting a honeymoon in some exotic place or another?"

"I will."

"What about the Republic of Ireland?"

"That would be fine. That's the place I had in mind."

"You'll marry me, then."

"I will."

"Would it please you if the Blakes were to witness the ceremony?"

"If they'll overlook my suspicions of them, which were never as strong as my doubts about *you*."

Tommy winced. "I deserve that."

"You do."

"Will you be pursuing your television career? You may if you like," he said grandly.

"I think I've had enough acting for a long time. I'll be perfectly content to trudge after you, carrying your guitar case and taking care of Balor."

There was an odd small silence, with the four of us standing there amidst that untold wealth of the ages and thinking of such prosaic matters as marriage and love and happily sacrificed careers. Then Alanna said, "If we turn our backs, O'Flaherty, do you think you can work up the nerve to kiss the girl? Seal the bargain, you know?"

"If she'll kiss me back in her abandoned American fashion," said Tommy. So they did, and he did, and I did. "You *will* marry me, then? Are you sure of it?"

"I am."

"Can't you say 'yes' like any normal foreigner?"

"I can."

"Why don't you?"

"I will not. I'll repeat the verb from the question, like any good Irishman, for that's what I'm to be."

"Lord but you speak like one already," said Tommy. "Look here, you know, love, I have my faults, just as everyone does, and you've seen only a part of them; so if you believe you should wait a bit—"

"I'll take my chances," said I. And I have never been sorry that I did.

There is little more to tell. The scar on my cheek was worked over by an excellent Dublin surgeon, and there's only a thin white line to remind me now and again that one appalling night I fought a battle with one of the Dread Women of Moher on the edge of the worst precipice in the world.

The multitude of relics from Dragon's Keep, the jewelry and weapons and artifacts, the bracelets, torques, necklaces, collars, badges and rings and girdles, the set of red and white chessmen that some king had carved from the bones of his enemies, the silver hand and the glorious chaplet, Red Macha's gold and crystal crown, the Early Christian chalice and the immeasurably old pagan idol, the silver and gold and amber and bronze and copper and enamel work, arrowheads and lance points, the blue-tempered gold-hilted swords, the carbuncle-studded basin chased with animals like leopards, the billiard balls and cues made of brass and judged to be nearly two millennia old, all the fantastic things laid down for us by Bran Roe O'Conor (who is well on his way to becoming a national hero to rival Finn Mac Coul and Dan O'Connell), are gradually finding their way into the museum. Even our mummified captain of gallowglasses has a place of honor there with his ax, and badly startles the unsuspecting visitor.

Experts at restoration are still working on the damaged and deteriorated articles, and will do so for years to come. Alanna occasionally helps with this when she isn't out on a dig somewhere in the back of beyond. Terence is at present, I gather, redesigning the city of Cork for his own amusement.

I believe it took the government about twelve seconds to forgive the lot of us for our unauthorized investigations in a medieval castle. I can illustrate their attitude by one final word.

The scythe chariot of the warrior-queen Macha Mhong Ruadh, the last of its kind in the world, stands where you cannot miss it in the center of the National Museum's great hall. There is a discreet card on its glass case with the following notation: "Discovered on behalf of, and presented to, the Republic of Ireland by Mrs. Thomas O'Flaherty, in Dragon's Keep on the Cliffs of Moher."

Recommended Reading from SIGNET

- [ ] **HAGGARD by Christopher Nicole.** (#E9340—$2.50)
- [ ] **SUNSET by Christopher Nicole.** (#E8948—$2.25)*
- [ ] **BLACK DAWN by Christopher Nicole.** (#E8342—$2.25)*
- [ ] **CARIBEE by Christopher Nicole.** (#J7945—$1.95)
- [ ] **THE DEVIL'S OWN by Christopher Nicole.** (#J7256—$1.95)
- [ ] **MISTRESS OF DARKNESS by Christopher Nicole.**
  (#J7782—$1.95)
- [ ] **THE WORLD FROM ROUGH STONES by Malcolm Macdonald.**
  (#E9639—$2.95)
- [ ] **THE RICH ARE WITH YOU ALWAYS by Malcolm Macdonald.**
  (#E7682—$2.25)
- [ ] **SONS OF FORTUNE by Malcolm Macdonald.**
  (#E8595—$2.75)*
- [ ] **ABIGAIL by Malcolm Macdonald.** (#E9404—$2.95)
- [ ] **HARVEST OF DESTINY by Erica Lindley.** (#J8919—$1.95)*
- [ ] **CALL THE DARKNESS LIGHT by Nancy Zaroulis.**
  (#E9291—$2.95)

  * Price slightly higher in Canada

Buy them at your local bookstore or use this convenient coupon for ordering.

THE NEW AMERICAN LIBRARY, INC.,
P.O. Box 999, Bergenfield, New Jersey 07621

Please send me the SIGNET BOOKS I have checked above. I am enclosing
$_____ (please add 50¢ to this order to cover postage and handling).
Send check or money order—no cash or C.O.D.'s. Prices and numbers are
subject to change without notice.

Name _____

Address _____

City_____ State_____ Zip Code_____

Allow 4-6 weeks for delivery.
This offer is subject to withdrawal without notice.